W9-AXM-990

ART'S BLOOD

"Lane's sharp eye for detail gets put to good use in this second installment of her Appalachian series. . . . The widow Goodweather is a wonderful character: plucky, hip and wise. The dialogue sparkles with authenticity, and Lane generates suspense without sacrificing the charm and mystique of her mountain community."
—*Publishers Weekly*

"Lane mixes the gentle craft of old-time quilting with the violence of a slaughtered innocent."
—Greensboro *News & Record*

"Lane is a master at creating authentic details while building suspense."   —*Asheville Citizen-Times*

SIGNS IN THE BLOOD

"Vicki Lane shows us an exotic and colorful picture of Appalachia from an outsider's perspective—through a glass darkly. It is a well-crafted, suspenseful tale of the bygone era before 'Florida' came to the mountains."
—SHARYN MCCRUMB

"*Signs in the Blood* turns the beauty of the Appalachian hills and a widow's herb and flower farm into the back-drop for modern menace. This clash of the traditional and the modern makes for an all-nighter of satisfying suspense."   —*Mystery Lovers Bookshop News*

"For readers familiar with the sound and feel of mountain life, this book rings with a resonance that is true to the life it describes. For everyone else, this book opens a peephole into a world both hauntingly strange and achingly beautiful. . . . Regional mystery lovers, take note. A new heroine has come to town and her arrival is a time for rejoicing."   —*Rapid River Magazine*

The Full Circle Farm Mysteries of Vicki Lane

SIGNS IN THE BLOOD
ART'S BLOOD
OLD WOUNDS
IN A DARK SEASON
THE DAY OF SMALL THINGS
UNDER THE SKIN

Under the Skin

A Full Circle Farm Mystery

Vicki Lane

BANTAM BOOKS TRADE PAPERBACKS
NEW YORK

A Bantam Books Trade Paperback Original

Copyright © 2011 by Vicki Lane

All rights reserved.

Published in the United States by Bantam Books, an imprint of The Random House Publishing Group, a division of Random House, Inc., New York.

BANTAM BOOKS and the rooster colophon are registered trademarks of Random House, Inc.

This book contains an excerpt from the book *Old Wounds,* originally published by Dell, an imprint of The Random House Publishing Group, a division of Random House, Inc., in 2007.

LIBRARY OF CONGRESS CATALOGING-IN-PUBLICATION DATA
Lane, Vicki.
    Under the skin : a novel / Vicki Lane.
        p.   cm.
    ISBN 978-0-345-53365-4
eBook ISBN 978-0-345-53024-0
1. Sisters—Fiction. 2. Family secrets—Fiction. 3. North Carolina—Fiction. I. Title.
    PS3612.A54996U53 2011
    813'.6—dc23   2011031801

Printed in the United States of America

www.bantamdell.com

9 8 7 6 5 4 3 2 1

Book design by Caron Harris

For Ann Collette, who believed . . .
For all the readers who waited . . .
And, of course, for John

A Sister can be seen as someone who is both ourselves and very much not ourselves—a special kind of double.
—Toni Morrison

I don't believe an accident of birth makes people sisters or brothers. It makes them siblings, gives them mutuality of parentage. Sisterhood and brotherhood is a condition people have to work at.
—Maya Angelou

Acknowledgments

At last! The resolution of the cliff-hanger that ended *In a Dark Season*! When I wrote that book and ended it with a puzzling message from Aunt Dodie, I was fairly confident that no more than a year would pass before I continued with the story—indeed, I'd already written the first and last chapters of this very book.

Alas, it was not to be. Miss Birdie insisted on having her say, and *The Day of Small Things* came next—and late at that. I began to feel very, very bad about that cliff-hanger: What if something happened to me and I never finished this book? My readers would never know the truth about Phillip. So I wrote a touching blog post, to be published in the event of my untimely demise and including the already written final chapter of this book.

Thank heavens, I can delete that post now. Many thanks to all you patient readers for hanging in there with me. I'll never write another cliff-hanger.

There are several others I need to thank for helping this book come to life. Karen and Pete Nagle gave me a tour of their beautiful Mountain Magnolia Inn and shared its history with me. Dr. Marianna Daly and Bryan Robinson gave me medical and psychological advice for one of my characters. Thanks also to Vic Copeland and to Pepper Cory for adding two wonderful new phrases to Phillip's vocabulary: "bitch wings" and "nets a-flaring."

Anthony Cavender's fascinating book *Folk Medicine in Southern Appalachia* was extremely useful to me, and I appreciate his allowing us to reprint a page. Byron Ballard, a hereditary Appalachian witch, told me about the burn spell and tried to help me understand more about the Earth religions.

A big thank-you to Martin T. Hodges, my blog friend across the pond, who read the chapters with Giles of Glastonbury and made sure he sounded properly English.

Many thanks to the gang at Random House: Connie Munro, my copy editor, does a great job of ensuring that my continuity makes some sort of sense, and she catches the typos and other gremlins that creep into a manuscript. Victoria Allen is responsible for the lovely, haunting cover art. And my patient editor, Kate Miciak, is responsible for making me a better writer.

Under the Skin

Chapter 1

A Complicated Person

Tuesday, May 8

I should have known Gloria would come up with something like this right before our wedding. It's just like her. I swear, she's . . ."

. . . crazy as the proverbial shithouse rat were the words on the tip of my tongue but I bit them back.

Without looking up from the paperback he was reading, Phillip made a questioning sort of sound. "Hmm? . . . What was that, Lizabeth? Gloria's what?"

I dropped the phone onto the table and glowered at it as if it were responsible for this new and unwelcome twist in my life. "She's . . . complicated," I hedged, rejecting the coarse country phrase, apt though it might be. "Complicated—which is a polite way of saying I don't understand her at all. She must be—"

I couldn't go on. But the voice in my head, never at a loss for words, finished the sentence for me. *She must be out of her rabbit-ass mind, as Ben would say.*

I stood there glaring at the innocent telephone. *It's not* FAIR! I wanted to shout, in a whining echo from my childhood. *Glory always messes* everything *up!* I wanted to throw something, to stamp my foot, to fling myself to the floor and have a screaming, kicking tantrum.

Instead, I made a strenuous effort to sound composed

and adult as I tried to explain things to the back of Phillip's head.

"It's just that with all the farm work right now, not to mention getting things ready for the wedding next month, this isn't exactly a good time for *anyone* to come for an open-ended visit, especially Gloria . . . she's so bloody high-maintenance."

All the old feelings were just below the surface: bitterness, guilt, annoyance, a touch of envy, and guilt again—an evil stew of emotion ready to break into a full boil.

Not attractive, Elizabeth, I warned that nasty inner child who was still quivering with righteous indignation. *Aren't you about forty years too old for this kind of adolescent reaction to your only sister . . . your only sibling?*

I took a deep breath, forcing myself into the mind-set of rationality and general benevolence that I like to pretend comes naturally. Usually, it does. But now . . . oh, why the *hell* does my sister always bring out the worst in me?

Two more deep breaths and I was able to say, "On the other hand, if things are so bad between Gloria and her husband . . ."

I was thinking out loud now, trying to make sense of the just-ended conversation and trying also to ignore the tagline from Tennyson that was running through my head—" *'The curse is come upon me,' cried the Lady of Shalott.* "

". . . if it's so bad that she's actually contemplating staying *here* for a month or longer, what can I do? And things must be seriously awful. Glory hates it here at the farm—'too much *Nature*,' she always says, as if Nature was something you wouldn't want to step in."

Phillip, comfortable on the sofa with a dog on either side of him, his sock feet propped on the old cedar chest that serves as a coffee table, finally looked up from his after-supper book with that calm, amused expression he's so good at.

"This guy—he's what—your sister's third husband? So problems with married life aren't entirely new to her. What's the big deal this time?"

He wouldn't be so calm and amused if he had any idea of what Glory's like, I thought, wondering if this could be some elaborate joke of hers. But the thing is—my sister has no sense of humor. None. Never has.

"Well," I told him, thinking at the same time that, after all his patient courtship, Phillip deserved better than this, "according to Gloria, the problem is that Jerry's trying to kill her."

He wants me dead, Lizzy, she had whispered into the phone, her voice hoarse with what might be fear . . . or might just be Glory's usual histrionics. The only thing that tempted me to take her seriously was that not once did she put me on hold—though I heard the telltale beep several times during the lengthy conversation.

Phillip lifted a quizzical eyebrow and, after carefully marking his place with an envelope, laid his book on the coffee table. Harlan Coben again, I noticed.

"Why don't you tell me exactly what she said?"

His dark eyes were intent on me—one of the things I like so much about this man I'm about to marry is the way he can switch from a comfortable-as-an-old-shoe, easygoing sort of a guy to a seriously focused police detective. And vice versa, thank god.

Already he was worrying at the problem like one of the dogs with a bone. "Your sister thinks her husband wants to kill her—does she have anything concrete to base that supposition on? Or is it just a general feeling? I'm guessing that if he'd laid hands on her, she would have had the sense to get the law involved. Just what did she say?"

Phillip was studying my face with what I took to be professional interest. "Well," I began, "there were several things . . ."

Standing there by the sofa, like a schoolgirl called on for recitation, I repeated what Glory had told me, trying to use just the words—leaving out what seemed to me Glory's typical exaggeration. And leaving out, as well, my skeptical reaction. No eye-rolling—just the facts, Detective Hawkins, sir.

These little things keep happening, Gloria had insisted, her voice breathless and hurried. *The slick place at the top of the stairs, the food poisoning; the brakes on the car going out all at once—the trooper said it was a miracle that I wasn't killed—and that's only three—there were more and they weren't all accidents. I'm sure of it now. Jerry wants me dead. I know too much about his so-called businesses.*

When I came to the end of my account, Phillip nodded.

"Interesting." He nudged Molly to dislodge her from her place by him. When her usual ploy of turning reproachful amber eyes on him was to no avail, the red hound gave a resigned sigh, rose, stretched her elegant body, and, with no evidence of hurry, made a graceful descent.

Phillip patted the vacant spot. "Come sit down, Lizabeth, and tell me what you think. Do *you* believe this story your sister's telling?"

I sank down at his side, nestling close and savoring the solid reassurance of him.

"Do I believe her? . . . Well, I guess I believe that she *thinks* she's in danger. But Glory's life is *always* such a drama—no, not a drama, more of a soap opera."

Phillip gave my ear a friendly nuzzle then put an arm around me and began to rub my neck. "Yeah, I got that impression from a few things Ben said . . . his dad was her second husband, right?"

"Umm," I nodded, closing my eyes. "That feels good. Yep, Ben's dad was her second marriage. Or maybe it was technically her first since the other one was annulled."

Was there any need to get into that episode of the Gloria Show? I wondered. Phillip's hands moved to my shoulders. Since he isn't asking, I decided, we'll just fast-forward.

"Ben's dad was a respectable young lawyer—nice enough but spectacularly boring—at least, that's what Sam and I thought. And I guess Glory got bored with him herself because she divorced him after only a few years. Ben was really little—maybe two or three—when that happened." I leaned forward. "Right on down my spine, if you would. Ben and I were transplanting starts for most of the day and my body seems to have decided that fifty-five is the new eighty-five. All my joints have kind of seized up."

As Phillip's strong fingers dug into my stiff muscles, I wondered if Ben knew about his mother's plans to visit. My nephew has worked on the farm since a few years after my husband Sam's death and I made Ben my business partner a while back. His choosing my lifestyle over his mother's is only the most recent of Gloria's many grievances against me. "Taking my only child from me" is how she put it during one particularly nasty phone conversation.

"About Ben's dad . . ."

There was real curiosity in Phillip's voice and I could almost hear the items being added to the file in that orderly cop-slash-detective mind of his: *Gloria: Elizabeth's younger sister, city girl, second husband, Ben's dad . . .*

"Ben's dad's still around, isn't he?" Phillip's hands were beginning to stray as so often happened and I swung my feet up on the sofa and stretched out with my head in his lap.

"Oh, he's around, but Ben doesn't see much of him. Benjamin Barton Hamilton the Third—and that's how the dad introduces himself, just to give you some idea of how stuffed his shirt is—anyway, he's a partner at some big important firm in DC. I think he was kind of disappointed in Ben's career path—he'd hoped his son would carry on the family tradition of lawyering. But BBH the Third's remarried now to a woman not a lot older than Ben. They have three young children and he's just not a big part of Ben's life anymore."

"Is he the guy your sister's money comes from? Ben mentioned something once about his mother being so rich that she was out of touch with the way real people live."

"No, the *big* money came from Harold. Harold Holst came after BBH the Third."

And was, very probably, the real reason Gloria left him. When she met Harold in connection with some charity do she was organizing and found out that not only was he recently widowed, but he had more money than God on a good day, that pretty well did it for old boring Benjamin the Third. Gloria and Holst were married before the ink was dry on her divorce papers.

Oh, mee-yow, Elizabeth! What a catty bitch you are, to be sure!

I closed my eyes, remembering the handsome white-haired man and his magical effect on Glory. During the ten years they had together, before Harold died so suddenly, my sister had been a different woman—softer, gentler—and happier than I'd ever known her.

Amazing what a having few million dollars for mad money can do.

Evidently that brat of an inner child was still whining and kicking. I bit my lip, then went on.

"Harold was a really nice guy. And he and Gloria truly adored each other."

Phillip's roaming hands fell still and I was amused to note that the cop was winning out over the lover. "So, if we count the annulment, this is her fourth husband that she's running away from . . . What's he like?"

"I've never met Jerry—two of Glory's weddings were enough for me."

That sounded pretty cold, I thought. It seemed hard to admit how little I knew of my sister's life; I fumbled around for what scraps I could offer.

"Ben told me he was surprised by Jerry because he didn't seem like Gloria's usual kind of guy. I got the impression he's maybe a little . . . *uncouth*. From some other things Ben said when he came back from spending a little time down there, evidently the relationship was pretty intense—either Jerry and Gloria were yelling and throwing things at each other or they were carrying on like hormone-crazed teenagers. No middle ground."

Sitting up, I swung around to face Phillip.

"Oh, here's one interesting thing—Ben kind of wondered if maybe Jerry was . . . you know . . . *connected*. Ben said there were these shady types who would drop by the house and Jerry would take them outside to talk business. Ben seemed to think"—*and now I'm the one sounding like a soap opera*—"that maybe Jerry was part of the Mafia or whatever they call it these days."

Phillip raised an eyebrow. "Really? That *could* be interesting. Ben's not the kind of kid to make up stuff like that. What did you say Jerry's last name is?"

I spelled it out and he wrote it on the inside cover of the paperback. The schoolhouse clock in the den struck the hour and Phillip gave a Pavlovian yawn and then another. Glancing at his watch, he frowned and shut the book.

"Hate to do it but I better turn in—early meeting tomorrow. But after that, I'll make a few inquiries—see what I can find out about this Jerry Lombardo."

Phillip was already in bed and I was making my last prowl through the house—turning off lights, putting dogs out for one last pee, and picking up odds and ends. I was moving the stack of Phillip's paperwork—tedious cop stuff, he calls it—off the cedar chest when I noticed the corner of an airmail envelope sticking out from under one of the files. The spidery handwriting of the return address was familiar.

Sure enough, it was a letter from Aunt Dodie that must have gotten mixed in with his things when he picked up the mail—a part of Phillip's routine when he comes home, saving me the half-mile trip to the mailbox for what's usually nothing but bills.

But why airmail? I turned the light by the love seat back on and sat down to see what my honorary aunt had to say. I had my finger under the flap when it hit me—the stamp was wrong.

The return address was Aunt Dodie's own—in New Bern—but the postmark was from the UK—Chipping . . . and something smudged. What in the world? I wondered, ripping open the flimsy envelope.

Her spidery handwriting was clear—unlike her thought processes. But as long as I'd known her—which was roughly forever as she'd been my mother's best friend—Aunt Dodie had been a fluttery, scatterbrained little woman. And her infrequent letters were always marvels of exclamation points and underlining, dizzying changes of subjects and frequent long-winded asides. This one was no exception.

Elizabeth, dear,

Believe it or not, here I am in England!!! As I told you when I left that message on New Year's Eve, there I *was thinking about the <u>Inevitable</u> and starting to put my house in <u>death order</u> (!!!) when the next day—New Year's Day—I had a call from my granddaughter Meredith!!! (Sarabeth's oldest, you know.) Well, Meredith married a <u>charming</u> young Englishman a few years ago (so handsome, just like Leslie Howard, you remember, the one who was Ashley Wilkes in "Gone With the Wind" but not nearly as good-looking as that devil Rhett Butler) and the dear child arranged for me to fly over with her mother and father and make a <u>nice long visit</u> and that's exactly what I have done!!!*

I can hardly believe that I've been here four months and am only now getting around to writing you but the children have kept me <u>on the run</u>! They've taken me to see so many things!—the Crown Jewels in the Tower (a little <u>gaudy</u> for my taste, and I expect the dear Queen feels the same) and to Stratford-on-Avon (Anne Hathaway's cottage is <u>charming</u> though, I fear, damp) and to a cricket game where I rather embarrassingly <u>dozed off</u>!

The letter rambled and nattered on for two more violet-scented pages of cream teas, Liberty fabrics, biscuits not really biscuits at all but cookies—*"very <u>nice</u> cookies too, though why called <u>digestive</u>, I couldn't say."*

My eyelids were getting heavy and I was just skimming the waves of words when the last paragraph stopped me.

My neighbor forwarded your <u>sweet</u> letter with all your news—it makes me <u>so happy</u> to hear that everything's all right with you and your beautiful Full Circle Farm and that you are still planning to marry your Mr. Hawkins. I'm just a <u>silly old woman</u> at times—

I should have known there couldn't be any connection between your nice police detective and the mysterious Hawk poor Sam was SO *worried about!! I don't know what got into me. But when I found that puzzling letter of Sam's in the Old Gentleman's desk—well, I suppose I just wanted to get it off my mind which is why I called.*

Of course I recognized Sam's hand at once—that beautiful <u>clear</u> printing like architects do and I thought I'd see if there was anything in the letter that you or your girls might be interested in. Sam and the Old Gentleman struck up <u>such</u> a friendship when you two visited—talking Navy talk nineteen to the dozen or is it twenty? But <u>evidently</u> they continued to correspond for in this letter Sam mentions having written before—though I haven't found any other letters.

The <u>peculiar thing</u> is that Sam spends most of this letter telling the OG about some strange "detached duty" he and this other man had been sent on. He asks the OG if he has obtained any information on "the matter I mentioned in my last letter" and then goes on to say that he's not sure if he can TRUST *the other man whom he calls <u>the Hawk</u>! Really, too mysterious!"*

So <u>that</u> was why I called. And then when the trip to England sprang up and I hadn't heard back from you, I just popped the whole thing, along with a few pictures of boats and things that were with it, into a mailer I had—bright red, I remember because Sarabeth had sent me some <u>lovely</u> family photos in it—to get it in the mail to you before going to England. I knew you'd want to make sure . . . but we won't talk about that now! <u>All's well that ends well</u>, as the Bard says!!!

By now you've read it for yourself and are probably

shaking your head at your <u>foolish</u> old Aunt Dodie!
I'm sure there was a <u>perfectly logical</u> explanation and
that your Phillip has helped to clear it up. It was just
that the names were so <u>similar</u>.

In the stillness of late night, the ticking of the school-house clock in the next room was the only sound I could hear. I sat up straight and read through the letter again.

It was like coming into a theater at the midpoint of a movie. *What* letter of Sam's was Aunt Dodie talking about? Yes, Aunt Dodie's late husband, aka the Old Gentleman, and Sam had become unlikely friends and correspondents. The Old Gentleman, a retired admiral, had seemed to enjoy hearing about the Navy from Sam's considerably more lowly point of view. So it wasn't impossible that there might have been some letters left in the Old Gentleman's desk and Dodie had thought . . . what exactly *had* Dodie thought? The mysterious Hawk . . .

And for that matter, as I reread the letter a third time, *what* phone message at New Year's? Surely the last time I'd talked to Aunt Dodie had been in December when I called her a few days before Christmas . . .

I thought back to New Year's Eve: Phillip and I had been here alone all evening. We had watched distant fireworks from the front porch at midnight, I had told him I wanted to marry him—had accepted the proposal he'd made long before. We had drunk champagne and gone to bed. If there'd been a phone call . . .

Was it the first of the year when the answering machine went out? I don't understand how these things work—I just remember at some point months ago, it didn't—work, that is—and eventually I switched to voice mail.

And why didn't I ever get this mysterious letter in the

bright red mailer? Where had *that* gone—down the same rabbit hole as the New Year's Eve message?

Yawning and shaking my head, I folded the flimsy sheets back into the envelope and tucked it under the calendar on my desk. *Dodie is battier than usual, I'm afraid. I'll see if it makes any more sense in the morning.*

Chapter 2

You Can Always Hope . . .

Friday, May 11

Good morning, Lizzy! Don't you just love this dewy early morning time? The sky at sunrise, the blaze of color . . ."

I watched as Gloria paused in the kitchen doorway and waved a vague hand at the window—the *south*-facing window. Yawning luxuriously she headed for the coffeemaker, baby-blue silk mules clicking on the wooden floor. Like our mother before her, my sister has never been one to leap out of bed and dress for the day—she prefers to spend the morning lounging about in some charming negligee before dressing to go out to lunch. Just now she had on a knee-length robe covered with clouds of embroidered pastel hydrangeas, each small petal tinged with delectable melting shades of palest greens and pinks, faintest blues and lavenders. It was heart-breakingly beautiful and set off her fair skin and blond hair to perfection.

A picture of the shabby terry-cloth bathrobe hanging on my closet door popped into my head and I gave the lump of dough I was kneading a final savage thump before I scooped it from the countertop and plopped it into the greased bowl awaiting it.

I glanced at the clock. "It's 10:53, Gloria. The sun

came up about five hours ago—in the east, as it usually does around here. And don't call me Lizzy."

My sister had been at the farm for less than twenty-four hours and already she was getting on my one last nerve.

On Wednesday morning, there had been a second frantic call from Gloria: this time to say that Jerry had just left the house and a friend was coming to take her to the airport.

"I hate leaving my Beemer but it would be too easy for Jerry to trace me—he has contacts everywhere. I'm literally throwing a few things in a bag and walking out . . . No, I don't have a ticket yet. I'll get one at the airport and I'll call you when I know what time I get in."

This, of course, had resulted in a day of frantic house-cleaning and reorganization—the guest room having become the repository for Phillip's belongings. Now that he worked full-time for Marshall County's High Sheriff Mackenzie Blaine, Phillip had finally given up his rented house in Weaverville and moved in with me—and though he had very few possessions, there were some that we hadn't yet found the right place for and these were, of course, piled on the guest room bed. Actually, we'd been talking about turning this quiet room at the back of the house into a study for him—but now that would have to wait. .

So I had spent the day chasing cobwebs, airing pillows, moving the boxes of Phillip's belongings to the basement, scouring the bathroom—all with an ear out for the phone call that would tell me when I would have to make the hour-plus drive to the airport and pick up Gloria.

A phone call which, I might add, didn't come till late that night. Gloria was in Atlanta, having decided to do a little shopping before continuing her trip.

"And the *good* news is you won't have to meet me after all! I was in the taxi heading for the hotel and I suddenly had a *brilliant* idea. I just had the driver take me right to the BMW dealership and I got myself the *perfect* little car for the mountains! I know you're going to love it, Lizzy."

"Oh yuck, this coffee's cold—I'll just make a fresh pot."

Before I could stop her, Gloria was pouring the coffee down the drain—coffee that normally I'd have drunk iced at lunchtime—and the grinder was chewing up a fresh batch of beans.

"Where's that good-looking cop of yours?" she asked, leaving the coffeemaker to fold herself into an elegant leggy pose on the cushioned bench at the end of the kitchen. "I was hoping to talk to him about my situation. We hardly said more than hello last night before he disappeared off to bed."

I wiped off the countertop and hung the dish towel on the rack. "Phillip had to be at work early this morning. Besides, I expect he thought you and I had some catching up to do and he'd just be in the way of our girlish confidences. Look—do you want some breakfast? There's eggs, bread for toast, juice, yogurt . . ."

"Is it Greek yogurt? That's really the only kind worth eating. I usually have it with fresh figs and—"

"It's probably made by Greeks in New Jersey," I said through gritted teeth, as I opened the refrigerator door. "And the fruit of the day is dried cranberries."

Her nose wrinkled in disgust. "Do you know how much *sugar* dried cranberries have? Never mind, then; I'll just have coffee. Is there some skim milk?"

I put the yogurt back, noting that it was, in fact, *appellation* New Hampshire—though still not Greek—and reached for the milk.

"That's two percent milk!" Gloria waved away the carton in something very close to horror. "Don't you have skim?"

I felt my teeth beginning to grind again. "No, and in my opinion, putting skim milk in coffee is about like adding dishwater. This is what I've got . . . or some dishwater."

"Oh, but I always add a splash of half-and-half *with* the skim milk—never mind, Lizzy, black will be fine— I don't want to be any trouble. If you'll drive me down to my car later, I'll run out to the grocery and do a little shopping. You know if you'd just have a little work done on that road, I could get my car all the way up here. Then I wouldn't have to bother you."

"For someone who's supposed to be hiding out, my mother isn't exactly low profile, is she? Are you going to have to ferry her up and down the hill every time she takes a notion to go somewhere?"

Ben and I were watching as Gloria's bright yellow Mini Cooper maneuvered around a water break and continued down the road with a cheery *toot-toot* of its horn.

"You know, I think that all of this area seems so like the back of beyond to your mom that she can't imagine that she could run into anyone who knows her. And she's probably right. Besides, she's just going up to the grocery on the bypass to get a few things. I've got plenty to do in the workshop that will keep me busy till she gets back—it shouldn't take her much over an hour."

Ben hefted the flat of lavender starts into the bed of the utility vehicle and I followed him over to the cold frame to get the rest. Out in the bottom Julio and Homero were preparing the new lavender bed, raking it smooth and tossing out the inevitable rocks that had surfaced in the wake of the tractor. *Thank god for these guys,* I thought. *With any luck, Full Circle Farm will perk along, providing fresh arugula, tarragon, nasturtium petals, and all those other delicacies to Asheville's ladies who lunch, while I deal with Gloria.*

In the beginning, it had been just Sam and me—with a little haphazard help from my girls. After Sam's death, things were pretty difficult—the girls were in college and I had been almost at the point of admitting that perhaps I couldn't manage alone. So when Ben showed up, wanting to learn the business, I'd welcomed him as something between a miracle and a knight in shining armor. With Ben's help and with the growing number of restaurants in Asheville, the business had doubled and then some. So now we had Julio and Homero—Mexican workers who shared the rental house just above our main growing field.

As so often happened, Ben seemed to be attuned to my thinking. "Listen, Aunt E," he said, taking the last flat of fragrant little gray-green plants from me. "You really don't need to worry. The guys and I can handle the work. And Amanda's willing to help too. You have plenty to do getting ready for the wedding and babysitting Mom."

"I don't know," I said, pinching off a single lavender leaf. I crushed it with my fingers and brought it up to my nose. The pungent smell filled my nostrils—calming and strengthening at once. "Since she's got a car, I have a feeling she'll find plenty to do that doesn't involve me."

"She'll find plenty to do, that's for sure." Ben laughed and climbed into the driver's seat of the little vehicle. Over the noisy clatter of the engine, I could just make out the words, "You can always hope it won't involve you . . ."

It was a pleasure to be in the cool quiet of my workshop and an even greater pleasure to know I had a

Gloria-free hour ahead of me—a whole hour of not being told a better way to do things. Already she had suggested that I gut my kitchen, get rid of the wood-stove, add a dishwasher—*I have two dishwashers,* I had told her, holding up my hands, but she had ignored me, moving on to weigh the merits of granite against soap-stone, dismissing my wooden countertops as out of date and hopelessly unhygienic.

Outside I could hear Ben and Julio laughing and jok-ing in an odd combination of poor English (Julio) and worse Spanish (Ben). The distant putter of the tractor let me know that Homero was mowing the lower pasture in the eternal fight against thistles and the vile prickly un-named weed that had evidently made its way to the farm in hay purchased in Tennessee.

I moved about the big room, taking inventory of wreath-making supplies on hand. Some of the dried ma-terial left over from last year was getting pretty ratty looking—most herbs and flowers really need to be dried fresh every year for maximum color and fragrance. I began to cram the pallid leftovers into a feed sack, plan-ning to add them to one of our many compost piles. Soon enough there'd be fresh cuttings hanging in the drying room; there was no need to hold on to this sad stuff.

Other materials, however, keep well for years—as long as they're protected against dust—and things like lotus pods and the pretty brown and cream seed cases from Siberian iris, branches of curly willow and corkscrew hazelnut, and a variety of pinecones were in good supply. As I lifted the lid on the last bin of pinecones, an unwelcome odor filled the air. Just under the lid, a ragged hole in the pale blue plastic showed where the invaders had gnawed their way in. All the cones were chewed and tiny black mouse droppings were everywhere.

At least there's no nest of babies, thank goodness. I hate killing anything—mice, even rats. But left unchecked . . . I dumped the reeking contents into another feed sack, took the bin outside and hosed it clean, then left it to dry in the sun. More check marks on my list and I moved on.

The bin for lavender held only a handful of battered-looking stems and a scattering of purple buds. These too were faded and their aroma was little more than the ghost of a memory. Still, lavender was too precious just to toss into the compost. I found an empty gallon glass jar and shoved the stems into it, crumbling them into bits. If I goosed up the fragrance a tad with lavender oil, then these little crumbs could be added to potpourri or to lavender sachets.

Lavender . . . it always made me think of Aunt Dodie . . . Dodie and her standing order for a new lavender wreath every year . . . and her signature lavender stationery.

That letter—what did I do with that weird airmail letter from Dodie? I forgot all about it in the upheaval of getting ready for Gloria. I put it somewhere . . . I'll have to look for it when I get back to the house.

I continued on with my inventory: *plenty of wreath forms; order more hoop pins; that's more florist's tape than I'll use in five years—what was I thinking? It must have been on sale; print more tags; need more wreath boxes*—but all the while an undercurrent of troubling questions kept pace with my list making.

What was it Dodie said? She was happy I was still planning to marry my Mr. Hawkins and glad there wasn't any connection between him and someone called Hawk that Sam was worried about. What was that about?

Sam and Phillip served together in the Navy during the Vietnam era, and only a few years ago I had learned from Phillip that their tours of duty had not always been the innocuous "waiting-off-the-coast" support role that Sam's letters had suggested. Indeed, there had been a dark chapter that I learned of only after Sam's death— *and evidently, there's still more I don't know,* I thought.

Inventory completed, I pulled up the chair to my desk and began to page through the calendar for the coming year—Ben handled the part of the business that supplied herbs and edible flowers to restaurants in Asheville and he kept those records; my responsibility was the wreath making and flower arrangements—sometimes fresh flower and herb wreaths or arrangements for weddings or parties, but usually wreaths or arrangements fashioned from dried materials and meant to last at least a year or two.

There were two small weddings I'd promised to do, bouquets for brides and bridesmaids—yellows and blues for one at the end of May, pink and orange for the other one in early June. And sometime in June, another small wedding—ours.

Phillip and I had decided to wait till then so that his children, both still at college, would be free on summer break. We hadn't set a firm date yet, beyond saying it would be toward the end of the month. And it would be here at the farm.

. . . still planning to marry your Mr. Hawkins . . . What had Aunt Dodie meant by that? Why *wouldn't* I be still planning on it? Heaven knows it had taken me long enough to accept his proposal. In a reversal of the expected male/female roles, I had been the one avoiding commitment, perfectly happy—no, *eager*—for Phillip to move in with me but somehow reluctant for a formalization of our relationship. It had been Phillip who had persisted until finally somehow I'd had a change of heart.

The winter solstice—the anniversary of Sam's death

and, as always, I wanted to be out of the house. So we drove up to Max Patch—there was rime ice . . . and sunshine . . . and something about the day just turned me around and I saw that what Phillip and I had was worth honoring . . . was worth a ceremony and a solemn pledging . . .

I flipped the calendar to June. June 21, the summer solstice, was on a Thursday. I had thought about a weekend but after all, what did it matter? All the guests would be neighbors and family . . . if we planned it for early evening, once the sun was down . . . a picnic supper afterward . . . and the longest day of the year . . .

The symmetry of the whole thing struck me as being perfect. I'd check with Phillip but I was sure he'd agree. Plucking a pencil from the jar at the back of the desk, I circled the date.

There. Done. It's really going to happen. I won't let Gloria change that.

Like a mocking echo, I remembered Ben's words: *You can always hope.*

I~*The DeVine Sisters*

Hot Springs, NC~May 1887

"*Mama?*"

The tentative whisper wavered in the rose-scented dusk of the darkened room. One of the heavy draperies covering the tall windows quivered slightly, allowing light to spill across the thick-piled carpet in a bright stream that vanished almost as quickly as it had appeared.

"*Mama?*"

Hands linked around the tapestry-covered table, the seated figures remained motionless as the child's wistful voice called, first from one side of the room then from another. Above the table a soft, luminescent shape hovered just over the chimney of the low-turned oil lamp— a dancing will-o'-the-wisp, an otherworldly flame that swirled, glowing and dimming, coalescing and dissolving.

There was a choked cry and one of the women half rose. "It's my Julia—Julia, my darling! Mama's here!"

The woman stretched out a tentative hand, but the phantasmal apparition moved higher, as if to escape the searching fingers.

"Madam, you must not!" The gentleman on the bereft mother's right caught at her questing hand and pulled her down to her chair. "You break the circle.

Without our combined energies, the drain on the life force of the medium is insupportable. You must resume your seat."

Across the table the medium groaned and writhed in her chair. Her eyes showed white in the lamp glow and her beautiful countenance was contorted into a mask of suffering.

The grieving mother's face remained upturned but she allowed her neighbors to take her hands once more. The pale phantasm hung above her and from all sides came the pealing of silvery bells.

The child spoke again, this time her voice brimming with pleasure. "Mama, so you've come! But the bells say that my time is almost up and I must go back soon. Will you truly-ooly promise to visit me another day?"

"Oh, it's she . . . my Julia." The words were sobbed rather than spoken but the mother's face was radiant with joy. "My angel child, yes, yes, truly-ooly! But my darling, tell me before you go—are you happy . . . where you are . . . over there?"

"Silly Mama, everyone's happy in Heaven. Truly-ooly . . ."

The bells sounded again and the child's voice grew softer, dying away as the light in the room dimmed and the apparition grew more and more indistinct.

It was a whisper in the still air that breathed into the mother's ear. "I miss you and Papa and the boys but I know that we'll be together again. And when I can speak to you like this, why then the waiting doesn't seem so dreadful. And did you know—I have Tip here with me now. He's all well again and we have ever so much fun, playing in the beautiful garden . . . Mama, I love . . ."

"Julia?" Once more the weeping woman pulled free of her companions' hands. She raised tentative fingers to

her cheek. "She kissed me . . . I felt her touch . . . like the brushing of a feather."

Across the table, the medium slumped senseless in her chair.

"And by the by, Dorothea, the animal's name was Nip, not Tip—when I go to the trouble of collecting useful information for you, the least you can do is to remember it correctly."

The tall dark-haired young woman in the deep violet dressing gown took a book from the jumble of illustrated papers and volumes that shared space on the center table with the remains of a substantial luncheon. She seated herself in the upholstered rocking chair next to the window seat where her sister was nestled amid a mass of silk and velvet fancy pillows.

Dorothea, her sister's mirror image but for the emerald of her dressing gown, did not look up but continued buffing her fingernails. "I don't believe it made a particle of difference, Theo. I could have called the animal Pip or Rip or Gyp—Mrs. Farnsworth heard what she wanted to hear. After the 'truly-ooly'—which I collected myself—she was convinced."

Dorothea stretched out an elegant hand, turning it this way and that, the better to admire her work. "She's booked again for Thursday, is she not, Renzo? And do put out that vile cheroot—the odor is perfectly disgusting!"

The swarthy gentleman lounging on the divan by the window blew out a long plume of blue smoke and, with a dramatic flourish, tossed the smoldering cigar out the open window.

"As always, milady's slightest wish is my command. And yes, La Farnsworth is panting for another kiss from her Julia."

Reaching under the divan, he drew out a short black-

painted rod and gave it a practiced twist. He smiled with satisfaction as the shaft extended in length to something over a yard long. At its end quivered a small black feather.

"I love you, Dorothea." The young man's pleasant baritone shifted to a honeyed falsetto, as the feather tip brushed the ear of the woman in the window seat. "And I love you too, Theodora," he continued in his normal voice, bringing the feather to the cheek of the other sister, who scowled and batted away the wand tip with an unladylike expletive, "though that frown's enough to frighten away even the friendliest of spirits. And your language—what would our dear mother say?"

"I doubt our dear mother would say much, having perished of the drink so many years ago," Theo snapped. An angry flush stained her pale face. "But as to what your mother might say—"

"Theo! Pas devant la domestique!" Dorothea rapped out the warning as a wiry woman of indeterminate age appeared in the doorway. "Have you finished the bedchambers, Amarantha?"

The chambermaid paused, shifting the heavy box of cleaning supplies from one arm to the other. She did not meet the young woman's eye but seemed to be looking at something just beside her. "I reckon that I have. I still got to dust in here and sweep the carpet. The housekeeper wouldn't have sent me along if she had knowed you folks wasn't going to the baths today. I kin come back later—"

"The baths!" Dorothea sat bolt upright amid the cushions. "Good heavens, what time is it? We're booked for three."

She shot an accusing glare at her sister, who was already on her feet and moving toward the bedchamber, tugging at the satin sash of her purple dressing gown.

"Whatever made you ask for such an early appoint-

ment, Doe? You know we always . . ." Her voice trailing behind her, Theodora whisked past Amarantha and into the bedchamber.

Lorenzo pulled a pocket watch from his fob and clicked it open. "It's a quarter till," he called after the pair. "If you girls are able to forgo your usual primping, I should think that—"

The slam of the chamber door cut short his pronouncements as the second sister hurried to ready herself for the baths.

"Like I said, I kin come back later." The chambermaid, standing like a patient work animal, addressed the young man in her flat mountain accents.

His eyes slid over her spare frame and gaunt face and he yawned. "No need—pray, go on with your work— I'll take a stroll while my sisters enjoy the healing waters."

Lorenzo stood and stretched. His hand went to an inner pocket of his morning coat and withdrew a cigar case of fine Moroccan leather. After retrieving his hat and walking stick from the lunette table by the door of the suite, he paused. With a sigh of resignation he retraced his steps, past Amarantha who was kneeling to brush the ashes of a dead fire into a dustpan. At the closed door of the bedchamber, Lorenzo raised his cane to rap on the door but it opened at once and the sisters, now clad in walking dresses of lavender and spring green, burst forth, exchanging muttered recriminations.

"If you would have the decency—"

"Decency! You have the effrontery—"

Lorenzo stepped back to let them pass then followed them out the door into the hotel hallway. "Ladies—I'll see you in the dining room at six-thirty. You do remember, Theo, that the recently widowed Mr. Harris is eager for a consultation—"

Amarantha looked up as the door closed behind the trio.

"Furriners," she commented to the empty room. "Dressed so fine and with money to burn. Think I can't see what's before my eyes? I reckon I could say a word to the manager—and him a strong Baptist—and he'd turn these three out. If that Lo-renzo's the brother of them two huzzies, well then I'm a Tennessee mule . . . But it ain't none of my concern. I got my rooms to do."

Giving the pale marble hearth a final polish with her rag, the woman stood and gazed around the sitting room of the Mountain Park Hotel's third-best suite.

She crossed to the window seat, where she began to plump and rearrange the scattered pillows, placing them in exact alignment.

"There, that's better, now ain't it?" she said to the air. "I like to bust out laughing—her thinking she's so smart and all the while, you making faces at her. You ought not to do me thataway. I ain't fixing to mess with them three."

Amarantha replaced the last cushion and drew the curtains shut. Her faded blue eyes narrowed and came to rest on the black feather protruding from beneath the divan.

"Still and all . . ." Amarantha mused, weighing the possibilities.

THE NEW MOUNTAIN PARK HOTEL

Is North Carolina's all-new, improved resort in the charming mountain village of Hot Springs (formerly Warm Springs).

Set in a 100 acre park, this magnificent edifice in the Swiss-Gothic mode boasts 200 gas-lit, steam-heated bedrooms, 1,000 feet of verandas, including 125 feet of glassed sun parlors.

The natural mineral baths, heated by Earth's own inner fires to temperatures from 96 to 104 degrees Fahrenheit, flow into private marble-lined tubs in the specially designed bathhouse.

Milk from our own dairy; food from our own farms; a resident physician and all appliances for medical treatments, in addition to the healthful mountain air make The Mountain Park a specific for recuperation.

All the amenities for a gay social life are here as well: a grand ballroom, an elegant dining room, music room, gymnasium, amateur theatricals, and our own orchestra, in addition to riding, hiking, archery, bowling, billiards, and many more entertainments for our guests.

Easily accessible by rail from all points.

For an illustrated brochure and further information, including rates and available treatments, apply to: Mr. Steve B. Roberts, The Mountain Park Hotel, Hot Springs, North Carolina

Chapter 3

An Old Friend

Sunday, May 13, and Monday, May 14

Brice! Thank god! I've been trying to get you for hours . . . No, I hate voice mail so I just hung up . . . anyhoo . . . here I am and so far, so good. Not a peep out of Jerry . . . Have *you* heard anything . . . Well, no, I didn't expect he'd exactly broadcast it that I'd left but I thought he might be asking around . . . Did he show up at the club for the usual poker game? . . . Really? . . . Did he mention me at all? . . ."

Gloria swatted at the moth fluttering near her head then started at the sound of scuttling on the deck just below the front porch. Instantly she leapt out of the rocking chair, abandoning the outdoors for the relative safety of the house. Inside, all was quiet. A single comforting light burned in the kitchen, another in the living room.

"Can you still hear me, Brice? I was out on the porch, trying for a stronger signal, but there was some creature stomping around . . . *I* don't know—I didn't stay to make friends . . . god knows, it could have been anything . . . you wouldn't believe this place! This morning I saw *snakes*, at least five of them, lying out in plain sight around this dinky little goldfish pond just off the front deck. I asked my sister why she didn't get an exterminator or something and she looked at me like I was out of my mind.

"Well, no, they weren't *poisonous*—at least, Lizzy said they weren't. She got out a book and showed me pictures of them and went on about natural balance in the fish pool yadda, yadda, but *still,* why in the world . . . Oh, I'm in the dining room now, by the open window . . . no, of course there's no A/C—I told you what this place is like—*primitive.* No A/C, no dishwasher . . . would you believe, no television . . . well, there is a *television* but no cable and no reception worth a hoot—they just use it for movies now and then.

"Good, I can hear you perfectly now and thank god! I'm about to go out of my mind—the tedious things they talk about here—chickens and gardens . . . Oh, that reminds me: you remember I told you that Amanda Lucas . . . you know, Lawrence and Ronnie's daughter . . . well, she's Ben's live-in girlfriend . . . yes, the gorgeous blonde who used to be a model . . . Would you believe she's given all that up to be a *gardener*—making gardens for some of the people moving into this area . . . Yes, she designs them but she gets involved in *all* of it . . . digging in the dirt, weeding . . . She came in the other night all sunburned and filthy . . . Well, it would break her mother's heart to see—

". . . no, Ben has a cabin—really a shack—though the way he and Elizabeth carry on about its history, you'd think it was—what's-its-name—Tara from *Gone With the Wind* . . . Oh, I don't remember the details—something to do with a grave Ben found when he was—god, I can't believe I'm telling you this—digging a hole for an outhouse."

Gloria held the phone away from her ear. An explosion of laughter sounded in the quiet of the dining room.

"Don't be crude. Of course, there's indoor plumbing here in Lizzy's house. You can't imagine I'd . . . No, but not in Ben's shack . . . I offered to pay to have plumbing installed for him but he just went on and on about being too near the creek and drain fields and gray water till I said, 'That's just fine, Benjamin. If it's your choice to live in Third World squalor, then so be it . . .'

"No, as a matter of fact, I *haven't* been able to spend much time yet with Ben—he's always busy with the farmwork. I swear, he might as well be a slave. I offered to take them all out for dinner tonight but Lizzy had planned a big family dinner—my niece Laurel, that's Elizabeth's younger daughter, came out from Asheville and there was Ben and Amanda and Elizabeth and her fiancé Phillip . . .

"Oh yes, he's living here full-time now with my saintly sister; I almost fell over when Lizzy told me; she's always seemed so . . . he's a cop . . . well, with the sheriff's department . . . kind of quiet . . . I think he looks Italian—dark skin and eyes, big shoulders . . . kind of heavyset but not fat . . . Of course he's not my type, Brice—he's *balding*! . . .

"No . . . no . . . but I have to say that there's something in the way he looks at my sister sometimes . . . Oh, Brice, you're *awful*!

"*Any*hoo, here I am all by my lonesome. Everyone's gone to bed but me—you wouldn't believe the hours they keep . . . Hush now, don't say things like that . . .

"I thought you'd met Lizzy . . . Well, maybe not, it *has* been several years since she came back to Tampa . . . and when she did come down, she never wanted to go anywhere, not even to the club for lunch . . . oh, she's *presentable*—but no clothes sense at all and she wears her hair . . .

"Dark brown, but, I'm sorry to say, starting to show some gray and she won't even consider doing anything about it. And she wears it in a long braid down her back. Or, if she's getting what she calls dressed up, she'll wrap the braid around her head like some Scandinavian milkmaid . . . No, we're very different—I take after Mother, who was petite, and Lizzy's tall like our father . . . and of course, she's *older* than I am."

Gloria giggled. "You big flatterer . . . you always did know how to get to me . . . Well, then I guess it's a good thing I'm here and you're there . . . I wouldn't want to keep you *up* after your bedtime . . ."

As she listened, however, her smile faded and her face grew serious. Finally she broke in. "Really, Brice . . . I meant what I told you that last time . . . Yes, you've been a good friend to me—and more than a friend. I know I can count on you . . .

"I'll let you go now but can I give you a call tomorrow—about this time? . . . You're literally my only link to civilization . . . No, this is a new phone—different number. I tossed the old one in the bay before I left Tampa for fear that Jerry could somehow trace me if I had it with me . . . I thought so . . . Well, I'll let you go . . . Till tomorrow then . . . Me too."

Gloria flipped the little phone shut, then held it between her hands as if drawing strength from it. She stared into the darkness beyond the dining room window. Then, with a deep sigh, she allowed her body to sag.

Was this a huge mistake? I had to make up my mind in such a hurry . . . I didn't really think it through. How long am I going to have to stay here? If it weren't that this is the very last place in the world Jerry would think to look for me . . . and that this cop friend of Elizabeth's may come in handy . . . I wonder . . . Maybe I could get an apartment in Asheville . . . at least there'd be cable . . . Lizzy's idea of entertainment . . . What was that weird movie they put on after supper tonight . . . a cartoon, of all things . . . something about triplets . . . three old hags . . . and in French. And there's Elizabeth and that cop of hers holding hands like a pair of lovesick teenagers. Doesn't she understand how utterly ridiculous . . .

Gloria pondered the enigma that was her sister. Elizabeth's husband Sam had been killed in a plane crash back in 1999, and it had looked as if she intended to remain a grieving widow forever. Then Phillip Hawkins had come on the scene—was it three years ago? Elizabeth's infrequent letters hadn't mentioned him at first. But Ben had let slip something about an old friend of Sam's who was evidently very interested in the widow Goodweather. And eventually, in her letters or in their phone conversations, Elizabeth had begun to mention "Sam's friend Phillip Hawkins." This had slowly changed to "my friend Phillip," then just "Phillip," and at last, a few months ago, the casual mention of plans for a wedding in June.

Glancing at the elegant little watch on her wrist, Gloria made a face. *Ten o'clock! If I get in bed now, I'll just lie there and stare at the ceiling . . . Maybe there's a decent magazine to look at . . .*

The chest in front of the sofa offered two hefty stacks of periodicals and she began to go through them. *Backyard Poultry, Countryside, The Herbalist,* were rejected, as were *The New Yorker* and *Smithsonian.* A newspaper—*The Marshall County Guardian*—caught her eye and she paged through it briefly.

God! I'm trapped in a place where it's a front-page headline when a double-wide catches fire.

Pausing at an ad for a tanning and beauty salon, Gloria clicked her tongue in disapproval at the photo of the owner/stylist—a middle-aged woman with Dolly Parton hair surrounding a haggard face—and reached up to pat at her own carefully arranged coiffure.

Tomorrow I'll spend the day in Asheville. Another day out here with Lizzy and I'll go stark raving bonkers.

I'll get something to read and some Perrier—they all carry on about how wonderful the water is here but I don't trust water that comes out of the ground. And I'll have my hair done—what was the name of that place Eleanor raved about when she visited Asheville? The Kindest Cut—that was it.

Tossing the newspaper back onto the chest, Gloria went to Elizabeth's tall secretary and found a notepad and pen. She seated herself, clicked on the desk lamp, and began a list.

"How was your day? Did you like Asheville?" Elizabeth glanced up from the stove where she was stirring something in a giant wok.

Gloria noticed, with a dainty wrinkling of her nose, that her sister hadn't bothered with an apron and that several grease spatters had marked her shirt. *Though with that faded old rag, I guess it hardly matters. You'd think, though, she could at least make an effort . . .*

Phillip put down the knife he had been using to chop broccoli stems and moved to the refrigerator. "Can I get you a glass of white wine, Gloria?"

"A glass of wine would be *lovely,*" she answered, flashing him her most radiant smile before brushing the cushions of the bench at the end of the kitchen free of dog hair. Phillip wasn't her type but it never hurt to let a man know that he was appreciated—something Elizabeth didn't seem to understand.

As Phillip handed her the wineglass, she let her fingers brush against his and smiled up at him from under her eyelashes—that special *intimate* glance that Princess Diana had used so well—but when he turned back to his kitchen chores without any response, Gloria sank down onto the bench, grateful to be off her feet. Perhaps, she thought as she slipped off her heels, the red Jimmy

Choos hadn't been the very best choice for a day of shopping in Asheville—which had turned out to be unexpectedly hilly.

And then moving all those packages out of her little Mini and into the Jeep— *Quel schlep!* as her friend Eleanor would say. She had counted on getting the Mexican help to do that for her but oh, no, they had been pulling out of the driveway just as she returned. Typical.

"Did you find the beauty parlor you were looking for?" Elizabeth dumped a bowl of chopped vegetables into the sizzling wok and whisked them around in a colorful swirl. The smell of garlic and ginger filled the air.

"Well, if you'd look up from cooking for half a minute . . ." Gloria preened, turning her head to display freshly highlighted hair gleaming in subtle striations of bronze, copper, and gold, ". . . you'd see that I obviously did. And I have to say that I was *very* pleasantly surprised. Nigel is a real *artist*—far better than I expected in a place the size of Asheville. Of course, he's from England—he trained with Sassoon."

"Sigfried Sassoon?" Elizabeth asked with an air of innocent surprise. "The World War I poet? But I thought—"

"*Vidal*, you backwoods frump, *Vidal* Sassoon, only the most important stylist—oh, I see that look. You know who I'm talking about—you're just trying to annoy me, aren't you, Lizzy?"

Gloria turned to Phillip. He had taken a seat on the other bench and was watching the two with somewhat alarmed amusement. "I tried to talk Lizzy into going with me—my treat, of course—but I couldn't make a bit of headway with her. You'd be amazed at the change a decent hairdo could make in her looks. She was actually rather striking as a young woman with her dark hair and blue eyes. Nigel could get rid of the gray and give her an attractive cut, something more suitable for a woman of her age. What do you think, Phillip? *I* say it's a shame to see a woman let herself go—"

" 'Let herself go' . . . what does that remind me of?" Elizabeth's voice, brimming with malicious innocence, broke in on her sister's harangue. "Something . . . what was the name of the workshop you took last year—out in California, wasn't it?"

She continued to stir the vegetable mélange, crinkling her brow as if making an effort to remember. "A fancy spa and a very expensive workshop—you emailed me all about it. You said it was led by someone who'd studied with a famous Tibetan lama and that it was life-changing for you. What was the name . . . oh, now I remember—*Letting Go of Self*. So, how's that working out for you, Glory?"

Chapter 4

To Be Fair

Monday, May 14

She really does bring out the worst in me!

I sprawled at one end of the sofa, just breathing in the silence. The day's mail lay unopened in my lap. The dishes had been done—to the unwelcome accompaniment of Gloria's repeated protestations that only a dishwasher could get them *really* clean, along with dire warnings about salmonella and hepatitis C, not to mention leprosy and possibly dengue fever. Phillip had made several trips out to the Jeep to bring in the fruits of Gloria's day in Asheville—shopping bag after shopping bag as well as assorted groceries—including skim milk, half-and-half, Greek yogurt, and a case of little green bottles of Perrier.

Now, at last, we had settled down to our individual pursuits. Gloria was in the guest room, sorting through her non-food purchases—and judging from the shopping bags, it had been a busy and expensive day. Phillip was in the little office, busy with his never-ending cop stuff/paperwork. As for me, I was happy with the quiet doggy company of Molly, stretched out on the sofa beside me, and sweet, shaggy black Ursa, sleeping at my feet.

That was another thing. Gloria was not a dog person. Oh, she pretended—talking to them in high-pitched baby talk and dispensing cautious pats when they came in range—even actually picking up James and holding him like a baby. But you could tell . . . For their part, Molly and Ursa seemed to have summed her up as harmless, if a little odd.

To be fair, I think she actually does like James. He's such a little suck-up—he loves the baby talk and the cuddling. He's probably back there with her now, exerting his canine wiles.

To be fair. That was the problem. *Could* I be fair? After a childhood spent playing "the tall plain one" to Gloria's petite prettiness, I'd taught myself to dismiss my sister as a ditz in high heels, a poster child for conspicuous consumption, a walking dumb blonde joke.

But I had to admit she wasn't the total airhead that she seemed. She had actually been quite clever in arranging her "getaway"—leaving a note for Jerry saying that she would be gone for a month, that there'd been a last-minute vacancy at an exclusive spa in Arizona where she'd been on a waiting list.

"And they're very careful about their clients' privacy at Horizon d'Or," she'd told me. "If Jerry were to call to see if I was there, they wouldn't tell him. Brice—he's a friend of mine who's a cosmetic surgeon—Brice told me that lots of celebrities go there after they've had work done and the staff absolutely will *not* confirm whether someone is there or not. Jerry can curse and bluster all day long but they'll just keep saying that they aren't at liberty to share that information. It's kind of like that thing with priests and Swiss banks."

No wonder Gloria felt safe, tooling around Asheville in her snazzy little car—Jerry thought she was in Arizona. Too bad she wasn't.

You're starting to grind your teeth again, Elizabeth. Get off it and look at your mail.

I'd picked up this lot on my way back from the grocery store and hadn't had the time or energy till now to remove the rubber band around the roll of magazines and envelopes. Bills . . . as always . . . invitations to subscribe, to donate, to buy . . . and a familiar lavender envelope. Another letter from Aunt Dodie? That seemed odd as she rarely writes more than two or three times a year.

But maybe there'd be something to explain that last baffling communication sent from England. I glanced at the stamp—U.S., honoring Longfellow.

Now totally confused, I opened the letter. The familiar lavender pages—and an enclosure on lined paper. I could hear the printer beginning to whir in the little office where Phillip was at work as I began to read:

Elizabeth, dear,

Well as you can see, I'm back at my <u>Home Sweet Home</u>. What's that rhyme—"<u>North, south, east, west, Where e'r you travel, home's best</u>!" But oh, my! Such a wonderful, once-in-a-lifetime trip it was! I'll write you all about it but for now, just a note to explain the enclosed. It seems to be a follow-up to the letter I sent you before I left—the one in the bright red mailer?

In the <u>rush</u> to get ready to fly to England—my passport had expired and I needed traveling clothes and I had to close my house up and, well, with one thing and another, I never finished cleaning out the desk. So just today, I tackled it once more and found this little note which I'm sending along. It seems to refer to the other longer letter which you already have. Of course, you've already "sorted" the matter (that's a phrase I picked up from Meredith's charming husband—so <u>veddy British</u>!)

Oh, Elizabeth, I do hope you can get to the Cotswolds someday! It's absolutely the most beautiful

*place I ever saw! You would love the gardens! And all
the <u>sweet sheep</u> and the beautiful houses of that
golden stone. Like a fairy tale. And the cream teas!
I'm afraid I was quite greedy when faced with hot
scones and jam and clotted cream.*

*But here I'm running on, <u>as usual</u>! When I get my
pictures of the trip back I'll send you a nice long account of my adventures. Though really, I wish you'd
come for a visit, I know how <u>busy</u> you always are but
I'd love to see you, dear.*

The letter nattered on for another page, but with a
sinking feeling I unfolded the enclosed piece of notebook paper. The clear, slanted printing was like a blow
to my stomach—Sam's handwriting. How long had it
been . . .

*Sir, just a few lines to say that I followed your sug-
gestion. I believe the matter will be resolved soon,
with as little adverse effect to the Navy as possible.
The fellow I told you about is hard to pin down—but
I think we have the goods on him this time.*

*Thank you again for your advice and help. I'll let
you know how this plays out.*
Sam

There was no date. It couldn't have been earlier than
'72—Sam hadn't met the Old Gentleman till our honeymoon trip. And the Old Gentleman had died—it would
have been toward the end of '75—I remember that I was
heavily pregnant with Rosemary and so we didn't go to
the funeral.

But Sam was out of the Navy before we married—so
what was this all about?

*I'll reread that letter Dodie sent from England—
maybe the two of them together will make some sense.*

And what *bright red mailer? How could I have missed something like that?*

Hauling myself off the sofa, I went to my desk to look for Dodie's previous letter. From the back of the house floated the sound of music—Gloria had evidently made good on her threat to purchase a CD player for the guest room. Show tunes were her favorite—I hate show tunes.

At last I found the letter lurking under my desk calendar. No matter how hard I squinted at the smudged postmark, I still couldn't make out the name of the town. But the date seemed to be March 19.

March 19 and I had just found it in Phillip's paperwork last week. How could it have taken an airmail letter almost two months to get here?

"Phillip," I said, walking into the office, "I was wondering—"

He was sitting at the computer with his back to me and looked up with a start. At the same time, whatever he had been reading vanished, replaced by the screen saver.

And at the same time, I felt a cold stab of doubt.

You've been down this road before, Elizabeth—back when you first met him. Things weren't what they seemed. Still . . .

I shoved the letter I'd been going to ask him about into my pants pocket and extemporized. "I was just wondering if you had to work next weekend or not—I was kind of sketching out some plans . . ."

He leaned back in the chair, hand still on the mouse. "I don't know for sure . . . It'll depend—" The sound of Gloria's heels tapping on the wooden floor of the living room stopped him.

"Lizzy?" she trilled. "I have a surprise for you! Lizzy, where are you?"

"Just a minute," I called back. Summoning up a weak smile, I nodded at the computer screen. "Sorry I interrupted you—it's no big deal about the weekend anyway."

Phillip shot a curious glance at the bit of letter sticking out of my pocket but said nothing. He turned back to the computer as I headed for the living room and my sister and James, who had followed her from the bedroom, the clicking of his toenails echoing the tapping of her heels.

She was standing there with a gift-wrapped box held out before her—shiny deep purple paper, almost surely the shade known to designers as *aubergine*—wrapped with an intricate arrangement of silk cords in pale green hues.

"I found the most wonderful store—Bravissimo or something like that. *The* most gorgeous clothing—'wearable art' they call it. And when I saw this"—she placed the box in my hands—"well, I immediately thought of you! Go on—open it!"

"Gloria—you don't need to get me stuff." I sat down on the sofa and began to undo the cords. It seemed like sacrilege to destroy the lovely web they made. Somewhere in the back of my mind I was wondering what sort of wildly expensive, completely unusable thing she had gotten for me.

I had been to Bravissimo—a kind of fusion between an art gallery and a high-end boutique—dragged there by Laurel when a fellow artist friend of hers had a series of innovative little jackets on display in the elegant shop. Gorgeous little jackets—with astronomical price tags, as I recalled. Beautiful one-of-a-kind handmade garments fit for Oscar night or the sort of event *I'd* certainly never be attending.

Gloria perched on the other end of the sofa and watched as I pulled off the last cord and set it to the side. Her face was glowing with a pure, unselfconscious delight that made her look somehow younger and softer. James snuggled at her side.

"For goodness' sake, just rip the paper off, Lizzy!" Gloria urged as I carefully peeled off the gold seals at either end of the package.

"It's so pretty—I'll save it to use again," I answered, removing the thick glossy paper, rolling it up, and tying it with one of the silk cords. As I lifted the top of the white rectangular box, a hint of a clean, crisp fragrance wafted out from the folds of rustling tissue. Putting off the moment when I would be expected to gush over some costly, inappropriate, over-the-top piece of clothing, I smiled at my little sister. She obviously meant well. And I was going to do the right thing, even if it meant lying.

"Glory, this is really sweet of you—"

"Lizzy, if you don't open your present this very minute, I'm going to *scream*!"

And so I did. I laid back the crackling leaves of tissue to see a shimmering of silk—periwinkle blue, lavender, blue-violet, cobalt—the most delicious shades of blue and purple all in one amazing fabric.

Carefully—no, reverently—I took the wonderful thing out of the box, stood, and shook out its glimmering folds.

A kimono—quite possibly the loveliest garment I'd ever seen. The colors—like all the irises of spring . . . like a mountain lake . . . like—

"I *knew* it was right for you," Gloria crowed. "Go look in the mirror—hold it near your face and just see what it does for your eyes."

"I don't know what to say, Glory. It's . . . it's magnificent."

And it was—I had thought I was beyond caring about clothes, but this . . . "What is this fabric? It's incredible."

"There's a little folder in the box that tells all about it—it's handwoven ikat silk—ikat is where they dye the silk threads in all different colors before they ever start to weave. The man in charge of the shop explained the process very nicely. That's how they get all those shades fading into one another."

I was staring in the mirror—maybe I was imagining it but my eyes *did* seem changed when I held the robe up to my face—deeper, with a hint of violet. The thought of how the silk would feel against my bare skin, of the delicious sensation of—

"Glory, I know how expensive things are at that place. You really shouldn't—"

"Oh, hush! I knew you'd say that." She beamed at me, still full of that happy goodwill. "Just think of it as a little something for your trousseau—and while we're on the subject, tell me about your wedding plans. You said next month—but where? And what will you wear? I saw a lovely dress—"

There was a sudden coldness in the pit of my stomach. *Of course, you've already "sorted" the matter,* Aunt Dodie had written.

But I hadn't. And now all the doubts that had tormented me before came boiling up out of the hidden places to buzz and chatter in my head.

"I . . . we wanted to wait till the end of June when Phillip's kids and Rosemary could be here. We haven't actually picked a day but—"

"Well, you'd better get cracking so you can send out a Save the Date card—no, it's really too late for that. Might as well just go on and send the invitations."

The old Gloria had returned.

I began to fold the lovely kimono, savoring the luxurious slide of the fabric against my fingers. With a last appreciative look, I laid the beautiful gift back in the tissue.

"The wedding's only going to be small—a few phone calls or emails will take care of inviting people. We plan to be married here—"

"*Here?* Are you sure?" Gloria frowned. "Well, I suppose your garden is pretty enough but what if it rains? Let's see, you could put the tent—"

"No tent," I said. Suddenly it was an effort to talk about what had been an occasion I'd been looking forward to, keeping a surreptitious list that I amended from time to time. "Like I said, really small. If we had to, it could be right here in the living room. But nothing's set in stone just yet."

Nothing at all.

Chapter 5

Looking for Comfort

Monday, May 14, and Tuesday, May 15

Phillip was still at the computer when I told Gloria good night and headed for my bath. There has always been an unspoken pact between me and the rest of the world to the effect that no one bothers me when I'm in the tub—no phone calls, no messages, no questions. Even when the girls were very little, it was Sam who was on call while I zoned out in my bath for a half hour or so. This time of respite has kept me reasonably sane through various rough patches and I guard and treasure it. The old iron claw-foot tub where I can run the water hot and high, then relax with a book till the water gets too cool, has always been my safe place, my comfort and sanctuary where cares are left on the other side of the door. Unfortunately, however, this time I'd brought them in with me.

A friend had recently sent me a bottle of some wonderful-smelling orange-ginger bath gel and I dumped a generous dollop under the flowing faucet and watched the bubbles froth higher and higher. They seemed an apt reflection of the thoughts and suppositions, the hints and allegations that were threatening to overflow my mind, but hoping that the warm water would work its usual magic, I pulled off my clothes, pinned my braid atop my head, and stepped into the bath. My reading material—the latest *New Yorker*, as well as both of Dodie's letters—lay on the edge of the wash basin but I ignored it all in favor of lying back, eyes closed, for a long thoughtful soak.

How could I, in Aunt Dodie's words, "sort things" without making Phillip think I was having second thoughts, without making him think I didn't trust him? *Or,* I mused, *without letting him know what I'm worried about—in case it's true . . . What if Phillip* is *the mysterious Hawk that Sam didn't trust? What if* I *shouldn't trust him?*

There was so much in the past . . . lies and half-truths . . . first from Sam . . . later from Phillip. Even in the beginning—Phillip's moving to Asheville and looking me up—there'd been a hidden agenda.

All of that had been resolved, explained away by Phillip . . . at least, I'd *thought* it resolved. But I knew from bitter experience that the past has an ugly way of persevering . . . and becoming the present.

I stared at the white billows piled high atop the water, trying to put my unspoken questions into words: What exactly was in that first letter of Sam's, the letter that had gone missing in its bright red mailing envelope? Wherever it was, why had it made Aunt Dodie think that I might not be going to marry "my Mr. Hawkins"? She had obviously believed there might be a connection between Phillip and this person called the Hawk, this person Sam had been worried about . . .

You need to read that letter from England again.

Sitting up, I reached for my towel, dried my hands, and took the airmail letter from its hiding place between the pages of the magazine. *Hiding place? Is that how you're really thinking . . . already? Sounds like you've made up your mind.*

Skimming down the page, I stopped at this paragraph.

The <u>peculiar thing</u> is that Sam spends most of this letter telling the Old Gentleman about some strange "detached duty" he and this other man had been sent on. He asks the OG if he has obtained any information on "the matter I mentioned in my last letter" and then goes on to say that he's not sure if he can TRUST the other man whom he calls <u>the Hawk</u> . . ."

That was it—the thing that was unsettling me. The strange "detached duty" Sam and this other man had been sent on, the other man Sam said he wasn't sure he could trust—the man he called the Hawk.

It was years after Sam's death when I had learned the truth about his time in the Navy during the Vietnam era—had learned that rather than serving aboard a supply ship, as he had told me, Sam had been "in country" and witness to a sickening atrocity.

And Phillip had been with him. Phillip *Hawk*ins.

And it was Phillip who'd given me the full story—though Sam's nightmares and the eventual diagnosis of post-traumatic stress disorder had made it obvious that there was more to his time in the Navy than he was willing to tell. I had always hated the fact that he wasn't open with me—

Yes? And are you being open with Phillip?

No. I absolutely was not. The longer I lay in the cooling water, watching the scented foam disintegrate, the more warning bells went off. Phillip had come into my life for reasons I wasn't made aware of till several years had gone by. He had not been what he seemed—

That all got straightened out, remember?

Maybe. But I had learned, to my sorrow, that though Vietnam was in the past, the evil brought to life by tragic events from that time was still alive, still dangerous. And though Phillip had seemed to be on the side of the angels, who could say if the scenes that played out two years ago were the final act?

Get off *it, Elizabeth! You're like a bloody rodent on an exercise wheel.*

I grabbed the washcloth and wiped at my already clean face, trying to put these increasingly repetitive thoughts aside.

The Hawk . . . Mackenzie calls Phillip "Hawk." It's a logical nickname.

Did Sam ever call Phillip anything but Hawkins? They got together a few times after Vietnam—that time Sam met his Navy buddies in DC to see the Vietnam memorial . . . I'm pretty sure Sam always referred to him as Phillip—maybe Phil—or just Hawkins. And if he didn't trust him, why did he go on keeping in touch with him?

This is bullshit, Elizabeth. You know *this man.*

I could hear him moving about the bedroom, the jingle of coins as he slid out of his slacks, the creak of the springs as he lay down, and the click of the reading light. He would be reading that Harlan Coben paperback, no doubt.

The water was cold now. And I'd decided. There would be no more secrecy, no more wondering. I would ask if he'd seen the red mailer, ask why he didn't give me the airmail letter, ask if he'd ever been called the Hawk . . .

And we'd laugh at Aunt Dodie's overwrought fears and I'd put on my beautiful gift from Gloria, sliding it over my freshly bathed body, and wait for him to notice how it turned my eyes to violet-blue . . .

I pulled the plug and hurriedly stepped out of the tub. As I toweled myself dry, I remembered that I hadn't brought the kimono into the bathroom with me. There was just my usual oversized T-shirt—the magical garment was in its tissue-lined box, on a shelf in my closet.

Never mind—just go in there and show him this silly letter.

When I emerged from the bathroom, my teeth brushed, my hair loosed from its braid, my body soft and fragrant with lavender-scented powder, there he was, sound asleep, a book open on his chest and his reading glasses on his nose. He didn't wake as I removed the book and the glasses, but when I crawled in beside him, he reached out a hand to give me a perfunctory pat on the leg, then, muttering something about an early start, rolled on his side and returned to the deep breathing of heavy sleep.

When I awoke he was gone.

I sat up and glared at the sun which was already well up—I'd lain awake for quite a while last night in spite of repeatedly reminding myself that there was nothing to worry about, that in the morning we'd straighten things out. And so I'd overslept.

Maybe he was in the kitchen fixing some breakfast . . . maybe there'd be a moment to talk before Gloria appeared in *her* lovely robe, makeup subtle but perfect, blond hair just *slightly* tousled . . . but no. There on the chest by the bed, where I'd put his book and glasses last night, was a note: *Mac needed me early and we may be out of touch all day. I'll try to call if I won't be home at the usual time. Love you—P.*

I frowned. *Out of touch* usually meant that some big bust was under way: a patch of marijuana hidden back on national forest land, a fence with a hoard of stolen chain saws, a meth lab, or even a moonshine still. This last was rare but a few hard-core fellows held to the old ways and turned out their white liquor in spite of the fact that you could buy cheaper stuff at any ABC store. What had begun simply, as a "value added" way of making a living from the corn that was one of the few crops easily grown in these mountains, was now almost a niche market. "Artisanal" moonshine, packaged quaintly in Mason jars half filled with peaches, blueberries, or some other fruit, was the drink of choice for a certain set.

I crumpled the note in my hand. Well, hell. But maybe he'd get home before Gloria—she had already informed me that she was going back into Asheville for a visit to a spa. "I knew I'd be worn out from a day of shopping, so I went on and scheduled a half-day treatment. Sometimes, I just need some 'me time,' you know, Lizzy?"

Good, I thought. *Let her have her precious "me time." As if there's ever any other kind for Glory. It'll give me a chance to go see Miss Birdie.*

"Why, look who's coming! What's a-gonna happen?"

It was Miss Birdie's standard greeting whenever more than a week or two passed without my stopping in. It *had* been longer than usual—the gardens were demanding at this time of year . . . and then I had to get ready for Gloria. I'd been going to stop several times but on one occasion Birdie's truck had been gone and another day I'd seen Dorothy's car and a strange vehicle there and had decided to postpone my visit. It always seems to me that with the quiet life she leads, Birdie'd probably rather not have all her visitors at once.

"Hey, Miss Birdie!" Grinning at my little neighbor as I climbed the steps to the cabin's porch, I gave my standard response. "You remember who I am?"

"Come on in and git you a chair, Lizzie Beth," she directed, her wrinkled face beaming as she held the screen door wide. "Wherever have you been all this time?"

Visiting Miss Birdie is always a comfort, from the predictability of her greeting to the unchanging décor of her living room—the recliner facing the television set, the Bible and the telephone on a table beside the recliner, the feed store calendar and the fly swatter sharing a nail on the wall by the kitchen door, and the shelves filled with the little wooden animals her son Cletus had carved. It was in the wake of Cletus's untimely death that I had really gotten to know Birdie and to appreciate her strength and wisdom. I only hope that when I'm her age—somewhere up in the eighties—that I can be as happy in my skin as she is in hers.

"Ben and that pretty Amandy stopped in day before yesterday." Birdie took her place on the recliner as I dropped onto the plastic-covered sofa. "He said you and Phillip was planning a wedding next month and I said I knowed that sooner or later you was going to come around and I was glad to hear it."

Par for the course. I don't think I've ever managed to be the first to tell Miss Birdie any news. She seems to attract it like a magnet. Usually it's her friend Bernice who keeps her informed about local goings-on—how many times has Birdie greeted me with the details of some late-breaking event, prefaced by "Bernice's boy heard it on the scanner"?

"Well, that Ben! He beat me to it." I was in defensive mode now, already a little guilty at not having stopped by earlier. "I was going to tell you as soon as we decided on a date but my sister—"

Birdie studied at me over the top of her glasses. "Ben *told* me his mommy was making a long visit. I seen a shiny little black and yellow car going down the road yesterday and again this morning. Reckon that must have been her."

I explained that Gloria was a city girl and not used to shopping only once a week or less. "She's still just getting settled but I'll bring her over soon so she can meet you," I promised, wondering what these two would make of one another.

"Now I'd like that just fine, Lizzie Beth." Birdie's

bright blue eyes twinkled at me then turned to peer out
the window. "Law, there goes that Roberts boy again;
he's up and down this road every whipstitch." She
watched the truck out of sight then turned back to me.
"Tell me about your sister, Lizzie Beth. Seems like I remember you saying she lives in Florida. You uns haven't
seen much of one another over the years, now have
you?"

"No . . . it's hard for me to get away, and Gloria . . ."
*Gloria hates it here. She wouldn't have come if it
weren't for this supposed death threat.* ". . . Gloria stays
pretty busy too."

"Ay law, that's a cruel shame." The sharp blue eyes
grew misty. "I had me four sisters but they every one of
them married and went off while I was still just a little
thing—me being the least un. The only one I remember
at all is Fairlight—and they's ever one of 'em dead and
buried long since. No, talking of sisters, I'd say Belvy—
you remember the one they call Aunt Belvy, her at the
Holiness Church over to Tennessee?"

Oh, yes, I remembered Belvy—a formidable presence
who spoke in tongues and prophesied when the Spirit
took her. Little chance I'd forget Belvy.

I nodded and started to answer but Birdie wasn't pay-
ing any attention to me. She was staring at the gray
screen of the silent television, just as if she were watching one of her stories unfold.

"Belvy was my playmate growing up and as close a
thing to a sister as there is. And though we've gone our
different ways this many a year and don't hardly see one
another but once in a great long while, I always knew
that in time of need . . ."

Her voice trailed off and she shook herself as if waking. "I do go on, don't I? But I'm proud that you and
your sister will have some time together now. You know,
Lizzie Beth, a sister's a comfort and a treasure in good

times . . . and she'll always look out for you when times is bad."

It was early afternoon and I was weeding the nasturtium beds down at the lower place when I heard the scrape of metal on rock. Looking up I saw Gloria's Mini Cooper bucketing up the dirt and gravel driveway—far too fast for the low-slung car to negotiate the ruts and water breaks.

With a final *clang* as it wheeled into the parking spot beside the corncrib, the little car stopped, the door swung open, and my sister—*my comfort and treasure*—leaped out.

"Lizzy!" she shrieked and began to run toward me, her high heels teetering on the uneven terrain. "Lizzy! He was there!"

II~*Amarantha*

Cripple Tree Holler~May 1887

"Come three angels from the North,
Take both fire and frost."

The boy stood before the gaunt woman, his bared arm outstretched, his hand held in hers. The burn was on the inner arm, an angry red that reached from wrist to elbow with watery blisters covering much of its surface. As she spoke the words a second time, Amarantha waved her free hand over the burn, fanning the heat away from the trembling boy.

"Come three angels from the North,
Take both fire and frost."

The boy shut his eyes as Amarantha bent to blow on the burned area but his companion—a younger brother, to judge by their identical bowl-cut, carrot-colored hair and shirts cut from the same blue-checked homespun— leaned in closer to watch.

"Zeb! Them blisters, they's—" he began in great excitement, only to be silenced by a sharp glare from the burn doctor. Once again she repeated the charm.

"Come three angels from the North,
Take both fire and frost."

*And again she waved her hand and bent to blow on
the reddened forearm. Finally, she straightened. "Well, I
believe we've drawed the fire out. Now you uns wait
here whilst I go to the house and get some balm to dress
it."*

*The two young boys nodded and stood transfixed,
their eyes following the witchy-woman as she climbed
the log steps to her front porch. When she had disappeared into the dark interior, the younger whispered,
"Zeb! Them blisters just dried plumb up! I was watching while she spoke the words. I seen it!"*

*Zeb was examining his forearm with openmouthed
awe. Only a faint reddening remained of what had been
an angry and painful burn.*

*"Well, I be . . . and hit don't hurt no more, not one
little bit." He tapped a cautious finger up and down the
length of his forearm, repeating the words. ". . . not one
little bit."*

*"Reckon she really is a witch, like old man Henderson
done said." The younger boy's eyes surveyed the bare-
swept dirt of the yard where a few yellow hens
scratched, the looming boxwoods near the branch, the
iron wash pot upside down on three big fire-blackened
rocks. "Her place don't look noways different to most
folkses' places. Seems as how a witch'd ought to—"*

*"Hsst!" A sharp jab from his brother's elbow and the
younger boy's mouth snapped shut as Amarantha reappeared at the door. A basket on her arm, she de-
scended the steps with measured tread and solemn face,
having found that her charms always worked best if the
patient was a little afraid of her.*

*Setting the basket on the ground, she lifted out a
small dark brown crock filled with yellow ointment. A*

smooth wooden handle protruded from the waxy-looking substance.

"Hold out your arm again, boy," she directed. "This balm'll seal the healing in."

Zeb did as he was told, wincing slightly at the first cold touch of the ointment but then relaxing as the small paddle slid gently up and down, spreading the greasy stuff over the wound.

"Now," said Amarantha, returning the crock to the basket and taking out a little cloth bag, "let's us see about your brother."

She fixed the younger boy with a stern gaze. "You want to get rid of them ugly warts on your hand, young un?"

Instantly the little brother whipped his right hand behind his back, ready to deny its very existence, but Zeb answered for him.

"Thanky, ma'am, we'd be obliged. Mommy purely hates the look of them things on Clete's hand. I told him not to go fooling with them old toads but—"

"How many warts are there, young un?" Amarantha's clear blue eyes held young Clete with an uncompromising stare till he produced a grubby hand for her inspection.

"Reckon they's five . . . ma'am." The boy stared at the ground to avoid the icy gaze. "But they ain't—"

"They ain't gone trouble you much longer." Amarantha was already reaching into the cloth poke and counting out five kernels of corn. "Hold these in t'other hand and don't drop them. Now I want you to close your eyes tight and count out loud. I want you to count to five, five times, you hear?"

Clete, both hands extended, began to count in a shaky voice. Zeb watched wide-eyed as Amarantha reached down and withdrew a silver needle from the hem of her *apron. In a lightning blur, her hand darted out and pricked the largest of the warts.*

". . . four, five. One, two, three, four, five. One, two, three, four, five." The count was finished and the boy appeared not to have noticed the needle's sting. On the largest wart, a drop of bright blood was forming.

"All right, young un, you done good. Open your eyes and pour the corn over to your other hand and don't you dare to drop it. You see there's a bitty of wart blood—you want to get it on the corn . . . Good. Now say after me, 'You grow and you go.' "

"You grow and you go," Clete quavered, his hand trembling but still outstretched.

"That's a good boy. You're almost done—now cast the corn to the ground."

Hardly had the red-stained kernels hit the dirt than the hens were at the boy's feet, gobbling down the corn.

"You grow and you go," Amarantha repeated, watching with satisfaction as the last piece of grain disappeared. "Now you boys get on home—leave that balm on till this time tomorrow, Zeb. And you, Clete, wash your hand in branch water for the next five nights and them warts'll fall off afore the week is out."

She watched them go, tumbling over each other in their eagerness to be well away from the witchy-woman. But just before they reached the trees that ringed the cabin site, the older boy slowed and turned. "We thank you, ma'am!" he called, and the younger echoed him.

"Thanky, thanky . . ." The words still hung in the air as the two plunged into the woods and vanished from sight.

Amarantha's stern expression softened. "Fine young uns . . . My, how I wish . . ." She left the sentence unfinished. With a sigh, she climbed the steps to return the contents of the basket to her cabin. With only one day in the week free from her work at the hotel, there wasn't time to stand about considering the what-ifs.

She set the crock on a shelf amongst others then tied on a faded blue poke bonnet. "I got to get on down the mountain after them merkles," she muttered. "That cook said he'd pay high for as many as I could bring him. What did he call them—mo-rels. Funny how many names them things has. I've known some to call them honeycomb musharoons and others name them wood fish. Hit don't matter what he calls them, long as he pays. And they's bound to be a mess of them in the old orchard round the Gahagan place."

"What a peculiar name! Why Cripple Tree, do you suppose?"

The woman's voice was raised to be heard above the steady clip-clop of hooves. Amarantha could see the riders clear: a dark-haired young woman and a portly older man. Struggling to prevent his gelding, one of the Mountain Park's more obstinate hacks, from pausing to browse every few seconds, the man answered in little bursts of polite words to the woman, interspersed with loud invective directed at the wayward horse.

"Who can tell about these outlandish names? . . . Come up, sir! . . . The natives appear to delight in the drollest and quaintest designations for their remote creeks and coves . . . Leave it, you vile creature, fit only for glue . . . Forgive me, I was going to mention Bone Camp, Spillcorn, Shake Rag, and Shut In—but a few that I've noted."

The man yanked at the reins and with repeated kicks urged his nag alongside his companion's mount.

"Miss DeVine . . . or may I say Miss Dorothea . . . ?"

The young woman pulled her horse to a halt and turned to look at the petitioner. She made an elegant picture atop the bright bay mare, deep green twill riding *habit draped over her mount's shining russet flank, and her slender torso, encased in a severe high-buttoned basque, rising straight and elegant. Behind the half-veil of her modish little hat, long eyelashes fluttered like captive birds.*

"Mr. Peavey . . . our acquaintance is hardly an old one, only a week and a day, I believe. But at a genteel resort such as this, where one meets one's friends daily, surely a little . . . familiarity is allowable . . ."

Mr. Peavey, his ruddy face wreathed in smiles, pressed his horse closer. "My dear Miss Dorothea, how wisely you speak—" He reached for Dorothea's gloved hand.

Eluding his grasp with a lift of her reins that put the bay mare to a walk, Dorothea giggled, a liquid burble of merriment. "Mr. Peavey, we are approaching a fork in the trail. Pray, which way do we go? To the left or to the right?"

Kicking the gelding into a marginally more rapid walk, Mr. Peavey squinted ahead. "Let me think . . . I was here last week with a local guide . . . Oh, yes, now I remember, we take the right and downward fork—it joins another trail a little farther on and that trail leads back to the stables."

The truth of this statement was verified as both horses strained toward the right-hand fork. Dorothea reined in her mare and looked longingly up the other trail.

"But I wonder what lies that way? Perhaps we should explore—"

"My dear Miss Dorothea—the guide warned us against taking that road. He was quite adamant—claimed that a witch—or as he put it, a witchy-woman—lives up there."

Dorothea's eyes were sparkling with lively delight as she tugged at the reins to turn her mare. "Then we certainly must explore. A witch—how delicious!"

Peavey pulled his mount to a stop, blocking the way.

"But, Miss Dorothea, have you forgotten? I am engaged to support my friend Harris when your sister attempts to summon the spirit of his late wife. He is relying upon me."

Dorothea's mouth fell open and she clapped a gloved hand to it. "How could I have forgotten! Of course we must return at once. Your poor friend—he's quite low in his spirits, I believe you said?"

As the two horses moved down the trail, the man's earnest tones rose above the brisk tattoo of the horses' hooves.

". . . If only your sister can fulfill poor Harris's longing to communicate with his wife just one last time. The carriage accident that took her from him was cruel enough. But he lives daily with the memory of his parting words to her—hasty words said in the morning; words that would undoubtedly have been kissed away in the evening. He still carries with him the diamond bracelet he had purchased earlier on that fateful day, hoping to win her forgiveness . . ."

As the sounds drew away, Amarantha shook her head. "A man's a fool for a pretty face like hers," she murmured. "By the time they're back to the hotel, she'll have turned him inside out and she'll know ever last thing he knows about poor old Mr. Harris. I see how them two huzzies work it. But it ain't right."

BURN DOCTORS

The testimonial below was obtained in 1989 from a fifty-five-year-old male, a resident of eastern Tennessee. The incident described, however, occurred in the 1970s in West Virginia. *We had people who could talk the fire out of you. I don't know how they done it but they did. I seen them do it. Stood there and watched them. I couldn't believe it, but, anyway, grease all over the woman's hand. I mean, it just burnt her whole arm and the guy sits there and took a hold of her hand and just talked and the damn thing [the burn] just went away. I mean, the blisters just went away and everything . . . Yes, I sat there and watched him, J.B., do it. L.J. jerked a pan of grease back and it went all over her arm. Her hand is burned up! There's blisters all over it and he sits there and talks and the blisters are going away. I said, "What are you doing?" And he's holding her hand and, I swear, the s.o.b. is sitting there holding her hand, and he's talking, you know, and the burn is going away. L.J. said, "I still don't believe it because I ain't got no scars or nothing." Anyway, you can go to Talledega Alabama Central Prison and see him and talk to him about it.*

It is likely that the burn doctor in this case used a charm well known in the region, and in English folk medicine as well, to "talk the fire out," a version of which is the following: "There came an angel from the east bringing fire and frost. In frost, out fire. In the name of the Father, the Son, and the Holy Ghost." Another version collected in 1939 in western North Carolina substitutes "salt" for "frost": "God sent three angels coming from the east and west. One brought fire, another salt. Go out fire, go in salt. In the name of the Father, the Son, and the Holy Ghost."

Chapter 6

The Monkey in the Middle

Tuesday, May 15

What about it, Hawk, have you two set the date? I need to work out the duty rosters for June."

Sheriff Mackenzie Blaine—high sheriff of Marshall County, in the old-time parlance—stood in the doorway of Phillip's tiny office, a cubicle partitioned off from a conference room, frowning at the clipboard in his hands. "You said you wanted to take a week sometime in June . . . that'll work . . . long as it's not the first week . . . Travis's put in for leave then—his wife's due the end of this month. So, when do you want me to put you down for?"

Phillip rolled his chair back from the computer. "You got me, Mac. We were waiting to find out when the kids would have some time off. Now it looks like they're all available anytime after the middle of June. But Lizabeth hasn't actually settled on a date. There's been a distraction . . . and her name is Gloria."

Blaine's brown eyes widened and he stepped into the cubicle, closing the door behind him. "You want to talk about this? I thought—"

"Have a seat, Mac." Phillip reached over and swept an accumulation of paperwork from the chair next to the desk. "I need to bring you up to speed."

* * *

". . . so I've been doing a little online snooping re this Jerry Lombardo—the husband Gloria swears is out to get her. And no," Phillip held up a hand as Blaine started to speak, "I haven't tried to contact anyone with the Tampa PD—according to Gloria, old Jerry's pretty tight with them. And what's more, according to Lizabeth, it's possible that Gloria's making the whole thing up."

The sheriff said nothing but Phillip felt Blaine's shrewd brown eyes on him. "What?"

The sheriff tapped the clipboard on his lap. "I was just wondering . . . is everything okay between you and Elizabeth? Back at the first of the year when you told me you two were going to make it official, you were—hell, I don't know, Hawk—without getting all sensitive, I'd have said you were as happy a fella as I'd ever seen. But recently . . . well, it seems like something's changed. Is it the cop work? That always gets to spouses sooner or later. One reason I've never thought about remarrying—"

Phillip broke in, shaking his head. "Yeah, I felt that way too . . . After Sandy and I split I swore there was no way I'd ever get myself into that situation again. But then I got to know Lizabeth . . ."

And she got to me . . . in spite of all the reasons not to get involved . . . and especially not with her.

Setting aside those troubling thoughts, Phillip shrugged. "It's not the hours—hell, Lizabeth keeps pretty long hours herself. And the woman's as independent as a hog on ice—those years alone after Sam died, she pretty much got into the habit of not needing anyone. So if I'm out late or leave home early, she just rolls with it."

Blaine raised his eyebrows but Phillip ignored his boss's skeptical expression. "No, Mac, it's not the job. What it is . . . well, at least part of it's her sister Gloria. You never saw two more different women—I don't know how the hell they came out of the same family.

And even though Lizabeth is trying really hard, Gloria's always making these little comments and suggestions . . . I don't know, I guess she means well but it rubs Lizabeth the wrong way and it's making her . . . well, short-tempered . . . and sometimes a little . . . if it was any other woman, I'd say she was acting bitchy. Plus she's gotten kind of distant—like something's on her mind. And when she and Gloria start sniping at each other, I feel like I'm the monkey in the middle."

Blaine put down the clipboard and leaned closer. He kept his voice low. "Listen, Hawk, it's none of my business—except that I don't like having my number two guy distracted by personal problems—but it sounds to me . . . sounds like someone's having second thoughts."

A silence hung between the two men. At last Phillip ran a hand over his bald scalp. "If it wasn't for—" he began but Blaine waved aside his explanation and stood.

"Like I said, none of my business. You doing any good finding out about this Lombardo character? If I can help—"

"Thanks, maybe later. So far I can't find anything against him. He appears to be a legitimate businessman but evidently there've been some investigations into his operations. Some of his associates have been nailed but he's got a Teflon hide—nothing seems to touch him."

Phillip reached for a printout that lay beside his computer screen and handed it to Blaine. "Here's one thing that might be significant: Lombardo's first wife—woman he'd been married to for years—died in a hit-and-run accident back in '03 and the driver was never found. This was right before he got together with Gloria—who, by the way, was a very, very rich widow at the time. Lombardo had always maintained a pretty lavish lifestyle but in recent years he's had some setbacks. I suppose Gloria could have been the answer to his problems. "

Blaine scanned the page, then looked up. "Tampa, you said? You know anyone down there? Anyone you can trust?"

"Afraid not." Phillip glanced at his watch and pushed his chair back. "I'm done here for now. I'm due in court to testify in that drunk driving case. Should be back in plenty of time for our little expedition. I told Lizabeth I might be late."

As he sat in the crowded courtroom, awaiting the call for his testimony and half hearing the lawyers' opening statements, Phillip's mind skimmed the surface of his memory like a flat pebble skipping over a still pool. The Navy years, the training camp where he met Sam . . . must have been the end of the sixties . . . Sam showing him the picture of the dark-haired girl with the amazing blue eyes . . . Sam's Liz . . . now his own Lizabeth . . . or so he hoped.

The younger lawyer—*hardly old enough to shave, that kid*—was addressing the jury. "The settlement of the insurance claims . . ."

The awkward beginning . . . she with all her defenses up . . . the necessary lies . . . *Please, God, don't let that shit come back to bite me in the ass* . . . the deepening emotional involvement . . . her clueless bravery in the face of evil.

"We will show that my client could not have been behind the wheel as the state has stipulated but rather that . . ." *The kid's got the moves, though. Looks like he's spent a little time watching courtroom TV.*

Then they had become lovers . . . but she had evaded his offers of marriage with a dogged determination to remain unattached . . . eventually revealing that she'd taken Sam's death as a kind of betrayal and feared that a second marriage would leave her vulnerable again.

The plaintiff was on the stand now, denying up and down that he had been behind the wheel of the wrecked car. A skinny, grinning clown of a Marshall County good ol' boy, he had been outside the courthouse earlier, laughing and joking with his cousin, the defendant—who also claimed not to have been driving.

Both men had been injured, or so they had claimed, when the vehicle left the mountain road and plowed into a tree. Phillip had been the first law officer on the scene. He and the EMS had arrived within seconds of each other to find that the injured pair had crawled away from the car and were sprawled side by side in the dimming glow of the shattered headlights.

Like my daddy always told me, the good Lord protects drunks and fools, the EMT had muttered as she strapped the neck brace on one semiconscious victim. *I believe these two qualify on both counts—they got double protection. Ain't no other reason they ain't both of 'em dead.*

The thought came to him that Lizabeth would enjoy this story—two good old boys, each trying to get the other's insurance company to pay for his injuries . . . and each with the identical defense: "No sir, Your Honor, I know for certain sure that it weren't me driving that night. I was *way* too drunk to drive!"

I guess she'd enjoy it . . . I don't know if she's enjoyed much of anything since Gloria's phone call. All the cleaning and commotion—the dogs had to be bathed, every last spiderweb vacuumed up, god knows what else. Plus the usual farmwork. Wearing herself out and for what? Women! What is it with them that they always—

He was being summoned to the stand now. As he walked to the front of the courtroom, he was struck with the realization that this was the first time he'd thought of Lizabeth that way—as one of that vast and unknowable sisterhood summed up by the quasi-expletive "Women!"

The thought of home was like a beacon light at the end of the tunnel of the day. Home, a shower, and a beer . . . maybe put his feet up and finish that paperback. He'd had to stop just when the wisecracking hero was in a hell of a fix. Phillip knew it would be okay because the hero had left his concealed cellphone on with his psychotic, preppy sidekick on the other end and, no doubt, on the way to provide a little lethal backup.

He grinned in anticipation. Reading murder mysteries wasn't usually something he enjoyed—too easy to nitpick over proper procedure and implausible coincidences. But *this* series—something about the blend of smart-ass humor and breakneck pace allowed him to just read for the fun of it without analyzing everything. Still, he did wonder about that stunt with the cellphone . . . would you really be able to hear what was going on if . . .

The house was all alight as his SUV crawled up the road. Phillip glanced at the clock on the dashboard. Ten-twenty—later than he'd expected to be. But that last-minute task of transferring a prisoner to a neighboring county had fallen to him. Then on the way back, there'd been an accident and he'd stopped to lend a hand. Good thing he'd called and left a message. Normally Lizabeth would have gone to bed by now. But there were lights on in seemingly every room so that as he looked up the road, the house appeared to float above him. *Like the mother ship in that movie—what was it,* Close Encounters . . . *something like that?*

As he turned into his usual parking spot under the big pear tree, Ursa and Molly padded out to meet him. The shaggy black dog rubbed against his leg like a cat but the elegant red hound merely stood in front of him, presenting herself to him for a patting opportunity. He could hear James's shrill howl a little way off.

"Hey, girls, what's up? Thought everyone'd be in bed by now."

The dogs were noncommittal but they followed as he made his way up the path and climbed the now familiar steps to the porch, where James was waiting and wagging. From within the house he could hear Gloria's voice, raised in a nonstop harangue. *My god, but that woman can talk.*

Squaring his shoulders, he opened the screen door and stepped in.

"I tell you, I know what I saw— Hold on a minute, Brice."

Gloria, cellphone in hand, swung round to stare at him. "Well, *you* sure put in a long day. If I were Lizzy—"

Thank god, you're not, he thought. Summoning a smile he said, "Hi, Gloria—has Lizabeth already gone to bed? I left a message and told her not to wait up—"

"I'm still up." Elizabeth emerged from the office and came toward him. "Did you have something to eat on the road? I can fix you a sandwich . . ."

She hesitated, then brushed his cheek with a kiss as Gloria moved back into the dining room to continue her telephone conversation.

"Hey, Lizabeth," he whispered, "c'mere." Catching her wrist, he pulled her to him and wrapped his arms around her. "I've missed you, sweetheart."

Did her body stiffen briefly at his touch before she melted into his embrace? Was there just a moment of hesitation before she laid her head on his shoulder and whispered back, "I've missed you too."

"Well, Elizabeth, if you can spare Phillip for a *moment*, I'd like to tell him about what happened today in

Asheville." Gloria was standing in the dining room doorway, hands on hips and glaring at the back of her sister's head.

Elizabeth pulled away from him instantly like a guilty teenager. The beginnings of a blush showed under the tan of her cheeks. "I think you should hear this, Phillip. I can go fix you a sandwich while Gloria tells you what happened in Asheville—"

"Thanks, but that's okay—I ate a burger a while back and it's riding pretty heavy."

Dropping his briefcase into a chair, Phillip sank down on the love seat and propped his feet up on the old cedar chest. Elizabeth came and sat beside him while Gloria ostentatiously swept invisible dog hairs from the sofa before arranging herself decoratively on its cushions.

"Well, so there I was and at first I thought it was just some guy flirting with me and I made a big point of letting him know I wasn't interested, thank you very much, by looking away, but then I took out my compact to check that my lipstick wasn't smearing—oh, I should have said—I was in a Starbucks grabbing a skinny latte and I'd gotten a pastry—way too greasy, by the way; you would think—"

"Glory," Elizabeth interrupted, "could you get to the point? It's been a long day and Phillip and I need our sleep."

Phillip tried to keep his face expressionless as the sisters looked daggers at each other.

Gloria backed down first, turning away and waving her hand as if to break the spell. "*Any*hoo," she went on, as if there'd been no pause, "I was looking in my compact mirror and I could just see this guy who'd been watching me. He'd taken off his sunglasses and was cleaning them and then I saw the eyebrow and knew that I'd seen him before. So I—"

Phillip interrupted. "I'm not sure I'm following you.

What's this about an eyebrow? One of those pierced jobs or—"

"Oh, heavens, no, this is a man in his *forties,* maybe older. When I said *eyebrow,* that's what I meant—all one eyebrow—like a mustache across the top of his face. Eleanor and I used to laugh about it."

I think my brain is going to explode. Phillip took a deep breath. "And Eleanor is . . . ?"

Gloria sighed and spoke very slowly, as if to a not-very-bright child. "Eleanor is my best friend. Back in *Tampa.* But Eleanor doesn't have anything to do with this, Phillip. You need to *focus* on what I'm saying. The point is, this guy with the eyebrow is one of my husband's so-called *associates.* I never actually met him— I've only seen him from a distance. There'd be a call for Jerry and Eyebrow Man would be waiting in a car parked out on the street. Jerry would go out and sit in the car and talk to him. When I asked why he never had his friend come in the house, Jerry just said that he didn't like bringing business home with him. But I saw the guy a couple of times when the light was right and you can't miss that eyebrow. It was him, I'm certain, there in Starbucks and watching me."

There was a snorting sound at Phillip's side and Elizabeth stood up, abruptly dumping a surprised James to the floor. "I'm going to bed," she said.

That too sounded like a snort.

Chapter 7

Getting Jesuitical

Wednesday, May 16

I gotta say, your sister has more sense than I would have given her credit for."

It was after midnight when Phillip finally came to bed. I didn't look up from my book but I could hear him pulling off his bathrobe and tossing it onto the hook fixed to the bedroom door. With Gloria in the house, he'd had to abandon his habit of padding around in the wee hours bare-ass naked. The bed creaked as he lay down beside me and the usually enticing aroma of freshly bathed male filled my nostrils.

"She was lucky that there was a back entrance near the ladies' room," he continued. "*And* that she was so near the parking garage. She said she was pretty sure that no one had followed her out here to the farm."

"If there was actually anyone following her in the first place." I turned a page. I could feel his eyes on me.

"Lizabeth, you want to put down the book and tell me what's going on here?"

He was speaking very softly now. The guest room is just across the hall but as I could hear the sound of some high-pitched voice wailing about *tomorrow, tomorrow,* I didn't think there was a chance Gloria was listening to us.

I closed the paperback but kept a finger in it to mark

my place. "How do we know," I said, looking down at him over the top of my reading glasses, "that she's not just making all this up? Believe me, she's capable of it. Anything to be the center of attention—"

Capable. Phillip's soft brown eyes are capable of making me feel weak in the knees on certain occasions. Now they made me feel ashamed. I knew what I sounded like—a sharp-tongued bitch—and I hated it.

He lay there with his head on the pillow beside me. One hand reached for my braid and tugged at it.

"Lizabeth, let's save Gloria till tomorrow. Come here."

It's that scent of soap that does it every time.

Only when I was drifting off to sleep, did I remember I'd meant to straighten out the matter of Aunt Dodie . . . Aunt Dodie . . . and the Hawk . . . circling and circling, its tail flashing red . . . red as blood against the clear blue sky.

"Well, sleepyhead, I thought you were always up before dawn. Phil said to tell you that he had to go in early but since you were sleeping so hard he didn't want to wake you."

Phil? I watched in something like amazement as Gloria plunged her rubber-gloved hands into the dishpan and began to wash a mixing bowl.

"What are you doing, Glory?" I managed to say, even though it was, of course, obvious. I hadn't slept well— weird, troubled dreams and then a long period of lying awake in the dark, listening to the regular sound of Phillip's breathing punctuated by the occasional snore from Ursa. And when at last I'd fallen asleep, it had been that hard, almost drugged sleep that leaves you exhausted in the morning. I was pretty sure that there were dark circles under my eyes and sleep creases on my face.

Gloria, on the other hand, was as perky, cheerful, and

immaculately dressed and made up as ... as one of those smiling female hosts I remembered from morning TV, back in the days when I had time to watch TV.

"Well, I got up early—you know I have a lot to do today—and since there was poor Phil with no breakfast, I just fixed him some beignets."

She waved a foam-frothed purple glove toward the stove. "I put some in the oven to keep warm for you. And Phil fixed the coffee. I found a shop in Asheville with some really good Ethiopian dark roast—Phil was just over the moon about it."

Was he. How nice.

I realized that I'd been breathing the delectable country fair smell of fried dough and sugar coupled with rich deep coffee undertones and, rather than question a miracle, I pulled open the oven door.

A dozen small plump brown squares sat on a paper towel, each covered with a drift of snowy powdered sugar. The aroma—was that a hint of cinnamon?—wafted out with the oven's heat. My mouth began to water.

I turned to get a cup of coffee—*Ethiopian coffee, not that crap you always fix, Elizabeth*—but Gloria was already taking down my largest mug.

"There's some milk on the stove," she chirped. "I'll just heat it up—you need to have café au lait with these."

The words *No, I don't need anything of the kind* were on the tip of my tongue when I realized that a big cup of strong coffee and hot milk was exactly what I needed to accompany those seductive little indulgences.

"Thank you, Gloria," I managed to say as she handed me a plate. "That would be great."

I sat myself on the cushioned bench and watched my sister bring the milk just to the edge of a boil and then pour it into the mug along with the coffee.

"They're delicious, Glory." I swallowed the last airy bite of the first beignet and reached for another. "When did you learn to make them?"

"Oh, Lizzy, you know me—they're from a mix I bought the other day." She handed me the steaming mug and plopped down on the other bench, letting out a little involuntary sigh as she did so. For a moment she slumped and I could see the pallor behind the makeup and the small signs of aging at her neck. Then she straightened and flashed a bright smile.

"I guess all that walking yesterday caught up with me. You know, Lizzy, as women get older, they should guard against making those little tired sounds like I just did. Sophia Loren said that nothing ages a woman more— I remember reading that somewhere years ago."

A snarky observation concerning Sophia Loren and her pronouncements was hovering on my lips but I restrained myself and took a sip of the fragrant coffee. It was a revelation! I'd gotten out of the habit of milk in my coffee but this . . . this was perfect. And I had to admit . . .

"Glory, the coffee's wonderful. Where did you say it came from?"

Her face brightened and I was reminded of how thrilled she'd been when I'd praised the kimono she bought for me. Suddenly I saw myself through her eyes—grumpy, hard-to-please, self-righteous, opinionated older sister. As I looked at her, scenes from my childhood—*our* childhood—flashed into my mind. Me, barricaded in my room with my books and my record player, shutting the door against my little sister who wanted me to play dolls with her; me, making a gagging sound and pretending to throw up when she danced into my room to show me the frilly pink dress she was wearing to a birthday party; me, ignoring—

". . . Ethiopia," the here-and-now Gloria was saying,

unaware of my guilt trip into our mutual past. "I think it's grown by some kind of monks or something. I'm so glad you like it, Lizzy."

We were smiling at one another in an unexpected moment of sisterly regard—a moment cut short by the buzz of my telephone. As I stood and started for the office, Gloria grabbed at my arm.

"It could be Jerry!" She was whispering as if I'd already picked up the phone. "I just realized . . . if the Eyebrow told him he saw me in Asheville, Jerry knows you live in the area. He might . . . maybe you shouldn't answer it . . . or you could screen it."

I shook loose from her grasp and hurried from the kitchen, calling back over my shoulder. "Relax, Glory— it's probably Laurel. She's coming out to do some sketching this morning and she usually calls to see if I need anything from the store."

Laurel is way too impatient to wait through more than six rings and I was in need of some lemons for a dessert I'd decided to fix for Phillip—*beignets, indeed*— so I scrambled to reach the phone by the fifth ring.

"Laur," I gasped, "three lemons . . . or a bag, if they look okay."

There was silence and I thought I'd missed her. Then a deep voice asked, "Is this Elizabeth . . . Elizabeth Goodweather?"

I had never met nor even spoken with my current brother-in-law but something convinced me that this was Jerry Lombardo and I was going to have to lie convincingly that I had no idea where his wife was.

I hate lying. Maybe because I'm not very good at it. I avoid it too because of all the complications that can arise from a lie—"Oh what a tangled web we weave," as the old saying goes, "when first we practice to deceive."

"This is Elizabeth." My voice was cautious. Actually, I'm usually cautious when there's a stranger on the other end, as I tend to assume that it's a telemarketer trying to sell me aluminum siding.

"Great! Listen, Elizabeth, this is Jerry Lombardo. I need to speak to Gloria—it's very important."

My first impulse was to say "Jerry who?" Instead I opted for the evasive, "Gloria? Did you think she was *here*? Don't you know how much she hates the country? Anyway, didn't she tell me she was going to a spa somewhere?"

Not quite a lie. She *had* told me that . . . once.

There was a deep chuckle. "Listen, Elizabeth, I tried to call Ben but I just keep getting his voice mail. I really need to talk to my wife. We had a little . . . misunderstanding and Gloria took off. She left a note with the name of a spa but she's not there and never was. I've checked with all her friends and I have good reason to believe that she's with you. Just put her on the phone and I'll straighten out—"

"Jerry," I interrupted resolutely. "If Gloria calls me or Ben, I'll make sure she knows you're trying to get in touch. If you two have had a falling-out, she's probably just taken herself off for a while—maybe the spa thing didn't work out or maybe she's there under a different name . . ."

I still hadn't told an outright lie. But my Jesuitical inventiveness was wearing thin and I dreaded the outright question *Is Gloria there?*

A peal of barking from James provided the necessary interruption. "Uh-oh, I need to see what that dog's up to—sorry I couldn't help you, Jerry. As I said, if I hear from Gloria, I'll let her know what you said. Bye now."

I gabbled through this nonsense at light speed, ignoring the sputtering of protest at the other end and mashing the off button almost before the last words were out. Then I set the ringer at its lowest volume. If Jerry Lombardo called back, I'd let the voice mail deal with him.

But the thing was, he really did sound worried. And, what's more, he sounded *nice,* whatever that puny word means.

James's barking had reached frenzy pitch and as I came into the living room I could see him dancing and wagging in front of the screen door. The door squeaked and my younger daughter bounced in.

Tall—almost six feet—and lean to the point of boniness, with the typical redhead's angular facial planes, Laurel invariably turns heads wherever she goes. She's not beautiful, but, as a wistful friend once said, "Who'd want to be beautiful when they could look like *that*?"

Shucking off her bulging backpack and dropping it in a chair, she flashed a brilliant smile in my direction. "Back again, Mum—is there some coffee still hot? I'd love a cup before I head up the mountain."

"Coffee's hot and even better—" I gave her a quick hug. "Go look in the oven and see what your aunt Gloria's been up to."

As Laurel exclaimed over the remaining beignets, I realized that she was sporting a new look. The two fat short braids she had twisted her unruly red hair into made me smile. "I like the new do, sweetie—you make me think of Pippi Longstocking."

"Oh, Mum . . ." Laurel's words were accompanied by an indulgent smile. She reached for another beignet.

Leaving Laurel to her late breakfast, I went to look for Gloria. When I tapped on her door, she emerged from her room, her face taut with apprehension. "It was Jerry on the phone, wasn't it? And what was the little dog barking at?"

"James was welcoming Laurel, who's getting ready to go up the mountain and do some sketching. She's in the kitchen now, enjoying the last of the beignets. And yes, it was Jerry. But I left him with the impression that I had no idea where you were. Come on back in the kitchen; I'm in need of some more of that great coffee."

Laurel was rinsing her dishes when we returned, doing a little hip-waggling dance at the sink as she hummed some rhythmic tune. Catching sight of us, she swung around and swiped her hands on the bib of her paint-smeared overalls.

"Morning, Aunt Glory! Those doughnutty things were *awesome*! Mum, listen, I've been thinking . . ."

When Sam was alive, those words were a cue for us to roll our eyes and prepare to batten down the hatches of our peaceful life. I forced a smile and braced for what might come.

Laurel leaned against the sink, her head bathed in the morning sun that streamed through the window at her side. Curly tendrils of red hair that had escaped the braids flamed into an aureole around her head as she fixed me with a beatific smile. "So, Mum, I was thinking about your wedding and I know you want it simple but I had a brilliant idea."

I needed to slow this down. I opened my mouth to do so, but Laurel was bubbling over with her idea.

"*Handfasting*, Mum, wouldn't a handfasting be cool? I know a Wiccan priestess who could perform the ceremony. We could do that thing with all of us joining hands and dancing in a circle around you and Phillip. And I bet Lisa could design some really amazing outfits for both of you!"

Is there a woman in the world who doesn't feel that she could plan the perfect wedding? Even I had a few ideas that had been slowly simmering on the back burner of my mind ever since I'd asked Phillip to marry me. And when I'd realized that the summer solstice would be a good date, I'd even begun to assemble a tiny, tentative list.

"Well, Laurel," I began, only to be interupted by Gloria. She too had ideas and was able to set aside her worries about Jerry long enough to make a few Gloria-like pronouncements as she sat on the bench filing her already perfect nails.

"Here's what we'll do. I'll call Keith; he planned my last wedding and it was marvelous! He did the most *artistic* arrangements—all the flowers flown in from Bali or Fiji or someplace like that. Lizzy, if you're still determined to have it here and not at the Grove Park or someplace really *nice,* at least we can do it with a little style. Keith will organize the food and the decorations. You'll love him. It'll be my gift to you. But you need a theme . . . let me think. "

"Have you and Phillip picked the date yet, Mum?" Laurel dried her hands and tossed the dish towel on the counter. "Rosemary emailed me yesterday and was wondering."

"Not yet," I admitted, "but—"

Without waiting to hear the rest, Laurel ducked into the pantry and untacked the *Old Farmer's Almanac* calendar from the wall.

Frowning slightly, she ran her finger along the weeks of June. When she had traversed most of the month, she let out a squeal. "Do you believe this, Mum? June thirtieth is a full moon *and* a blue moon—the second full moon in the month! And it's a Saturday—*sweet!*"

Gloria jumped up to peer over Laurel's shoulder at the calendar. "A blue moon—there's your theme, Lizzie; so suitable! *And* your color! At your age, white would be too silly. And with your eyes, blue's absolutely perfect!"

She pulled out her minuscule cellphone and began to punch in numbers. "I'll just check with Keith—if by some miracle he's not booked . . . blue flowers . . . What were those gorgeous blue flowers he used on the tables at Eleanor's birthday luncheon . . ."

I started to protest that *I* had thought the summer solstice would be a good time and then, like a leaden bell tolling, the voice in my head started up again. *What* was *Dodie trying to tell me?*

"Gloria, stop right there," I heard myself saying in a harsh tone I didn't recognize. "Nothing's definite yet. *Nothing.* You two just back off."

Chapter 8

A Lot You Don't Know

Wednesday, May 16

They stared at me as if I had just kicked one of the dogs. The shocked looks on their faces quickly gave way to a bustle of subject-changing small talk. Laurel asked her aunt how the beignets were made and, at the same time, Gloria began to quiz Laurel about her bartending job.

"I'm sorry," I said, my voice choking. I grabbed the bucket of scraps for the chickens. "I didn't mean to sound so . . . I had trouble sleeping last night and I guess I'm a little . . . Oh hell, I'm going down to feed the chickens."

They broke off their chatter and turned wide eyes on me as I croaked out another *Sorry* and hurried out the door before I had to hear their soothing reassurances . . . or their questions. I made it off the porch before the tears came.

Crying doesn't come easily to me. I've always fought against it, especially if I'm around anyone else. Maybe I see it as betraying weakness—I don't know. I do know that it's something I do best in private. And even then, only rarely. But when the tears come, despite my best efforts, they come in a torrent—as if to make up for a long drought.

So I picked my way down the steep gravel road, eyes

streaming, nose running, snuffling and sniffling in a way that I'm sure Sophia Loren would have had something to say about. I wasn't crying because my wedding was in danger of being hijacked by Gloria and Laurel and their ideas and their themes—well, maybe that was some of it—but the thing that had me in its grip was the thought that, after all this time, after I'd finally made the decision to marry Phillip, to trust him—oh, bloody hell!

By the time I reached the place in the branch where a little trough over a rock allows me to fill a bucket with water for the biddies, I'd pretty much run out of tears and was reduced to gulps and the occasional hiccup. The inviting patch of grass by the branch was out of sight of the house so I plopped down in the shade of the trees and tried to regain some measure of calm. After wiping my face on my T-shirt, I closed my eyes and began to take deep breaths.

So many thoughts were fighting to surface—my feelings about Gloria . . . Why was I turning into such a bitch? And Phillip—*no*, Phil, *all of a sudden he's Phil.*

Was I jealous of my sister?

Oh, please. I'm not the jealous type. Am I?

And that mocking inner voice whispered, *Not the crying type either, are you?*

Something bumped against my shoulder and I opened my eyes to see Ursa. Shaggy, muddy Ursa, who had evidently been taking her ease in the little pool lower down the branch, was rubbing against me with what I chose to interpret as doggy concern rather than an attempt to dry herself.

I put an arm around the big dog, ignoring the dripping fur. I'd already trashed my T-shirt wiping my eyes and my runny nose—at least now I could cover up the evidence of my uncharacteristic crying jag.

Ursa sat down beside me with a heavy thump, then laid her head in my lap and promptly went to sleep.

"Our Zen dog," Laurel calls her; whether it's the result of philosophy or just a slow metabolism, Ursa's approach to life is admirably laid-back.

Sitting there with my hand on Ursa's flank, watching it rise and fall with her breathing, at last my mind slowed and faced the real problem—not when the wedding would take place nor what its theme would be. No, the real conundrum I'd been mentally dancing around was Aunt Dodie's question about the Hawk—the guy Sam hadn't trusted. Why the hell hadn't I dealt with this? It wasn't my usual policy to ignore painful necessities—and that's what this was.

I knew that I loved Phillip, that he was who I wanted to spend my life with. But if I asked him about the Hawk . . . oh god . . could I trust his answer, whatever it might be . . . would there be a wedding at all?

I dawdled away half an hour or more, feeding the chickens, gathering the eggs, even pausing to do a little weeding in the bed of daylilies and black-eyed Susans that fronts the chicken yard. By the time I'd cleared the bed of incipient devil-in-the-garden, crabgrass ("crap grass" as some of the old-timers call it), and all the other weeds that had taken root in the rich soil, there was a huge pile of fresh green stuff for the biddies' eating pleasure.

When I dumped the armload of weeds on the dirt of the chicken yard, Gregory Peck, the handsome Ameruacana rooster, began at once to scratch through the stems and leaves, all the while making encouraging clucking sounds to summon his harem. I sat myself down in the doorway of the chicken house and watched as he went through the always enchanting rooster routine of picking up choice bits, then dropping them so the hens could eat first.

The birds were still scratching and exclaiming *Oooh!*

A lovely bug! in their pile of fresh greens when I started back up the road. I felt sure that by now the telltale reddening would have faded from my face and eyes and that I would be able to deal with my sister rationally and unemotionally. Just as I would, in the fullness of time, deal with the questions raised by Aunt Dodie's letter—rationally and unemotionally.

"Mum, where's that burn ointment we used to have—the white gunk in the blue plastic jar?"

Laurel's voice floated out of the pantry. Gloria was nowhere to be seen but from the back of the house I could hear the sound of music—and a man's mellow voice exhorting the listener to climb every mountain.

"Did you burn yourself?" I asked, setting down the wire basket with the morning's collection of eggs. "I kind of think I threw it out—it was almost empty and what was left had turned a funny color. It was only about twenty years old—probably its use-by date expired ages ago."

I could hear the sound of Laurel rooting around on the crowded pantry shelves. "No, I don't see it . . . maybe you have something else . . . peroxide, calamine, antibiotic ointment, cough syrup . . ."

"Let me see the burn, sweetie," I said. "I'm afraid I haven't gotten around to replacing that white gunk yet. I went on a rampage a while back and got rid of all the expired medicines. Believe it or not, the shelf is much tidier than it was before. How bad is the burn? I have a first-aid kit down at the shop. There might be some—"

Laurel emerged from the pantry with a cobweb draped across the top of her head—the medicine shelf is the topmost one, a holdover from our childproofing days.

"It's Gloria who has the burn, not me. She said it was from the hot grease when she was frying the little whatchamacallits. It's not that bad but it was starting to bother her some."

Laurel downed the last of her coffee and shrugged on her knapsack. "I need to move along if I'm going to have any time for my sketches. It'll take me twenty minutes anyway to get up to the top of Pinnacle and—"

"Laurel." I caught at her arm and followed her out to the porch. "Listen, sweetie, I'm sorry I snapped at you. I'm sure a handfasting is a lovely ceremony but I'm no more a Wiccan than I am a Christian. Having a religious ceremony would seem . . . well, hypocritical. Will you have a sandwich with us when you come back down? I promise to be in a nicer frame of mind."

" 'S okay, Mum, no biggie." My daughter looked at me with a motherly kind of affection and gave me a one-armed hug. "It's probably natural for you to be a little on edge, with the wedding coming up and all."

With a glance toward the door, she added in a conspiratorial whisper, "And I can see how Aunt Glory would get right up your nose—no wonder Ben doesn't go home more often. She's already suggested that I change my hair, dress better, and think about getting a *real* job, maybe receptionist at a law office. Somewhere I'd meet someone *nice*.

"But anyway," Laurel continued cheerfully, "I made myself a peanut butter sandwich and snagged a cider to take with me. I don't have to be at work till five so I can stay up there till around three-thirty. Sweet!"

Another brisk hug and she was off, bounding down the steps, Molly and Ursa trotting after her. I watched them go, then turned to lean on the rail and stare for a bit at the distant mountains, listening to a persistent towhee calling from the shrubs below and allowing my thoughts to drift like a feather on the wind.

I was in a much better mood when I pulled open the screen door to return to the house. *New game. Now for*

Gloria. Apologize again and try, politely but firmly, to make sure she doesn't bring in her florist friend from Florida.

The silly alliterative phrase made me grin and I began to think of ways to improve on it. *Fancy florist friend from Florida . . . fancy florist friend from freakin' Florida . . . fancy f—*

All f-words fled—well, almost all—at the sight of Gloria, in skintight turquoise and fuchsia, lying on the living room floor doing something slightly obscene with a fat iridescent purple ball. James was making little darts at her face with his tongue and she was fending him off with one hand while raising and lowering the other arm. It was quite a picture. Freakin' funny, as a matter of fact.

"Lizzy!" Gloria gasped, removing first one and then the other leotard-clad leg from atop the ball and waving them about in the air. "I just don't know if this is going to work."

I called James off and put him outside but Gloria had stopped her . . . whatever it was and had assumed a cross-legged position on the mat beneath her. I began to apologize for my ungraciousness at her kind—though unnecessary—offer to help with the wedding but she waved my words away.

"Not a problem, Lizzy. I remember how touchy Mother was when she was going through menopause. You know, exercise can do wonders for your mood, as well as help with weight control . . ."

She cast a significant glance at my hips and continued. "I was going to suggest you might like to try Pilates but I think Pilates works better in a less . . . cluttered atmosphere. At home I go to this beautiful studio—very simple, very Japanese—a scroll on the wall, an ikebana arrangement on a low table, and one wall, completely glass, looking out on a meditation garden—all rocks and moss and just a tiny trickle of a waterfall into a koi pond—"

"It sounds lovely, Glory," I interupted, wondering if gritting my teeth every few minutes was going to damage them. "And you certainly have stayed in good shape. But, I tell you what, why don't we take a walk together? That would be exercise."

Of course a walk involved a change of outfits for Gloria and then I had to suggest that her choice of a sports bra and very short shorts was not a good idea for walking a mountain trail.

"Oh, but we need to go down to the paved road and walk there," she insisted. "It'll be a much better cardio workout—we can really move along. Do you have some hand weights?"

Not me. But Gloria did and we strode along in fine fashion: she, holding the little gray dumbbells and pumping her arms furiously; me, stretching out to keep up with her. I had to admit, my little sister was, indeed, in good shape. She could set a brisk pace and talk at the same time.

". . . go to Hot Springs—that's near here, isn't it, Lizzy? Nigel—the one in Asheville who did my hair— he's a psychic, by the way, and he was telling me about this really fabulous inn in Hot Springs that's going to have a weekend psychic retreat. Nigel said there was this amazing man from Glastonbury—England, you know— who's going to be in Hot Springs doing a retreat. Nigel says this man is known in the spiritual community as a really tuned-in medium who can put people in touch with their departed loved ones. Well, I started thinking and it seemed to me that—"

"Gloria?" I panted, "I didn't know you were into . . . when did you get interested in this stuff?"

My sister has always been a devotee of self-improvement workshops, often with an exotic spiritual slant: Tibetan color—or was it colon?—therapy, Mayan massage, Shinto chants for rejuvenation, Bulgarian bulge reduction—okay, I made that one up. But, *séances*? It just didn't seem like her thing.

Still, Asheville *is* known as a New Age vortex—"the Sedona of the East" as one magazine article put it. It evidently hadn't taken long for Glory to get sucked into that vortex—with Nigel's help, I suspected.

Gloria looked sideways at me and replied without missing a beat. "There's a lot you don't know about me, Lizzy."

The words were said in a matter-of-fact way and not, I thought, intended to wound. But they did.

"Glory," I said, grabbing her wrist and pulling her to a stop, "listen—"

"Let go!" she squawked, coming to an abrupt halt and shooting me an accusing glare. "You're hurting my burn!"

I pulled my hand away and began once more to apologize. How could I have forgotten so quickly? We had checked the first-aid kit in my shop for burn ointment and come up empty but Gloria had insisted we take our walk first, saying she would run in to the drugstore later. Now the burn was an angry red with a weeping blister, popped, no doubt, by my stupid hand. And I was winded.

We were about a mile down the road from my driveway—almost directly in front of Miss Birdie's place. And her truck was there. Thank goodness I'd convinced Glory to put a T-shirt over the sports bra and change the shorts for longer pants. Miss Birdie seemed to take modern life and fashion in her stride but still . . .

"Gloria, we really need to put something on that burn, especially now that the blister's open. That's Miss Birdie's house there across the branch and I'll bet she'll have some ointment. I was going to bring you down to meet her anyway. Birdie's one of the last of the old-timers around here and one of my favorite people in the world."

It didn't take much convincing—I think the burn was hurting more now and maybe, just maybe, Glory was a little winded herself.

We had crossed the bridge and were passing the hedge of tall rhododendrons at the edge of the yard when I heard Gloria's sharp intake of breath. She was frowning slightly and staring down the road. All at once her eyes widened and I felt her fingers dig into my arm.

"Oh my god! Quick, Lizzy, we have to *hide*!" she gasped and, before I could protest, tugged me into the interior of a giant rhododendron. Peering through the screen of dark green leaves and deep red blooms, I tried to see what had put that note of panic into my sister's voice, what was causing her to tremble so violently. The first vehicle we'd seen since we began our walk—except for the old guy who went by in an ancient pickup as we were coming out of the driveway—was coming up the road in our direction.

I nudged her, trying to get her to stop hyperventilating and talk to me. "Is it that Hummer you're so stressed about, Glory? Hey, I hate them myself, stupid, ostentatious gas-guzzlers, but why should we hide from—"

The boxy, tanklike vehicle crawled along the road like an ominous black beetle, slowing at each clump of mailboxes. As it passed I saw the white license plate with the orange Florida silhouette in the center. The driver seemed to be lost—a familiar sight.

"It's only another Floron," I reassured Glory. "He's looking for the place his friends bought or the place he thinks he might buy. We get that all the—"

But Gloria was shaking her head. "He's from Florida, all right—I *know* that car." Her voice was flat and resigned. "Don't you understand, Lizzy? That's the Eyebrow—the one I saw in Asheville—and he's looking for me."

Gloria pulled at the slender chain around her neck, bringing from under her shirt a little gold heart. She clutched at it like a talisman as we watched the Hummer disappear around a corner, heading for Full Circle Farm.

III~*The DeVine Sisters*

Hot Springs, NC~May 1887

"*Has she gone?*" Dorothea whispered to her sister.

Theodora, who had been leaning down to unlock the traveling trunk at the foot of the bed, paused. She straightened and looked toward the bedroom's open door.

"*The chambermaid? Heavens, I don't know. Perhaps she's tidying Renzo's lair. What does it matter? She wouldn't have the least idea . . . but close the door if it troubles you.*"

When the heavy oak door had been shut and latched, Dorothea returned to her sister's side, a finger laid to her lips. "*She's just finishing up—but do keep your voice down till she leaves. Perhaps I'm being overzealous— you're right; I doubt the poor old thing has the wits to understand any of this.*"

The stately Theodora turned the key in the trunk's lock and pushed open the lid. After a brief perusal of the odd assortment of objects before her, she nodded thoughtfully. "*No, I believe you're right to be cautious. There've been some unpleasant revelations and expo- sures in the Spiritualist community of late. You remem- ber that insistent young reporter at the hotel during our last engagement—*"

"*Indeed I do!*" Dorothea's silvery laugh rang out in a

merry peal. "Did I not find him hiding in my closet? You saw how he tried to brazen it out by pretending that he was smitten by our beauty but I had the hotel detective escort the wretch to the street with a warning never to return."

Theodora's face remained grave, unmoved by her sister's laughter. "It was a near escape. My wardrobe had been searched thoroughly and there were telltale scratches all round this lock. Fortunately, that young man was as poor a locksmith as he was a liar and our . . . materials went undiscovered."

Dorothea drew closer. "What shall we use for your next session with Harris? The trumpets again?"

Reaching into the tray at the top of the steamer trunk, she withdrew two yard-long cones fashioned from heavy paper. One was pure black, the other white. The larger opening of the white cone was smeared with some creamy substance.

Lifting the black trumpet to her lips, Dorothea began to speak. Though hardly above the level of a whisper, the deep voice that she affected resonated within the cone, causing it to vibrate as she spoke.

"Who calls Guiseppe from the Elysian fields, back to the earthly plane, back to this dark place of travail and woe? Is it another in search of a guide?"

Still considering the contents of the trunk, Theodora didn't bother to look up.

"No, I think not. Not the trumpets. We used them last time. Familiarity breeds, I'll not say contempt, but rather, curiosity. And where there's curiosity, there's danger." She pushed aside a folded length of pure white silken gauze and brought out a small shellacked board. On it, in an elegant italic hand, were painted the letters of the alphabet and the words YES and NO.

"I think that for tonight, we'll employ the planchette and the message board. If I have to listen again to Harris's late wife calling for her Wodwick to speak to her, I fear I'll burst into laughter at the most inopportune moment. Really, Doe, sometimes you go too far."

"What would you have me do then? His name is Roderick. And the solicitous Mr. Peavey did tell me that the dear departed Mrs. Harris had just such a way of speaking—tho' he called it 'prattling like a pretty child.'"

"Harris did seem much moved." Theodora dipped into the trunk yet again and brought forth a tiny table-like affair. Balancing the letter board on one outstretched palm, she placed the planchette atop it, her delicate fingers riding lightly on the little tabletop.

"Indeed, 'twas quite affecting, the way he pressed that bracelet on the empty air. A lovely piece of jewelry, was it not?"

Her face grew thoughtful as the planchette beneath her fingers slid from letter to letter. Then her blue-violet eyes glittered and, with a sudden swoop, the little device raced to the upper right-hand corner and stopped on the YES.

In the adjoining room, Amarantha finished brushing the carpet, gave the mirror a hasty swipe with her glass rag, then attacked the surfaces with a feather duster. She had already emptied the chamber pot and spittoon, made the bed, and tidied the clutter of masculine items atop the massive dresser. Now she collected the articles of men's clothing that lay carelessly draped over the bench at the foot of the bed. One by one she examined them and consulted the printed list that had been left atop the heap.

"Two shirts to wash, three missing buttons to sew on, medium starch; one pair drawers—" She shook out the grayish white garment and sniffed. "Seems this fancy feller ain't so particular about what don't show."

A pair of trousers was next and she began to go

through the pockets. "This un's more careful than most. He's done emptied his pockets—no, now reckon what this is here in the fob?"

A small round metal device about the size of a silver dollar emerged from the inconspicuous slit at the waist. Amarantha held it between two cautious fingers and studied it. As she turned the disc this way and that, the innocuous-appearing object suddenly emitted a loud crack! The mountain woman started and almost dropped the thing but, recovering herself, stared at it more closely.

Cocking her head to one side as if in response to a call, she turned toward the window. In the shaft of light that streamed between the heavy draperies, a low rocking chair was moving slowly as if someone were sitting in it and gently rocking. In the dancing dust motes, a shadowy form wavered.

"You here?" Amarantha asked as she dropped the little round thing into her apron pocket.

THE NEW PLANCHETTE

....

A Mysterious Talking Board and Table

"Planchette is simply nowhere," said a Western man at the Fifth Avenue Hotel, "compared with the new scheme for mysterious communication that is being used out in Ohio. I know of whole communities that are wild over the 'talking board,' as some of them call it. I have never heard any name for it. But I have seen and heard some of the most remarkable things about its operations—things that seem to pass all human comprehension or explanation."

"What is the board like?"

"Give me a pencil and I will show you. The first requisite is the operating board. It may be rectangular, about 18 x 20 inches . . . The 'yes' and the 'no' are to start and stop the conversation. The 'good-evening' and 'good-night' are for courtesy. Now a little table three or four inches high is prepared with four legs. Any one can make the whole apparatus in fifteen minutes with a jack-knife and a marking brush. You take the board in your lap, another person sitting down with you. You each grasp the little table with the thumb and forefinger at each corner next to you. Then the question is asked, 'Are there any communications?' Pretty soon you think the other person is pushing the table. He thinks you are doing the same. But the table moves around to 'yes' or 'no.' Then you go on asking questions and the answers are spelled out by the legs of the table resting on the letters one after the other. Sometimes the table will cover two letters with its feet, and then you hang on and ask that the table will be moved from the wrong letter, which is done. Some remarkable conversations have been carried on until men have become in a measure superstitious about it. I know of a gentleman whose family became so interested in playing with the witching thing that he burned it up. The same night he started out of town on a business trip. The members of his family looked for the board and could not find it. They got a servant to make them a new one. Then two of them sat down and asked what had become of the other table. The answer was spelled out, giving a name, 'Jack burned it.' There are, of course, any number of nonsensical and irrelevant answers spelled out, but the workers pay little heed to them. If the answers are relevant they talk them over with a superstitious awe. One gentleman of my acquaintance told me that he got a communication about a title to some property from his dead brother, which was of great value to him. It is curious, according to those who have worked most with the new mystery, that while two persons are holding the table a third person, sitting in the same room some distance away, may ask the questions without even speaking them aloud, and the answers will show they are intended for him. Again, answers will be returned to the inquiries of one of the persons operating when the other can get no answers at all. In Youngstown, Canton, Warren, Tiffin, Mansfield, Akron, Elyria, and a number of other places in Ohio I heard that there was a perfect craze over the new planchette. Its use and operation have taken the place of card parties. Attempts are made to verify statements that are made about living persons, and in some instances they have succeeded so well as to make the inquirers still more awe-stricken."—*New York Daily Tribune,* March 28, 1886: page 9, column 6.

Chapter 9

Talking to Miss Birdie

Wednesday, May 16

Gloria watched the black Hummer out of sight. *Goddam Jerry and his goddam business associates.* She mouthed the words as she pulled her cellphone from her fanny pack.

"Lizzy, I'm going to call Ben and warn him that creep might be coming; why don't you call the Mexicans and tell them—they have a phone, don't they?"

"First let's get into Miss Birdie's house." Elizabeth was tugging at her sleeve and backing gingerly out of the depths of the big bush. "Anyway, your cell probably won't work down here. If it really is the guy you think it is, let's get inside before he comes back."

Gloria glared at her sister. "If it really is—" *Why doesn't she ever believe me? It's always the same,* she fumed as she allowed herself to be hurried toward the little log house.

A curtain twitched and a shadow moved away from the nearby window. Seconds later the storm door was opening and a voice was calling out, "Lizzie Beth? Whatever in the world were you doing in that ol' laurel? You and your sister come on in and git you uns a cheer."

As they crossed the immaculate little yard, Gloria tugged at Elizabeth's sleeve and whispered, "What did she say? Come on in and do what? And what's *yuns* mean?"

"It's *you uns*—like we say 'you all'—she's saying get a *chair*. It's what she always says when someone shows up. It just means she's inviting us to come in and sit down," Elizabeth hissed.

They stepped through the doorway and Gloria saw a low-ceiled room, cluttered with cheap furniture and an old television set. Miss Birdie, a plump little woman in a faded print housedress, stood waiting, her bright blue eyes shining with delight in her wrinkled face.

Gloria's first thought was that she doubted she'd ever seen anyone that old. And her second was an unsettling visceral response to the gaze: *I wish my mother had ever looked at me like that.*

The old woman beamed at her. "Aye, law, so you're Lizzie Beth's little sister. And ain't you a purty thing—like a little doll. How proud I am you uns come by!"

Elizabeth hugged her neighbor. "This is Gloria, Miss Birdie. She's staying with me for a while."

Gloria held out her hand. "Elizabeth's told me so much—" But the polite formula was cut short as the little old woman took the hand and turned it over to reveal the ugly burn at the wrist.

"Why, honey, whatever have you done to yourself? Does it pain you right much?"

Gloria felt about four years old as her eyes began to well up and prickle. "Yes, ma'am, it does." *And when was the last time I called anyone ma'am?* "I was going to go to the store to get something to put on it—Lizzy didn't have anything . . ."

The little old woman was looking deep into her eyes and Gloria fell silent. All at once there was a hush in the room and she had the oddest feeling of being drawn into the heart of some thing or some place. For a moment it was as if she and this ancient woman were standing, hands clasped, alone on some high misty place, far away from the real world.

"Iffen you want," the words were soft and strangely seductive, "I can draw the fire out of that burn and soothe it. I learned how from my granny."

"Why, Miss Birdie!" Elizabeth's light teasing voice shattered the moment of perfect rapport. "I didn't know you were a witchy-woman."

The feeling of isolation fell away and Gloria returned from the mysterious mountaintop—*What was that about?*—to the here and now of the tacky little living room with its vinyl recliner and plastic-covered sofa. She saw her sister's mouth parted in a mock O of astonishment and she realized that her own mouth had been gaping open in a most unbecoming way.

Miss Birdie kept a firm hold on Gloria's hand and shot an amused look back at Elizabeth. "Reckon there's some would call me a witchy-woman though I didn't have aught to do with none of that for many a year. It was on account of Luther didn't like me using Granny's charms—he said it weren't in Scripture. But I believe he's done changed his mind now."

A puzzled frown replaced the O. "I don't see how—"

Just like Lizzy to forget the whole reason we're here, thought Gloria as she overrode her sister's protestations. "Really, Lizzy, don't you think you ought to call Ben? And those Mexicans of yours too? Warn them to be on the lookout."

"Their names are Julio and Homero and they're not *my* Mexicans," Elizabeth snapped. "Miss Birdie, may I use your phone?"

"Why, you go right ahead, honey. Me and your little sister'll step into the kitchen and I'll put some bam gilly on that burn."

Gloria let herself be led into the adjoining room. Behind her, Lizzy was saying, "If you get this message . . ." Obviously Ben or the Mexicans hadn't picked up.

In the kitchen a comforting smell of baking hung in the air, teasing her nose with familiar scents—sweet, spicy, but nameless. Like cookies or cake—that was the best she could do to identify the tantalizing aromas. A shiny white wood-burning cookstove, its vast black surface crowded with pots and pans, radiated an enveloping heat that seemed, somehow, pleasant rather than oppressive. Just inside the door a dinette set occupied half of the floor space. The turquoise and gray plastic-topped table with matching chairs was straight from the fifties, she thought, and so tacky that it would probably be called "retro" by some designers.

"Come over here by the back door, honey, where we can get the breeze," the little woman urged her and Gloria did as she was told.

"I finally got hold of Ben," Elizabeth announced a quarter of an hour later, coming into the kitchen where Miss Birdie was spreading a yellowish, sweet-smelling ointment over Gloria's inner arm. "He was down in the lower pasture sawing up a tree that had fallen on the fence. The Hummer must have gone up our road while the saw was running because he didn't see it till it was coming back down and heading for the hard road. Ben said that bothered him so he jumped on his four-wheeler to try to catch the vehicle and find out who it was. But just as he was about to catch up with it, the Hummer got to the hard road and took off around the mountain."

Miss Birdie looked up from her doctoring. "Are you talking about that great black vehicle? Was that what you uns was hiding from?"

Then, of course, there were explanations—of a sort. Gloria wondered why the little old woman didn't ask more questions as Elizabeth sketched out a brief version

of why Gloria was in hiding but Miss Birdie simply nodded and offered to let them know if she saw "that great
ugly black vehicle" another time.

"And she will too," Elizabeth had promised. "Miss
Birdie's a one-woman Neighborhood Watch. She always
keeps an eye on the road and pays attention to who's
going where."

The Neighborhood Watch had insisted on driving
them back to Full Circle Farm. "Iffen that feller's such a
fearsome somebody that you uns had to hide up in my
laurel bush, then it wouldn't do for him to find you
walking on the road and no one in sight, now would it?"

Even Lizzy didn't argue—it was obvious, thought
Gloria, that no one argued with Miss Birdie—and they
had all three climbed into the old pickup for the short
ride up the road to the farm's driveway.

There had been no further sign of the Hummer and
Miss Birdie had let them out at Elizabeth's workshop.
Gloria watched the truck as it rattled down the driveway, Miss Birdie's white head barely visible in the rear
window.

What was it about this old country woman that was
so calming . . . so . . . almost . . . *wise*? Gloria was reminded of a spiritual workshop she had attended where
a yoga teacher had had just such an effect on her—
briefly causing her to imagine laying a trusting hand in
the brown palm of the guru and following wherever he
led.

Fortunately that feeling had passed. She couldn't
really imagine a life of chastity, simplicity, and chanting.
But during the short time she and Miss Birdie had been
alone together, that same seductive feeling had crept
over her. She had felt like a little girl again, safe in an
adult's comforting embrace.

Miss Birdie makes me think of Gramma. I used to be-

lieve that Gramma could do anything. Lizzy was her fa-
vorite, though. She and Gramma were thick as thieves. I
remember Mother saying that. "Thick as thieves, those
two. Your sister would rather listen to your grand-
mother talk about that wretched little dirt farm she grew
up on and the smelly chickens—chickens! I ask you.
Never mind, Gloria, you and I'll have a girlie day to-
gether in town shopping . . . and if there's time, we'll get
our nails done . . ."

". . . or I can take you up to the house. Glory, did you
hear me?"

Elizabeth was staring at her with real concern on her
face. Gloria shook herself out of the reverie.

"Sorry, Lizzy, what did you say?"

"I asked do you want me to drive you up to the
house? I need to get an order ready before Julio does the
delivery run. It won't take long and it's not lunchtime
yet . . . if you wanted to hang out with me, we could
talk . . ."

Lizzy actually sounded apologetic and a little . . .
humble? Was that the word? *Maybe she believes me*
now about Jerry. The Eyebrow showing up proves
Jerry's after me. Gloria looked toward the barn with the
faded red paint.

"Sure," she agreed. "I'd like to see what it is you do in
here." She followed Elizabeth into the cavernous workshop, filled with bins and baskets and several huge tables. Shelves lined two of the walls, overflowing with
mysterious jars and containers. A large flat basket
draped with a damp towel lay on a workbench to one
side.

"Rosemary and lavender trimmings," Elizabeth said,
pulling back the towel to reveal a pile of sweet-smelling
sprigs of green-gray foliage. She reached to switch on
the overhead lights. "It's really too early to be pruning
them but the woman having this party was willing to

pay whatever I asked if she could just have six little fresh wreaths as centerpieces. She mentioned some spiritual reason it had to be fresh rosemary and lavender but I forget what it was. Anyway, I named a price so outrageous that I thought she'd back out but it didn't faze her. So Julio cut these for me this morning."

Elizabeth rummaged in a blue plastic bin and emerged with six fat rings of some dark green material.

"This is great stuff—it's been soaking in water and now we just stick the herb sprigs all over each wreath form and voilà—a fancy-schmancy fresh herb wreath!"

She placed the green rings on a long rectangle of mottled white plastic that was spread on the big worktable. "This is where my old shower curtain liners go when I can't get the mildew off them anymore. So, Glory, want to make a wreath?"

Gloria protested that she was no good at crafts, that she would mess it up, that she didn't think she—but Elizabeth paid no attention and handed her a ring to work on.

"Like I said, just jab the stems in the foam. You want to kind of alternate the rosemary and the lavender and put them close enough together that none of the green foam stuff shows, okay?"

And Elizabeth turned away and began poking the little sprigs into the damp foam of the circle before her. After watching for a moment, Gloria reached for a silvery sprig and sniffed at it. So this was lavender! It smelled just like the divine French paper that lined her lingerie drawers and linen closet back home.

She made a tentative stab into the green material. To her surprise, the stem sank in without the least resistance.

A sideways glance revealed Elizabeth working with steady precision, her right hand implanting a sprig as her left reached for another. About a third of the ring bristled with the fragrant herbs.

With her left hand, Gloria reached for the rosemary.

They worked in a companionable silence. Gloria found herself enjoying the task—the sight of the little wreath growing beneath her fingers, the pungent smell of the herbs, the rhythm of her movements, and the muted sound of classical music on the radio.

She became aware that her sister was watching her— that deep blue gaze that could make her feel so uncom- fortable—and she stopped, a sprig of lavender poised just above the partially finished wreath. "What? Am I doing it wrong?"

Elizabeth's expression softened. "No, Glory, it's per- fect. I was wondering if the burn was still bothering you—maybe we ought to go get some real burn oint- ment."

"It's quit bothering me completely." Gloria turned her hand palm up to show the tender inner arm. A few pale yellow streaks of Miss Birdie's concoction remained but the skin beneath was no longer red.

Elizabeth leaned in for a closer look. "But there were blisters . . . I saw them. Weren't there? . . . What was in that ointment anyway?"

Gloria returned to the rhythm of her wreath. *Pick up, push in, pick up, push in.* "Miss Birdie called it bam gilly. It's crushed-up buds of balm of Gilead, whatever that is. She said that her grandmother used to mix them with bear grease or hog lard but she uses sweet oil— whatever *that* is—and petroleum jelly."

She couldn't help noticing that Elizabeth was still staring at the place where the burn had been, staring and shaking her head in disbelief.

"There were blisters. It was a bad burn, I know it was.

And she just put this . . . this stuff on it and it healed, is that what you're saying?"

Gloria wedged in a final piece of rosemary. "Actually, first she said some words—something about angels and fire and frost—while she kind of fanned at the place with her hand. She called it drawing the fire out. She said the words over and over and by the time she put the ointment on, the blisters were gone and the redness had faded. She's an amazing healer, Lizzy, just like this holy man I met at a spiritual retreat in California."

"Really?" Once more Gloria felt the penetrating blue stare. "So you and Miss Birdie hit it off right away?"

Was that a note of disapproval in Lizzy's voice?

Gloria lifted her chin. "Yes, as a matter of fact, we did. She reminded me of Gramma . . . and she was so easy to talk to. I told her about—"

"*Perdóname, Elizabeta,* the truck, it is ready."

It was one of the Mexicans standing in the doorway— a short, square, dark-skinned man wearing new jeans, a freshly ironed blue cowboy shirt, and shiny cowboy boots. He ducked his head at Gloria and smiled.

Gloria watched as the two wreaths she had completed—*They're just perfect, Glory! Excellent work!*— were packed with the others into a plastic box and handed over to Julio. *I wonder what Lizzy gets paid for these. I've never done anything to make money—except get married.*

"These are the directions." Elizabeth handed Julio a printed sheet. "It's two streets after the turn to El Chalapa. That's where you and Homero usually stop for lunch, right?"

Julio nodded. "*Sí,* we eat in the room with the TV *grande.* Homero, he likes the *telenovelas. Pero yo—me gusta la lucha libre. El Scorpion*—"

A whistle shrilled outside. *"Hombre, vamos! Mira la hora!"*

Julio grinned and picked up the box of wreaths. "Today they show his favorite: *Los Ricos También Lloran*—'The Rich, They Cry Too.' "

As he hurried out the door, Gloria heard his words echoing in her mind. *The rich, they cry too.* She felt her eyes filling with tears and lifted her hand to brush them away. The scent of rosemary clung to her fingers.

Chapter 10

The Green-Eyed Monster

Wednesday, May 16

Gloria was uncharacteristically silent as we drove to the house. Usually she's doing that southern lady thing of not letting a silence fall. But she sat quiet in the passenger seat, not even responding as we jolted over a freshly dug and particularly deep water break.

Ben had been out with the tractor early that morning, cleaning ditches and redigging the water breaks. I'd suggested earlier that he and Amanda join us for breakfast while Gloria was here but he'd just laughed, saying that their days had to start much earlier than his mother's. Dinner now and then, he added, would be the best thing for all involved.

I knew what he meant. I'd seen him bristle under Gloria's annoying, though well-meant, interference and had seen him bite his lip more than once as his mother began to question Amanda about her sudden decision to abandon a lucrative career in modeling for life on the farm. *"Really, Amanda, back home everyone's wondering . . . I heard you had an eating disorder and your doctor absolutely forbade . . ."*

Amanda, with far more forbearance than I could ever have shown, had maintained a cool and unruffled calm through the interrogation, laying an admonitory hand on Ben's when he looked as if he might explode as his mother asked yet another prying question. *"Was it the kind where you don't eat or was it the other one—where you eat a lot and then make yourself throw up?"*

That beautiful long-fingered hand and a sideways glance had been all it took to remind Ben that Amanda was perfectly capable of fighting her own battles. But he had pleaded too much work on almost every occasion I'd asked the two of them to dinner and consequently Gloria had seen very little of her only child.

Suddenly I felt sorry for my little sister.

And found myself doing the southern lady thing as the silence in the Jeep began to seem oppressive.

"You know, Glory, I'm really glad you liked Miss Birdie. I wasn't sure you two would find much to talk about but—what *did* you talk about anyway? She and I usually stick to beans and gardens and quilts—all the old-timey stuff, I guess. We—"

"She told me about her angels." There was a strange, eager excitement in Glory's voice as she continued. "You know, all those babies that died before the last one finally lived? She told me how she talks to them, up in the graveyard . . . all her lost babies . . ."

Her voice cracked and she turned away. As soon as I pulled to a stop in the shade of the pear tree, her door was open before I'd turned off the ignition.

"I'll grab a quick shower before lunch, Lizzy."

And she was gone, power walking her way up the path, leaving me dangling somewhere between confusion and jealousy. *Jealousy is so unattractive. What's the bloody matter with me anyway?*

I took a deep breath and got out of the car to follow her. It occurred to me to wonder if the Hummer had made it up this far before turning around but the gravel of the driveway held no clues. A powerful vehicle like the Hummer could creep slowly up the steep road, without any telltale spinning and gravel-spraying.

And if it really was this Eyebrow fellow, wouldn't he have waited and confronted Gloria? What would be the point . . . ?

There were too many unknowns in this problem. *If it is a problem and not just more of Glory's histrionics. She really didn't seem that worried, once I told her Ben had seen the Hummer leave. I thought for sure she'd be wanting me to call Phillip and get the sheriff involved. Have him put out an APB or something.*

Remembering that I needed to fix lunch, I abandoned my scrutiny of the uncommunicative driveway and headed for the porch. As I drew near, I could see Ursa and Molly wagging a welcome at the top of the steps but there was no sign of James. *Probably followed his new love into her room,* I thought, dropping into a rocking chair to give my faithful girls a little attention.

Did Glory get that right, I wondered, about Birdie talking to her dead babies? Miss Birdie'd never told *me* she did anything like that. Of course I knew about the children she'd lost—had even gone to the cemetery with her on numerous Decoration Days and left a flower on each tiny grave.

So common, those little graves—back when the mountain women mostly gave birth at home with nothing in the way of prenatal care and not much money to pay a doctor should a child fall ill.

Molly nosed at my hand, inviting me to scratch behind her long ears. As I did, first automatically checking for ear mites, the thought came to me: *My dogs have probably gotten far more medical attention than the mountain people of Birdie's youth—more and better too.*

What was the disease that Birdie had told me accounted for so many of those sad little graves in the family cemeteries at most mountain farms? Some form of diarrhea or infant dysentery . . .

Oncet hit takes a hold, she had said, *every drop of milk just runs right through them. That's what took my first, my Britty Birdsong. Aye law, the summer complaint, hit was a cruel hard thing—*

Oh, yes, Miss Birdie had told me about her lost babies . . . and yes, she'd called them her angels. But talking to them up in the graveyard? Glory must have misunderstood—she hadn't been here long enough to get the hang of the accent. Talking to dead babies didn't sound like the Birdie I knew.

I was putting the salads on the table—my first plan had been pimento cheese sandwiches but the memory of Gloria's comments about weight control and her meaningful glance at my hips had won out—when she reappeared, freshly bathed and shampooed, and wearing a sleeveless caftan sort of thing in a delicate pale coral. Embellished with intricate silver-threaded embroidery at the neckline, it was pretty enough to be an evening gown but evidently my sister saw it as loungewear.

Lunch was a somewhat silent ordeal. Gloria picked at her salad, still in an unnaturally quiet mood. At first I resisted making small talk but, finally, the stillness began to feel oppressive again and I tossed a conversational ball into the air.

"What was that you were telling me about a weekend workshop in Hot Springs? Is it something you're planning on going to?"

That didn't come out well. It sounds as if I'm trying to get rid of her.

But she perked right up at the question. Abandoning the pretense of eating, she planted her elbows on the table and began to sing the praises of someone called Giles of Glastonbury.

"Nigel, you know, the one who did my hair, says that Giles is the most amazing medium—Nigel attended one

of his readings years ago, right after his mother died,
and he was able to talk to her through Giles and find out
all sorts of things he needed to know about her estate. I
mean, there was *real* communication—she told him
where she'd hidden some important papers and she
warned him about his then-boyfriend who was stealing
from him and *anyhoo*—I was telling Nigel how I sometimes wished that I could just call up Harry and talk to
him about my problems—he was so wise and patient
and fatherly—at times I think he's the only one of my
husbands I ever really loved . . ."

Harry—otherwise Harold Holst—had indeed been
old enough to be Gloria's father. Since our own father
had decamped, never to be seen again, when Gloria was
only four, it was perhaps not so strange that she would
have been attracted to this kind older man . . . And
then, of course, there was the money.

Stop it, Elizabeth, and listen to what she's saying.

". . . of course Harry tied things up very nicely, I'm
sure, but sometimes his children . . ."

Oh, yes. Those grown children of Holst and his late
wife. They hadn't been a bit pleased when Poppa, as
they all called him, had married a young wife, capable of
bearing any number of half brothers and sisters to share
in Poppa's bounty. But, as it happened, that *hadn't* happened—though I know it wasn't for lack of trying, as
Gloria had made clear.

I wondered what the terms of the will had been—I remembered Gloria saying that there had been some dis-
pute but she was obviously exceedingly well off.

". . . and I do miss him so much. If I could just have
one little talk with him and ask him what to do about
Jerry. You know, Harry was always so marvelous at giving advice. He made me feel safe . . . and he understood
me . . ."

Gloria's turquoise-blue eyes were just at the edge of

tears and once again I found myself pitying my poor little rich girl sister. Two times in one hour had to be a
first. I reached for her hand but could manage only an
awkward pat. "I'm sorry, Glory. I wish there was something I could—"

The turquoise-blue eyes steadied on me. "As a matter
of fact, Lizzy, there *is* something . . ."

"Hey, Mum, it was brilliant up there! You and Aunt
Gloria should have come too."

I looked up from the pile of unfolded laundry on the
bed to see Laurel, her stubby braids adorned with wilt-
ing daisies, grinning at me from the bedroom door. My
mind had been so busy with trying to figure out how to
get out of the promise I'd just made my sister that I
hadn't heard Laurel return.

"Hey, Laur—Glory wanted to walk on the hard
road—we only went as far as Miss Birdie's. But listen,
when you were at the top, did you happen to see a big
black SUV come up our road?"

Laurel dropped her knapsack. "Nope, I couldn't see
the road. I was down at the northern end of the fence
line." She came and stood by me and began pulling the
dish towels from the pile of laundry and folding them
neatly.

"By the way, Mum, the fence at that end needs some
work. Some of the barbed wire is lying on the ground. I
hunted around till I located the staples that had popped
out and banged them back in with a rock but the repair
job is seriously sketchy. One of the guys probably ought
to go up with fence tools and fix it before a cow leans on
it again."

She flapped a blue plaid linen dish towel to shake out
some of the wrinkles. "What black SUV are you talking
about? Were you expecting someone?"

I gave her the brief version of the mysterious Hummer

and Gloria's insistence that it was one of her husband's friends looking for her. Even before I'd come to the end of my tale, Laurel was shaking her head.

"What do you want to bet it was some lost sightseer? Or Witnesses with *Watchtower*s? A stalker? Boy, Aunt Glory's something else—"

Laurel clapped her hand over her mouth and looked toward the doorway. Her voice dropped to a whisper. "Oops! Where is she anyway?"

"On the front porch, making some phone calls," I said. "Making reservations."

I smoothed out a stiff and scratchy sun-dried towel and began to fold it, not trusting myself to go on in an adult fashion. I like to think that my daughters and I have no secrets from each other but though I like to think it, I know it isn't so. There is much I don't know about their love lives; sometimes I've learned of a new man only after he's been discarded—or done the discarding. I only know what I'm told and I try really hard not to ask.

By the same token, I don't tell the girls everything. I try to present a façade that is strong and serene, above such petty emotions as curiosity . . . jealousy . . . annoyance . . .

Right.

"Reservations? Like for dinner somewhere?" Laurel plucked the napkins one by one from the heap of clothes and linens. "You don't iron these everyday ones, do you?"

"Not those. Just folding them will be fine. No, the reservations are for a weekend workshop in Hot Springs—a *psychic* workshop with someone called Giles of Glastonbury."

Laurel's lips quirked. My skeptical take on such things is well known to my family and friends. I don't insist that *all* such stuff is made-up baloney. In fact, I've had a couple of very strange experiences that I can't really explain—yet another part of my life I don't talk about. But I do believe that at least some of the New Age gurus infesting the Asheville area are little more than scam artists.

"I know, Mum—don't get you started. But at least it'll give you a break from Aunt Gloria for a few days."

"Not really." I was struggling to fold a fitted sheet—an origami-like skill that has always eluded me. "She wants me to go with her."

"... *late again ... all night ... later ...*"

The message on the voice mail had been left while I was down closing up the chickens and Gloria was on the porch in the midst of another interminable phone call. The words had been garbled—wherever Phillip had called from, the reception was poor. Not unusual, in this county of mountains and valleys and deep, dark hidden coves. Not surprising either, since these hidden coves are exactly the sorts of places the sheriff and his men often find themselves—called to break up family disputes, sur-veilling (is that a word?) suspected marijuana patches or the far worse meth labs.

I looked at the lemon pound cake waiting on the counter and the remains of supper drying out on top of the stove. The long and erratic hours a cop had to keep, Phillip had once warned, invariably put a strain on his relationships.

Invariably.

Was this what I wanted?

Suddenly the idea of a weekend in Hot Springs at the elegant Mountain Magnolia Inn seemed appealing. Glo-ria could commune with her late husband and I . . . well, I could spend some time thinking about this wedded state I was about to enter—and about Phillip Hawkins.

I scraped the unappetizing remains of the dinner into the chicken bucket and went in search of the letter from Aunt Dodie. This time I would read it and pay attention.

The shriek was part of the dream I was having—Aunt Dodie's response to my telling her I *had* to get married. But the persistent knocking, followed instantly by a hand on my shoulder shaking me awake, had no part of my dream chat with Dodie.

"Lizzy! He was *there*! Right in my bedroom! For god's sake, where's *Phillip*?"

Chapter 11

The Queen of Hearts

Thursday, May 17

Gloria stood gibbering beside the bed as I pulled myself into consciousness—only to realize that Phillip still wasn't home, though the luminescent dial on the clock at the bedside proclaimed the hour to be 4:23.

It was mid-morning when he finally showed up, obviously exhausted after an all-night stakeout of a suspected meth lab, culminating in the arrest of four suspects and an abortive chase up a wooded mountain slope after three more. Phillip was filthy, smelly, and uncommunicative, saying no, he didn't need any breakfast—just a long hot shower and some sleep.

And Gloria was freaking out, insisting that he listen to her story of the man she called the Eyebrow and the thing she'd found under her pillow. Grabbing Phillip's arm, she positioned herself in front of him to prevent an escape and began to pour out her story.

"Lizzy went to bed but I sat up, hoping you'd get back soon and I could tell you about this creep who's trying to frighten me. But you didn't get back and you didn't get back and finally I just gave up and decided to go to bed. I fell asleep right away . . ."

Phillip's red-rimmed eyes drifted toward the hall leading to our bedroom but he stood patiently listening to Gloria's story.

". . . so it wasn't till after four that I woke up and realized there was something under my pillow, something lumpy. Well, of course I leaped out of bed—it might have been a mouse or god knows what—out here in the wilds I know anything's possible and Lizzy's so careless about—"

"Gloria." Phillip held up one dirty hand and I could see the scratches across its back, evidence that the chase had led him through the cruel briars and brambles so common in abandoned fields. He looked utterly exhausted. "Could you show me what it was you found?"

My sister seemed for the first time to notice his state of complete fatigue. Without continuing her dissertation on my failures as a housewife, she led the way back to the guest room.

"*There* it is!" She whisked away the pillow to reveal her find: a beheaded Barbie doll in a gold lamé evening gown. Lying a few inches away atop a half-torn card— a queen of hearts—the blond head smirked up at us.

"You see! This *has* to be Jerry's doing. On my last birthday he threw a big party for me at the club and that was the theme—the Queen of Hearts—invitations, centerpieces, they were all done with big blowups of the card with my head on the queen's body."

Gloria leaned in for a closer look at the doll. "I even had a gold lamé dress—but not tacky like this one." It was hard to tell if fear outweighed annoyance in her tone as she regarded the bizarre little display. "He must have walked right into the house—I *told* Lizzy she ought to have an alarm system but she just laughed and said she'd lost the key to the front door years ago. Well, I ask you . . ."

When I tried to stem the flow of my sister's rambling narrative, suggesting that perhaps it would be kind to let Phillip get some sleep before we pursued this case of the

Barbie Who Lost Her Head, he ignored me—*they* ignored me.

Phillip went into full cop mode—checking the French door that led from the guest room to the outside, bagging up the Barbie pieces along with the card—and all of the time treating Gloria's babbling as seriously as if a major crime had been committed.

At last he had finished and my sister had allowed him to get a shower. I followed him into the bedroom, Molly trailing close behind.

"Sorry about last night, sweetheart." Phillip yawned hugely and planted a perfunctory kiss on my cheek. "We were in a dead zone and I couldn't call earlier . . ."

He yawned again, tossed his robe to the foot of the bed, and slid between the sheets. "Just a few hours and I'll be good to go . . . tell your sister I'll . . ."

His voice trailed off and I could see that he was half asleep already.

"Phillip," I said, keeping my voice low. "I'm wondering . . . how do we know Gloria didn't put that silly doll under her pillow herself? I sure didn't see any signs of—"

He was curled on his side, his face covered by his arm to block the light from the uncurtained windows. I could hear his breathing, slow and regular as if he were already asleep.

I stood and watched him for a few moments, torn by contradictory emotions. Part of me wanted to lie down beside him, inhale that clean soap smell, and be soothed by the sound of his breathing.

The other part of me was completely and irrationally ticked off that he'd paid so much attention to Gloria's so-called fears, that he'd been gone for so long, that he'd ignored—

"Lizabeth, listen, sweetheart . . ."

The half-mumbled words made me jump. I'd been

sure he was alseep. But he continued, the drowsy, muffled words seemingly dragged out of him. His eyes were still hidden in the crook of his elbow and he was talking into the pillow, but I could understand him.

"You got to get past this . . . this thing you have about your sister. It's . . . messing with your . . ."

The last word was enveloped in a sudden snore and I realized that I'd been tuned out. Across the hall I could hear Gloria's music starting up again and suddenly I felt like a prisoner in my own house . . . and worse, in my own mind.

As I watched him sleep, I considered this man in my bed—*our* bed for quite a while now. Annoyed though I was at his inability to see through Gloria's obvious attempts at manipulation, still, I was deeply in love with him—this man with whom, for better or worse, I was about to promise to share my life.

I knew he was gentle; I knew he was kind. That he was patient, I had ample opportunity of knowing, none better.

Even the sight of his bald, nut brown scalp, ringed with graying dark hair, inspired the sort of tenderness in me usually reserved for puppies and small fluffy creatures. I knew how I felt—no doubt about my feelings . . .

I heaved a sigh and sat down on the bench at the foot of the bed. Feelings were all very well. *But what,* I asked myself—that fluttery teenager-in-love self who kept wanting to ignore the adult self asking the hard questions—*what do you really know about Phillip?*

Staring out the window at the familiar beautiful view, it was hard to focus on the ugly possibilities raised by Dodie's letter. The view from my window was, as always, an invitation to meditate—the woods and fields of the farm laid out below me with green fold upon green fold in the nearer distance and then blue shading to rich violet as the ridges marched toward the horizon.

Had it been only three years ago that he had come into my life?

An uneasy memory of the somewhat duplicitous nature of his reason for invading my world—the safe little world I'd built for myself of hard work and grief—nudged at me. *You see! He wasn't what he said. Even though it all got explained—*

The springs creaked as Molly leaped up onto the bed, did the obligatory circling and, sighing heavily, lay down in the crook of Phillip's knees.

There—what about that? The dogs have trusted him from the beginning. Of course James would cuddle up to an ax murderer. But Molly and Ursa have always seemed much more discerning. And how many men would put up with three spoiled dogs the way he does?

He has, in fact, fit into the life here with barely a ripple. No furniture or collections to find a place for, no personal stuff except for a few pictures of his kids. I couldn't believe how simple moving was for him—a couple of duffel bags of clothes, three boxes of books and odds and ends, and a file cabinet that fit on the backseat of his car. When I asked where the rest of his stuff was, he said that was all there was.

Was it realistic for a man in his fifties to have so little baggage—literal or otherwise? I knew about the ex-wife, now happily remarried; had met the children briefly before they'd vanished off to Australia to pursue whatever it was they were pursuing. Marine biology for Seth, I reminded myself, and Party Hearty 101 for Janie, if her infrequent emails to Phillip were any guide.

The horrible things that Sam and Phillip witnessed in Vietnam decades ago seemed not to have haunted Phillip. Sam had suffered through terrible nightmares, flashbacks, depression, but as far as I could tell, Phillip had put that episode behind him forever.

Different men—different ways of dealing with things,

I told myself, watching the resident pair of redtail hawks wheeling against the deep blue sky. One screamed and dove toward the slope below the house, the sun striking copper glints from his tail feathers. The second continued her lazy arcs then abruptly changed course to head for the tree line of the ridge to the south.

A gang of crows exploded from the trees where the second hawk had gone. Like bits of cinder against the sky, they swirled and coalesced, then moved away in a ragged line.

Behind me Phillip was snoring. Across the hall, another of Gloria's interminable show tunes was playing—a full chorus this time.

Suddenly I had to get out of the house. Let Gloria weep out more of her story when Phillip finally wakes up, I decided. They don't need me here for that—the obvious *thing* I have about my sister is too likely to get in the way.

I pulled off my stained workaday T-shirt, replacing it with a cleaner, newer model, and headed out.

"Gloria," I called over the racket in her room. "I'm off to the grocery store. For god's sake, let Phillip get his sleep—you can tell him the rest of your story when he wakes up."

"Naw, Daddy ain't doing no good these days. But he's dead set on keeping the trout business going long as he can. It gives him something to get up for of a morning."

I'd been engrossed in the magazine covers there beside the checkout counter—wondering who all these people were anyway and why it mattered if they were cheating on each other. But that familiar voice . . . almost at my ear . . .

The two men behind me had exchanged the ritual farewells—*Let's go to the house*, the first voice had said.

And *Reckon I best stay here and pay for these groceries,* the other had answered.

Harice Tyler—Brother Tyler to the congregation at the little church I had visited several times for Miss Birdie's sake—was standing just behind me. Harice Tyler—whose bedroom eyes and slow sensual smile had been so enchanting to me for a brief mad moment that I had imagined—

I could feel a flush rising on my face as I remembered what I had imagined. I inched my cart forward and began shoving my groceries along the motionless belt toward the scanner. The previous customer had paid but now her cellphone was out and she and the cashier were cooing and exclaiming over all forty-three pictures of the new grandchild.

"You got any grandbabies yet, Miz Goodweather?"

This was ridiculous. I couldn't pretend not to know who it was. Taking a deep breath, I turned and summoned up a polite smile.

"Mr. . . . Mr. Tyler? I thought I recognized your voice. It's been quite a while."

Did his eyes seem to burn into mine? Why was I suddenly so exquisitely *aware* of this dark-eyed preacher from the Church of Jesus Love Anointed—the *snake-handling* church in Tennessee?

I couldn't help making a quick inventory of his shopping cart—canned biscuits, Treet meat, a bunch of bananas, dried pinto beans, margarine, two loaves of Bunny bread, four pouches of chewing tobacco, a gallon of cherry vanilla ice cream, and a box of Little Debbies.

He caught me looking. "Been doing some shopping for Daddy," he said, his voice low and confidential as if we were sharing some secret. "They's a widder woman in the next holler that brings him soup or a big pot of stew now and again, but Daddy, he's a fool for them Little Debbies."

What was it in his sleepy-eyed gaze that had me tongue-tied and ransacking my brain for something innocuous to say?

"Did I hear you say your father still has the trout farm?" I finally managed. "I keep meaning to go get some but—"

"Ain't nothing better than fresh trout," Harice Tyler assured me. "You come on over this evening, Miz Goodweather, I'll see you get treated right."

A nice change, I thought as I pushed the cart out to my car.

And immediately wondered what, exactly, I'd meant. Trout, trout for supper—that would be a nice change, I told myself as I put the groceries into the back of the car. No need to hurry home—for once I'd remembered to bring a cooler with ice packs for the cold groceries— there'd be room for some trout . . .

In the next row of cars, Harice Tyler was sauntering toward his truck, two bulging white plastic bags in each hand. Dark-haired, slim-hipped—what an older Elvis might have looked like if no one had ever told him about deep-fried peanut-butter-and-banana sandwiches.

Almost as if he'd heard my thoughts, Harice Tyler stopped, swiveled around, and fixed his gaze on me.

"I'm on my way to Daddy's place right now—you come along, Miz Goodweather, and I'll fix you up. All the trout you want—it won't take no time."

I could feel my face flush again, as if he'd just made an indecent proposal.

"You remember how to get there, don't you?" he persisted.

It took me a minute to find my voice. *Why* did this man have this effect on me?

"Yes, I do remember. But I—"

"I thought that you would. You just come along if

you've a mind—I got to get going afore this ice cream melts—Daddy asked for it special."

And I found myself following his truck out of the parking lot onto the road that led back to the bridge at Gudger's Stand. By the time I got to the bridge, I told myself, I would have decided whether or not I really wanted trout for dinner. That's all.

IV~*The DeVine Sisters*

The Mountain Park Hotel~May 9, 1887

At the Mountain Park Hotel
Hot Springs, North Carolina
May 9, 1887

My dear sister,

Yours of the 29th ult. received three days ago. They tell me that such speedy mail service is still a nine days' wonder here, the rail not having been laid till the year '82.

Pray, dear Nell, put yourself at ease as regards my health. The bracing mountain air, the health-giving baths, the sumptuous meals—these have all helped to heal my body. You would not credit the change that has been wrought. The pale, debilitated skeleton that you bade farewell at the train station has all but vanished and I am, for the most part, close to regaining my former strength.

The other trouble—that melancholy, which has held me in its iron grip since the loss of my dearest Emmeline—while still a daily companion, has not now so strong a hold on my mind. I attribute this in part to the continuing solicitude of my friend Peavey and to my wonderful good fortune of having made the acquaintance of Miss Theodora DeVine.

No, dear sister, rest assured, 'tis not a matter of the heart. I doubt I shall ever love again. It is that I have at last been able to communicate with my Emmy, to beg forgiveness for my harsh words on that fatal morning and to hear, in the sweet lisping tones I know so well, that she forgives me and is waiting on the other side.

Miss DeVine is, you see, a medium—a bridge between our world and the next. And although she and her similarly gifted sister are here at the Mountain Park precisely to recuperate from their labors (for labor it is—Miss Theodora is quite wrung out at the end of a successful sitting), good Peavey (who is, by the by, fairly smitten with Miss Dorothea) prevailed upon the sisters to take mercy on me and vouchsafe me an interview with my lost Emmeline.

Oh, Sister! Could you but have been one of the hand-clasp'd circle round the table in that darkened room; could you but have heard the beautiful young medium calling for the guide! Could you but have seen the pale trumpet floating before our astounded eyes, alight with an unearthly glow! Could you but have heard the voices of the departed speaking through it!

My eyes overflow. My heart is too full to go on. Trust me, dear Nell, to relate the story fully on my return and believe me to be—

Your loving brother,
Roddy

"I believe that our fish is well and truly hooked, my dears."

Lorenzo refolded the creamy pages and replaced them in the envelope, taking care that the resealing of the flap should leave no traces.

Theodora extended a graceful hand and studied her narrow bare wrist. "Indeed, I can almost see that lovely bracelet now." The sleeve of her deep amethyst robe fell back to her elbow as she made a regal gesture in the air. A thought seemed to strike her and she frowned.

"Renzo," she said, lowering her hand. "Need we be in a great hurry to dispose of the bracelet?" Her voice was light and cajoling. "For one thing, who would buy it in this backwater? And for another, I should very

*much like to wear it on tour this winter—think how ef-
fectively it would catch the light onstage. Paste jewels
are all very well but—"*

*"You don't have it yet, Theo, so you can stop playing
the great lady." Dorothea looked up from the wispy garment she was hemming with tiny even stitches. "Counting your chickens before they hatch is dangerous—as
you should know. Besides, it's one thing to take a little
gift of money in return for bringing comfort to the bereaved. What you and Renzo are contemplating is more
akin to theft—"*

*"Higher stakes require higher risks." The elegant
Lorenzo's tone was stern and reproving.*

*He sauntered over to the window seat and leaned
down to inspect Dorothea's needlework. "Just as the
tangible evidence afforded by this cherubic nightshirt
will no doubt give some bereaved mother a lasting so-
lace—and may I say that those slits for the putative infant wings are an especially nice touch—would it not
bring comfort to poor Harris if he could believe that his
late lamented Emmeline accepted the jeweled token of
his apology and that its earthly brilliance would grace
her heavenly wrist through all eternity?"*

*He leaned lower still, till his mustachioed face
touched Dorothea's hair. "Perhaps we should discuss
this later. I'm sure I can win you to my point of view."
He drew in a deep breath, savoring the scent of her hair.
"Ah, Dodo, I feel the most unbrotherly affections on the
rise. Your—"*

*Laughing, the green-clad young woman brandished
the almost invisible needle she held in the direction of
Lorenzo's crotch.*

*"Take care, Renzo, lest I prick those rampant affec-
tions in the—"*

*A clatter of knocking on the sitting room door inter-
rupted the foolery and the two women glanced at one*

another. With silent accord the sisters rose and hurried to their bedchamber, leaving Lorenzo to answer the door.

"Express letter for Mr. Lorenzo DeVine."

The voice was young—betrayed by an adolescent crack on the second syllable—and a pronounced twang hinted at the local origin of the speaker.

Feeling in his pocket for a coin, Lorenzo strode to the door. He opened it, received the missive, and silently tipped the messenger, closing the door firmly as the boy struggled to express his appreciation.

Carrying the bulky envelope over to the window seat, Lorenzo took a small mother-of-pearl-sided penknife from his trousers pocket and slit open the thick brown envelope. He extricated the contents—a single folded sheet and a sheaf of newspaper clippings.

He was frowning at the contents of the letter when Dorothea emerged from her room.

"Has Murchinson secured another engagement for us? I had thought that our fall schedule was already tight-packed. And what are these? More reviews from the Charleston engagement?"

Laughing, she picked up the topmost paper—the front page of The Charleston Courier—*but the laugh died as she saw the headline. Quickly she scanned the first few lines of the story, and then glanced at the engraving illustrating the article.*

Her eyes widened and a choked sob escaped her lips. Shaking her head in negation, Dorothea thrust the page at her companion.

"Renzo, this isn't our Mrs. Waverly, surely? Please—"

He looked at her a long moment before nodding. "I'm afraid it must be, Doe. But—"

He broke off his attempt at reassurance as he saw Dorothea sway. At once he was on his feet, hands out-

stretched to assist her but too late—uttering a despairing
little cry, she had slumped to the carpet in a faint.

NOTE FROM THOS. C. MURCHINSON,
THEATRICAL AND BOOKING AGENT

Here's a hell of a thing, DeVine. All Charleston was
singing the praises of your sisters and clamoring for a return engagement at the earliest possible date. I'd secured
some very favorable terms for a suite at the best hotel—
Theodora let me know pretty sharply that the boarding-
house wasn't up to her high standards. The girl has a
short memory, is all I can say.

But now that's neither here nor there. Here's one
of your recent clients—a grieving mother—gone and
hanged herself. You can see for yourself in the clippings
I enclose. "Distraught with grief when the comfort of
communication with her departed child is revealed to be
nothing more than a heartless hoax—"

"Angelic garment 'materialized' from the other side
proves of earthly origin."

"I done found it on the floor in their rooms where it
had fell behind a table. I put it back in Miss Dorrythea's
workbasket. I knowed it wuz hers for they wuz more
of the same fine cloth folded up in there." Testimony
of Negro chambermaid. "I wondered whuffo she had
made them slits there on the back."

Read it for yourself, DeVine. Of course Charleston is
out in the future—the whole southern seaboard is likely
out. And in these days with communication as rapid as
it is, you might consider a change of name or relocation
to the West Coast.

Yours, etc.

TCM

P.S. My friend RB tells me there was some talk in the taverns of Charleston of tar and feathers! In all likelihood, he exaggerated. Still, a word to the wise . . .

P.P.S. Damn and blast that careless sister of yours! I am at a stand as to where to place your act this fall.

Chapter 12

Mrs. Robinson? Mr. Hawkins?

Thursday, May 17

There's no sign of any Hummer; I think it would be safe for you to sit up now."

Phillip glanced across at his passenger, slouched low in her seat. A bright green scarf covered her hair and big goggle-like dark glasses hid her eyes. *Damned if she doesn't look like some weird bug,* he thought and fought back the grin that was starting to spread over his face.

"Are you positive?" Gloria inched a little higher and peered cautiously up and down the almost deserted highway. "Aren't we there yet? That sign said that it was only fourteen miles to Hot Springs. It's been almost a half hour."

"This isn't Florida, Gloria. Mountain miles are different."

The bug eyes turned and fixed him in their black lenses. "Phil, I know for a fact that's not true. And, by the way, I am *not* a dumb blonde, whatever my sister may have told you."

He suppressed another smile. "All I meant is that you can't make the kind of time on a twisting mountain road that you can on a sixty-five-miles-per-hour highway. I've noticed you Florida people always seem to think that twenty miles means twenty minutes."

Gloria sighed and looked away. "I guess I do think

that way. I just can't quite get used to how long it takes to get *any*where up here—at home almost everything is five or ten minutes away."

Was that a note of wistfulness in her voice? he wondered. She was gazing out the window at the wooded mountain slopes flashing by.

"See that overhead bridge up ahead? That's the AT— the Appalachian Trail." He pointed at the footbridge spanning the highway. "It runs through Hot Springs— we're almost there."

He had awakened earlier from a blissful sleep and stumbled blinking into the kitchen in search of food, only to find that Elizabeth was gone and Gloria was in the living room—with a pile of luggage waiting by the door.

"I decided that I can't sleep in that room another night." Her tone of voice said that this was not a matter for discussion. "Knowing that creature was there—well, I'm sure *you* understand, Phil. *Any*hoo, I called the Mountain Magnolia again and fortunately they had a room free tonight. If Lizzy hadn't slammed out of here in such a hurry to go to the grocery, she could have run me over but—"

Still stupid from the unaccustomed daytime nap, he had rubbed his eyes and offered to take her and her suitcases down to her car.

"Oh, no—I need a *ride* to Hot Springs, Phil. Couldn't you do that for me? I thought it would be best not to take the Mini because the Eyebrow is on the lookout for it. And if he comes back and sees it, he'll think I'm still here."

Really, it had been worth the aggravation, Phillip thought as he followed the innkeeper and Gloria up the stairs of the big Victorian house. Get Gloria away from the farm for a while and maybe Lizabeth would stop acting so strange. A little normal, quiet time together would do it. There would be a Gloria-free week ahead in which they could restore the harmony they had enjoyed till so recently. He would happily have toted twice as many suitcases up twice as many stairs if he could have the old sweet-tempered, easygoing Elizabeth back.

"And this is the Rose Room," the innkeeper announced, swinging wide the door to a luxurious-looking room, "and there's your private balcony and in *here*," she gestured with a bit of a flourish toward the bathroom, "is your two-person Jacuzzi. It's very popular, especially with our honeymoon couples," she added, looking at them with obvious meaning.

"We're not—" he began, only to be cut off by Gloria.

"Thank you so much, I'm sure we'd enjoy it. But poor Phil won't be staying with me. Too sad, but the old sweetie pie can't get free till later in the month. Of course, my sister will be joining me next weekend for the psychic workshop—I reserved a room for her when I called earlier."

Phillip stared at Gloria and shook his head as if clearing his ears. *What* had she just said?

The young woman nodded eagerly. "Oh yes, we have her down for the Sycamore, beginning Thursday the twenty-fourth and running through Sunday."

"That's fine then. Now, if you'd be a dear and bring up that champagne I ordered earlier . . ."

"Certainly! It's on ice right now. Back in a jiff, Mrs. Hawkins!"

Mrs. Hawkins? Phillip sat down abruptly in the less delicate-looking of the two armchairs by the fireplace. As the innkeeper bustled off, Gloria closed the door and turned toward him.

Unable to find the words right away, he raised both hands before him as if to fend her off. "I don't know what you have in mind here, Gloria, but it's not . . . well anyway . . . And another thing—you want to tell me why that girl called you Mrs. Hawkins?"

She regarded him with a look that managed to be both amused and skeptical—a look that brought to life a hitherto unnoticed resemblance between her and Elizabeth—strange to see that expression of suspended judgment on this perfectly made-up face.

"Well, think about it, Phil. Obviously I didn't want to give my real name when I made the reservations, and I went with the first thing that popped into my head. And then, since you were here with me, I thought it wouldn't hurt for people to believe that I had a husband around. You aren't upset about that, are you?"

He considered, wondering where this was leading. But Gloria, standing there, hands on hips, was waiting for an answer.

"Okay, I guess that makes some kind of sense." He was still uncertain, though, as to what exactly was going on . . . the whole thing with the champagne felt like a real *Are you trying to seduce me, Mrs. Robinson?* moment.

All at once he realized that he had shrunk back in his chair with his arms folded protectively across his chest, *seriously* w*impy body language there*. So he sat forward with his hands on the arms of the chair and, clearing his throat, leaned forward to take charge of a situation that seemed to be eluding him.

"Just tell me what the hell you want, Gloria." His voice was harsher than he'd meant it to be but she only laughed . . . and again he was reminded of Elizabeth.

"What I *want*, Phil, is a relaxing glass of champagne to help me settle in. You can join me if you like."

Sinking gracefully into the other chair, she explained. "You see, my late husband Harold and I traveled a lot and Harold always insisted on ordering champagne whenever we checked into a hotel. He said that was one sure way of getting good service during a stay: Start by ordering champagne—*good* champagne—and tip well. And it really is a lovely way to slow down a bit and unwind—that's all. Good heavens, what did you think I had in mind?"

There was a tap at the door and Gloria sprang up to open it.

"Oh, lovely!" she cooed at the innkeeper and the silver tray with a pair of crystal flutes beside a dewy silver wine cooler. A gold-foil-covered cork peeked from the snowy napkin that swathed the bottle's neck and a bowl of smoked almonds completed the presentation.

"Just set it there," Gloria directed, pointing at the table between their chairs, "Phil will deal with opening it."

Her hand went to her pocket, there was the flash of a folded bill, and the young woman, now Gloria's willing slave, turned to go.

Though the cork put up a fight, Phillip was relieved that he managed to open the bottle with no more than a discreet *pop*—no showy foaming, thank god. *Real French champagne too,* he noticed; *how much do you reckon they'll charge for that? Ah, well, like they say— if you have to ask, you can't afford it.* Again, he found himself wondering just how rich Gloria really was.

"I know you're in a hurry to get back, Phil, but at least you can have one glass before you go."

He accepted, partly out of a curiosity as to what "real" champagne was like and partly with an ulterior motive—there were things he wanted to find out.

On the drive over Gloria had resisted all his attempts to get her to talk about who, other than her current husband, might wish her harm. Her only response had been to say that she was sure there wasn't anyone like that. And she had clammed up when he'd asked about earlier romantic entanglements. So, he told himself, leaning back and savoring the crisp dry wine, let her get a few glasses of this down the hatch. Maybe that will relax her enough to answer a few questions.

It worked almost too well, he decided, glancing at his watch a half hour later. Gloria had slugged down three glasses while he had sipped at his first, cautious as a maiden aunt. And now it had come, a flood of words that had him wishing he could reach for a notepad.

He was shaking his head in disbelief as almost an hour later he climbed into his car for the trip back to Full Circle Farm. For a moment he just sat, replaying the scene just ended. Then he reached for his cellphone and rang the house. There was no answer, only Elizabeth's cautious message on the voice mail repeating the phone number and inviting the caller to leave a message after the beep.

He left a message after the beep.

"I'm on my way, sweetheart. Your sister insisted on being taken to Hot Springs and she's safe and happy there. In the Rose Room, for cripes' sake. I'll explain when I get there. Love you."

Flipping the little phone shut, he started the car. As he was pulling out of the parking area, he saw Gloria come down the front steps of the inn, deep in conversation with a white-haired woman at her side. She pointed toward his car and waved briefly, then the two women continued their stroll out to the lawn.

Phillip breathed a sigh of relief and continued on down the drive. After a quick stop at the Hot Springs police department and a few words with the officer on duty, he drove through the tiny town, noticing the summer profusion of lean hikers and chubby day-trippers wandering in and out of the little shops and eating establishments. On, across the railroad tracks and past the entrance to the spa, modest successor to a once magnificent hotel, and back to the highway.

Gloria—what a piece of work! To look at her, you'd think she really was the dumbest of dumb blondes but he had to give her credit, she'd weathered some rough times.

Again there was the resemblance to Elizabeth . . . the independence . . . the reluctance to share private problems . . . and yes, the strength too. It seemed that beneath the fancy clothes and brittle façade, there was a woman far more like his Elizabeth than not.

Driving more or less on autopilot, his mind busy rehashing some of the things Gloria had told him, he was surprised to find himself already crossing the bridge at Gudger's Stand. He slowed to see if the great blue heron was visible—he had caught the habit from Lizabeth, who was oddly superstitious about that bird—and scanned the lower reaches of the river. No luck.

But just as he was almost to the other side, he was startled by a harsh creaking cry to his right and the sudden appearance of the heron rising on huge wings from the riverbank below the bridge. Phillip slammed on the brakes and sat watching reverently—another thing he'd caught from Lizabeth—as the great bird, long legs trailing, went flapping his stately way right over the car to continue upriver.

As he turned onto Ridley Branch, Phillip found himself humming. Things were going to work out; he was sure of it. A quiet dinner for two—that would be nice. He had some time coming after last night—he could tell Mac that he needed tomorrow morning off . . .

He was still humming as he got out of his car and headed for the house. Lizabeth's Jeep was there with the hatch door open to show several canvas bags of groceries sagging against one another. Evidently, she had just gotten back from the store. Grabbing the rest of the bags, he took the porch steps two at a time, happy to be back home.

Through the window on the porch he could see Elizabeth moving about the kitchen and he called out, "Hey, sweetheart!" He didn't hear an answer but he wrestled his load of bags through the mudroom and into the kitchen where he plonked them down on the bench where the other bags sprawled.

"Hi, honey, I'm home!" He grinned at her expectantly but she didn't look up from what she was doing—which was taking what looked like freshly cleaned trout from a cooler and putting them into individual freezer bags.

Trout? Where'd that come from, he wondered but before he could ask, he caught sight of her face.

Unless he was badly mistaken, Elizabeth was angry. Very, very angry. Tight-lipped and quivering like a plucked string in a way he'd never seen.

"Sweetheart," he ventured, "what's wrong? Didn't you get my message?"

At last her eyes met his. Their icy blue sent a chill through his body.

"Oh, yes," she replied, just a little too evenly, "I got your message. And so I thought I'd give Glory a call to see how she liked it over there. But when I reached the Mountain Magnolia Inn and asked to speak to Mrs. Lombardo, there was a little problem."

His heart sinking, Phillip tried to say something but she continued, ignoring his attempt to break in.

"No Lombardo here, they said. Oh, I thought, she's probably using her maiden name or maybe she's gone back to Holst. So I told them that the guest in question was my sister and she had just checked into the Rose Room."

Another silvery fish slid into another plastic bag and Elizabeth ran her fingers along the seal. Her face was stony and he dreaded to hear the rest of her story. But he was like a man under a spell, unable to do anything but listen.

"Imagine my surprise," she continued, busy with the fish and not looking at him, "when the person on the other end giggled and said oh, of course, that nice Mrs. Hawkins. She—the person on the phone—had just delivered some *champagne* to that nice Mrs. Hawkins and her husband but she could find out if Mrs. Hawkins was available . . .

"I told the person on the phone not to disturb the Hawkinses and I hung up." She turned toward him, the last shiny fish drooping in her hand. "Maybe *you* can explain what's going on, *Mr.* Hawkins."

Chapter 13

Emergency Champagne

Thursday, May 17

There I was, threatening Phillip with a dead fish and feeling as though the Wicked Witch of the West was in possession of my body and speaking through my mouth, about to cackle *I'll get you, my pretty!*

What was I *saying*? What was I *thinking,* for god's sake? Did I really believe that Phillip was fooling around with Gloria? Or was this some strange reaction I was having to the lust I had felt in my own heart (thank you, Jimmy Carter) a few hours earlier.

Even as the words left my lips, I knew I'd made a mistake. The man I love was standing there, staring at me in utter amazement.

"Who *are* you?" he asked, after a few uncomfortably silent moments had ticked by. "And what have you done with Lizabeth?"

Covering the distance between us in two steps, he grabbed me by the shoulders, not roughly, but not particularly gently either. He ignored my gasp of surprise and brought his face close to mine, looking into my eyes as if searching for something. Stunned into speechlessness, I closed my eyes to escape that penetrating gaze. Then, without a word, he wrapped his arms around me and pulled me so close that I could feel his breath in my hair and the beating of his heart against my body.

Held tight in his embrace, I felt all the righteous anger—anger that I had knowingly stoked to flame by my imagination—flicker, sputter, and go out, leaving behind just the black ash of regret. The fish in my hand slipped to the floor and I put my arms around his neck. We stood there swaying slightly.

"Hey, Lizabeth," he whispered in my ear, "you want to hear a funny story?"

"So there I was, shrinking back in that chair like a frightened virgin—hell, I did everything but cross my legs . . ."

We were on the sofa, our feet up on the cedar chest, completely happy and completely relaxed. I had retrieved the fish from the floor and put it in the fridge to await cooking while Phillip had gone to the basement for one of the bottles of emergency champagne that I keep in the second refrigerator down there.

Yes, emergency champagne—well, okay, sparkling wine—usually a Spanish Cava. Because you never know when there may be something to celebrate. Our family has always been big on celebrations—a needed rain, the first daffodil, the first snow, a bird-watching trifecta (i.e., spotting a male goldfinch, a male cardinal, and a male indigo bunting all at the feeder at the same time)—any of these served as an excuse to break out the cheap champagne.

A narrowly avoided disaster is another good reason and it seemed to me that this was such an occasion. Besides, if Phillip was going to drink champagne with Gloria in the afternoon, it seemed only fair he drink it with me in the evening.

The story, as he told it, was hilarious—from his driving my sister "disguised as a giant bug" to Hot Springs to his reaction when the innkeeper called Gloria "Mrs. Hawkins." By the time he got to the part where he was sure she was about to make an assault on his virtue, I was helpless with laughter and the Wicked Witch had melted away—forever, I hoped.

"There's the Lizabeth I know and love." He planted a kiss on the top of my head. "You want another glass of bubbly or do you want to save it to have with dinner?"

"Dinner—now, there's a thought." I untangled myself from him and stood up, a little woozy with the champagne and the emotional roller-coaster ride I'd been on all afternoon.

"That nice-looking trout you were waving at me—is that on the menu?" He trailed me into the kitchen and stuck the open bottle in the refrigerator.

"Was I waving it? Well, at least I didn't throw it at you. Would you get them out? They're in a plastic bag right there on the top shelf. I thought I'd grill two and freeze the rest."

He brought out the pair I'd saved back for tonight and studied them with a professional eye.

"These didn't come from the grocery. I'd bet another bottle of that champagne they were swimming around this morning." He leaned down and sniffed at them. "Maybe as late as midday— Where'd you get them?"

Deep breath. What *had* I been thinking? Harice Tyler's bedroom eyes flickered at the edge of my memory and disappeared.

"There's a trout farm up on Bear Tree Creek. You know where it is—just before that Devil's Fork place, remember?"

"I'd rather not." Phillip grinned. "That was another time you caught me in a hard-to-explain situation. Thank god, we're okay now . . . aren't we?"

Not waiting for my answer, he went on. "I don't remember you ever getting trout there before, but I think it's a great idea. Did you fish for them or . . . ?"

"Or," I admitted. "The guy in charge threw in a little food and netted them for me. And killed and cleaned—"

"Oh yeah, old man Tyler—I was out there one time last year. He'd called the department about someone getting into his ginseng patch. Quite a character but he'd talk your ear off. You want me to go light the grill?"

While Phillip was tending the trout on the grill, I defrosted some of last year's roasted cherry tomatoes, steamed some asparagus, and sizzled sliced almonds in butter to top the fish. A big salad of red and green lettuce with baby beets and carrots, chopped green onion, vinaigrette, and we were good to go. And the rest of the champagne, of course.

As we took our places at the table, outside the dining room window a gentle rain began to fall and I felt blessed in all things. *God's in His Heaven; Gloria's in Hot Springs; all's right with the world.*

"Phillip, I've been such a bitch—" I began, but he stopped me by lifting his glass.

"To us," he said.

"To us," I agreed.

We sat in the rocking chairs on the porch, savoring the lingering twilight and the refreshment of the rain— the welcome coolness, the clean smell, the calming patter on the metal roof. Molly and Ursa came hurrying up the steps, back from an early evening adventure, shook off the droplets that trembled on their fur, and settled at our feet. James, of course, was already ensconced on a pillow on one of the rockers.

I listened to the rain and the chirping of the frogs down in the little fishpond and thought about the past few weeks . . . the letter from Dodie . . . was it having Gloria around and the poisoned effect of her doubts about her husband that had caused me to take seriously the scattered ramblings of a very sweet but sometimes rather loopy old woman? God knows, Gloria's visit had revealed an unpleasant, snippy, arrogant aspect of my personality—why shouldn't it be paranoid as well?

Something clicked in my wandering thoughts. I turned to look at Phillip, who was rocking, eyes closed, completely relaxed and utterly at peace. Poor guy, I thought, he's got to be exhausted after being out in the woods all last night. He couldn't have gotten much of a nap.

By unspoken mutual consent, we had avoided talking about Gloria during dinner. And it would probably have suited both of us to stay off the subject at least till the morning.

But still, I had to ask.

"Do you think she'll be okay over there?"

He didn't open his eyes but yawned and nodded. "I don't see why not."

"But this Eyebrow character . . . what if he—"

Phillip's eyes came open and he gave me a sharp, police detective look. "This morning—was it just this morning? Geez, seems like a week ago. But this morning you said that Gloria might have set up the whole Barbie doll thing."

I blushed, remembering my selfish annoyance at the whole affair.

"I know, I did say that. But what if I was wrong? What if there really *is* someone after her? Is she safe over there?"

He reached for my hand. "Sweetheart, I didn't want to make a big deal of it but when I was looking around outside Gloria's room, I found a man's footprint on the little porch. I know Ben comes that way sometimes, but he always wears boots with cleated bottoms. This was a smooth sole—like a man's dress shoe."

I thought about this. "Okay. I'm not saying I doubt

you but . . . a footprint? This is the first rain we've had in over a week and the ground is—was hard and bone dry. How'd he manage to leave a footprint?"

Phillip raised my hand to his lips and kissed it, then gently nudged at the sleeping Ursa with his toe. "Remember how Gloria was complaining the other day about the girls pooping right outside her door . . ."

While I was still giggling, Phillip hastened to assure me that he had alerted the Hot Springs police force—such as it was—to be on the lookout for a black Hummer with Florida plates and had explained that the driver might be a stalker.

"I told them that it was my future sister-in-law that was his target and that she had registered as Mrs. Hawkins in an attempt to throw this guy off. Nah, she should be fine—in a place as small as Hot Springs, this Eyebrow fellow's bound to be pretty damn conspicuous. I gave them a description of him too."

"Stinky shoe and all," I muttered. "Could they arrest him?"

"Afraid not—he hasn't actually done anything that we could prove," Phillip explained. "Can you imagine going into court with my strongest evidence a shoe with traces of dog poop on it? I asked Gloria if she wanted to get a restraining order but when I found out she doesn't even know the guy's name . . . besides, I'm not convinced that this Eyebrow fella is the whole story. From some of the things your sister said when she finally started talking, I'm guessing Jerry's not the only one with a motive for doing her in."

He stood and tugged on my hand. "Let's go inside. I'd like to stretch out while I question my next witness. Gloria told me a good bit about her various marriages—why don't you give me your take on these different husbands?"

As we arranged ourselves on the sofa, me at one end

with his head in my lap, I had my doubts as to how long he would stay awake. But he stretched luxuriously, closed his eyes, and said, "Let's start with number one—the Latin lover who got annulled. What can you tell me?"

I leaned back and tried to assemble my thoughts . . . to remember. This whole episode was hardly real to me—all my information was second- or thirdhand, and not from particularly reliable sources.

"Let's see . . . When Gloria was . . . I guess she would have been nineteen . . . she ran off with a foreign student she'd met at college. I'm pretty sure his name was Arturo but I don't think I ever knew his last name. You see, Sam and I were married by then and he was out of the Navy and in college. We weren't living in Tampa so I really didn't know much about what was happening with Glory beyond some late night phone calls from my mother who seemed to think Glory's elopement was somehow *my* fault because Sam and I hadn't had a big fancy wedding.

"The next thing we knew, my mother had managed to get the marriage annulled and Glory back in school. By the time Sam and I returned to Tampa, no one was talking about the elopement; Arturo, or whatever his name was, had moved back to Colombia; and Glory was engaged to Ben's father."

Phillip nodded. "Yeah, you told me about him before. Skip him and tell me about the rich husband—Harold. Or not so much Harold but his kids. They'd be Gloria's stepchildren, right?"

"I guess—but there was never any kind of family feeling between them. They were all grown and off with their trust funds and she rarely saw them. None of them were happy about Gloria marrying their dad—particularly since she was more or less their age. I think they were afraid of her presenting them with some half brothers or sisters who would get cut in on the eventual inheritance. I mean, there was so much money—it could have been split a hundred ways and everyone would have still been rich. But the Holst kids acted like a bunch of kindergarteners squabbling over toys."

The memory of the brief visit Sam and I had made to the Holst estate for the wedding, and the drunken toast the younger son had given at the wedding breakfast, made me shiver. It had been obvious that relations between the newlyweds and the Holst younger generation would never be good. Still . . .

"Except for Harold, the Holst family was the most unpleasant group of people I think I've ever met. But after one incident, Harold made sure they were polite when they were visiting—"

"Hang on, what incident would that be?" He was wide awake and alert now—full-tilt cop mode.

"It was, actually, at the wedding. Nothing you could prove, but Gloria was convinced that one of the Holst gang had made sure that her serving of lobster thermidor was slightly off. She ended up that afternoon at the emergency room having her stomach pumped. But, like I said, there was no way of proving anything and she didn't want to start off a marriage accusing her husband's only daughter of attempted murder."

"Food poisoning . . ." Phillip murmured. "Probably not a murder attempt—more of a malicious mischief kind of thing." He yawned. "So then what?"

"Nothing. The real tackiness didn't start till Harold dropped dead one day on the golf course. Then his children contested the will and started all kinds of unpleasant rumors about Gloria. Harold had fixed things so that she came in for a good chunk of his estate—but only in trust for her lifetime. It'll revert to the Holst family eventually. She does very well on the interest though."

Phillip considered this information briefly then looked up at me. "Any other men in her life? Before she married Lombardo?"

"Hmmm. Let me think . . ."

I thought about it. Gloria had never wanted for an escort to the major events that defined old Tampa society, especially all the Gasparilla carrying-on—Tampa's version of Mardi Gras. But had any of those "dates" been more than that?

A memory stirred. Dr. Brice Sterrings. *"We met cute, Lizzy,"* she had told me in a phone call years ago. *"I was in his office to see if it was time to have some work done—he's a cosmetic surgeon—and he told me that I was perfect just as I was and invited me out that weekend. Anyhoo, things are getting pretty serious and I just thought I'd let you know . . ."*

"There's a guy—a Dr. Sterrings. I know they went to Aruba together and then on some cruise. Gloria seemed to think that it was just a matter of time before . . . Then the next thing I knew she'd married Jerry. I don't know what happened but I'm pretty sure I heard her talking to him on her cell the other night. Very flirty conversation."

Phillip's eyes were closed again and he was quiet for so long that I thought he'd gone to sleep. Then his eyes opened.

"Did your sister tell you that she's also been in touch with Arturo recently—that he's back in the States?"

I was amazed. "No, she didn't mention it," I had to admit. On reflection, I realized that the time she called about Brice had been a kind of anomaly. For the most part Gloria had never told me much of anything about her life. Probably because I'd always made it silently clear that I disapproved of both her lifestyle and her taste in men.

Miss Birdie's words popped into my mind: *A sister's a*

comfort and a treasure in good times . . . and she'll always look out for you when times is bad.

A comfort and a treasure—I'd been neither. And though taking Gloria in when she needed refuge might count as looking out for her in bad times, I'd done it in such an ungracious, unpleasant way that it was small wonder my sister had escaped to Hot Springs at the first opportunity.

Phillip's head moved in my lap and his mouth opened slightly. His breathing became regular and I knew he was asleep.

Sighing, I closed my eyes again. The day had brought far more self-knowledge than I felt able to deal with. I'd managed to right things with Phillip—or so I hoped. But now—could I learn to be the kind of sister Miss Birdie was talking about?

I resolved that when I went to Hot Springs next week to attend the—I could hardly allow myself even to *think* the words—*Exploration of the Other Side* workshop with Giles of Glastonbury, I would go with an open mind—and a closed mouth. My eyes would not roll; I would not smirk. I would be a loving support to my sister; my actions would be my apology and a new beginning for our relationship.

Tell you what—self-knowledge sucks.

Chapter 14

Baby Steps

Thursday, May 24

I don't know what I'd been expecting—some Merlin-like figure with a blowing cloak and a wizard's staff, maybe—but Giles of Glastonbury certainly wasn't it.

I'd just arrived for my long weekend with Gloria at the Mountain Magnolia and was extricating my suitcase from the backseat when a car pulled in next to mine. The window slid down and a mild, slightly rabbit-like face blinked at me.

"Hello—are we meant to park here? I'm staying for the weekend."

"I'm not sure," I told him. "I just arrived myself. Are you taking part in the . . . the workshop?"

"Well, sort of." He cut his ignition and climbed out, then stood studying the house and stretching as though stiff from long hours on the road. He didn't look like someone interested in spirit communication. He looked like—oh, an optician, maybe . . . or an accountant.

My interest piqued, I did a quick covert assessment of the newcomer. Fiftyish, at a guess, of medium height, medium weight, close-cropped sandy hair, he was completely ordinary, from his clothes—brown trousers, tan polo shirt—to his car—beige rental.

Clasping his hands behind his neck, he swiveled his

head from side to side then backward and forward, keeping his eyes fixed on the building before us.

I followed his gaze. The inn, built as a private residence just after the Civil War, had been rescued from dilapidation by its current owners. Set amid beautiful landscaping, it was an impressive piece of restoration, from the five-way paint job—siding a muted light green, accents and ornamental trim in dark green, mauve, mustard, and white—to the arched windows, balcony, and tower topped by a trumpeting angel as weather vane. Scattered over the looming roofline, elegantly shaped lightning rods that incorporated glass balls added a vaguely steam-punkish note. I had to admit it looked like a congenial place—for the living or the departed.

"A lot of sadness there." The words were half muttered—I didn't think he meant them for me. But suddenly he brought his neck-stretching exercise to a close and held out his hand.

"So sorry—I'm Giles Mellish—the chap running the workshop. Are you a Seeker—one of the participants?"

I stared at him, openmouthed. Of course the English accent should have been a tip-off. But I'd been expecting someone, well, a bit more exotic-looking. This mild-mannered nonentity, Giles of Glastonbury? Where was the Arthurian aura? Where were the mists of Avalon?

I closed my mouth and took his offered hand. "My sister's a participant—Gloria . . . Gloria Hawkins. I'm Elizabeth Goodweather. I'll be . . . sitting in. Gloria wanted me with her. But I'm not exactly . . ."

My sentence dangled as I struggled to define my role and I resorted to a noncommittal shrug.

"No, you're the skeptical one, aren't you?" He bobbed his head and smiled. "*You'll* not be caught up in any otherworldly codswallop, not you." The words were perfectly friendly but he kept a firm grip on my hand and stared into my eyes in a most disconcerting manner.

His eyes—what color were they? Gray or brown or neither? They gave nothing away but seemed to be taking in everything. The moment—and it was no more—ended and the eyes released me, just as Giles Mellish released my hand.

"The time may come," he continued in a matter-of-fact tone, as if advising me on new reading glasses or my tax return, "when you'll realize that you too are a Seeker. Oh, yes, most definitely."

"Lizzy!"

There was a cry from the house and I looked up to see Gloria hurrying down the walkway.

"I'm so glad you didn't back out." She hugged me and went on at top speed, totally ignoring the inconspicuous man who had moved to open his car trunk.

"The medium—Giles of Glastonbury—is going to be here soon! The innkeeper told me they'd had a call from him and he was just outside Hot Springs. I swear I'm so excited I could wet my pants! I wonder what we call him? At some of the workshops I've done, we called the leader 'Master' or 'Sensei' or—"

"Just Giles would be fine."

Setting his suitcase on the ground, Giles of Glastonbury advanced on my sister with a quiet smile and outstretched hand. For a moment I thought she was going to curtsy but she recovered herself.

"It's wonderful to meet you at last. Nigel told me how you . . ."

Her voice trailed off as the psychic began the eye-lock treatment I had so recently experienced.

It takes a lot to render my sister speechless. Giles accomplished it with one look. I began almost to look forward to the coming workshop.

At last, as he had done with me, the psychic released

Gloria's hand. "My dear," he said, "I hope to bring you good news tomorrow—good news and heart's ease."

Then, reverting to the everyday, he picked up his suitcase.

"Ladies, a pleasure to meet you. I've had a long drive and am ready for a bit of a rest. I believe an introductory session is scheduled for this evening at eight-thirty. So until then."

And with a polite nod, he made his unremarkable way up the walk and into the inn.

Still silent, Glory watched him go. She seemed to be holding her breath. As Giles of Glastonbury disappeared through the front door, she turned to me with a happy exhalation.

"*Well!* Did you hear what he said? Good news and heart's ease. Oh, I knew this was going to be just what I need. Do you know, Lizzy, when he was looking into my eyes, there was the strongest feeling of connection . . . that he was seeing right into my soul. Nigel was right: I'm sure this man is very spiritually gifted. Didn't you feel it?"

Her eyes were wide and expectant. I grabbed my suitcase and the carrier bag full of reading material I had so optimistically packed. *Loving support,* I reminded myself. *Open mind, closed mouth—that's your mantra, Elizabeth. Do this for your sister.*

Besides . . . I *had* felt . . . something. I was ready to believe that there was considerably more to the mild Mr. Mellish than met the eye.

"I believe you're right." I smiled at her, seeing again something of the little sister I remembered from so long ago. "Yes, this is going to be an interesting weekend. I'm glad you asked me."

I'd heard of the Mountain Magnolia, of course, but this was my first time to see it in person and I was definitely impressed. As Gloria hustled me inside, through the hall and up the stairs, I caught glimpses of medallioned ceilings, Oriental rugs, shining white crown molding, period furnishings . . .

"You're in the Sycamore Room." Gloria brandished a large key and opened a door. "This was the only room still available—it's a little small, but the wallpaper reminded me of the room you always stayed in at Gramma's. I hope you like it." There was a wistful tone in her voice and I remembered how when she was little she had begged to be allowed to stay at Gramma's like I so often did.

"It's lovely," I assured her. "I know I'll like sleeping here." I studied the wallpaper—rich cream with a small green pattern repeated on it. "You know, it could be the exact same pattern that Gramma had."

Gloria gave a satisfied nod and gestured at my suitcase. "You go on and get unpacked, then come to my room—just down the hall—the Rose Room. We'll have a glass of wine so you can relax and then maybe we'll take a walk before dinner, okay?"

Without waiting for my answer, she darted at me, brushed a fleeting kiss against my cheek and whispered, "Thank you so much for coming, Sissy."

And was gone before I could answer.

Sissy—that was the first word Gloria had spoken, even before *Mama,* so family legend went. I'd been three when she was born, delighted to have a real live baby doll to play with. And as soon as she could walk, she had toddled after me, a willing pawn in whatever game I might devise.

When did things change—was it when I went to school? Or was it when Papa left and I turned to Gramma for comfort?

I looked again at the familiar wallpaper and felt tears welling up, missing Gramma, missing Papa, missing the little sisters that Glory and I had been. *It's not too late. I've been given another chance . . . with Gloria, at least. But I'll have to take it in baby steps—we've grown so far apart and have so little in common—if we ever did.*

The wallpaper pattern swam and blurred in my vision and I turned to unpack my bag and hang my few garments worthy of the attention in the closet. Including the gorgeous silk kimono—this was surely the perfect venue for its debut. I trailed my fingers along its silky surface, marveling again at the shimmering colors.

As I crossed in front of the window to set my reading material on the nightstand, I felt a cold draft and wondered if an unseen air conditioner had just kicked on. Beyond the window was a sycamore tree and a row of gray-green pines—*nothing like the view from my bedroom at home,* I thought but something about the scene held me there. Was that a child, just slipping behind the big tree?

I watched a moment longer without seeing anything more of the elusive form, then recalled that Gloria was waiting for me.

"This is where the old hotel was—actually, *hotels.* There were several back in the 1800s—one after another because they kept burning down. And there was a nine-hole golf course *here* and a little lake over there."

We were standing on the grounds of the Hot Springs Spa. I knew the history of the succession of grand hotels, the wealthy visitors who'd flocked there, at first by stagecoach, jolting along the Buncombe Turnpike, and later by train, to soak in the healing waters. But Gloria was enjoying the role of tour guide so I nodded and said, "Oh, really?" and "What about that!" and "How amazing!" as she related the history of the spa.

"The old bathhouse is still there but they don't let people near it—it's pretty much a ruin. Swan, she's the masseuse I've been going to, told me that the marble tubs are still there—some of them six feet deep! Now, instead of a bathhouse, they have modern Jacuzzi hot tubs that they fill fresh from the springs—I've signed us up for a soak and a massage on Saturday."

The champagne we had sipped in Gloria's room had done a thorough job of relaxing me after my supposedly *exhausting* half-hour drive from the farm to the inn. It had also mellowed me out to an astonishing degree, making it easy for me to fall in with Gloria's plans. But as she chattered of exfoliation with Dead Sea salts and botanical mud wraps with crushed flower petals and hot-stone therapy with smooth, mineral-water-warmed basalt stones, I held up a finger to interrupt her rapturous descriptions.

"What about the workshop with Giles of Glastonbury? When does that happen? If we're going to be lolling about in mud wraps—"

"Not a problem." An airy wave dismissed my objections. "The workshop sessions are from nine to eleven in the morning and three to six in the afternoon. And then after dinner there's another session. There's plenty of time in the middle of the day for us to have a little 'me time.' "

Me time is one of those phrases that, especially when uttered by a woman of leisure, make me want to get up on a soapbox and start ranting about the terrible lot of women in various Third World countries, not to mention that of poor women in our own US of A. But such were the calming powers of half a bottle of champagne (*real* champagne, I'd noticed), as well as my resolution to behave, that I merely smiled meekly and said that a visit to the spa would be lovely.

As we wandered about the grassy field where a grand hotel once stood, my eye was caught by a little clump of trees that seemed to be growing around and, in one case, out of an unusual grouping of shoulder-high boulders. Closer examination revealed narrow pathways into the formation ending at an open center. Wild ferns and grasses clustered about the outer edges of the rocks and thick mosses covered some of the shaded surfaces. The paths and the center were clear except for some litter of dead twigs and fallen leaves.

Nor was there any of the litter I might have expected. This looked like the sort of place that would be a magnet for children—a playhouse or fort, depending on the kids in question.

"Do you know anything about this place, Glory?" She had followed me into the center of the formation where she stood, keeping her distance from the rocks and looking uncomfortable as I peered about, trying to determine what made this place so fascinating to me.

"I know I don't like it." She hugged herself as if she was chilly—which on a May day was fairly ridiculous. Still, she was used to Florida temperatures, I reminded myself, and here in the shade of the trees, it was a little cool.

"Besides, there might be snakes." She cast an apprehensive glance at some of the deeper crevices in the nearest rock. "And don't give me that 'They're more scared than you are' crap. Could we just get out of here? Besides, I need to get back and take a bath before dinner."

As we walked up the path leading to the inn, I stopped by a high-arching clump of grass to admire a fuzzy yellow caterpillar teetering at the end of a glossy green blade. He had reared up and his tiny pink feet—the front six of them—were questing in search of their next step.

"Glory, come look at this guy and his adorable little feet!" It was worth a try, I thought. I'd learn to love Dead Sea salt exfoliation and maybe Gloria could get a little appreciation for Nature.

"Adorable?" My sister leaned down to see my find, wrinkling her nose in fastidious disgust. "Those creepy little feet? If you killed that thing and stuck it with pins to some sort of board and looked at it under a microscope, you would see that those feet are anything but 'adorable'—they are vile little buggy mutant feet that look really gross close up." She glanced at her watch. "We've got forty minutes before dinner. You can stay and visit with your yucky little friend; I'm going to go have a bath."

Well, it was a start. In the past she'd have wanted to stomp—no, make that wanted *me* to stomp my yucky little friend.

Baby steps, I reminded myself, as I watched my sister disappearing through the front door of the inn.

V~Amarantha

The Mountain Park Hotel~May 11, 1887

It's better money than chambermaiding—being a bath attendant and giving them massage treatments. And that was where I started, when I was younger. Before the old hotel burned, they had a whole slew of foreigners working here but it was hard to keep them on—seemed like they didn't take to the place and after a month, or whatever it took to earn their fare, they'd light out for the city. So Mr. Roberts the manager was always on the lookout for any of us mountain folk who could talk polite and do the jobs the foreigners was quitting.

At first all I did at the bathhouse was to help the ladies with their clothes—them stays they wear need a strong somebody to pull the laces tight and give them that narrow middle they all want. I done that and I helped the ladies getting in and out of them deep old tubs. But then it come about that Greta, this one woman massager, she sprained her wrist whilst clambering over them Injun rocks on her day off. So she showed me how to give a massage, not wanting to have to cancel any appointments and get in trouble with the boss.

I already knowed something about it, my papaw having been took bad with the rheumatics as he aged. Some mornings he'd wake all twisted up and just groaning with the pain and I'd rub at his poor old legs till they *loosened up to where he could stand. Ever one in the family knowed that I had a healing touch. Papaw always said it was the warmth of my hands done the trick more so than all the rubbing.*

So at the hotel, it weren't long afore word got round and more and more of the women asked for me by name. I was making good money and my ladies was always giving me little presents and the manager was like to bust, he was so happy at the way they all went on about "Amarantha's magic fingers."

It was fine, bringing relief to some of them sickly females, and the money was fine too. But it got to where sometimes my hands told me more than I could bear— a cancer growing that couldn't be stopped or a confusion of the brain that I might ease for a time but never cure. Knowing that the woman under my hands would carry these ills with her to the grave was sad. Yes, bitter sad, but I could have borne it, knowing that I'd given the poor thing a moment's ease.

Yet there was worse—a blackness at the heart or a twisting of the soul that I could feel—that seemed to cling to my fingers like an ugly smell. Such times fair sickened me till I would go home and drink the black draught to purge myself of the ugliness and scrub my poor hands with lye soap till they was raw.

It weren't worth it to me. And so I asked the manager to let me be a chambermaid instead. He looked at me like I was crazy but I made up some story and at last he agreed. Though he made me promise that I would take a turn in the bathhouse whenever they was short-handed.

Today was one of them times. When I come to work this morning and went to get my cleaning things, the head housekeeper told me that she was training a new girl and they would do my afternoon rooms.

"Mr. Roberts said for you to get over to the bathhouse

by two and get changed into a uniform—Selma's not come in nor has she sent word."

I dreaded it when I saw that my first lady was one of them DeVine sisters. I didn't know how she might take it to have her treatment from a chambermaid. But I had on the white dress and apron with my hair up under my cap and when she swept into the changing room all fine in her lilac walking dress (for it was the sister called Theodora), she never seemed to notice that I was the same one as made her bed and tidied her rooms.

"A quarter of an hour in the tub will be long enough today," says she, turning to let me undo the buttons at the back of her dress. "And when you begin the treatment, I'd like you to spend some extra time on my neck. I slept awkwardly last night and there's a certain stiffness. Your treatment last time was relaxing, to be sure, but I'd prefer a more vigorous approach to work out the kink in my neck."

I mumbled my yes ma'am, like we are told to do, and once her stays was loosened, stepped into the tub room to put the towels ready. When she opened the door, she had the bathrobe wrapped around her decent enough but then, without looking at me once, she marched straight to the edge of the tub and dropped the robe. Most ladies generally keep it on; some wears a bathing costume, but not this one. There she stood naked as a jay but for the big cap that covered her hair. She took no more mind of me than if I wasn't there, just set down and slipped into the tub, being careful to keep her head well out of the water. I picked up the robe and laid it across the little stool by the tub.

"Will that be all, madam?" says I, standing waiting by the door of the treatment room.

She had already settled into the steaming water and she stood there with her arms out to the side, a-waving them slow like up and down under the water. With her long slim neck and the great puffy white cap sticking up above the water, she put me in mind of one of them fancy water flowers they used to be in the pond by the old hotel.

"You can go now, Selma," she said, "but come back for me in a quarter of an hour."

I like to laugh out loud when I closed the door behind me. Selma is a hand's breadth shorter than me and a good bit heavier. Me and her don't favor in the least. But all that Miss DeVine saw was the uniform. Oh, she had taken the trouble to learn the names of us who did for her—but all she saw was the white dress and it was Selma; gray calico with an apron, now that was Amarantha. There hadn't been no call to worry that she'd know me.

This was my first appointment of the day and I looked about me to see what needed doing. The treatment room is a little box of a place—there's a chair and the leather-covered table, a big clock on the wall, and a cabinet where the creams and lotions and folders for the different patients is kept. All the walls and wood is painted white and for a moment I took a notion that was I to stand still, all in white as I was, I might sink into them white walls like a raindrop into a pool.

Notions. I shook my head to clear it of such foolishness for there was things to do. The windows, which is set high so's can't nobody peer in at folks whilst they're having their treatment, was shut so I used the long pole with the hook to open them and let some air in. And there was the creams and lotions to set out and the clean sheets for the treatment table.

Next I looked at the paper that said how many was down for treatments—five in all. A right full day. My own back would need a massage when it was over but that wasn't likely to happen.

I set myself down in the chair and took up the folder

marked T. DeVine to see if there was anything special Selma had been doing for her. They neither one of them sisters looked sickly and it didn't surprise me none to find a big R stamped in green ink on her file.

Professor Swann is the director of treatment here at the Mountain Park. He wears a white coat and little gold glasses and it's him who talks to every new guest and draws up a plan of treatment for them to follow during their stay. When he marks a folder with the green R for Regular, it mostly means that these is healthy folks who feel they need a rest. These folks generally like to have a fuss made over them. They drink the waters twice a day and soak in the tubs and get a massage but it ain't like there is aught to cure. These R folks is generally the easiest for me and I was some relieved to see that Miss DeVine was one of them.

I looked at my list for the day and checked the folders of each one—two R's, one O, which just means too fat and calls for sweating and extra-hard massage. These ones is told to keep to a special diet but when I worked in the bathhouse regular, I had many an O woman offer to pay me would I bring something for them to eat when they came for their treatments. There was one wanted a whole pie—"Any kind you can get"—and another that was crazy for hard candy.

Next was a C, and I shook my head. C is for Cancer. Which usually means they are seeking anything they can find after being give up on by their regular doctor. There have been a few times where I think I may have helped one of these C's—when the growth hadn't gone too far and when they was of the sort who was amenable to being helped. But for the ones I can't heal, there is another way I can help them.

Some of them poor C women is plumb starved for touch, their husbands fearing to cause them pain—or, worse, fearing that the cancer's catching. And too, there's many a man can't bear the sight of his wife's body after the surgeon's knife has been at it. No, I can't cure these women but at least I can let them see that I don't shrink from them and I can let them feel the touch of a gentle hand on their bodies. There has been more than one woman weep and tell me how long it had been since anyone had touched her.

The last folder was a N. These is the ones I always dread, for what it means is the doctor don't have no idea of what's wrong. The N is for Neur-as-thenic—I had the professor to write the word out for me but I disremember how to speak it. These N women is always tired and sad and sometimes a little addled. Now and again they will be calmed by the treatment but mostly they is hard to please.

Looking up at the clock, I saw there weren't but a minute left before I had to go after Miss DeVine so I put the folders back in the cabinet and pulled my cap down a little lower, hoping to let her go on thinking I was Selma.

Miss DeVine was standing by the bath with the robe loose around her when I opened the door. She didn't say nothing, nor did she look at me but walked through and dropped her robe again without even waiting for me to turn away. She stretched out facedown on the table and just lay there, not bothering to pull a sheet over herself like most would. So I draped her the way I was taught and put the special oil on my hands.

"Shall I begin with the back, madam?" I tried to make my voice soft like Selma's and speak the words like we was taught.

"By all means—and remember, extra attention to the neck."

I laid my hands on her draped shoulders for a moment, to accustom her to my touch—same as you'd do with a young unbroke mule. Then I put aside the drapes that covered her back and began the long stroking motions, always toward the heart, light and easy at first and growing a little firmer after a time.

My hands was tingling some but I figured that was on account of I hadn't given no treatments in some time. Miss DeVine's flesh was firm and healthy-feeling and her skin was creamy white, without a spot, except for a little sickle moon of dark brown moles—five in all—on her left hip. I wondered did her twin sister have the same marking.

Next came the part that is like kneading bread and I could feel the stiffness in her shoulders giving way. I worked them muscles hard, and when she didn't seem to mind I went on to the next step, digging deep and pressing with my thumbs, all the while moving them in little circles. She made a little squeaking sound and I slacked off, not wanting to hurt her.

"Don't stop," says she, "I believe that's helping."

And on I went, stroking, kneading, digging, and on to the tapping and the shaking—all the different ways I'd been taught to work on a body. There is foreign names for each of these—"effloory-something" and "tappy-something else"—those are two which I learned once but they have a foolish sound to them and I can't hardly make out to say them right nohow.

She was easy to work on—lay still, didn't complain nor nothing. But the longer my hands stayed on her, the more it seemed to me that there was something wrong deep inside that fine-looking body of hers. There was the feeling of wrongness, of something black and rotting inside and as I labored over her, I could feel it drawing up through my fingers and into my own body.

At last the time was up. I still had to help her with her

stays and such but while she was putting on her shift, I excused myself to step outside for a breath of air. I was weak and trembling and my stomach heaved but didn't nothing come up but a little yellow bile.

Back in the dressing room she was waiting and she spoke right sharp when I couldn't pull them stays as tight as she wanted. But as she left, she handed me a quarter—with most ladies it would have been a dime or a nickel.

"My neck feels much better, Selma," says she, sweeping out the door. "Put me down for the same time tomorrow."

I got through the rest of the day somehow but the bad feeling wouldn't leave me, no matter how much I washed my hands. When finally I got home that evening, I washed them with lye soap in the hottest water I could bear. Then I mixed a black draught and drank it down.

Later, after I'd purged myself and my hands was raw and red, I set the milk for the fairies and went up to the spring, aiming to look in the little round pool for an answer to what was ailing Miss Theodora DeVine.

Basic Techniques of Swedish Massage

1. *Effleurage:* Preliminary gliding strokes with palms, thumbs, or fingertips. Always toward the heart to promote circulation.
2. *Petrissage:* Kneading and compressing muscles to drive out toxins.
3. *Friction:* Penetrating deep circular movements with thumbs or fingertips. Used near joints and bony areas to break down adhesions within the muscles.

4. *Tapotement:* Quick repeated tapping of the muscles, using the edge of the hand, the fingertips, the cupped hand, or the closed fist to relieve tension or muscle spasms.

5. *Vibration:* Shaking the muscle with fingertips or full palm to relieve tension.

Chapter 15

Getting to Know You

Thursday night, May 24

Gloria looked around the room at her fellow Seekers. They had gathered in the parlor of the inn, for
what Giles had called an informal chat. "Get to know
one another a bit—that sort of thing." Giles Mellish—
she really couldn't think of him as Giles of Glastonbury
anymore—was seated in a wing chair with a cup of coffee, silently observing as the various participants—nine
in all—milled about the room, helping themselves to
coffee and cookies from a side table and chatting quietly
as they took their seats.

Gloria glanced at her sister. Elizabeth was sitting next
to her, wedged into the corner of the long sofa, apparently engrossed in studying the fancy medallion on the
ceiling. She had, Gloria thought, the look of someone
pretending she wasn't there.

"Is that place taken?"

A pleasant-faced woman with white hair and shining
blue eyes was pointing to the empty space between Gloria and the large henna-haired woman of indefinite age
who had staked out the farther corner and was whispering to the woman in the chair beside the sofa.

Gloria smiled and inched a little closer to Elizabeth.
"It's all yours—there's plenty of room."

Carefully balancing her cup of coffee, the woman

lowered herself to the sofa and turned to Gloria. "I'm Sandy Secrest—I just got here. My friends and I drove from Wisconsin. We're staying at the campground and they wanted to get the RV hooked up before dark. Have I missed anything important?"

Repressing a shudder at the thought of campgrounds and RVs, Gloria nudged Elizabeth to bring her attention back from the ceiling.

"No, you haven't missed a thing. This is the introductory meeting. Giles said we'd get started in a few—"

"I believe we'll begin now."

Giles Mellish, still wearing the same nondescript clothing he'd traveled in, was on his feet. The several conversations that had been in full swing ceased and the parlor fell silent. Across the hall, where the dining room was being set for tomorrow's breakfast, the rattle of cutlery and soft clink of dishes was suddenly audible.

Two youngish women who'd been standing by the table with the coffee and cookies hastily seated themselves and every face turned toward the psychic. He lifted his hands in a gesture that reminded Gloria of a priest greeting the congregation and looked around the room, gathering in the participants one by one.

"Well come. You are all *well come* to this time and this place."

For just a moment, Gloria thought, he seemed taller. Dropping his hands, he resumed his seat and the momentary awe she had felt was replaced with a simple *liking* for this most unassuming of men.

"What I'd like to do tonight," he began, his voice pitched low so that all of them leaned forward to catch his words, "is to go around the room and give each of you Seekers the opportunity to introduce yourself. You might tell us a little bit about your reasons for coming here; maybe what you hope to gain from this weekend. The investigations we plan to undertake require the united energies of the group—the more united we are, the more successful the weekend will be. Tomorrow morning at nine, we'll be doing some trust-building exercises before we begin our explorations. But tonight we just need to get to know and feel comfortable with each other."

The henna-haired woman was waving her hand. "Do we tell about who we're hoping to contact?"

"Not this evening. We just want to hear a little about you—Christian name, where you come from, and a bit more. I'll begin, shall I?"

He took a sip of his coffee and went on. "Good evening, I'm Giles and I'm your, shall we say, *guide* for this weekend of discovery. I'm from England and when I'm not traveling to workshops, I live in Glastonbury, which as I expect some of you know is a rather magical place. But as I drove here from the airport, winding deeper and deeper into these most ancient of mountains, it became increasingly obvious that this too is a place of old magic—perfect for our journeying."

Giles fell silent and looked toward the man on his right. Gloria had particularly noticed the deeply tanned, wiry man in hiking shorts earlier—hard not to when he had brusquely declined coffee and cookies. "White sugar is poison to me, and caffeine is an addictive drug. I'm very particular about what I put in *my* body!"

Upon which he had waved aside an offered chair and, moving to Giles's right-hand side, had crossed his sinewy legs and sunk effortlessly to the Oriental carpet, there to assume a full lotus position. He had not responded to friendly overtures from the others as they moved about in search of seats but had closed his eyes in apparent meditation. Now, obedient to Giles's glance, he spoke.

"I'm Xan—that's X-A-N. I moved to Asheville from Sedona about five years ago. My main interests are a healthy lifestyle and sacred geometry. This weekend I hope to gain deeper understanding of some past influences on my life . . ."

He looked up at Giles. "Is that enough?"

Giles reached out and patted the waiting Xan on the shoulder. Almost, thought Gloria, as if he were saying *Good dog*. But rather than speak, the medium looked at the next participant and nodded.

"Me?" The shy-looking woman perched on the edge of one of the Windsor chairs, borrowed from the dining room for extra seating, started when Giles's gaze fell on her. "Oh, I see, we're going around the room. This way. Widdershins."

She moved one hand in a counterclockwise circle, let out a nervous giggle, and clasped her hands together. "Okay, seriously now. I'm Ree . . . from Raleigh. I work in a bank but I'm very interested in the paranormal and . . . and all kinds of psychical stuff. My friends got together and gave me this weekend as a gift for my fortieth birthday. And I . . ." She paused, evidently at a loss, then brightened and concluded with a triumphant smile, "I hope to broaden my horizons this weekend."

The introductions continued. The henna-haired Charlene was a student of tarot seeking to broaden *her* horizons as well. Originally from Pittsburgh, Charlene was now living with her husband and her four shih tzus in Fairview, a community near Asheville. Sandy from Wisconsin proved to be a recently retired librarian and a mystery buff, looking for a different sort of vacation.

Now Giles was looking at *her* and Gloria found herself unexpectedly tongue-tied. The mild gaze held her and she took a deep breath.

"I'm Gloria from . . ." Suddenly she didn't want to say Tampa, and settled for a lame ". . . from Florida. I'm looking for . . . I'm looking for answers."

A brief smile flickered across Giles's face then his attention turned to Elizabeth.

Gloria tensed, hoping Lizzy wouldn't do one of her typical sarcastic speeches. It would be so embarrassing if—but no, Lizzy was saying, in soft and rather un-Lizzy-like tones, "I'm Elizabeth and I live here in Marshall County, over near Ransom. I came for the weekend to be with my sister . . . but I wouldn't mind some answers myself."

After Elizabeth came Dawn and Steve—owners of a bed-and-breakfast in southern Alabama, here on a sort of working holiday.

"Dawn's into this New Age shit, excuse my French." Steve gave her partner's leg a gentle slap. "And I thought it might be something we could run at our place." She shot an appraising look at Giles. "No offense meant, Mr. uh . . ."

"None taken, I'm sure." Giles's eyes twinkled but his face remained serious. "I'll try to make the weekend worth your while."

The last of the circle was Len, a sixtyish man with thinning gray hair pulled back in a wispy ponytail. A tie-dyed T-shirt with the dancing skeletons of the Grateful Dead logo was stretched across a substantial paunch. He too wore shorts. Inwardly, Gloria had summed him up as yet another of the aging hippies who seemed to infest the area. Her jaw dropped slightly as Len described himself as an executive with Microsoft—on a sabbatical and hoping to satisfy a long-held interest in spirit communication done via computer. He was just launching into a story of some strange cybercommunication that he'd had with the late Jerry Garcia when there was the sound of a bell, the hurried steps of the innkeeper in the hallway, the door opening and more footsteps.

All eyes were on the arched doorway as a slim figure in baggy jeans and outsized shirt burst through and

stood, looking from one to the other of the circle. His—
or was it her?—head was bandaged with just a few
strands of dark hair showing at the back. The strangely
androgynous face bore a puzzled frown which dissolved
into an angelic smile as Giles stood and beckoned.

"Master," the newcomer panted, leaning against the
elaborate woodwork of the doorframe. "Master Giles,
I'm here. I'm Joss."

"An interesting assortment of people in this . . .
workshop."

Gloria watched as Elizabeth studied the lavish bowl
of fruit that sat on the small table between the two
chairs. *Here come the snarky comments,* she thought.
But Elizabeth just yawned and muttered, "Do I dare to
eat a peach?" as her hovering hand came down and se-
lected a plump specimen.

"I don't see why not, Lizzy. They're all organic and
perfectly ripe. I have to have my fruit before bedtime
and I specified—"

Elizabeth grinned and waved off the assurances as she
took a bite. "It's delicious, Glory—a nice idea for a little
something before bed. If I can just keep from getting
juice all down my front . . ."

Gloria stepped into her bathroom and returned with a
terry hand towel. "Use this, for goodness' sake." She
studied the assortment and, choosing a plum and a small
cluster of green grapes, settled in the other chair.

"It seemed to me," she began, "that the men were
much stranger than the women—that hippie type—
what was his name?"

"Len? The guy with Jerry Garcia in his computer?"
Elizabeth reached for a plum. "He seems nice enough
but computer people are another breed altogether. And
what's his name, Xan with an X—Mr. Fruits and Nuts—

I bet he'd like to come along for a fruity organic nosh—
you should have invited him up, Glory."

Glory recognized the wicked grin as a bit of sisterly
teasing and relaxed a very little bit. If they could just get
comfortable with each other, without the constant spar-
ring . . . The secret she'd kept all these years was going
to have to come out this weekend and she owed it to
Lizzy to tell her first—before sharing it with a roomful
of strangers.

". . . and speaking of strange, what about the male-
to-female ratio? Three men—well, four, counting Giles—
to seven women? Are women just more interested in
this . . . stuff? Or are they more adventurous? Or do
they just have more free time?" Elizabeth slipped off her
sandals and wiggled her toes.

"*Four* men?" Gloria frowned at her sister. "Giles
and Len and Xan: That makes *three*. That Steve person
isn't a—"

"Glory, I know that—but that crazy-looking one who
showed up late is. Joss is a guy. You wanna bet?"

It was just what she had hoped for, Gloria thought.
They had moved from the elegant but not particularly
comfortable chairs to the big walnut bed and were
propped up with the pillows against the headboard,
chattering and gossiping like a couple of teenagers.
*Maybe if there hadn't been the age difference. Three
years seems like nothing now but back then . . . and
Lizzy started school early and Mama kept me back that
year I had rheumatic fever . . . We were hardly ever at
the same school at the same time. And she had her
friends and I . . .*

Still there were some happy shared memories: the
family trips to the beach . . . Lizzy was chuckling over
the recollection now.

"Do you remember the time we saw a sign for a

restaurant that had boiled shrimp? It said 'Peel 'em and eat 'em' and for some reason we both thought that was the funniest thing in the world. We bounced up and down shouting 'Peel 'em and eat 'em! Peel 'em and eat 'em!' over and over till Mama reached around and smacked me."

"I remember that! Do you remember the sign on a motel . . . the 'Welcome Inn'—"

Elizabeth threw her head back, choking with laughter. "And we said 'Well, come in!' all the rest of the way to the beach. Lord, no wonder the first thing Mama did when we got there was to fix herself a stiff drink . . ."

The mood shifted abruptly as both remembered the almost invariable sequel to Mama's stiff drink in the afternoon. From the corner of her eye, Gloria could see that Elizabeth's face had gone solemn. Gloria reached out and squeezed her sister's hand.

"I'm sorry, Sissy," she whispered. "You always got the worst of her temper. I wish . . ."

Elizabeth returned the pressure and managed a small smile. "It's in the past, Glory. It took a long time but I think that Mama and I finally understood each other a little better in the last years of her life. And when . . . when Sam died, it really came home to me how Papa's going away must have changed everything for her. Even though he fixed it so there was plenty of money, she really didn't deal with being alone very well. And because I took after Papa . . . I guess I was a constant reminder of the man who'd abandoned her."

Papa. The mystery man. Mama wouldn't talk about what happened but her bitterness had been a daily companion, an unseen member of their little family.

"Lizzy, in all these years, have you ever heard from him? Mama never ever mentioned him and I didn't like to ask . . ."

Elizabeth's grip tightened and she slowly shook her

head. "Never the first word. For all I know, he may be dead." After a long moment she asked, "Do you remember him at all? You were only four when he left."

"I think I must—there weren't any pictures of him but I think I remember a big man with blue, blue eyes and dark hair. He rode me on his shoulders. But that's all. You must have a lot more memories of him."

"I do." Elizabeth's voice was hoarse. "He . . . he was . . . my hero. I thought he could do anything. And then . . . one day he was gone."

There was another long silence as the two women sat side by side on the big bed, holding hands and staring into the past.

Finally, gathering her courage, Gloria began, "Lizzy, I need to tell you about when I married Arturo . . ."

Chapter 16

Midnight Revelations

Friday, May 25

Where am I?

Something had awakened me—had there been a cold draft? Had I imagined that sound of low hopeless sobbing? Opening a bleary eye, I was completely confused to see dim half-light and the wallpaper of my bedroom at Gramma's house—the refuge of my youth.

I lay still, waiting for reality to reassert itself, studying the well-loved old pattern and expecting it to dissolve into the familiar windows of my own bedroom. When, however, it showed no sign of vanishing I shut my eyes again.

You're still in the dream—it's just done one of those quantum jumps that dreams sometimes do. Relax and go with it . . .

In the dream I'd been having, I was deep in conversation with Gramma, sitting next to her in the big comfy chair that was our special place. The worn copy of Gene Stratton Porter's *Freckles* lay open on her lap but she had paused in her reading aloud to answer my question . . . my question . . . what was my question? Something about Gloria.

Gloria.

In a dizzying readjustment of reality, I sat up and

looked around. Not my room at Gramma's—long lost, miles and years ago—but a room in the Mountain Magnolia. What time was it? Just barely daylight, according to the light beyond the window.

The clock on the bedside table said 5:43. I groaned and lay back down. And then I remembered last night. My sister . . . my poor little sister . . .

"I wish you'd been around back then, Lizzy," she'd said. "You could have helped me be stronger. But of course, in the end it didn't matter so much."

The pre-bedtime chat was Gloria's idea and it had been wonderful. We had giggled and carried on like girls at a slumber party. Like sisters, in fact. But then the shared good memories led to the subject of our father— our father which art . . . where? And when there was nothing I could tell her about the man she has only the faintest recollection of, Gloria dropped her bombshell.

"You weren't around when I married Arturo. And by the time you came back, it was over. How much did Mama tell you about me and Arturo?"

I had tried to remember. It hadn't been much. The whole Arturo thing had been just a tiny detour in the path Mama had mapped out for Gloria—the path to marriage with the right sort of man. The right sort, it went without saying, was a fellow WASP—a white, Anglo-Saxon Protestant, preferably of a Good Family, and necessarily wealthy. Gloria had been (and still is) a beauty and I had known that Mama had several eligible young men in mind as potential suitors for Glory.

But then, fate, bad luck, hormones, or some toxic combination thereof took control. Seventeen-year-old Gloria, off to the University of Florida for her freshman year, fell madly in love and before that freshman year was over, she had eloped with a decidedly dark and probably Roman Catholic engineering student from Colombia.

"What did Mama tell me?" I had hedged, trying to edit out some of the worst of the language and accusations—those venomous late night phone calls, fueled by far too many stiff drinks. "Well . . . she thought that Arturo had taken advantage of your innocence and had probably married you to get his citizenship. She said that she had 'friends in high places' who'd hinted that Arturo might be part of one of those drug cartels . . . That was the main reason she was so insistent the marriage be annulled."

I felt that chill draft again and pulled the bedspread up around my shoulders. Last night's sisterly chat had covered the rocky ground of many lost years and I had seen a side of my little sister I'd never even guessed at.

As I'd finished my meager little recitation of the case against Arturo, I'd been appalled to see tears trickling down my sister's cheeks.

"Glory! I'm sorry . . . I had no idea that you still had any feelings for him. I had the impression that you were relieved . . . you certainly seemed happy enough when you married Ben's dad—"

"That's not why I'm crying, Lizzy," she had said, shaking her head and twisting at the little heart on a chain that she so often wore around her neck. I had suddenly realized that she'd worn that same simple little trinket for years and years—a rather un-Gloria thing to do—and for the first time wondered if it had some sentimental value.

"Did Arturo give you that?" I had said it as gently as I could and was startled when she let out a bitter laugh.

"Not exactly. Let me go blow my nose and I'll tell you the part Mama left out."

In spite of the mild May morning, I shivered under the covers, going back over the story Glory had told me—the secret she'd kept all these years.

She'd returned from the bathroom in complete control of herself and, in an almost emotionless voice, had traced the events of 1973, the year I'd been too busy with Sam and school and my own happy life to come home for a visit.

Arturo Rodriquez had been an assistant in her Spanish lab. Handsome and charming, he had gone out of his way to help her and they had begun dating in the fall of '72. By December she knew she was pregnant and Arturo had insisted they get married right away, fearing that her mother might force her to get an abortion.

"He was right; when she found out, that was exactly her reaction," a dry-eyed Gloria told me. "We went to Georgia one weekend and got married just before the Christmas break. He wanted to come home with me, to be with me when I told her but I was afraid . . . I knew how she'd be. So he stayed in Gainesville and I went home. I thought if things got too bad—and I knew they would—at least I could look forward to going back early so Turo and I could celebrate the New Year and our new life together."

A new life.

"Gloria," I ventured, "what happened when you told Mama you were pregnant?"

"Well, of course she pitched a fit. Then she went and made a bunch of phone calls and came back and told me she'd fixed everything and that we'd be going in to her gynecologist the next Monday. 'You're not very far along,' she said. 'This early it's nothing, just a D and C—no worse than a bad period.'"

"So you went," I said, knowing the hold Mama had always had over Gloria.

"I did not! But I didn't argue. I just got up early the next morning before she was awake and drove back to Gainesville, back to Turo. He had the funniest little apartment—a converted garage behind a house and right on an alley. There was a little hand-painted sign over the door that said *Chalet in the Alley*. It was so tiny that the bathtub was in the middle of the kitchen, covered by a wooden top . . ."

Her voice had trailed off. Her face was frozen into a beautiful expressionless mask. "But when I got there he was gone. I hadn't called—he didn't have a phone. And the apartment was a wreck—drawers pulled out and things thrown all around. When I went to the landlady to ask what had happened, she said that some men from the government—Immigration or Narcotics or something, she wasn't sure—had come that morning and taken Turo away. They had said that he was here illegally, that he was suspected of drug trafficking.

"I asked if I could use her phone to make some calls before I went back to tidy up the apartment and she just frowned at me and said the lease was with Turo and she wanted me off her property. It was clear she was terrified. So I found a phone booth and called everywhere I could think of. I finally found a lawyer who would see me right away.

"I had to take a room in a motel—and I was there for a couple of weeks while I waited for this lawyer to find out something. I was running low on money and knew that by the time I paid the lawyer, I wouldn't have enough for my next semester's tuition.

"When he finally called to tell me that Arturo Rodriquez had been deported to his native Colombia, I was beaten. Worry and sadness and morning sickness had worn me down. I'd maxed out my credit cards and all I could do was to crawl back home."

Gloria's words had cut deep. To think that I'd never . . .

"Glory, why didn't you call me? I could have . . . we could have . . ."

"I called and the phone just kept ringing . . . over and over. Later I found out that you were with Sam's family for the holidays. So I went home to Mama."

"And Mama got her way about the abortion . . ."

"No. Oh, no." Gloria had wrapped her arms around herself and was shivering. But she lifted her chin and went on. "I let her yell and carry on and say terrible things—you know how she could be—but I told her I was going to have the baby no matter what. She threatened and pleaded and tried to bribe me but at last she realized I wasn't going to change my mind. So we made a bargain. I would go live with Aunt Dodie in New Bern and have the baby there. And then we would decide what to do. She talked about all the nice couples anxious to adopt but I told her we'd just wait and see."

My heart ached at the thought of my sister separated from her child all these years. "And when the baby came, I'll bet there was a nice couple lined up. Maybe it was the best thing—I mean, look how young you were. But have you ever . . . a lot of adopted children are eager to know who their birth parents are . . . I just wondered—"

Gloria had shaken her head. "No. That's not what happened. Oh, she had a nice couple eagerly waiting all right. But I hadn't signed anything . . . I felt like I couldn't decide till I saw the baby . . ."

"Oh, Glory! What an awful decision to have to—"

"I never had to." Her voice was still flat. "The baby was born dead. They said the cord had strangled it—that it never took a breath."

I had listened in abject misery, aware of how badly I'd

failed my sister so long ago but unable to put together any words. And then Glory turned luminous eyes on me. "You see, Lizzy, that's the other reason I'm here. Of course, it would be wonderful if I could talk to Harry and get his advice. But the real reason for this weekend is my baby—if only I could reach my baby . . . if I could tell my baby how sorry I am . . ."

Chapter 17

Trust

Friday, May 25

When I knocked on Gloria's door the next morning, she opened it almost immediately. There was no sign on *her* face of the late night that had left dark circles under my reddened eyes. It was almost as though the revelations that were still spinning through my mind had never been spoken. Glory was crisp and fresh and perfectly made-up and she greeted me with a radiant smile. Before either of us could speak, however, Steve and Dawn emerged from the Walnut Room and we all went down to the dining room for breakfast, exchanging pleasantries about the beauty of the old house, the fineness of the weather, and the interesting weekend that lay ahead.

Xan, the fruit and nut eater, was in the dining room when we got there, sitting alone at a table and silently working his way through a bowl of mixed fruit and a smaller bowl of raw almonds. He didn't acknowledge our entry in any way but continued his methodical mastication. I was pretty sure he had some rule about chewing each bite a certain number of times.

As the rest of the group filed in—some still sleepy-eyed, others obnoxiously cheery and talking about the brisk hour's walk they'd just taken—we helped ourselves at the buffet and found seats at the various small tables. Gloria and I joined Sandy from Wisconsin and henna-haired Charlene. These two had evidently just discovered a common interest in murder mysteries and were tossing titles and authors' names back and forth.

Next to us, Len had snagged a seat by Giles and before long the whole dining room was treated to Len's theories on ITC—Instrumental Trans-Communication.

"I figured I needed to experience communication through a human medium—then I can use that as a kind of a template for a program I have in mind. Of course, I'm not the only one out there working on this; there's a fellow in Virginia named Atwater; though he's pursuing a different . . ."

Concentrating on the delectable soufflé-like thing on my plate—an airy bit of heaven called Chili Egg Puff—I congratulated myself on my choice, all the while wondering how tacky it would be to go back for a little taste of the very righteous-looking French toast that Gloria had chosen.

"Good, is it?" I asked, noticing the look of bliss on her face. "Blueberries and pecans, is that right?"

She rolled her eyes, smiled, and nodded. "Only the best thing I ever put in my mouth."

I saw Xan give a little shiver of disgust as he finished his healthful breakfast and, passing the laden buffet table with averted eyes, removed himself to the front lawn. There, as we could see through the French doors, he proceeded to go through a number of gyrations which Gloria informed me were yoga poses.

"They're called asanas," she explained. "I learned a bunch of them in that workshop in California a few years ago. See—he started with the mountain pose. That's *tadasana* in Sanskrit. And now he's moving into downward-facing dog . . ."

We sipped our coffee and I munched on the small (really just a taste) portion of French toast I'd convinced myself I needed to try. Savoring the fruity, nutty confection and trying not to think about the calories I'd just downed, I watched in fascination as Xan arranged his wiry body into a series of poses ranging from very silly-looking to somewhat obscene to a bit alarming. Still, I had to admit, he was as flexible as a cat. Something I'd never be, especially if I ate like this every day.

Sandy and Charlene excused themselves to go back to their rooms and brush their teeth and I was finishing my second cup of coffee when, just like last night, the ambiguous-looking person known as Joss appeared in the dining room doorway. This time however, instead of flinging himself (I checked—there was an Adam's apple) at Giles's feet, he simply filled a plate and looked for a place to sit. I noticed that he had a somewhat shuffling gait, more suited to an old man than to the thirty-something he appeared to be, but put it down to whatever accident had caused the head injury he'd mentioned the night before.

"Would it be all right . . ." he asked, looking at the empty seats at our table, and when we said that yes, certainly it would, he lowered himself cautiously into the chair.

Seeing our concerned expressions, Joss reached up to touch the heavy bandage that covered much of the right side of his head. "It's not as bad as it looks. I was in a car accident a few days ago and I'm still feeling a little banged-up. I made them let me out of the hospital though. I've been told that this workshop will be life-changing for me and I don't want to miss a minute of it. But I keep having these blackout moments, where I forget where I am and what I'm doing—that's why I was late last night and again this morning."

He applied himself to his food and Gloria and I exchanged a glance.

"Are you sure you're going to be up to all the activities, Joss?" Gloria's voice was unexpectedly soft. "We're supposed to go outside in a few minutes for the trust-building session. Do you think—"

Our tablemate paused, his fork hovering in mid-air, and stared at my sister as if memorizing her features. "You're . . . Gloria, right? All those names last night, I . . ."

His unabashed scrutiny of her face continued and I saw her look down before answering "Yes, I'm Gloria and this is my sister Elizabeth. And we know you're Joss. But seriously, do you think—"

His dark eyes seemed to blur momentarily. "I think this session is necessary. I need very badly to learn to trust. I've needed it all my life—to trust and be trusted. Will *you* trust me, Gloria?"

The way he looked at her made me a little uneasy. A hungry look. I studied him covertly. What age was this Joss, anyway? Late twenties or early thirties would be my best guess but he was just so *young*-looking. Far too young to pique Gloria's interest, I thought; she's old enough to be his mother.

"Trust is an essential element in a gathering like this. We must all feel the freedom to ask questions long unasked, to speak truths long unspoken. We meet as strangers but we must forge a bond so that we can make use of the united energies of the group. Our success will depend on this bond."

We ten *Seekers,* as Giles referred to us, were gathered in a loose circle on the green lawn in front of the inn, listening to his explanation of the so-called trust-building exercises that would precede our psychical explorations. I was trying to pay attention but the view of the mountains and the perfection of the colorful flowerbeds at the edge of the yard were far more compelling to me than the idea of forging some hypothetical bond with this group.

My mind wandered as I studied the flowers and Giles's voice seemed to segue into the sleepy buzzing of the bees that were working the early blooms. *Trust . . . buzz, buzz . . . group bonds, buzz, buzz . . . trust . . .*

Trust. The absolute core necessity in a relationship— not sex, not wit, not income, not usefulness, but trust. The bone-deep knowledge that a person is what they seem, will *continue* to be what they seem. If a person— If Phillip—

"Lizzy!" A sharp elbow in my side and Gloria's hiss in my ear brought me back to the here and now and Giles's soft voice.

". . . so we'll begin with simple eye and hand contact. You may be surprised at your reactions to this basic exercise. I'd like you to take the hands of the person opposite, look into his or her eyes, and count to sixty. If you need to blink, that's fine, but don't look away. Len and I will start around the circle, with me moving to the right and Len to the left . . ."

What followed was a stately promenade of Seekers as the circle turned itself inside out and each of us gazed into ten pairs of eyes, one after another. Dark eyes, gray eyes, all shades of blue eyes, turquoise eyes (Gloria had worn her tinted contacts), and hazel.

I was surprised at how amazingly personal it felt, how difficult it was not to look away—and how very long sixty seconds could be. When at last I'd faced them all and held hands—soft, calloused, dry, clammy, warm, or icy—with each of them, it was true, I was more ready to trust any one of them simply by the fact of having shared that interminable minute. Even odd Xan, from whom I'd expected an impersonal and clinical contact, seemed more likable now as he blushed slightly and I felt his hands tremble in mine.

Giles put us though a series of these trust-building exercises. We led and were led blindfolded about the lawn; we made our way, blindfolded again, through a "minefield" of paper cups, no longer led but responding to our seeing partner's spoken directions. It was interesting to see how difficult it was to direct—how aware of your partner's gait and response time you had to be—and how very tiring it was to give your complete attention to the task.

There were more exercises and the day grew warmer. We were all glad when Giles called a halt and suggested that we return to the covered porch where water and lemonade would be waiting.

"And in the interval before lunch," he said, leading our little gaggle of Seekers back to the welcome shade, "I'll talk a bit about the multidimensional universe and astral spirits."

I sipped at the tall glass of fresh lemonade and drew a spiral on the bedewed glass. The trust exercises had been one thing; now, I was being challenged to absorb a mass of Spiritualist information of the sort that my nephew Ben termed New Age shit. But I had promised myself to approach this weekend with an open mind for my sister's sake. Okay, then, I'd make an effort to understand this New Age . . . stuff.

The multidimensional universe, according to Giles, who spoke of it with the familiarity of a frequent flyer, was composed of various planes, all of different densities and vibrating at different rates. The first plane, he informed us, is the physical.

"This," he waved his hand to encompass our surroundings, " 'this goodly frame the earth,' as Hamlet calls it, is of the densest matter and accordingly, it vibrates at the slowest rate. Beyond the physical plane lie the various levels of the astral plane and it is there that the astral spirits we hope to communicate with have their being."

As Giles explained it—". . . and this is just a construct, mind you; these concepts are more easily grasped with a map of sorts . . ."—we would be attempting to communicate with spirits who had left the earthly plane—died, in other words—and moved on to the astral plane.

One of the astral planes, that is. According to Giles, there are three—high, middle, and low, with multiple levels within each. These astral planes act as a buffer zone between the dark earthly plane and the realms of celestial light and mental-causal inspiration.

Or something like that. I was trying hard to follow his explanation and not roll my eyes. As he spoke, I began to visualize a three-layer cake, sitting on an ugly lumpy cake platter (the physical plane). The bottom (and somewhat soggy) layer of the cake was the lowest astral plane, where the unenlightened (unen*light*ened, as Giles put it) went after "passing over" (the words *death* and *dying* being somehow taboo). These dark spirits on the bottom layer had been unable to make a good transition from life—in fact, they might not even realize that they had died and, in consequence, might keep trying to return to Earth. Ghosts, in other words.

The middle layer—er, plane—was described as a rather pleasant place where most spirits go for R & R before moving on up. A kind of Earth with all the bad parts left out. It sounded like my sort of place and I hoped that my vibrations matched it.

The thing about vibrations, here again, as Giles described it, is pretty much like Karma. Or the biblical *As ye sow, so shall ye reap*. During life, a person's thoughts and beliefs determine their vibratory rate: pride, anger, wrath, and all the other Seven Deadly Sins, for example, are low-vibration thoughts while love and spirituality yield very high vibrations.

"And, just as the lowest astral plane is similar to Hell or Purgatory, the highest would be akin to the Christian Heaven. Many Spiritualists call this Summerland. It is somewhere within these planes that we shall seek the spirits . . ."

I looked around the group. Everyone was rapt—some openmouthed and wide-eyed, others nodding in agreement as if this was familiar ground to them. Gloria, her eyes alight, leaned forward. Her hands were palm to palm, fingertips at her lips. I could see that she was clasping the little locket she had shown me the night before. A tiny gold heart and inside, where a picture ordinarily would be, a wisp of dark hair. Engraved on the other side in minuscule letters was the simple inscription: *Dana—7/28/73—Always, Mama.*

Dana, the name she'd given that long-ago stillborn baby—the baby she longed so urgently to reach this weekend.

VI~The DeVine Sisters

May 11, 1887

"I won't! I tell you, I won't! Give her the money back! Tell her anything . . . say her Julia's busy on the other plane, playing with her horrid little dog; tell her I'm dead; tell her—"

The torrent of protest ceased abruptly and Dorothea fell back on the divan. The smartly administered slap had shocked her into silence and she curled up on the cushions, one hand to her stinging cheek. Her beautiful eyes brimmed with tears as she looked up at her attacker.

"Theo, you needn't have—"

Theodora gazed down at her sister in disgust. Then she turned and paced to the window where she put aside the heavy drapes and leaned her forehead against the glass. "Don't you understand, Doe," she said, her voice weary, "that our finances are not such that we can turn away clients? You saw Murchinson's letter. He has no more engagements for us. And when the month—"

"Oh yes, I saw Murchinson's letter . . . yes, and that dreadful newspaper story!" Dorothea's voice was low but urgent. "Theo, don't you understand? It's I who am responsible for that poor mother's self-destruction. How can I, after that, carry on with this . . . another deception? I'd always felt that I was bringing comfort, some assurance . . . but now, after this fiasco—"

The woman on the divan buried her face in the cushions and gave way to racking sobs. Her sister waited at the window till the fit had passed. At last, when Dorothea had subsided into sniffling hiccups, Theodora came and sat beside her, taking her sister into her arms and murmuring soothing words.

"Doe, Doe . . . it wasn't your fault. The Waverly woman was quite unbalanced . . . We all remarked upon it at the time. Of course it's regrettable that she— But think of all the mothers to whom you have brought comfort . . . women who now carry the precious memory of a last touch, a sweet adieu, and the knowledge of their beloved child's perfect happiness in that joyous land beyond the veil . . ."

Theodora stroked her sister's hair as she spoke. The honeyed words ran on and little by little Dorothea grew calm.

"I have helped those poor women; I know I have. I couldn't bear to think I should be so wicked as to play upon their sorrow and all for the money. Bless you, Theo, for reminding me . . . but, oh, need I see Julia's mother today? Pray, put Mrs. Farnsworth off till tomorrow or the next day. I'll be stronger then . . ."

There was the rattle of a key in the lock.

"Well, my dears, we have a new prospect." Lorenzo DeVine pulled off his gloves and dropped them into the hat he'd just placed with his walking stick on the lunette table by the entry. "Mrs. Farnsworth has been singing your praises, Doe, and she has a young friend who is eager for a sitting. A Miss Cochrane, from Pittsburgh. You may have seen her about—dark hair in a fringe, a decided jaw, and determined eyebrows. Not one of these shrinking southern belles but a forthright little Yankee— a girl after my own heart, by damn."

Smiling at some recent memory, he took a seat, crossed his legs, then fixed Dorothea with a stern gaze. "Has she come to her senses, Theo?"

The afternoon was warm and the two young women strolling about the spacious grounds bent their course past the croquet court where a lively game was in progress, making their leisurely way toward a little clump of trees and rocks.

"Shall we wander through these curious stone formations, Miss Cochrane? The shade would be agreeable— don't you find the sun rather warm even with a parasol?"

The keen eyes under the heavy fringe of dark hair peered at the narrow path. "Why, that would be most pleasant, Miss DeVine. I've been wild to take a look at these queer rocks—the porter told me they had something to do with the Red Indians who once dwelt here."

The two paced along the path, exclaiming at the oddness of the shapes of the stones. Miss Cochrane hinted at the unspeakable savage rituals that these same rocks might have witnessed then stopped her ready flow of speculation on seeing her companion's look of distress.

"Oh! My dear Miss DeVine! Pray, forgive me for running on in such an unladylike manner! I'd forgotten that one who is in daily contact with the mysteries beyond the veil is apt to be unduly sensitive . . . You look a little faint; would you rather we returned to the hotel?"

Theodora forced a smile. "Not at all. It's a touch of the sun and, if you'll forgive my mentioning it, my sister laced me a bit too tightly this morning. Perhaps if we sat on that bench just there in the open area . . ."

They settled themselves on the bench, a fantastic composition of twisted rhododendron limbs, and Miss Cochrane insisted on applying her little bottle of smelling salts to Theodora's nose.

"*I always carry it,*" *she explained, returning the useful item to her reticule. "If only I had my eau de cologne with me to put on your wrists; it's wonderfully refreshing.*"

Laughing now, Theodora assured her friend that she was quite recovered. "But how is it you are so well prepared? Are you here in attendance upon an elderly parent? An invalid aunt?"

Now it was the other's turn to grow quiet. Her lively expression slackened and she turned her head away for a moment before replying, "No, alas, I'm here alone. My darling mother passed away this spring. I was with her almost constantly during the last months of her life. She was quite ill and couldn't bear for anyone but me to attend her. By the time of her . . . blessed release, I was badly run down and Papa insisted I try the Mountain Park's rest cure for a month. He puts much faith in the mountain air and the mineral waters."

Theodora reached over and patted her new friend's hand. "My dear Miss Cochrane, Renzo—my brother— said that you were hoping to speak with a loved one but I had no idea your bereavement was so recent. I am so sorry, my dear . . ."

Miss Cochrane pulled a dainty handkerchief from her sleeve and patted her eyes. "It was most kind of your brother to introduce us. I feel as if I've found a real friend in you. Won't you call me Liza Jane, the way they used to . . . at home?"

"*Her mother suffered terribly toward the end. A cancer in the breast, a brutal operation, a prolonged period of partial recovery, and then a return of the growth in the other breast. The poor woman couldn't bear the thought of going under the knife again. She was kept under morphia much of the time but nevertheless her suffering was horrendous. Miss Cochrane has dabbled in Spiritualism and is much concerned to think that her dear mother may be trapped on the lower plane. There have been rapping sounds in the room where she died and the dead woman's wardrobe door often is found open in the morning when it was firmly shut the night before. Miss Cochrane—or Liza Jane as the family calls her—also mentioned a cold draft . . ."*

Theodora paused in her brushing of Dorothea's luxuriant mane. "Are you getting all of this, Doe?"

Her sister didn't look up from her notebook but her pen continued to scratch. ". . . family pet name, Liza Jane . . . rapping, wardrobe door, cold draft. Do go on brushing, Theo; that was never a hundred strokes."

NELLIE BLY
from
ONE HUNDRED AND ONE WOMEN WHO MADE A DIFFERENCE

Elizabeth Jane Cochran, who would later become Nellie Bly, intrepid investigative journalist, was born May 5, 1864, in Cochran's Mills, Pennsylvania. Her father's death when she was only six and her mother's subsequent marriage to an abusive man may have sparked her later interest in investigating situations where women were at risk.

Known at home by the nickname "Pink" due to her childhood fondness for the color, as a teenager Elizabeth Jane added an "e" to the family name, becoming Elizabeth Jane Cochrane.

When the family (her mother now divorced) moved to Pittsburgh in 1880, Elizabeth Jane wrote an angry letter to the editor of *The Pittsburgh Dispatch* in response to a sexist column. The editor was so impressed by her language that he offered her a position at the newspaper. It was here that she assumed the pseudonym Nellie Bly and launched into a series of investigative articles on female factory workers. When she was reassigned to the women's pages to write on gardening, fashion, and society, on her own initiative, at twenty-one, she traveled to Mexico as a foreign correspondent. After six months, she ran afoul of the dictatorship and, threatened with arrest, returned to Pittsburgh, where she was assigned to report on the theater and the arts.

She left *The Pittsburgh Dispatch* in 1887 and four months later took an undercover assignment for Joseph Pulitzer's *New York World*. Her *Ten Days in a Mad-House*, a firsthand account of the brutal conditions in the Women's Lunatic Asylum on Blackwell's Island, was published in September, 1887 . . .

Chapter 18

Journey to the Astral Plane

Friday, May 25

After lunch and some free time—napping or meditation was suggested—we convened in the parlor. Dark shades were drawn at the windows and a temporary drape had been rigged over the arched opening that led to a smaller room, making the space dim, but by no means dark. Once again we took our places in a ragged circle. And once again I was at the end of the sofa with Gloria on my left. The chairs had been drawn in closer to the sofa, I noticed, so that we were almost elbow to elbow.

Giles waited, relaxed in the wing chair, till everyone had taken a seat and then, in the most matter-of-fact voice imaginable, he asked, "How many of you have ever attended a séance?"

Several hands went up—Dawn, Ree, and Charlene.

"And how many of you had satisfactory experiences?"

Ree's hand came down at once. Dawn's hand came down, started back up, then came down again.

Giles nodded. "That's interesting. Now to begin with, a few housekeeping details. We'll be here for an hour or more; if anyone wants to visit the loo, this would be the time. And this is also the time to turn off your cellphones—right off. Not set to vibrate but entirely off."

There was a fumbling in pockets and purses and several people left the room for the suggested bathroom call. People were talking to one another in low tones as Giles moved around the group, speaking to each person individually. Gloria glanced over at me, her eyes bright with excitement.

"Oh, Lizzy, I've got such a positive feeling about this! I really think—"

"What about smudging?" Charlene's strident voice caught everyone's attention. She was offering Giles a little bundle of something that looked like dried leaves. "At the séances I've participated in, we always began by smudging the room to get rid of any negative energy."

There was an amused look on the medium's face. "If you like," he said. "I don't find it necessary but if no one here has a problem with smoke, then by all means . . ." He made a polite gesture.

"Oh, but shouldn't I wait till everyone's here—in case anyone's carrying negative energy?"

Negative energy. I hoped that wasn't me. I wasn't a believer by a long shot but I felt that I could keep an open mind. I had done so in the past . . . and I remembered the time I'd been called to a neighbor's house to stop a nosebleed by reading a particular Bible verse. I'd made a conscious effort to believe in what I was doing . . . or at least, not to scoff at it . . . to allow for the possibility. And it had worked. The nosebleed had stopped—whether because of or in spite of me.

"Elizabeth."

Giles was in front of me now, bending down to speak close to my ear. "Don't worry, Elizabeth. I feel sure that you'll be a stronger link than you might have imagined. If you can only look past the trappings . . ."

He nodded toward Charlene, who, now that everyone was assembled, had lit the little bundle of leaves and allowed it to flare up before she blew the flame out. Now she was waving the smoking bundle back and forth and muttering something as she walked clockwise around the room.

"The trappings and the terminology, as I said yesterday, are merely constructs—a way for us to deal with something far beyond our understanding."

I nodded and started to say that I'd do my best. But he had passed on to Steve and Dawn. It helped that Giles was so ordinary, that he didn't spout a lot of metaphysical stuff. Or, at least, if he did spout, I could comfort myself by thinking of it as a metaphor.

"Thank you, Charlene," he said as she completed her circuit of the room and stood at the doorway, one hand holding back the drapes while with the other she seemed to be shooing the smoke out of the room. "Well done. And now . . ."

With a scant tilt of his head, he motioned her toward her chair. As he took his own, a little shiver of anticipation ran round the circle.

"Now"—Giles spoke in that low tone that had each of us straining forward to catch his words—"I should tell you that while there are many different ways to conduct a séance, my . . ." he hesitated, "my particular method has proved to be satisfactory again and again. I will ask you all to keep that in mind as we proceed.

"For those of you who've never participated in a séance, you should be aware that spirits may communicate by knocking or rapping or some other nonverbal sound. Or the spirit may speak to one of you in your mind—and not necessarily to the one asking the question. If we're very fortunate, the spirit may speak aloud—through one of us."

"Wait a minute. Not just through you . . . but *any* of us?" Steve looked alarmed at the thought.

Giles hastened to assure her that it was only a remote possibility, then gestured at our circle. "We'll begin the session by joining hands. It helps us to focus but, contrary to what some believe, it's not a requisite. As the time goes on you may find that maintaining that hand clasp is causing fatigue which is working against your concentration. If you find this happening, please, let go. It will do no harm. Are there any questions?"

Giles looked around the circle of expectant but silent faces. "Very well, then. We'll begin with a few minutes of silent meditation. Each of you should concentrate on the spirit you hope to contact, as well as the question that you have for that spirit. At the end of this period of silence, I'll ask one of you to begin and we'll all bend our minds to trying to contact that particular spirit. Remember, we'll have one more session today and three more tomorrow so there'll be ample time for each of you."

So saying, Giles put out his hands and closed his eyes. Somewhat self-consciously, the group joined hands and we began.

The only meditating I've done has been in a bathtub of hot water. And it's been of the "think of nothing" variety. But this . . . would I be a spoilsport, a big old load of "negative energy," if I didn't try to contact someone? And which someone would it be?

Sam. Of course that's who Gloria felt was the logical choice. She had said something earlier about how good it would be if I could have "closure" with Sam. Maybe so. But how strange it would seem, assuming this contact occurred, to be speaking to my beloved late husband almost on the eve of marrying his best friend. Certainly there were unresolved questions I could ask—several battered at me. But did I want the answers? Moreover, did I want Gloria to be privy to my doubts?

No, I did not. Sam, wherever he was, would not be on my calling list. But then, who . . . ? My mother . . . no . . . Papa . . . oh, how tempting, but, again, too personal. And for all I knew, he could still be alive—no point seeking someone who hadn't crossed over, as they say.

At last I settled on Gramma. If anyone was going to speak to me or send me a message, I thought I'd like it to be Gramma. So I composed myself to meditate on Gramma, her comfortable plump figure, usually with an apron over her dress, her soft brown eyes, her . . . and I wandered off into days of remembered bliss . . . Gramma . . . Gramma . . .

"Let's bring our meditation to a close now. We'll begin by all concentrating on the spirit that Xan is hoping to contact. Xan, will you give us the name?"

I opened my eyes to see Xan, quivering like a greyhound as Giles looked at him. Xan took a deep breath and made his request.

"My brother . . . my brother Rob. Robert MacNaughten."

"Thank you, Xan." Again Giles's gaze swept round the circle. "Let us all hold that name in our minds and silently ask Robert to come among us."

And so we did. At least, I did. Mindlessly concentrating on the name Robert MacNaughten, over and over, I could feel Glory's hand trembling in my left hand and Dawn's, still and icy, in my right. Somewhere in the distance I heard the muffled rattle of a diesel truck starting and forced myself back to the task at hand.

Robert MacNaughten, Robert MacNaughten . . . Beneath this mantra ran a magpie jumble of thought. *Mac-*

Naughten sounds Scottish, Xan must be short for Alexander . . . Robert MacNaughten, Robert MacNaughten, Xan wants to talk to you . . . I wonder if this is an older or younger brother we're calling and how long he's been dead. Oh hell, I'm wandering . . . Robert MacNaughten, Robert MacNaughten . . .

I had closed my eyes in order to concentrate better but the absence of sight only seemed to sharpen all my other senses: the sound of the group's breathing and the prissy little sniff that appeared to be habitual with Dawn, the lingering smell of the smoke from the burning sage of the smudge bundle . . . *dammit, I'm wandering again . . . Robert MacNaughten, Robert MacNaughten . . .*

What happened next is hard to describe. At last my busy mind shut down and it was as if the words *Robert MacNaughten* were being played on a continuous loop. I was conscious of nothing more than the fact that my breathing had become very slow and steady and I had the feeling of being connected to something—almost as if I were a conduit of some sort. There was a central core of empty space and my being was wrapped around it and I was cherishing it and protecting it even as the words *Robert MacNaughten* pulsed through that core and . . .

A cascade of sound erupted from the piano standing in the bay of the room, a glissando—if that was the word for a tumble of notes from high to low, as if the pianist had run his thumbnail along the piano keys—and my eyes popped open and my head turned in the direction of the sound.

Again and again, an unseen hand made the instrument ring out. The notes crowded upon one another, deafening, maddening, till I felt that I would have to cover my ears, but just as they seemed to reach an unbearable frenzy, Giles spoke.

"Robert, thank you for joining us. Xan is here. Will

you speak with your brother? One note for yes, two for no."

All eyes were turned toward the piano and I heard a muffled sob that must have come from Xan. "Rob," he begged, "Rob, will you—"

A single plangent note rang out, reverberating in the stillness of the dim room.

Chapter 19

A Man Alone

Friday, May 25

Sorry, guys, it's just me. She won't be back till Sunday."

Three wagging tails slowed then drooped and the dogs looked beyond him in hopes of seeing Elizabeth coming up the path. Shaking his head, Phillip climbed the porch steps, threading between Molly and Ursa who seemed determined to ignore him. James, however, gave up the vigil and followed Phillip into the house, dancing and yapping as a reminder that it was well past feeding time.

In spite of the noisy little dog, the house seemed strangely deserted. On a normal day, Elizabeth would have been in the kitchen, putting the finishing touches on dinner while listening to an audiobook or to NPR and *All Things Considered*. There would be good smells and she would turn to him with a smile and . . .

James's barking grew more frantic. The smiling image faded and Phillip dropped his battered briefcase on the kitchen bench.

"Okay, buddy, I'll get the chow."

He was just setting down the third bowl of dog food on the porch when he heard the phone in the house ringing. Smiling at the thought that it would surely be Elizabeth, he hurried into the little office and snatched up the phone.

"Who's this?" was the abrupt response to his eager hello. A deep voice. A man's voice.

"Who are you calling?" he countered.

"Is this Ms. Goodweather's place?"

Phillip admitted that it was, adding that Ms. Goodweather wasn't in.

"Gone off somewhere with Gloria, I'll bet—no, don't bother making something up. You must be the boyfriend, am I right?"

Phillip took a deep breath. *And you must be the husband.* "This is Detective Phillip Hawkins of the Marshall County Sheriff's Office." *That'll give this sucker something to think about.* "Ms. Goodweather and I are getting married next month. And you are . . . ?"

"Well, I guess I'm your future brother-in-law, *Detective* Hawkins. You can call me Jerry. You know, I'm glad it was you that answered. There's something you need to know about."

"That's right, the same black Hummer I told you about before. I'm not sure what he has in mind—but if anyone spots the vehicle, let me or Sheriff Blaine know right away . . . Yeah, they'll be at the Mountain Magnolia all weekend—should be secure there but . . . Okay, then, 'preciate it . . . You too."

Phillip glanced at his watch: six-thirty. He needed to tell Elizabeth and Gloria about Jerry's call but it would have to wait. They were probably eating dinner or already in a workshop session. Besides, he knew from experience that Lizabeth would have left her phone in her bedroom, turned off. They had agreed to talk every night at ten—or every morning at seven.

He wandered kitchenward through the quiet house. Might as well get something to eat. Then he would put in some time with the never-ending paperwork that was part of modern law enforcement. The sound of his footsteps on the wooden floors seemed magnified in the silence; for a fleeting moment, he felt like an intruder in a strange house.

Lizabeth had insisted on leaving the refrigerator well stocked. He'd reminded her that he'd survived for many years as a bachelor but evidently she had no opinion of his ability to fend for himself and had left things in the refrigerator that he could heat up. She had carefully pointed out some meal options before she left: a container of chicken and yellow rice, ham and cheese for a sandwich, a creamy glob of noodles and something . . .

He ended up on the porch with a thick peanut butter sandwich and a beer. The dogs would clean up the crumbs and he'd enjoy the view and the frogs' chirping in the fish pool. The quiet of the country was still a novelty to him—there had been so few occasions that he'd been here alone for any length of time. Somewhere down the hill he could hear the *putt-putt* of the tractor—Ben, working late to take advantage of the cool of the evening. He'd seen Amanda making her way up the road to the cabin; she too put in long hours at this time of year, readying the gardens of summer residents so they could brag about their green thumbs to their houseguests all summer long.

This was an interesting sort of family he was marrying into, he thought, taking another sip of beer and giving each dog a bit of crust. Close—Ben and Amanda's cabin was in shouting distance—but careful to allow everyone space. God knows, they'd all made a point of seeming oblivious to his and Elizabeth's budding romance. And when he had moved in, it had been accepted as a matter of course. The next step—the wedding—had generated a bit more interest but aside from Gloria's unsolicited pronouncements about how things should be done, everyone had appeared happy to go along with whatever he and Elizabeth decided on. Very different from the dog-and-pony show that his ex-mother-in-law had turned his and Sandy's wedding into—so long ago and far away.

He rocked quietly, thinking about that long-ago marriage. It had been a train wreck: he and Sandy too young and his job as a new cop taking up all but a fraction of his time and energy. They would have grown apart anyway; two more different people didn't exist. But if he'd had a nine-to-five job, they might have hung on longer. Still, the kids had turned out all right. Seth was deep in his graduate studies and Janie, after some aimless years, finally seemed to have settled down, even going so far as to declare a major.

Fine kids, the both of them—and though they hadn't yet gotten a chance to spend much time with Elizabeth, they seemed happy enough with the idea of his marrying her. After all, he and their mother had divorced years ago and Sandy had remarried at once. They wouldn't begrudge him a shot at a happy life.

A happy life. That's what it had been, ever since he'd moved out here. If occasionally he remembered that he was sliding into the vacancy left by Sam's death—sleeping in Sam's bed, hanging his clothes in Sam's closet—he had tried to get past that. It wasn't as though he had a home to offer Elizabeth, a symbolic new start to a new life together. Even if he could have afforded to buy a house, and he couldn't, not on his pay, not with two kids still in college, he didn't think she wanted a new life. The farm was her passion—if he had asked her to choose between him and the farm . . . but then, he knew better than to even think of such a thing, didn't he? Better to be content that she had at last agreed to make him an official part of her life.

Brushing the crumbs from his lap, Phillip stood and

stretched. A thought occurred to him: the farm. It was a considerable asset. Ben was a partner in the herb and flower business and he and Amanda seemed to have every intention of making their lives together right here on the farm. Furthermore, both of Elizabeth's girls had expressed their firm intentions of eventually coming home and building their own houses somewhere on the hundred-plus acres.

Once he and Elizabeth married, though—if something happened to her, half of the farm would be his. How would—

Again, the ringing of the telephone broke in on his thoughts and he hurried back to the office. Maybe Lizabeth had had a little extra time between dinner and whatever weirdness this workshop was offering up . . .

"No, ma'am," he replied to the obviously elderly woman on the other end. "Elizabeth's away for the weekend. I'll be speaking with her later and can give her a message . . . yes, ma'am . . . yes ma'am . . . thank you."

On and on the caller went, in a sweet southern babble that threatened to stretch into tomorrow. Aunt Dodie—Lizabeth had spoken of her often, not an actual aunt but a school friend of Elizabeth's mother, living in New Bern.

"No, ma'am, we haven't settled on a date just yet—sometime next month, toward the end of the month, I think. But Elizabeth can . . .

"You are?" He began to grin in spite of himself. "No, ma'am, not at all. I'm sure Elizabeth will be . . . Oh, a surprise. Well, if you think . . ."

He dropped into the office chair and let the stream of the old woman's monologue wash over him, just interjecting a polite sound now and then.

"Well," he said at last when the flow seemed to be ebbing, "when I talk to Elizabeth later, I'll tell her you called . . . No? . . . Well, if you're sure, Miz . . . er . . . yes, ma'am . . . ah, Aunt Dodie."

Still grinning, he hung up the phone. So that was Aunt Dodie—the Admiral's widow. Listening to her had been like being spun around in one of those machines for making cotton candy. He could almost feel the sweet, sticky fluff wrapped around his head, stuffed into his ears.

He paused to examine some of the family pictures that hung on one wall of the office. Hadn't Lizabeth once pointed out an Aunt Dodie in this black-and-white and sepia collection of parents and grandparents, aunts and uncles, and still more distant forebears? Was it the young woman in correct riding apparel standing beside a haughty-looking tall horse? No, it must have been one of these bathing beauties: four young women lined up on a seawall in those monumental one-piece bathing suits of the type he could remember his mother wearing. More like old-fashioned corsets than something a person might actually want to swim in.

The small pretty blonde on the far right—that must be Lizabeth and Gloria's mother; there was a definite likeness to Gloria in the determined set of the jaw. Now which one was the young Dodie? The lanky girl with short dark hair? No, now he remembered. It was the plump little person linking arms with Lizabeth's mother—"best friends forever," Lizabeth had called them. "My mother kind of wore out most of her friends but Aunt Dodie never gave up on her," Elizabeth had said, with a strange downward turn to her mouth.

Aunt Dodie was still on his mind when, just at ten, the phone rang for the third time. *Don't mention her call to Lizabeth,* he reminded himself. *Aunt Dodie wants it to be a surprise when she shows up for the wedding.*

"Hey, sweetheart," he said. "I've missed you. How's

the exploration of the other side going? . . . Really? And soaking in hot tubs and massages too? You girls know how to live it up, don't you? But what's this Giles fellow like? . . . Has your sister gotten to talk to her late husband yet?"

As soon as those last words were out, he had the unsettling sensation of treading on very thin ice and hurried on. "But you can tell me all about it when you get back home. Listen, sweetheart, there was a call from Gloria's current husband Jerry : . . ."

He launched into as complete a recap of the call as he could manage but even as he spoke, the thought kept running through his mind: *Please tell me you're not being taken in by this psychic crap. Please tell me you're not trying to contact Sam.*

". . . so Jerry says to me that it's come to his attention that a former associate of his may have been responsible for his first wife's death and what's more, this former associate is thought to be in our area and if Gloria's up here, which he's pretty sure she is, she'd better look out for this guy because it looks like there's some kind of vendetta going on . . .

"That's right . . . Jerry said, 'Tell Gloria it's the fella she calls the Eyebrow—she'll know who I mean.' "

There was an excited squabble of sound on the other end and Phillip was forced to wait till it had slowed to explain that he'd already alerted the chief of police in Hot Springs and his boss Sheriff Mackenzie Blaine as well.

"But don't take any chances, okay? If you stay there at the inn, you ought to be fine . . . you're going back to the spa again? How far away is that? . . . well, I don't guess that would be too . . . yeah, I know what you mean . . . but keep your cellphone with you and keep it turned on, okay, Lizabeth?"

Phillip ran his hand over his head. "I don't know . . .

Sweetheart, is there any chance you could get your sister to cancel out on this weekend and you two come back . . . No, I see your point . . . But there's another thing—that doctor friend of hers you said she was talking . . . yeah, Sterrings, that was the name. Do you know if Gloria's heard from him recently? . . . Well, according to Jerry . . . No, I know Jerry may be playing his own game here. But my gut instinct was that he was telling the truth."

"Tell my wife this, Detective Hawkins," the gruff voice had said. "Tell her that her buddy, Dr. Brice we're-just-good-friends Sterrings, is under investigation for malpractice. Word at the club is he's facing the mother of all lawsuits and will be filing for bankruptcy soon. In fact, he may have skipped town, what I hear. So if little Gloria was thinking about him for husband number five, she should probably think again."

Chapter 20

The Woman in White

Friday, May 25, and Saturday, May 26

I had already made up my mind to wait to tell Phillip about Gloria's stillborn child. There were so many unknowns in the equation—maybe this weekend would make things clearer. But the news Phillip had couldn't wait. As soon as we'd said our good nights, I hurried to Gloria's room. It seemed important that she know right away about Jerry's call but she just waved off what I had to tell her.

"Oh, Lizzy! Don't you see? Jerry's just trying to sound like he's actually worried about me. That, and at the same time to put all the blame on the Eyebrow. Did Phillip actually believe him?"

She gazed at me over the top of her reading glasses—a blue-gray gaze, as the turquoise contacts had been removed for the night. She was propped up in the elegant bed, leafing through a copy of *Architectural Digest*. Several other glossy magazines lay on the sheet beside her, as did her cellphone, and I wondered if she was expecting a call.

"Well," I hedged, "he did say—"

At that moment, the cellphone emitted a throaty sort of gurgle and Gloria snatched it up. After a quick glance at its screen, she mashed a button, dropped it back down, and yawned, just a little too casually.

"That was Eleanor. She'll talk and talk and I really need my sleep. Thank you, Lizzy, for letting me know what Jerry told Phil, but really . . ."

She yawned again. "Could we discuss this in the morning before breakfast? I took an Ambien and I think it's starting to kick in."

I hesitated but she made a shooing gesture at me as she climbed off the big bed. "Go on, Lizzy. We both need our beauty sleep. I want to be very well rested for the sitting tomorrow morning. I'll bolt the door behind you, don't worry."

As she shut the door behind me, I heard the click and rattle of the little chain bolt. I stood there a moment, somewhat miffed by the reception my concern had gotten. Then, from behind the door, I heard the low murmur of Gloria's voice. Horrified at the thought that I was eavesdropping, I hurried across the hall to my room. *She probably decided to return her friend Eleanor's call,* I told myself as I opened my own door.

Except that what I'd heard had sounded awfully like *Hey, Turo, it's me.*

Back in my room I thought about the afternoon and evening sessions we'd just experienced. My skeptical nature had been shaken by what I'd witnessed and, even more, by what I'd felt. I was deeply weary—surprisingly so—and expected to fall asleep at once. But my night was unsettled—too much to think about, a cold draft in the room, and when at last sleep came, instead of dreams of Gramma, there was a woman weeping at my window.

In the dream I tried to console her but she was so wrapped in her grief that she couldn't seem to hear me. I tossed about, sliding in and out of sleep and in and out of this tedious dream till at last the morning light crept in the window and the weeper vanished.

I tried to think about the workshop ahead and Gloria's hope to contact that long-ago child. Assuming one believed all this astral planes stuff, where would a still-born child go? Would it go anywhere? Would it, as ghosts are said to do, have "unfinished business" and be lingering on that first plane?

Get a grip, Elizabeth! I threw back the covers and got up. Habit being what it is, I made the bed, though I knew that I would find on my return that it had been re-made by a far more professional hand than mine. I tried to arrange the pillows as they had been but giving it up as beyond my skills, I dressed quickly and went to Gloria's room. I hoped that we'd have a few minutes to continue our conversation of the night before.

With a discreet rap on her door, I called, "Glory? Are you ready to go to breakfast?"

No answer.

"Glory!" I rapped more loudly, wondering if the sleeping pill could have caused her to oversleep. "It's breakfast time. Glo—"

"She went out early," said a voice at my ear. "I think she was going power walking. She had those little hand weights, you know?"

It was Dawn, holding a laden tray with covered dishes, glasses of orange juice, butter and jam, a napkin-covered basket that suggested hot biscuits, and a steaming coffeepot. She grinned and nodded at the tempting display. "I'm treating Steve to breakfast in bed. Your sister was just heading out the front door when I went downstairs to get the tray, maybe ten minutes ago."

Cursing under my breath, I hurried back to my room, grabbed my shoulder bag, and headed for the stairs.

There was no sign of Gloria in the dining room or outside. I had briefly allowed myself to hope that she might have joined Xan in his postures. But he was alone on the lawn, twisted into an improbable pose. When I asked if he had seen my sister, he untangled himself long enough to tell me that she had passed by earlier, saying that she thought she could make it to the spa and back and still have time for breakfast.

I hesitated. I could get to the spa faster if I took the car. But Gloria would have gone down the one-way drive and then by footpath—where I couldn't take the car. I needed to make sure she wasn't there . . .

Shitshitshit! I cut across the lawn and negotiated the stone steps leading to the driveway.

"Gloria!" I shouted, my voice feeling like an intrusion in the still of the pristine morning. There was no answer and no sign of anyone on the tree-hung drive.

I called again, to no avail, then hurried back to the parking area for my car. Gloria's ten-minute head start probably meant that she was already at the spa and I had no illusions of being able to run all the way there.

The way out of the inn led me through the early morning back streets of the small town where only a few people were stirring. I kept a sharp lookout for the black Hummer—*though who's to say that the Eyebrow might not have rented another car.*

This was a sobering thought and I paid close attention to the drivers of the few vehicles that were on the town's main street. A vintage hippie type in a pickup, a family in a van with a Michigan plate, a young woman jabbering into a cellphone as she sped through a stoplight in her VW bug—none had any resemblance to the man Glory had described.

At last I was turning in at the gates to the spa—but still no sign of Gloria. The car's clock read 7:35; surely she would be heading back by now. I turned through the gates and started down the winding road toward the spa building.

The spacious grounds seemed deserted, just an open

swath of green with a few wisps of fog still lingering. No sign of Gloria, but the level drive that ran through the grounds and back behind the spa building suggested itself as the route she might have taken. I was reasonably sure that she wouldn't have been tempted by the clump of rocks we'd visited the day before so, with no more than a cursory glance down the narrow path to the center, I continued down the road.

Then, in the rearview mirror, I caught a flicker of movement among those strange rocks.

Slamming on the brakes, I reversed and came to a stop just where the narrow path ran into the center of the ancient stones.

"Glory?" I called, telling myself that what I'd seen was probably a bird or a squirrel, even as I reached into my shoulder bag for my pistol.

It had surprised me to find how easy it was to become a gun-totin' citizen. We'd always had some guns at the farm—a legacy from Sam and just a part of rural life. But a few years back, when there was a very real threat to me and mine, Phillip had insisted that I get certified for a concealed-carry permit and when I'd passed the written test, as well as the test at the firing range, he'd presented me with a handgun suitable for carrying in my shoulder bag—or in an ankle holster, should I prefer.

I'd practiced with this weapon and had taken great pride in my improving aim. Though what's needed with a handgun, according to Phillip, is not so much aim as resolve and a familiarity with the weapon. Two years ago I'd found myself in a position where I had used that weapon to protect myself. Ever since then, the ugly little snub-nosed .357 Magnum had been just another useful tool to keep around in case of need.

I sincerely hoped that this wasn't such a time but after Phillip's warning about the Eyebrow . . . My hand tightened around the pistol grip as an indistinct form seemed to coalesce back in the dim depths of the tree-shaded stones.

"Gloria? . . ." But even as I spoke the word, I could see that the woman in the shadows was not my sister.

No, this was a local countrywoman, by her looks—wiry, ageless. But she seemed to be in costume—white, all of it: the long skirt and loose blouse. There was a basket full of green stuff on her left arm and I wondered if there was a reenactment of some sort going on this weekend. She was picking leaves from some small plants growing at the base of one of the rocks and putting them in her basket. Suddenly aware of my gaze, she straightened and looked toward me.

"Good morning," I called to her. "I wonder if you've seen a small blond woman go by? She was—"

The woman in white's arm came up, pointing a long finger toward the clump of buildings in the distance. She didn't speak, however, and something about her blank gaze and motionless stance seemed odd—almost as if she were nothing more than a human signpost. Goose bumps lifted the hair on my forearms as a chill breeze, seemingly from the clump of trees and the rock itself, wafted through the car window.

But there was no time to puzzle over this wordless stranger. With a quick thank-you, I continued down the road.

It was too early for the spa to be open, so I followed the road around to the back and parked by the remains of the old bathhouse. It was a small, roofless shell of a building with gaping glassless windows and doorways blocked by wooden planking. Except for one, where the planking had been partially removed. There was no sign of Gloria, no sign of anyone. Stepping out of the car, I drew a deep breath, preparing to call her name, then stopped.

From within the bit of the building that was still

standing, I heard voices—low, murmuring, confidential. And one of them was my sister's.

I hesitated, torn between relief at having found her and annoyance that I'd been so worried. One of the other weekend Seekers must have had the same idea for an early morning walk and they'd decided to take a look at what was left of the old bathhouse. But it was time to get back.

"Gloria," I called at last, "how about a ride back to breakfast?"

The voices stopped and in a few moments Gloria appeared in the doorway, her turquoise tracksuit bright in the morning sun that had finally overtopped the nearby trees. Still carrying those hand weights, she stepped carefully around the barrier, blinking like a moviegoer emerging from an imaginary story into reality. She paused for a moment and then looked down at her wrist.

"What time is it anyway, Lizzy? My watch battery must have died." She motioned vaguely over her shoulder. "I got to talking to the most interesting woman in there . . . she knew all about the history of the place. I think she must be some kind of docent—she has on a long skirt and a white cap and a big white apron."

I frowned. "They do reenactments here sometimes. But surely someone would have mentioned it . . ." I stepped past Gloria to look into the interior of the old bathhouse. "Let's ask your friend what's up."

A quick glance revealed nothing but a small empty room, in the center of which was a long rectangular bath, half filled with murky water. The sunken tub's marble was stained and the floor—more marble?—surrounding it was cracked and uneven. In several places, accumulations of bird droppings hinted that the remaining rafters of the missing roof served as a night perch for birds of some kind.

Then a sudden shaft of light slanted through those rafters, hitting the water and illuminating it to a pale clouded green. I could see insects skittering over the top of the water and something seemed to move through the sunlight. For a brief moment, I had the eerie sensation of being just on the verge of—I don't know—maybe it was the verge of time. Instantly I could imagine this little room as it had been: a wooden chair, a stack of white Turkish towels, an enamelware basin, the gleaming marble tub, now brimful of clear water with wisps of rising steam on its surface.

No sooner had I registered this impression than it was gone. I was back amid the present dingy remains of past glory. The sunlight faded and I looked up to find that a cloud had moved to cover the sun.

"There's no one in there . . ." I began, turning back to Gloria. But she was in the car, carefully reapplying her lipstick with the help of the rearview mirror.

I looked again. No, there was no one. And no back way out of the roofless building. Unless I chose to believe that a woman in a long-skirted costume had somehow noiselessly climbed out . . .

Glory was still busy with the mirror, fluffing her hair now, and I made a quick circuit of the little building on foot, scanning the open area all around for any sign of the mysterious woman.

No sign. Unless the little scattering of fresh-picked leaves at the back of the building was a sign.

I peeked back into the old bathhouse just to make sure but, as I'd expected, there was no one to be seen.

"Hello?" I whispered, my voice echoing strangely above the marble tub. "Is anyone—"

"Lizzy!" The sharp sound of Gloria's voice made me jump and I turned to see her face at the car window. "I thought we needed to get back to breakfast. Who are you talking to, anyway?"

"Evidently, no one," I muttered as I climbed back into the car. "What happened to that woman in white? I don't see how . . ."

"Woman in white?" Gloria's brow wrinkled and she favored me with a long turquoise stare. "What are you talking about?"

Indeed.

I'd been there before—there on that misty boundary line between what is and what might be. For a person who prides herself on her rationality and who has, prior to giving in to Gloria, avoided all varieties of psychic exploration, I have to admit that there've been events . . . experiences . . . things I couldn't explain so I didn't try.

No more could I explain what had gone on in the two sessions yesterday. Apparently Xan had received messages from his brother via notes on the piano. I had heard the notes—and, I'm a little embarrassed to say, had lingered behind at the end of the session to look for hidden wires or something of the sort. Which I had not found.

And apparently Charlene had heard the voice of a departed friend—in her head. There had been some disappointments: No spirit had spoken through Giles, much less through any of the rest of us. But I had to admit . . . there had been something at work that I could in no way explain.

I started the car—we would just have time to grab some breakfast before the first session—and headed down the road toward the gate. As we passed the clump of trees and the odd rocks, I slowed but wasn't surprised to see no sign of the woman who had been there earlier.

"Glory, when you came by here this morning, did you notice anyone back in there?"

But Gloria wasn't listening to me. She was humming an odd little tune, simple and haunting and, I was pretty sure, not a number from one of her favorite Broadway shows. In a minor key, it had the feel of a mountain ballad to it. And I knew I'd heard it before . . . somewhere . . .

"What's that you're humming?" I asked.

She stopped abruptly. "That? Why . . ." Her face screwed up in concentration. "That's strange. I have no idea. It just popped into my head."

She hummed a few more bars. Unlike me, Glory can carry a tune rather nicely and as she continued on, I realized when and where I'd last heard it.

Almost eight years ago. I'd been in the kitchen, finishing up the Christmas baking when Sam had come in. There had been snowflakes on his Navy watch cap and he'd been grinning with delight.

"Listen to this, Liz," he'd said and had whistled a few plaintive bars. "Odus was playing it on his banjo when I stopped by this evening. I asked him what it was and he said it was 'one of them old love songs.' He sang some of it for me—all about a murdered man visiting his widow. But talk about a haunting tune—I can't get it out of my mind."

And we had laughed and hugged and planned to go back and get Odus to sing me the song. And Sam had whistled or hummed the melody till the girls had put their hands over their ears or turned up the radio to drown him out.

He'd been whistling it when he went out the door a few days later, on his way to meet an old Navy buddy and go flying in that buddy's little airplane.

The last time I ever saw my husband.

VII~Amarantha

May 12, 1887

"They want you at the bathhouse again," the house-keeper said when I come back to work the next day. "Selma's still down in the back—she sent word by one of her young uns that she can't hardly go. Mr. Roberts allowed as how you best count on taking her place today and all next week."

I had been dreading it, for my hands hadn't yet lost that queer ugly feeling that had come from Miss Theodora DeVine's white body. And after what I seen in the looking-glass pool, I knew that there was a doom hanging over her and over someone near her. But a body ain't always got a say in this life and I needed my job at the Mountain Park too bad to get choosy about whose back I rubbed.

When I looked at the list of my ladies for the day, though, Miss Theodora's name was scratched out and there was a Miss Cochrane wrote down instead. I was considerable relieved to see that she was an R—just here for rest.

Miss Cochrane was waiting for me when I got to the bathhouse and a more quizzy somebody you never did see. Where did I learn to do massage and how did I like doing it and what sort of folks had I worked on and where did I live and on and on till I was wore out with *answering. She had her a little notebook and she wrote down some of what I told her, saying she would be writing letters home and she liked to have things straight when she did.*

There was something about her that put me in mind of a bright-eyed little sparrow pecking all around for crumbs and I took to her right off. But there was something more, behind those green eyes . . .

I helped her with her clothes and took her to the tub. And all the time, them sparrow eyes was darting about, taking in everything there was to see.

"Amarantha," says she, "do you believe this water has ever cured anyone of anything?" and I couldn't stop myself from smiling.

"Well," said I, "it's cured several of being dry and cold."

She laughed like one thing at that but I hastened to say that I knowed it had made quite a few feel better for a time, at least, though I couldn't speak as to a lasting cure.

"And it ain't never harmed no one," I put in right quick. I was just as glad she'd left her little book back in the changing room for I wouldn't want my silly words used against me.

After she was safely in the tub, I went to the massage room and laid the things ready. The little bit I'd seen of Miss Cochrane had set me to wondering about her so I took up the small white enamel basin, poured it almost full of rubbing oil, and set it on the low table by the chair to where I could lean over it and take a look.

In some ways, oil is better than water for a seeing—of course, living water, like my little pool in the hollow of the rock, is what my granny swore by—though I've known her to use a mirror turned on its side, or a pan of ashes, or the blood from pig-killing time.

"Law, young un," I mind her saying, "anything'll

*work to get a seeing. The power's in the one what's
doing the seeing, everwhat they may use."*

I went to the door and peeked into the tub room but
Miss Cochrane was stretched out with her head back
and her eyes closed, looking like she was feeling mighty
good there in that steamy water. Leaving the door open
just a crack, in case that she might call, I went back and
set myself down at the little table with my elbows on
either side of the bowl and my face resting in my hands
where I could peer into the oil.

Used to be, it took some time for the pictures to come.
I would wait and wait and the least little thing would
pull my mind away—a fly buzzing, a worrisome
thought—but now it seems as if I can go to that place
between the worlds in no more than a few heartbeats'
time.

I let my eyes go foggy, looking without trying to see,
as you might say. At first there was just the shimmer on
the surface of the oil; then, as my breath hit it, lines and
patterns grew, one inside another and afore long the pictures begun to come. I seen Miss Cochrane, her dark
hair in a long braid down her back, astride a horse in the
midst of a gang of brown-faced men, all in white and all
wearing these great broad-brimmed straw hats. She
reined the horse around and lit out of there and the patterns changed and now, there she was, in her shift, it
looked like, with her hair all in a tangle, setting on a
wooden bench in a bare cold-looking room with some
of the sorriest-looking females you ever saw to either
side of her. It seemed like she was in a jail of some kind,
but whether this was a seeing of something already past
or of something yet to come, I couldn't tell.

I must of jostled the table for the pictures shifted and
I saw great boats, the like of which I have only seen in
some of the pictures on the walls here in the hotel. Great
boats and trains, there was Miss Cochrane again, in a

blue dress and carrying a hand satchel. And there were black men and strange long-necked beasts with great humped backs, and women with veils over their face, and more strange folks, and Miss Cochrane riding in a queer little two-wheeled cart pulled by a skinny little somebody and there was another great ship—

"Amarantha, I believe I'm sufficiently cooked."

Her voice was right at my ear and I jerked upright, pulled away from where I was wandering. She was standing there in her robe, head cocked to one side and studying my gazing bowl.

"I ask your pardon, ma'am," I said, all confused. "I didn't mean—"

She leaned closer, peering into the oil. Then she looked up at me, a sharp little glance like a hen that has spotted a likely bug, and clapped her hands together.

"You were fortune-telling, weren't you? Oh, what fun! I once knew a woman who could see all sorts of things in a bowl of water. Tell me, Amarantha, what do you see for me? The massage can wait—this is far more interesting. And I'll leave an extra-good tip, you may be sure."

With that, Miss Cochrane hopped right up on the table and set there cross-legged, just waiting for me to speak. I tried to pass it off and go on with the treatment as usual but she would have none of it. So I leaned back over the bowl.

Of course, I'd already seen aplenty that I could tell her. But I didn't want to let on that I'd been so curious about her, fearing she might take offense. I took my time and, sure enough, along come the pictures stronger than ever. It works that way sometime, that the pictures are clearer when the person they're about is nigh.

"I see you on a horse, in some far-off place," I told her. "And brown men with big straw hats . . ."

"Oh, but that must be Mexico," she said, "and that's

already happened. Tell me about the future—what lies ahead for me; can you do that, Amarantha?"

Well, I went on to tell of the other things I had seen: the big bare room with all the poor sad-looking women lined up on a bench and the great boats and all the trains and queer animals and folks I seen and all at once she jumped down off the table and threw her arms about me.

"Oh, Amarantha, you good witch, you! It hasn't happened yet but I promise I'll make sure it does."

Well, that was as queer a treatment session as ever I'd had. We just set and talked for what was left of the time and she asked could she come visit me at my home for she'd admire to see how a real mountain woman lived. She was so earnest and winning in her ways that at last I agreed and we set a time for Sunday evening. And when the hour was up, she give me a fifty-cent piece.

The next to come for treatment was Miss Dorothea DeVine, and though her chart had her down for an R, by the time she was on the table and under my hands, I knowed her for an N—weepy and wandering in her thoughts.

For a mercy, there wasn't that same deep-down ugly feeling that came off her sister. Though to look at they was as alike as two peas (except for the marking of the moles—Miss Dorothea didn't have that), my hands would have knowed one from the other at the first least touch.

This one was all wrought up about something. There was a trouble eating at her heart as bad as any cancer.

She lay there quiet as I worked on her back and legs, but when she had rolled over for me to tackle her arms, I seen they was tears, running out of the corners of her eyes and down her cheeks.

"Is the treatment paining you, ma'am?" I asked. "You must speak up if—"

"*Oh, no, it's fine; I'm just—*" And then for the first time she looked at me close.

"*You're Amarantha, aren't you?*" she asked, wiping her eyes with a corner of the sheet that was draping her. "*I didn't know you—*" and then the tears plumb busted loose.

"*Oh, Amarantha,*" cries she. "*I am so unhappy and . . . oh, whatever shall I do?*"

"*Excuse me, ma'am, I don't understand,*" said I, though my fingers had told me that it was the life she was leading that was eating at her, not any cancer. "*Is there some way I can help you?*"

She lay there still, the tears just streaming, and her lips pressed hard together.

"*Ma'am?*" I said again and reached to blot at her tears with a linen towel.

With that, she seemed to get herself in hand and, letting out a great sigh, she turned her head away from me. "*Thank you, Amarantha, I don't know what came over me. Female vapors, I suppose. Pray, continue with the massage.*"

Nellie Bly's Notes

Collected from various members (local residents) of the staff at the Mountain Park Hotel, Hot Springs, North Carolina, May 1887. Possible article?

Granny women in Appalachia (Note—correct pronunciation AP-A-LATCH-IA)

Scots-Irish—ties to Old Country—also some Cherokee influence?

Midwives, healers, can "dowse" for water

Belief in Little People (Leprechauns? Fairies?)—leave food for them

Haints—ghosts—"Haint blue" paint on a door will keep ghosts away

Ax under bed to cut pain of childbirth

Buckeye (horse chestnut) in pocket to ward off "rheumatiz"

According to those who know her, Amarantha can remove warts, cure "thrash," ease the pain of a burn, forecast weather, and tell your future by looking into a pool of water (or oil!).

Other granny women are said to use tea leaves, coffee grounds, a pan of dirt(!) for the same purpose. Cards, spiderwebs, clouds are also used for "getting a knowing."

I believe this woman is no charlatan—none here know that I am "Nellie Bly" and yet she described my ignominious departure from Mexico City . . . and her glimpse into the future gives me such hope for my Jules Verne stunt . . .

Chapter 21

Spirit Messages

Saturday, May 26

That odd little tune was stuck in her head, Gloria noticed, as she took her place for the Saturday morning session. So haunting and so familiar. Something that an old-fashioned music box might play . . .

Lizzy had already claimed her corner of the sofa but she no longer gave off that Lizzy-like impression of being an aloof and amused onlooker. Indeed, she had seemed to go into something of a trance at one point yesterday. At first Gloria had assumed that her sister was pretending—a subtle mockery to get back at her for insisting on this weekend. But it hadn't been an act; Gloria was certain of that now.

Giles was issuing the standard reminder about cellphones and bathroom visits—*done and done,* thought Gloria, eager to get on with the session. Perhaps it would be *her* turn this morning, her turn to name the spirit the group would call.

When she had broached the subject to Giles at breakfast, just to let him know that she was *prepared* but trying hard not to seem pushy, the medium had only smiled. He would know, he had said, when the spirits were ready to speak to her.

And now everyone was in place, taut with anticipation, and now Charlene was smudging the room again, intent upon her self-appointed duty, and now Giles was speaking to the group.

". . . a few of you have mentioned strange dreams and some . . . mmm . . . contacts . . . experienced since last night's session. It's a common enough phenomenon, the reason being that when one immerses oneself in the spirit world for any length of time, the veil between this plane and the next grows more . . . permeable. You may, indeed, have communication outside of these formal sessions. Take into consideration too that we are in an old house which may harbor resident spirits . . ."

Beside her, Gloria heard Elizabeth's sharp intake of breath. But when she turned, her sister's face was expressionless.

". . . In fact, I'm told there is a mischievous prankster at the inn who enjoys moving small objects about . . . so if your toothbrush ends up missing . . ."

A little ripple of amusement went round the group and Ree nodded. "I knew I hadn't left my glasses in the sink."

"That sounds like the work of a prankster, to be sure," Giles agreed. "And there may be another spirit on the premises, a mother, mourning a lost child . . ."

A *lost child.* The sleeping pain in the depths of Gloria's heart awakened, an old wound, never fully healed. But perhaps soon all that could be put right; perhaps the next spirit would speak to *her.* And she to it, at long last.

" . . . I know that those of you who haven't yet made contact with your particular chosen spirit are eager to do so. And there will be time, rest assured. But before we begin asking for a specific name, I'd like us to open ourselves to any spirits who, though they've not been called, may have messages for some among us."

Giles paused and frowned, as if deliberating. "How shall I explain it? It's a bit like putting out grain and seeds for the wild birds. You may wish only to attract the pretty songbirds but a swarm of rooks and pigeons will descend, frightening away the others. So we'll give any eager or importunate spirits out there a chance to be heard first. Otherwise, they could interfere with our attempts to communicate with the ones you have chosen. You see, gathered as we are . . ."

Oh, can't we just get going? Gloria had to bite her lips to keep from speaking the words aloud. *Please, I want my turn!*

Of course it wouldn't do, and she controlled herself as Giles went on at some length about the group dynamic and misdirected energy and restless spirits. But at last he was done.

Once again they all took hands and closed their eyes. This time, however, rather than concentrating on a name, they were asked to "think of a mirror, reflecting nothing. Try to hold that thought in your mind," Giles urged them, "making it a blank slate on which the spirits may write their messages . . ."

Minutes passed in the darkened room. Heavy breathing . . . a discreet cough . . . that repetitive little sniff from Dawn.

Really, if she'd just blow her nose, thought Gloria, abandoning for the moment her concentration on the nonreflecting mirror. *Isn't this taking a lot longer than the last time? Maybe there aren't any messages for anyone here and we can . . .*

And suddenly Dawn was giggling. It welled up and overflowed—a fountain of pure amusement. Gloria opened her eyes to see that all heads were turned toward the young woman whose shoulders were shaking as peals of mirth poured from her. Steve's mouth gaped open and she shot a questioning look at Giles who shook his head and put a finger to his lips.

"It's just *too* funny," Dawn gasped, between bursts of laughter. "She—Aunt Somebody—the prankster you

were telling us about—says she's torn out the last pages
of Sandy's mystery novel and hidden them somewhere in
Sandy's room. She won't stop laughing."

Giles addressed the prankster spirit, asking if she had
any message for anyone. There was a pause in Dawn's
laughter. "She says . . . Sandy should look in the fireplace . . . and she says . . . that it's the husband who's
trying to kill the wife."

Is that a message for me? Gloria leaned forward to
catch Dawn's next words but there were none. The
laughter stopped and Dawn's head drooped.

"I believe our prankster has moved on," Giles told
them. "Let her go and once more concentrate on the
mirror reflecting nothing . . . the empty slate. There may
be others waiting to speak."

Again the room fell silent except for the sound of quiet
breathing and muted rustlings as the group resumed its
vigil. Moments ticked by . . . endless moments . . .

There seemed to be a humming . . . so faint that Gloria dismissed it, at first, as a ringing in her ears. But then
she felt Elizabeth's hand jerk convulsively and heard her
utter a tiny squeak of exclamation. And then the humming became louder and with a jolt like a mild electric
shock, she realized that it was the same odd little tune
she'd had in her mind earlier.

And now Giles was speaking in his usual quiet tones,
sounding like a cautious fisherman who feels a nibble
at the end of his line. "Hello . . . I believe we have someone . . . Is there a message for one of us?"

The humming grew louder, no longer haunting and
lovely but fierce . . . grating . . . frightening in its intensity.

Then, abruptly, it stopped.

Gloria felt Elizabeth pull her hand free. Opening her
eyes, she was startled to see her sister, hands over her
face, slowly shaking her head as if refusing something.

Reaching out a tentative hand to her sister's shoulder, Gloria hissed, "Lizzy! What are you—"

Giles stopped her with a quiet "She's fine. Please, don't distract her. I believe she's receiving a message."

The whole group watched in tense silence as Elizabeth continued to shake her head. Then she grew still. She was breathing heavily, as if she'd been running . . . or engaged in some mighty struggle.

Alarmed at her sister's actions, Gloria turned and looked at Giles, her eyes wide with apprehension. He returned her gaze and, making a downward gesture with his hand, mouthed the word *Wait*.

They all waited, watching Elizabeth, who remained motionless, her face hidden. Then, just as the silence was about to be unbearable, Giles spoke.

"Elizabeth."

Dropping her hands, Elizabeth lifted her head. The pupils of her eyes were huge, almost eclipsing the blue, and she stared unseeing across the room.

"Elizabeth . . . please share your message with the group." Giles's voice was gentle but he obviously expected compliance.

There was a long hesitation and then Elizabeth blinked. Her eyes returned to normal as she straightened and turned toward the medium. "I'm sorry—there was no message for any of you. Nothing." Her unwavering blue gaze forbade further inquiry.

Gloria felt a little shiver run over her body. She was sure that Lizzy *had* received a message of some sort. And she was equally sure that her sister would not be sharing.

Elizabeth and Giles stared at one another. Finally Giles spoke.

"Very well. We'll move along to give some others a go. We'll begin with . . ." He closed his eyes, as if musing over a choice, and Gloria could contain herself no longer.

"Please, if I could just talk to my baby. They said I couldn't keep it, that there was a nice family who wanted to adopt; and then they said it died . . ."

She knew that she was perilously close to sobbing. She had already said far more than was necessary but the wall of secrecy, built up so many years ago, was crumbling and she was helpless to stop it. Her words flowed out in a great tumbling stream.

"They gave me anesthesia and when I woke up, they said that my baby had died. They never let me see it . . . They wouldn't even tell me if it was a boy or a girl . . . I thought I heard it cry but they said it was the anesthetic that made me dream that . . . Please, if I could just tell my baby how sorry . . . I couldn't help it. My mother . . . She didn't want it even to be born . . . She wouldn't let me keep it . . . I wasn't strong enough to fight her . . . All I know about my baby is its birthday, July 28, 1973 . . . I have it engraved on this locket. I named him . . . her . . . Dana."

Gloria was aware of disapproving looks from some of the circle, as well as pitying glances from others. Joss was frowning, fiddling with the bandages on his head. He opened his mouth as if about to say something then closed it again without speaking. Giles's expression remained neutral, noncommunicative, and she plunged ahead, all the years of pent-up sorrow distilled into a single entreaty.

"Please . . . is my baby there?"

She heard those last words striking against the silence like tiny mallets on a silver bell and it seemed to her that plaintive syllables hung reverberating in the air. A sudden vibration went round the circle of clasped hands and there was a startled gasp from one of the Seekers.

Across the table the medium let out a low moan. In

the darkness of the room, all that could be seen of Giles of Glastonbury was the vaguest outlines of his face. The medium's head rolled from side to side as a confusion of sounds issued from his parted lips. Then, all at once, his head drooped forward.

Gloria sat rigid, unmoving as a tiny surge of current went tingling through the locked hands of the circle. A breath of air stirred above her head and a silvery chime sounded once.

Then, from somewhere . . . from everywhere . . . came a hesitant voice.

Mama?

Chapter 22

Seekers

Saturday, May 26

"Mama?"

I blinked my eyes in utter confusion. Joss was on his feet and staring at Gloria. He had pulled free of the circle, leaving Len and Giles with empty outstretched hands. Suddenly the medium slumped back in the wing chair as if in a faint, and a murmur of voices ran round the room. Ignoring the obvious consternation of the group, Joss appealed directly to Gloria.

"This is . . . I have to talk to you . . . now! It's very important . . . the most important thing in the world!" Joss cried, staring at my sister with such hungry intensity that the other members of the group, some of whom had been trying to make him sit back down, grew silent.

Gloria, like all the rest of us, was dumbfounded at this outburst. As for me, I was still trying to get my bearings—to sort out the experience that had left my thoughts swirling in confusion. But whatever had happened to me just before Gloria began to call for her baby (if I was prepared to believe it *had* happened and wasn't some midlife hallucination brought on by suggestion and a close atmosphere) had to be forgotten for the moment.

"You need to get out of here now!" Charlene was on

her feet and tugging at Joss's arm. "Somebody help me!" She looked around the group as Joss refused to move but continued to stare at my sister.

"Listen, people," Charlene implored, "Giles is in trance. This interruption is draining all his energy—it could be dangerous if it goes on." She continued to tug and now Len was on his feet, catching hold of Joss's other arm. As he and Charlene began to propel Joss toward the door, Gloria stood.

"That's all right. Let go of him. Joss and I will go outside and have a talk, won't we, Joss?"

A few steps and she was at his side, taking his hand. Charlene and Len hesitated and then released their hold on Joss, who allowed Gloria to lead him in meek silence from the room.

Still stunned, I watched them go. Minutes ticked by and Giles began to revive. The circle of Seekers reformed, but moved at last by a deep irrational feeling of something wrong, that warning bell that insists on being heeded, I excused myself and hurried after my sister and Joss.

They were sitting at one of the tables on the porch, talking quietly. I don't know just what I'd expected— Joss seemed more or less loony but not especially violent. I couldn't understand, though, why Gloria had walked out of the séance just when she was on the brink of making this long-hoped-for contact with the child she'd never seen.

She looked up as I came out the front door and smiled. Her face was radiant—smooth and serene with a look that made me think of some potent female saint or perhaps the joyous earth mother of an older religion.

"Come sit with us, Elizabeth." She beckoned to me and I saw that she had the chain of the little heart locket wrapped around her hand.

Joss was sitting opposite her at the round table watching her with that same hungry intensity as I slid into the chair between them.

"So," I said, with a total lack of originality, "what's all this then?"

Gloria favored me with a saintly smile. It became her but I found it unsettling.

"Joss was just starting to tell me something that . . . Well, you'll have to hear it for yourself, Lizzy. Joss, would you start over? You said that you're a friend of Nigel's—remember, Lizzy? The stylist I went to in Asheville . . ."

The story Joss told was—well, I'd call it unbelievable but for one thing.

Glory believed it. Or desperately wanted to. From the minute Joss began the improbable tale, I could see the depth of her longing to accept it as true.

Joss was quivering with pent-up excitement, one leg jigging up and down and his fingers beating a nervous tattoo on the table as he began his story.

"Okay. So, I moved to Asheville about six months ago—I'm studying massage therapy and waiting tables at a place in Biltmore Village. I met Nigel at a party back in February and he was doing these intuitive readings. He put his hands on my head and right away told me that I was searching for someone very important to me—someone I hadn't seen in a very long time."

He turned his dark eyes on Gloria and I felt a chill at the intimacy of the shared gaze.

"Excuse me," I said, "but I thought that Nigel was a hairstylist. What—"

"Oh, Nigel's a psychic too," Gloria hastened to explain. "He told me that he'd always been gifted that way and when he worked on people's hair, he often got very strong impressions—"

Joss ignored my interruption and continued, his eyes

still fixed on my sister. "I told him I'd been searching for my mother ever since I learned that I was adopted, but that none of the databases could tell me anything. I'd begun to believe that maybe she really *had* died when I was born. That was the story my adoptive parents had always told me—they may have even believed it."

For a moment the young man seemed to be struggling for words. A troubled expression flitted across his face.

"Nigel and I got to be friends—he thinks we knew each other before—in a previous life, I mean. He's been really good for me, helping me understand who I am . . . and he's the one who suggested I come for this weekend."

Joss wrinkled his brow and reached up to adjust his bandage. "I think that's right. I think it was Nigel who said something about finding my mother . . . but since the accident, my memory is kind of messed up."

"I'd been wondering about the bandages," I said, wondering even harder where all this was leading.

"A car knocked me down when I was crossing the street," he explained. "I was lucky it wasn't worse— that's what they said. And my memory *is* coming back. It's just sometimes, there are two different memories . . ."

He looked at Gloria and a sweet smile spread over his face. "But that's not important anymore. All my important memories begin today, don't they?"

His smile widened. "I need to call Nigel right now and tell him what's happened—that his reading was right. He'll . . ."

Joss's voice trailed off and he stood, reaching for the cellphone on his belt. "I owe it all to Nigel . . . I have to call him right away . . ."

"Gloria, do you believe all that stuff Joss was saying?"

My sister and I were soaking in one of the hot tubs at

the spa, preparatory to going for our massages and whatever other treatments she had signed us up for. Though I hadn't been especially eager for the spa experience, I was glad that this previous appointment had cut short the increasingly emotion-charged conversation that Gloria and Joss had fallen into. And so, I think, was she.

Our tub was outdoors—tucked away amid the trees and close enough to the creek that its soothing murmur was an additional pleasure. Birdsong—sunlight glinting through leaves—an idyllic spot. For a brief, selfish instant, I wished that it was Phillip sharing this moment rather than Gloria.

"Do I believe that Joss is the child they told me was dead?" Gloria was stretched out in the gently steaming water, her head resting on the edge of the blue fiberglass tub, her eyes closed. She looked drained, as if she'd just completed some tiring journey.

Letting out a deep sigh, she opened her eyes. "Lizzy, I don't know what to think. I would love to believe it. And I did, for a moment or two."

She trailed her hands through the water, rippling the surface. "Back there, during the séance, when I heard the word 'Mama,' my body responded. Do you remember how just the sound of your baby crying would make the milk come in? I didn't nurse Ben long—it was just so inconvenient—but even after my milk had dried up, whenever he cried, suddenly my breasts would feel full . . ."

A tear appeared and slid slowly down her cheek. "And that's what happened when Joss called to me; it was like I was in a dream, a dream I've had over and over—except that in the dream, the baby I called Dana is a girl."

"Oh, Glory . . ." I pulled myself around to her side

of the hot tub and put my arms around her. My little sister . . .

I held her tight, without saying more. Then, after a long moment, "Listen," I said, "let's keep an open mind about this Joss. There are ways of finding out if he's who he says he is."

"I know that." Gloria put her hands to her face. "I've already been thinking of who I might call. But . . ." She gulped, regained her composure, and began again. "But maybe I'd rather just believe he *is* my lost child."

I kept my arms around her and tried to make sense of the situation.

"I hope that he is, Glory. But let's go slow here. He says he was adopted at birth by folks who live near New Bern. Just think how many adoptions there are every day. And he says that his birthday is the same as your baby's but he couldn't even show you a driver's license to confirm the birth date. That's awfully convenient."

It had been the first thing I'd thought of. If Joss's birth date was the same as the date Gloria's lost baby was born—well, it wouldn't prove a thing. But it would be a place we could begin.

Or so it had seemed to me. Joss, however, had shrugged his shoulders and explained, all too glibly, that the doctor who'd treated him for concussion after the car crash had warned him against driving until a return visit showed that it would be safe.

"I had a couple of blackouts—that was the problem— so I gave my license to a friend to hold for me so I wouldn't be tempted to drive. Back in Asheville, I can ride my bike to class and to work. It's no big deal," he had said.

Hmm. As Ben would say, the story about the license sounded seriously sketchy. And then there was this Nigel thing. I knew that many women saw their hairstyl-

ists as a combination confessor/girlfriend/shrink and
were likely to—

"Glory," I asked, "did you talk to Nigel about
the child? You're a very wealthy woman and it's just
possible—"

Gloria stiffened in my arms.

"You have such a suspicious nature, Lizzy! How
would Nigel or Joss know anything at all about my fi-
nancial situation?"

She stood and pulled herself out of the hot tub. "We
need to go back to the spa. It's almost one-thirty and the
Head to Toe I've signed us up for takes over an hour."

This conversation is over was the message.

A full-body exfoliation had sounded to me like a dire
medical condition, but I had to admit that being gently
scrubbed with a combination of Dead Sea salts and essential oils felt rather nice, though the warm herbal
wraps that followed—lengths of some stretchy fabric
saturated with more oils and herbs and wrapped around
my arms, legs, and torso, and then the whole of me covered in a thermal blanket—had me feeling like a pam-
pered burrito.

At least my body felt like a burrito. Just now my face
was receiving a hydrating treatment. Various liquids
were patted on and massaged in and wiped off. There
was warm stuff and cool stuff and cucumber slices over
my eyes and something that smelled like honey and almonds and something that tingled and something that
smelled minty.

"You want salad with that burrito?" I mumbled to
myself.

"Isn't this heavenly, Lizzy?" On the table next to
mine, my sister was receiving the same full-body treatment. She had booked us into a "couples" room so we
could enjoy the experience together but the presence of

the two busy massage therapists meant that we wouldn't be having any awkward conversations about supposed long-lost children.

"It's very . . . different," I answered, trying to put some enthusiasm into my reply. "I feel . . . very . . . relaxed . . . and clean."

Actually, that wasn't the whole truth. I'm not keen on having a stranger putting hands on me. I also felt a touch claustrophobic, firmly wrapped up and weighed down by the heavy thermal blanket as I was. It was a lot like being at the gynecologist's, where odd things are done to your body and, because you know it's in your best interest, you just breathe deep and put up with it rather than run screaming down the hall. It amazed me that people paid for this. But obviously, I was in a minority here.

Swan, the masseuse who'd been working on Gloria, spoke. "We're going to take a break before beginning the massage. You two just relax and let your bodies absorb the hydration. We'll be back in about twenty minutes."

I could hear the soft click of the door shutting behind the two women. The clean, glorious sound of a Bach cello suite filled the room, replacing the syrupy-swoony New Age/space music that had been playing.

Now was my chance. "Glory," I began, ready to tackle the subject of Joss again, "don't you think—"

"I don't want to think right now, Lizzy. This time is supposed to be for ultimate relaxation. I'm just going to drift away for a bit and so should you. It'll clear our minds. I promise we'll have a serious discussion later."

There was a yawn and a profound exhalation, then deep, regular breathing. My sister and I are both good at avoiding things, I thought as I pushed aside the memory of the humming and the voice that had been in my head during the séance. *Not now,* I told myself and allowed the music to sweep through me, the sobbing of the cello—Yo-Yo Ma?—like mental floss through my ears, sweeping my brain clear of all thoughts.

Buried alive—the grave clothes and the winding sheet clammy with underground ooze; the coins cold on my eyes. Bleak silence but for a slow dripping of some liquid. And the smell, not of the tomb but of honey and almonds and the herbs of the embalmers.

I twisted from side to side, trying to free myself from the grave and the darkness and the dream. The cucumber slices fell from my eyes and I was awake again, struggling to throw off the thermal blanket that had lost its heat and to divest myself of the mummy wrappings that had grown chill and slimy-feeling.

Turning my head, I saw that the other massage table was empty.

"Glory?" I spoke loud enough for her to hear me if she was in the little bathroom that adjoined this room.

No answer. The cello sang on.

Moving awkwardly in the oily wrappings, I sat up and called again, louder this time. "GLORY?"

Still no response. Surely the therapists on the other side of the door should have heard me. Grumbling to myself, I slipped off the table, draped a sheet around my partially wrapped body, and padded to the door.

Which was locked.

Chapter 23

In the Dark

Saturday, May 26

I grabbed the doorknob and gave it another savage twist but the door remained obstinately shut. Why in the world would it be locked? That had to be a violation of the fire code, at least. The claustrophobia began to inch its way back into my brain . . .

I gave the unyielding door a few stern raps. There must be an explanation for this.

"Kimberly? . . . Swan? . . . Hello? . . ."

No answer and my knocking became pounding. In the distance I could hear footsteps hurrying toward me and I pulled the sheet a little closer. A key rattled in the lock.

"What's going on? Where are the therapists?"

The manager, a sandy-haired woman who'd been behind the front desk when we checked in for our treatment, scanned the room as if expecting to find the missing Kimberly and Swan hiding under the massage tables. She shot a concerned glance at me. "Are you all right? Can I get you some water? Maybe you'd better sit down and—"

"I'm fine," I assured her, "but where's my sister?"

Again there was the sound of hurrying feet and Kimberly and Swan appeared in the doorway, disheveled and out of breath.

"Oh, my god, I'm so sorry, Ms. Goodweather. We—"

"Kimberly, this is completely unacceptable!" The manager's eyes narrowed. "Why was this room locked and where have you been and where is the other client?" Putting her hands on her hips, she waited for an answer.

"*We* certainly didn't lock the door. And we were down the hall in the break room." Swan was sputtering with righteous indignation as she tried to explain. "We were there for fifteen minutes and when we started to come back—"

"We couldn't get out! We were locked in too." Kimberly overrode her friend's words. "Or at least, someone had jammed one of those big supply carts in the doorway and we couldn't get past it. We ended up crawling out the window. When we were coming around the building to the door, I saw the linens truck driving off. I suppose it could have been them—the driver's kind of a practical joker . . . but where's Swan's client? Where's Gloria?"

We all looked at one another. Swan ducked into the bathroom and came back shaking her head. "Her clothes are still here. So are the robes. She can't have gone far wearing just wrappings."

Everyone snickered except me. Not only was I aware of how unlikely it was that my fastidious sister would be rambling around covered only by a few greasy strips of cloth, I was also aware that Gloria had a stalker. The Eyebrow. If he knew she was here and had somehow— And what about the other one, her buddy, the plastic surgeon—the one Phillip had told me about last night? Could he have—

"I need to make a call right away." I turned to head for the bathroom where my clothes and purse were waiting.

"You can use the desk phone. Sometimes cell reception is a little spotty here." The manager was holding out a robe for me so I backed into it, dropped my sheet, and peeled off those of my mummy wrappings that hadn't already dropped off.

The manager rattled off commands. "Swan. Check all the rooms—bathrooms too. Kimberly, you have a look outside. I'll call down to the hot tubs, just in case."

We were moving down the hall toward the front desk. I noticed that, in spite of that uneven reception, the manager was thumbing her BlackBerry. I figured she was hoping to find Gloria at the hot tubs before I called the law.

Which was, of course, what I intended to do. Phillip. He would know the quickest way to get things rolling. If I couldn't get him, I'd call the local police. But I had a feeling it would take a while to get their attention—and could already hear them telling me that they couldn't file a missing person report when an adult had been missing for less than an hour.

I was ushered behind the front desk by the manager who was still tapping away at her BlackBerry and frowning at whatever message she was or wasn't receiving. She pointed out the phone and mashed the button for an outside line, then moved a bit away—almost but not quite out of earshot. This was undoubtedly looking like a publicity disaster in the making for the spa and I sympathized with her.

Nonetheless, I wiped my oily hands on the fluffy robe and reached for the phone. I had just punched in the first three digits when the front door of the spa flew open to reveal a wild-eyed, sweating Joss.

"Have you found her?" he gasped and bent over, hands on his knees, struggling to catch his breath. The bandage on his head had slipped and was almost covering one eye, giving him the look of a demented pirate. "Nigel had a message . . ."

I put the phone down.

"Joss, how did you know Gloria was missing? What does Nigel have to do—"

He waved off my questions. "Later, just tell me, is she missing?"

"Yes, but—"

"Is there a cellar or some sort of underground storage around here?" This was addressed to the manager, who had dropped her BlackBerry and was staring open-mouthed at Joss. "Nigel said underground. In a box of some sort."

A chill ran over me. The dream I'd had back in the treatment room, the dream of waking in the tomb, buried alive—I reached out and grabbed the manager's arm.

"Please, just tell us—is there a place like that?"

She looked at me as if I were as crazed as Joss appeared to be. "The spa was built over part of the old hotel's basement. But we don't use it at all. It's too damp part of the year for storage and they only put stairs to it because there's some equipment from the old bathhouse rotting away down there. The owners think they'll eventually haul it out and use it for a display of some kind. But—"

"Please, just show us the stairs—*now*."

I was begging—and yanking none too gently at her arm.

"Okay, but I sure don't see . . ." Shaking her head at the strangeness of this whole affair, the manager led Joss and me back down the hall and into a large storage room at the rear of the building. I noticed that Joss's slight limp had become more pronounced, due, I assumed, to his having run all the way over from the inn.

"The door's behind that supply cart." The manager pointed to a tall, multishelved affair on wheels. Stacks of towels and robes, as well as paper supplies and trays of various bottles and jars obscured whatever was behind the cart but as Joss pushed it aside, a wide white-painted plywood door was revealed.

"But this door is always locked—only the owners have keys." The puzzled manager pointed at the cheap padlock hanging open from the hasp. "I don't understand . . ."

"She's down there—just like Nigel said!" Joss snatched off the lock. The flimsy door opened easily and a dank earthy smell oozed out into the room along with an unseasonal chill.

The stairs that led down into the gloom were of recent construction, I was happy to see. Unpainted treated lumber, dusty but sturdy.

"Wait." I grabbed Joss by the shoulder. "We're going to need some light. And we need to stay off of *that*."

There in the dust of the top steps I could see footprints—going down *and,* I was happy to note, coming up. While the manager was fetching some flashlights, I slid a tray of tiny brown bottles off the supply cart. One by one I placed the bottles on a nearby table, then turned the empty tray upside down and set it gently over one of the clearer prints.

"Let's just be careful not to step on the tray, all right, Joss? It could be important." As I spoke, I couldn't help glancing down at his shoes: pretty much standard running shoes, the kind that would have a characteristic tread. The prints on the stair, I thought, had been made by a shoe with a smoother sole—but a shoe of the same size.

As we waited for the flashlights, it occurred to me that the robe I had belted around my naked self was not exactly the best garb for descending steep stairs and exploring a long-unused cellar. It also occurred to me that it would be nice to have my gun.

With a word to Joss, I hurried back to the little room where I'd left my clothes. Throwing off the robe, I pulled on jeans and shirt over my exceedingly well-hydrated body. I didn't bother with underwear but shoved my feet into my sneakers, grabbed the little snub-nosed revolver out of my shoulder bag, and clipped its holster to my waistband. The loose shirt would cover it and I would be happier knowing that it was there, even if the leaver of the footprints was long gone. And that made me think of the laundry truck one of the therapists had mentioned.

As I came through the door to the hallway, I almost collided with the manager, who was hurrying back to the storage room.

"These are all I could find." She thrust two flashlights at me—one, a Maglite, heavy and black—of the type cops carry—and a smaller headlamp contraption with a maze of elastic bands. "Listen, I've got people checking in at the desk I have to deal with. I can't imagine you're going to find anything down in that old cellar but you might as well have a look. Swan and Kimberly are searching the grounds for Mrs. Hawkins and I'll call the Mountain Magnolia to see if, for some reason, she went back over there."

Mrs. Hawkins. I'd forgotten about Gloria's alias and something must have shown on my face for the manager put her head on one side. "Tell me, Ms. Goodweather, is your sister mentally unstable? Because if—"

Just then a bell rang up front and with a hasty warning to be careful on the stairs, she hurried back to the reception area.

Though my clothing change had taken less than five minutes, Joss was almost frantic. He had gone partway down the stairs but, realizing that he really couldn't see anything, had been forced to wait. He reached out and grabbed the Maglite from my hands.

"I called her name but didn't get any response. Maybe . . ."

But the maybes were too many and too unpleasant to

contemplate. He turned back to make a hurried descent into the old cellar.

Okay, I thought, hesitating before following him, *is this one of those Too Stupid to Live scenarios? Down into the dark basement with this admittedly strange young man in search of my sister—*

My sister. Those two words trumped the hesitation and the better judgment. If she was down there, I wanted to be part of the search. And, as the slightly uncomfortable lump at my waist reminded me, I was armed. Possibly even dangerous.

Pulling the headlamp onto my head, I realized what a stroke of luck it was that both my hands would be free for my gun. I took it from the holster and, holding it pointed carefully skyward, started down the steps.

Below me I could see the beam of Joss's light, dodging crazily around, illuminating a series of brick pillars, assorted barrels and boxes, and more dusty spiderwebs than seemed possible.

"Joss? How big is this place? Have—"

"There's another room back here." His voice sounded nearby but I could no longer see the beam of his flashlight, just a dim glow beyond another row of pillars. "Look down. You can see kind of a trail in the dust. That's what I'm following. If she's here . . ."

He was right. The floor was hard compacted clay but it was overlain with a thick layer of dust, just like all those boxes and barrels on either side of me. Keeping my headlamp trained on the trail, just barely discernible as a slight disturbance in the dust, I moved toward the pale light of the room beyond, then slowed to examine my surroundings for any traces of recent disturbance.

The ceiling was plywood subflooring laid atop new treated-timber joists. I could hear the muffled sound of footsteps coming and going above me, as well as the rush of water in the PVC pipe just above my head. That was today's world, up there. Down here was from another age. The brick pillars and arches, upon which had rested the grand old hotel, now supported nothing. The framework of the new building floated a foot or more above them, resting on a few utilitarian-looking concrete block columns—ugly behemoths but far stronger than the elegant brick.

As I moved deeper into the cellar, boxes and barrels gave way to strange machinelike things ranged on either side of this path in the dust. Draped in spiderwebs, they looked like medieval instruments of torture but I suspected they were nothing more than a previous century's Bowflexes and StairMasters. A clutch of dumbbells heaped to one side confirmed this suspicion.

A scurrying sound behind me made me whirl around, just in time to see a rat's bare tail disappearing under a stack of penitential-looking stools, and I shivered involuntarily.

"Over here!"

There was a thump and a clatter in the area ahead and I came around a corner just in time to see Joss lift the lid on an odd slant-topped box. The beam of his flashlight jittered on the ceiling and not until I was at his side could I see what was in the box.

At first it looked like nothing more than a pile of dirty towels but as Joss held the lid open wide, I saw that it was a body, wrapped in one of the thermal blankets, a baglike thing on its head. One limp hand was exposed, its fingers filthy but the elegant French manicure still recognizable.

Gloria. My sister.

VIII~*Amarantha*

Cripple Tree Holler~May 15, 1887

Miss Cochrane come, like she had said she would, just after dinnertime on Sunday. She was astride one of the hotel hacks, and no one with her, which let me know that she must be a good rider and a powerful good talker too, as Mr. Jameson who runs the stable mostly don't let ladies take out his nags on their own.

I was setting in my loom out at the end of the porch, working at a coverlid, but when I heard the clip-clop of hooves, I stood up and moved to a mule-ear chair and let on to be doing nothing. There's some folks mightily offended at the notion of weaving or any kind of work of a Sunday—I doubt that Miss Cochrane is like that but still . . .

As the long nose of the sorrel mare peeped around the big laurel bush where the trail comes in front of my cabin, I stood and threw up my hand. "Howdy," says I. "Light and come in the house."

When she gets down from the tall mare, I see that she has on a skirt that is divided in two—like britches but so loose that it looks like a skirt when she stands still. And it don't come down but to the top of her pretty high-polished boots and I think that in a rig like that, a woman could do herself justice atop a horse. I never kept nare horse—just a mule for plowing and cultivating—

and when I have rode, it's been astride and hanging on to the gears. Those fine ladies at the hotel, with their long skirts dragging as they try to stick on to one of them sidesaddles, have a time of it on our steep mountain trails.

"You see I found you, Amarantha," Miss Cochrane hollers as she hitches her mount to the post under the big beeches. "Your directions were perfect!"

"Come up and set," I say, setting out a chair for her.

She comes up the steps, them little sparrow eyes taking in everything, from the loom to the mule shoe above the door and the old boot I have nailed up to give the jenny wrens a place to make their nestes.

"Tell me what you're weaving here," she says, putting her head to one side. "And did you spin the wool yourself? I saw some sheep down in the meadow on the way up here."

I told her that I had my granny's old spinning wheel and I liked to spin of a winter. And I do, for spinning is one of those things that frees up your mind to where you can step to the other side and take a look. Oh, I've learned many a thing whilst I was a-spinning.

She leans over the web and studies the half-finished coverlid, then she catches sight of my draft that is embroidered on a piece of homespun and hanging from the crosspiece of the loom.

"What's this?" says she, looking more like a little bird than ever, and I tell her it is the rule I follow to make this pattern. "It tells me when to tromp," says I and then nothing will do but that I sit myself back in the loom and weave a piece to show her the way of it.

The pattern that I am making is called Wheels of Time and it has a white chain and white and indigo-dyed filling. Miss Cochrane marvels over it for a piece then asks was I making it to sell and I say, no, it's for my bed.

I wait to see will she try to buy it offen me like fur-riners generally does but she just nods and say that was she to make such a pretty thing, she'd not be wanting to part with it neither.

"What other sorts of things do you weave?" she asks me and I tell her about making jeans cloth and linsey and show her that my dress is of my own weaving.

I can see her eyes going to the door and I know that she is wishful of seeing the inside of my house. She don't want to ask but her face shows that she is eat up with wanting to know how I live.

"Would you like to see some more of my weaving?" I ask her. "There is a red and green coverlid on my bed and I have some other—"

"Oh, could I, Amarantha?" says she, clasping her hands together at her breast. "I'd love to see it."

So we make for the door and she is about to step through when she catches sight of the mule shoe that sets above the doorframe.

"I've seen that done before," says she. "Is the horse-shoe for good luck?"

"I reckon—it's been there all my life. The old people always did that—they said the open end must be up, to keep the luck from running out."

She studies it some more, them sharp eyes of hern taking it all in. "I wonder," she asks, "why they didn't use a shiny new one? This one's all rusted and worn so thin . . . wouldn't a brand-new one be better luck?"

"No, a new one ain't no use at all. The shoe's a charm to keep off mean witches of a night—the old folks used to say that a witch couldn't pass under the iron shoe un-less she first went and traced every step that shoe had taken. And if she couldn't do it before morning light, it'd be to do all over again the next night. So folks just naturally wanted an old worn-out shoe—one that had taken many a step."

She looks at me like she wants to ask another question. But instead she nods and steps into the house.

It ain't but the one big room and a loft upstairs. My bedstead is over in the corner and she makes for it at once.

"Oh, how perfectly lovely! Did you make this coverlet too?"

"It was my granny wove this one. She was a powerful weaver—it was her learned me how and it's her drafts I follow. Them drafts was writ on paper and all faded and nigh falling to pieces, which is when I decided to embroider them onto homespun so's they'd last my time."

"Does this pattern have a name?" she asks and I see that she is taking everything in and storing each word away.

"Granny called this one Bonaparte's March—he was some king or such over the water, who lost a war."

She wants to know about the dyes I use and how long it takes to spin the wool for a coverlid and all manner of things. Then she begins to look about the room.

There ain't much to see. No fine furniture, just what could be made by a man with an ax and a drawknife. A table and a pair of benches, three mule-ear chairs, and a stool. There's a big wooden chest where I keep my blankets and such, a corner cupboard for my few plates and bowls, and a dry sink. I figure that it must appear mean and low to her, after all the fancy fixings at the hotel, but she is looking all round and smiling as though she likes what she is seeing.

"I've never been inside a real log cabin," she says, wondering like. "How old is your house?"

I study on that for a time. "I couldn't rightly say," I tell her at last. "My people come into this country a good while back—not so long after the War for Independence. At one time, they owned a right smart of land *but most of it went, one way or t'other. I have the heart of it though. They's been a house on this piece of land as long as anyone can remember, though the first several burned down. The chimbley is the same though—you see there on that flat rock where the old people marked the date."*

She steps up close to the fireplace and runs a finger over the numbers. "1787!" says she, just a-marveling. "Your people have been here a hundred years—that's astonishing! Nowadays people move around so much— why, even my own family—"

And she falls silent and I can feel the dark unhappiness in her heart as she looks back to those times. Then she gives a little shake.

"And you live here all by yourself and you're not afraid?" she asks.

"Not a bit of it," I tell her. "I'm on good terms with all my neighbors—two- and four-legged alike."

She stands there staring into the cold ashes of the fireplace. There is something more she wants to say but she is having trouble getting it out so I ask will she take a sup of buttermilk or water. She asks for water and I step out to the springhouse to get some with the chill yet on it. When I come back in, she is looking at my charm papers that are tacked there on the log wall above the fireboard.

"I was just noticing all these names and dates," she begins and her face goes pink. "I'm terribly nosy—it seems I was born so."

It kindly tickles me to see her so bashful and I think to fun her a bit.

"Read 'em off," says I, "and tell me what you make of it."

She stands on tiptoe to peer at them and reads off, "Lovie Whiteside, August 4, '86, February 21, '87; Belle

Johnston, July 26, '86, April 3, '87; Omie May Gentry, August 9, '86, May 3, '87; Harce Clyborn, September 5, '86, April 17, '87; Benjamin Franklin Freeman, August 18, '86—"

She breaks off. "I don't see . . . Are these babies who died . . . or . . ."

I take pity on her and, instead of the made-up story I was fixing to tell, I say, "Them's all babies what are cutting their first teeth. Folks around here set a powerful store on me charming away the toothache. They bring their little uns round everwhen the first tooth breaks the gum. And I write down its name and the day it was borned and the day the first tooth showed. Then I pin up the paper above the fireboard for a charm. When all the teeth are in, I burn the paper—that's all they is to it."

Her head goes on its side again and she grins at me. "So you are a witch, like they said at the hotel. But if that's so, how do you get past the horseshoe?"

We go back out and set on the front porch and I explain that it's there just for bad witches, ones that tries to harm folks—the kind the Injuns called Raven Mocker. Of course, they must have had them over the water too, in England and Scotland and Ireland where most of the old people's folks come from for it was them knowed about the horseshoe.

Miss Cochrane is a quizzy somebody, sure enough, but with such a winning way to her that I find myself telling her all manner of things that I usual don't speak of. I tell her that most folks are like to call me a witchy-woman not a witch. And that there is water witches, who can find water with a forky stick; that my charms and such were passed down from my grandpap—who was a seventh son just as I am a seventh daughter.

"It weren't till I first begun to bleed that I got the powers," I told her, amazed to find myself speaking so

free, but this Miss Cochrane has such a way to her that I believe she is something of a witchy-woman herself.

We talk along like we was old friends and I find myself thinking that had my little girl lived, she'd be nigh the age of Miss Cochrane and the old wound tears open yet again. My mind wanders off in the land of might-have-been and I lose track of what Miss Cochrane is saying. Something about a woman at the hotel grieving for a lost child but that only turns my thoughts inward all the more until I hear the words, ". . . They are preying on these poor grieving mothers and it's not right. I need your help, Amarantha! Will you help me to show them for what they are?"

AN APPALACHIAN WITCH
By Nellie Bly

They call her a "witchy-woman" but their hushed tones hold more of respect than of fear. This is no hunched, black-clad, broomstick-riding beldam of myth nor yet the Bard's cauldron-stirring hag. Potions she may brew, but rather than "eye of newt and tongue of dog," these healing brews are composed from wholesome wild herbs, gathered in careful observance of ancient practice by herself from the meadows and woodlands about her cabin.

I found her at her loom, weaving a web of beauty in indigo and white, and her first words were a welcoming "Come in the house!"

This house, her ancestral home, built of mighty chestnut logs, is a Phoenix raised on the ashes of its predecessors; only the carefully laid stone chimney remains from previous incarnations. And on the face of one of the largest stones in that chimney, graven by some rough tool, the date "1787" gives notice of the witchy-woman's century-old heritage in these verdant mountains.

The mountain folk are kindly to strangers, but wary of sharing their secrets—and none more than the witch. Yet when, after some conversation, I proved harmless, this good creature consented to answer my importunate questions and to tell me something of her craft.

This witchy-woman is the local healer—able to charm away a wart or a boil, to soothe a toothache or an aching heart. She has cures for colicky babies and is held in high repute as a "thrash doctor," able to cure an infant of thrush by blowing in its mouth.

She speaks of the "little people" and relates how she leaves out a saucer of milk for them every evening—or a crust of cornbread if the cow should happen to be dry. But whether these are the little people—the fairies, brownies, pookas, or leprechauns—of the Old Country or the little people (Yunwi Tsunsdi) of Cherokee lore, she could not say.

The witchy-woman is an adept of the Old World practice of divination through examination of the surface of a bowl of liquid—"scrying" is the learned term but our Appalachian witch is ignorant of the word. She will "take a look" or "git a knowin' "—and in that look, she has been known to see past and future.

"Simpleminded superstition!" the city-bred, college-educated will exclaim. But when one speaks with this woman, her native dignity and wise, far-seeing gaze are such that . . . (cont. on page 12)

Chapter 24

Six Impossible Things

Saturday, May 26

"There is no use trying," she said. "One can't believe impossible things."

"I daresay you haven't had much practice," said the Queen. "When I was your age, I always did it for half-an-hour a day. Why, sometimes I've believed as many as six impossible things before breakfast."

—Lewis Carroll

G lory!"

I shoved my gun back into the holster and, pushing past Joss, I reached into the box where the shrouded form slumped against the side. Still, so terribly still. The bag or pillowcase or whatever it was covering the head came off with one tug, revealing my sister's pale face and half-closed eyes. She lolled forward.

"Glory!" I put my hand to her cheek. Warm—and then there was a fluttering of her eyelashes and a ragged indrawn breath. "Joss, help me lift her out of here."

"You take this." He thrust his flashlight at me and leaned over the box. "I'll get her."

Reaching into the cramped box, he scooped her limp body up gently into his arms and arranged the thermal blanket around her.

"Still breathing, thank god! Do you suppose she's been drugged? Maybe chloroform or something on the bag that was on her head?"

I sniffed at the bag that was still in my hand. "I don't think so. The bag is damp but all it smells like is laundry detergent. In books they always talk about a sickly sweet odor."

"Maybe it's something else then. I'm going to get her upstairs—you'll have to shine the light ahead of me." He turned, ready to retrace our steps.

Casting a hurried glance into the odd box, I looked to see if there was anything in it that would give a clue to Gloria's abductor. But, except for a stray leg wrapping, the odd little chamber was empty now.

What was *that box anyway?* I wondered, as I followed just behind and a little to the side of Joss so that I could keep my headlamp focused on the way ahead and the other light on the floor in front of him. The strange box had looked specifically designed for one person to sit in—high at one end with a low board as a seat, and about knee height at the other end. Puzzling. But not so puzzling as how my sister had gotten there.

We inched our way through the underground maze of pillars and boxes and shrouded shapes. Gloria, who had been so still, began to stir.

"Hang in there, Glory!" I reached out and squeezed her twitching foot. "We're almost out of here!"

As the foot of the stairs came in sight, I could hear Joss whispering to Gloria. "It's okay," he crooned, "everything's okay. I have you now, my little mother."

My little mother . . . Was this really happening? A psychic hairstylist had managed to get a son looking for a mother and a mother looking for a child to the same place . . . with this result. And this same psychic hairstylist had "seen" that Gloria was in a box in a basement. And she had somehow gotten there without anyone in this facility noticing anything amiss.

Who was it that talked about believing six impossible things before breakfast? Oh, yes, Lewis Carroll's Red Queen—I was going to have to work at this.

"Watch out for the—"

My warning was interrupted by the clatter of the tray falling down the stairs. The same tray I'd put there to protect at least one clear footprint of whoever had carried Gloria down the steps. Joss had stumbled momentarily and put out a hand to catch himself. A hand which was now, I could see, covered with the dust of that fine footprint. Had that stumble been intentional? Another thing to ponder.

As we emerged into the light of the storage room, Gloria spoke.

"Joss? How did you . . ." She put out a wondering hand and laid it on his cheek. "Never mind—she said that someone would come. But how . . . how *perfect* that it was you . . ."

She was gazing up at him with a look of such complete confidence and pure happiness that I hesitated before breaking into this communion. But I had to know what had happened.

"Are you all right, Glory? How did—"

"I'm perfectly fine, Lizzy. Joss, you can put me down now."

Gathering the thermal blanket about herself like a bulky sarong, my sister managed to look somehow dignified and radiant at the same time. I wanted to hug her—but I was also tempted to shake her till that beatific smile faded.

"What the bloody hell happened to you? Why weren't you hollering for help? Or—"

"Lizzy, could we postpone all this till I can get a shower? I'm unharmed and I'd just like to get into my clothes and out of here. Joss can stay with me while you go tell the manager we're canceling the massages. And for goodness' sake, don't make a big *thing* out of this."

I was bewildered. "A big thing! What was I supposed to think? I was just about to call the police when Joss showed up and said he knew where you were. *Of course* it's a big thing. I'm going to call them now so maybe we can find out who—"

"Elizabeth Grace Grey, do *not* call the police. We can talk this over with Phil—later. I think it might be a good idea to cut our stay short and go back to the farm."

For a single stunned moment I stared at her. Then I threw up my hands in surrender. "That suits me fine but what about the rest of the sessions with Giles? I thought you wanted to—"

Again with the beatific smile. "Not now, I don't." She reached up to touch Joss's face. "I have what I came for."

So I pulled the door shut, relocked the padlock, and shoved the supply cart back in place while Joss, sporting a matching beatific smile, accompanied Gloria back to the treatment room to get her clothing. I, meanwhile, went to let the manager know that we'd found my sister.

The reception area was full of people waiting to check in, all trying to talk to the manager. The poor harassed woman was so happy to hear we didn't want to stay for our massages (there was a honeymoon couple waiting for the double treatment room) that she didn't ask any hard questions.

"Tell your sister I'll adjust the bill and only charge her for the hot tub—we'll just strike off the Head to Toe." She tapped away at her computer and then lowered her voice to ask me, "Is there going to be a problem?"

Is there going to be a problem?

I was asking myself that very question as the three of us walked back through the grounds of the spa to the inn. Gloria, seemingly totally unfazed by her experience, and Joss were walking side by side, saying little, but apparently trying to memorize each other's features. I trailed a little behind, unwilling to intrude on this reunion of mother and son—*if that's what it really is*—and on the lookout for—for what? A black Hummer? A linens delivery van?

I was alone in my concern. Gloria was far more interested in the color of Joss's eyes and the set of his ears than investigating what had just happened. Joss's miraculous rescue of her had evidently tipped the balance in his favor and I wondered how my sister was ever going to tear herself away from this young man whom she had clearly decided was the long-lost Dana.

The answer was quick in coming. As we walked up the driveway to the inn, Gloria stopped and wheeled round. "Joss has to come back to the farm with us, Lizzy. You can understand that, I'm sure. That upstairs guest room—he could stay there? Just for a few days while I make some plans."

"I don't want to put you out." Joss gave me an apologetic look. "But if I could . . . There's so much to learn about my . . . my mother . . . and my real family."

His dark eyes were pleading; Gloria's were steely. I bowed to the inevitable and said that of course Joss could come home with us. And truly, the two of them were so transformed, so blissfully, gloriously happy in this newfound relationship that it would have taken a heart of ice to refuse.

Like a general deploying her troops, Gloria took charge. Joss was sent to go pack his belongings and meet us at the car in an hour.

"You and I both need showers, Lizzy, and . . . would you mind speaking with Giles? Look, he's over there on that bench beneath the magnolia. The next session doesn't start for"—she glanced at her watch—"a little while. Just run over and let him know we're ducking out early—you can explain why, if you like. I want to get a shower and start packing. It always takes me so long to do it right."

Whereas you just throw things in any old way—pack-

ing will probably take you all of three minutes was the unspoken part of her request. But her eyes were shining, so once again, I said that would be fine; I'd go speak to Giles.

"Thank you—Sissy." She gave me a hug. "You don't know how much this means."

Disengaging herself she added, "And let the innkeeper know we're leaving early, would you?"

I watched her trot up the steps to the porch with an airy wave in Giles's direction. He lifted his hand to her in a gesture comprised of equal parts of benediction and farewell then turned his gaze on me as I plodded toward him.

"So she and Joss believe their searches are at an end." Giles patted the bench beside him, inviting me to sit. I did, aware that I smelled powerfully of whatever fragrant oil had been on those wrappings while I was hydrating.

I nodded. "Yes, they do. Gloria has decided to cut short our stay here. She and Joss and I will be going back to my farm this afternoon."

Giles's brow furrowed but he didn't speak.

"I'm sorry—I hope this doesn't mess up the sessions. But my sister's made up her mind—she said to thank you . . ."

The medium looked away from me, rubbing his chin in that meditative way of a man troubled by something but unwilling to speak.

"The sessions were very interesting." I was doing that southern lady thing again—making nice, not letting a silence fall. I hurried on. "And, if it weren't for the coincidence of Joss—"

"Coincidence," Giles repeated. He appeared to roll the word around in his mind before speaking. "There are those who believe there are no coincidences. And I must say, I find this one a little troubling. But, Elizabeth,

I'm afraid I must burden you with something you'd perhaps rather not hear. I'd hoped you'd discover it for yourself in one of our next sessions"—the look he gave me was shrewd—"if, indeed, you haven't already received a communication."

The memory of my strange experience in the morning session came back in a rush—the beating of wings, the talons, and Sam's voice, sounding a warning in my head. I closed my eyes to escape Giles's penetrating gaze.

"Someone you were very close to—not a blood relation, I think, but a husband or a lover—is trying to communicate with you. The energy was so strong this morning that though the message was clearly directed to you, some of it came through to me.

"It's a bit like . . . like picking up a telephone and inadvertently overhearing part of a conversation. You clearly didn't wish to share your communication with the group and I'd have left it at that but for the fact that I've continued to feel . . ." He rubbed his chin again. "I feel that this spirit is trying to make sure you heed the warning he gave you."

Giles gave me an apologetic look. "It *was* a warning, was it not?"

I closed my eyes. "Yes. Yes, it was."

"I thought so—something about a large bird falling from the sky and danger—that was all I got. Is that similar to your message?"

"Yes, very similar." My eyes were still closed but I could see again the scenes that had assailed me during the morning session. I had seen a small airplane attacked by a giant bird and spiraling out of control to an inevitable crash in the green mountains beneath—just as Sam's plane had gone down.

We sat silent on the bench in the sleepy afternoon sun. Somewhere in the distance a lawn mower was purring; nearer I could hear the small rustlings of birds in the big tree behind us and the sharp warning cry of a blue jay across the lawn. Bees buzzed; from within the inn I heard the deep twanging chime of an old grandfather clock. The heat of the sun, the fragrance of new-mown grass, as well as the floral scents arising from my own body, were all combining to lull me into a drowsy state from which—

"There's another thing, Elizabeth."

I started, snapped out of the mesmerized, floating state I'd been in. "What? What other thing? Isn't a warning enough?"

Giles was staring across the lawn at the old stone steps that led down to the road. He didn't look at me as he spoke. "There's danger in the message—for you or someone near you. I felt I had to tell you that. But the other thing is this. Your sister asked to speak to her lost child, the child she'd been told had died at birth. And there was a response—"

"Well, yes—Joss jumped up and said *Mama*. We all heard him."

Giles continued to study the sunken stone steps. "No," he said at last, his voice soft, "I meant the first response. *That* came from the other side."

Chapter 25

Who? And Why?

Saturday, May 26

You see, Phil, Lizzy was sound asleep on the other massage table, snoring—yes, you were, Lizzy, snoring so loud that I was about to reach over and wake you up and then I heard the door open and I assumed it was the massage therapists coming back and the next thing I knew someone was pulling a wet bag of some sort over my head. Well, at first I thought it was part of the treatment but then I was being picked up and carried somewhere and this voice—"

Phillip watched as Gloria shuddered and wrapped her arms around herself before continuing. "This weird voice whispered that if I made a sound, he'd make sure it was my last. I could feel us going down some steps and then he dumped me in this weird box and shut the lid."

At his side, Elizabeth spoke up. "Okay, Glory, so you were afraid to make any noise at first. I can understand that. But when Joss found you . . ."

Joss. Phillip studied the intense, rather too pretty young man sitting beside Gloria, his dark eyes fixed on her. There was something about him, Phillip thought, something a little—was *manic* the right word? Maybe that wasn't fair. If this whole story was true, if Gloria and Joss had only recently found that he was her lost child, then that could explain the look of wild excitement. And then there was the bandage, sitting slightly askew on the young man's head—*that* added to the impression of a person a few bricks shy of a load.

For a moment, Phillip tuned out of the discussion and tried to organize his thoughts. First there had been the phone call a few hours ago; fortunately he'd been off duty and was at the dining table with paperwork spread out all around him when his cell beeped. Lizabeth hadn't said much, just that they would be home in about an hour, that she would bring stuff for dinner, and that a young man would be coming with them. That was it—she'd explain it all later, she'd promised. At least the part that could *be* explained, she'd added, before hanging up.

He'd rushed around, tidying up his clutter, making the bed, and doing the dishes that had been accumulating. He'd even thought about hauling out the vacuum cleaner but decided instead just to sweep the kitchen floor and let it go at that.

Lizabeth had taken him aside as soon as the three had arrived and swiftly filled him in on the story of Gloria's lost child and the "miraculous" events that had just taken place. And now here they were, all sitting around the living room like one big happy family. *Family*— Phillip wondered how Ben was going to feel about a newfound older half brother. The answer to *that* question would have to wait till Monday, as Ben and Amanda had taken off for a weekend music festival somewhere. And while it was great to see Gloria looking so happy, still, the cop side of Phillip's nature was deeply suspicious of the whole setup. Too neat, too—

He became aware that the story Gloria was telling had moved on. *I've lost the thread here. Where were we? Gloria was in some kind of box in a basement and Lizabeth wanted to know why she hadn't been hollering for help.*

"... the same woman?" Elizabeth was asking.

"Yes, the woman in white I met at the old bathhouse this morning. She came to me . . ."

Gloria stopped. Her brow furrowed. "But that doesn't make any sense—I was in that box, wasn't I? I swear though, I *saw* her and she told me that I was going to be fine, that someone was coming to get me out. She . . ."

Gloria was shaking her head now. "I know this sounds crazy . . ."

You got that right, thought Phillip. He glanced at Elizabeth. But her face was expressionless.

"No, go on," urged Joss, "this is amazing—just one more amazing thing in this amazing day." He picked up Gloria's hand and put a gentle kiss on her palm, then wrapped her fingers around it. Phillip realized that he found the intimacy of the gesture somewhat unsettling. What age was this Joss, anyway? Early thirties, by what Lizabeth had said, but he looked much younger. Whatever, this cozy, lovey-dovey stuff between Joss and his supposed mother was creeping him out.

Not Gloria. She favored Joss with a radiant smile and went on.

"Well, anyway, the woman in white was *there,* somehow, and she told me I was going to be all right. She *spoke* to me—I heard her voice—just like your Miss Birdie, Lizzy—and she said, *Honey,* only she said 'hawney,' *now you lay quiet fer a spell. Take a little nap.* And I curled up and fell asleep, just like that!"

Gloria patted Joss's hand. "The next thing I remember, I was being carried upstairs and out into the light. And then I saw it was Joss and I knew that all of this had somehow been *meant* to bind us together."

"Excuse me, I think I'm missing something here." Phillip could hold back no longer. "You're saying some unknown person or persons—"

"Person," Gloria corrected him. "I'm sure there was only one."

"Okay, an unknown *person* carried you off, dumped you in a box of some sort—"

"I've been thinking about that box . . ." Now Lizabeth was doing it. "It must have been a sort of early steam cabinet. There was a hose fitting—"

"What does that have to do with anything?" Phillip leapt to his feet and moved out of the cozy circle of family, feeling that if he didn't get up and walk around, he'd explode.

"Sorry, sweetheart." The look of surprise on Elizabeth's face made him lower his voice and he reached down to give her shoulder an apologetic squeeze. "But for the love of god, don't you folks understand that a crime's been committed here? Did anyone bother to call the Hot Springs police? I know the sheriff's office wasn't called."

They were staring at him now with expressions ranging from guilty embarrassment (Lizabeth) to indignation (Gloria) and what looked suspiciously like barely concealed amusement (Joss).

"I told Lizzy not to, Phil. Since I was the one involved, surely it was my decision." *And there's an end to it,* Gloria's tone said.

"When I first realized Glory was missing, I did start to call you. But then Joss showed up saying he knew where she was and . . ." Elizabeth lifted her hands in one of those *whaddayagonnado* gestures and concluded, "And then everything happened so fast and Glory—"

"I absolutely forbade calling any local yokel cops." Now Gloria was on *her* feet, hands planted on her hips and elbows waggling in that old familiar bitch-wings pose his ex-wife had majored in. Bitch wings seemed to work best, Phillip thought, with short, strong-willed women—the ones like little feisty dogs. They could waggle those elbows and stare a big man down in no time flat.

At least, Lizabeth looked like she understood why he was so ticked. Maybe it would be best just to back down for the moment and see where this was going.

The cellphone clipped to his belt began to vibrate and he reached for it.

"Excuse me, folks." Happy for the interruption, he headed for the office. "I gotta take this."

When he returned from his phone call, Elizabeth was on her way to the front porch. "I need to go check on a heifer—she's not due for a while but the cows are down from the mountain and handy over there in the pasture. I might as well take a look . . ."

We need to talk, her eyes said.

He nodded. "I'll come with you—do me good to stretch my legs. I've been swamped in that blasted paperwork for most of the day."

Leaving Joss and Gloria deep in conversation, he followed Elizabeth to the porch and waited while she pulled on boots. The dogs, well aware of her intentions, danced about while James made little darting attempts to lick her face as she leaned over to tie her laces.

When they reached the driveway, after glancing back to make sure that they were out of earshot of the house, Phillip began. "Lizabeth, there's something about this whole setup that—"

"*Setup!* That's exactly what I've been thinking from the beginning." Lizabeth's blue eyes were shining. "But you see how Glory is. She wants to believe that she and her lost child have been miraculously reunited."

They continued on through the gate to the tractor road that ran along the top of the pasture, Ursa and Molly leading the way. Up ahead, just at the edge of the woods, a dozen red cows were grazing.

"Is it one of those up there?" he asked, wondering how she could tell one cow from another anyway.

Elizabeth waved dismissively. "That heifer won't come in for another month; I just thought we needed to get out of the house." She reached for his hand. "You looked like you were about to explode right before that phone call took you away."

He looked back at the house. "Yeah, Gloria can be a little . . ."

"Yes, she can. So let's go on and have a walk and I'll try to fill you in on what's been happening."

As they walked along the path in late afternoon sun, Elizabeth recapped Gloria's story of the hushed-up pregnancy, the banishment to New Bern and Aunt Dodie, the arranged adoption, and the birth.

"They told Gloria the baby was born dead. She'd been under anesthesia for the birth and by the time she regained consciousness, dead or alive the child had been whisked away. Of course, since Gloria hadn't really wanted to consent to the adoption, it's possible my mother decided to tell her the baby died so she wouldn't make a fuss."

"Wait a second—would the doctor or the hospital or whatever have gone along with a big lie like that? And, anyway, for the adoption to take place, your sister would have to sign papers—"

Lizabeth gave him a pitying smile. "You never knew my mother. She always said it was amazing what a little money could do. And she would have forged Glory's name without thinking twice. She might have even told herself that it was better for Glory this way, just to believe that the baby was dead rather than to go on worrying about it. And do you imagine that an adopting couple, about to be presented with a healthy male infant, would ask a lot of questions?"

They had reached the edge of the woods and, after a

quick look at the heifer in question, Elizabeth paused to admire some little purple flowers that covered the ground below the path.

"It's a good thing the cows don't have a taste for wild iris." She swept her hand toward the swathe of bloom. "They trample a few here and there but at least they don't eat them. I look forward every year to seeing this. It always makes me think of a pool of water spread out here in the shade."

He watched as she bent to inspect a single fan of leaves that had been dislodged by a passing hoof. In an instant she had set it aright, patting the rich dirt around its roots, and then wiping her hands on her jeans as she stood back up.

"Oh, bloody hell, these are my good jeans! I forgot."

He reached for her dirty hand and drew her to him. "I like the way you know and love every inch of this place. And the way you tend to even the wildflowers—I've seen you leaving big patches of those lacy white ones when you're out with your weed cutter. It's . . . it's nice."

She stood, quiet in his embrace. Almost as tall as he—he liked that too—an armful of woman.

At last she said, "I can't imagine ever living anywhere but here. I enjoy seeing other places—and with Ben and Amanda and Julio and Homero to take up the slack, it's gotten easier to be away now and then. But you know, anytime I'm somewhere else, I'm always wondering what I might be missing here: the first crocus, the flame azaleas, those lovely Louisiana irises down at the pond . . ."

She fell silent and he closed his eyes and breathed in her fragrance—shampoo, soap, the woman herself—a smell that always oddly reminded him of fallen oak leaves—an elemental smell. Time seemed to stop as they clung to each other, just out of sight of the house and the questions waiting there.

Finally she pulled away from him. "But I was supposed to be giving you the backstory on Glory. Let's walk on."

As they moved into the wooded section of the walk the dogs trotted ahead, eagerly examining invisible trails and tantalizing scents. A squirrel darted in front of them and ran up a poplar tree to the first branch where it paused to flirt its tail and chatter abuse. All three dogs scrambled up the bank in futile pursuit then abandoned the hunt in favor of following their people.

"This abduction—your sister being carried off like that— Did she have any idea who it was—make any guesses?"

"No, none at all. When she was first missing, I figured it must have been that Eyebrow guy."

Phillip shook his head. "Not him."

"Oh, I know," Elizabeth continued. "When we found her in that cellar, I realized it really couldn't have been him. It would have to have been someone familiar with the place. But—"

"It couldn't have been Mr. Gregorio Lopez, aka 'Goyo'—the fella your sister calls the Eyebrow," he continued. "Because according to Mac—that's who the call was from—Goyo was stopped *yesterday* in a routine traffic check and the drug-sniffing dog evidently detected a trace of cocaine on one of the seats. One thing led to another and your Eyebrow friend got violent and he's sitting in the Buncombe County jail just now, awaiting transfer to Florida, where, as it turns out, there are several outstanding warrants."

He grinned. It felt just fine to be delivering good news for a change. But Lizabeth seemed to be deep in thought.

"So who? And *why*?" She kicked at a rotting branch on the path. "If it couldn't have been the Eyebrow, who was it? And why . . . to scare her? Did whoever it was think she would stay quiet? Were they going to come back for her? Or was it all some kind of setup—all so that Joss could be the hero who found her . . ."

Or, thought Phillip, *did your crazy sister set up all of this herself?*

But he didn't say it.

Chapter 26

In the Dark

Monday, May 28, and Thursday, May 31

Do you believe this shit, Aunt E?"
I looked up from the tray of seedlings I was transplanting to see Ben, looming over me and vibrating with emotion.

This was the first I'd seen of him since he and Amanda had returned late the previous night. Gloria had left a note on the door of their cabin, telling Ben to come over in the morning as she had some important news for him.

"I just can't *wait* for Ben to meet Joss. You know he always hated being an only child. And now he has a big brother! Won't he be thrilled?"

She actually believed that.

I wasn't so sure and suggested that it might be a better plan to break this news to Ben privately before presenting him with his ready-made older brother. I even offered to talk to Ben first but Gloria was having none of it.

"We'll do it my way, thank you just the same, Lizzy. I'll tell him when he comes over in the morning. Don't you dare call him or do anything to spoil my surprise, do you hear me?"

So, in a somewhat cowardly move, I'd gotten up early and fled the house, leaving a note to tell Gloria that I had urgent work to do. Phillip had been of the same mind and had left before dawn, swearing that he had an early meeting at the sheriff's office.

"Well, Aunt E? *Do* you believe that . . . *person* is who he says he is?" Ben picked up a spray bottle of insecticidal soap and began to toss it from hand to hand—a mindless activity that warned me that he was trying very hard not to give vent to all his suppressed feelings.

"I truly don't know, Ben. I wish I did."

I wanted to hug him, seeing not the handsome man he'd become but instead the lonely defensive little boy who had so often spent his summers at the farm while Gloria vacationed with the husband or boyfriend of the moment. But Ben, in this mood, didn't appear to want hugs. So I just tried to answer him honestly.

"At this moment, there's no proof at all—just some odd coincidences—"

His faraway, closed look told me that he wasn't really listening to me and that he wasn't done with his anger. "I never even knew my dad wasn't her first husband. You never bothered to let me in on *that* little piece of information either."

Without warning, he hurled the spray bottle to the ground. The plastic top flew off and the contents splashed out. And at once, the tension on his face and in his voice was gone and he looked at me with a rueful smile.

"Sorry, Aunt E. Mom *told* me she made you promise not to tell. She said since the marriage was annulled, it didn't count, which meant that legally my dad *was* her first husband—"

Thank you, Gloria, for that. I hurried to clarify my position. "And I never knew there'd been a child, not until a few days ago—you need to understand that, Ben."

He squatted down to pick up the pieces of the broken sprayer. I had the impression that he was near tears and

I went back to my transplanting to give him time to recover his equanimity.

"It's just . . ." His voice choked and he cleared his throat before going on. "This guy doesn't look anything like me or Mom. And he acts like . . ." Ben was still down on the floor, fiddling with the hopelessly cracked sprayer. "Is she going to take his word for *everything*? 'Welcome, Joss. Here, Ben, this is your brother.' Is that all?"

I was feeling near tears myself as I tried to reassure him that it was just a matter of time; that there would be DNA tests, and a search of birth records . . .

"All that takes a while and it'll have to be done. But right now—Ben, you have to understand that your mother's carried a huge load of guilt all these years, blaming herself for the supposed death of her child—as if it had died because she didn't want it. And now . . . there's this miracle. Don't you see? She's not ready to put it to a test, not yet. Give her a little time."

Ben did just that. He made himself scarce in the following days, citing a big job he had to help Amanda with—a job that had them leaving the farm early and returning late. Apart from an exquisitely uncomfortable and unavoidable family dinner Monday night, Ben's contact with Joss had been minimal.

At first Gloria seemed oblivious to Ben's deep unhappiness with the new situation. Her absorption in Joss was total—the two spent long hours just sitting and talking. She had gotten me to unearth my old photo albums and was bent on introducing Joss to all the members of the family, living or long gone.

And when they weren't building family memories for Joss, she was making up for lost time by spending money on him. Now that the Eyebrow was out of the picture—safely checked into Florida's penal system, according to Phillip—Gloria had no hesitation in whirling Joss into Asheville to outfit him in the kind of clothing she could never persuade Ben to wear. Furthermore, she had convinced Joss to quit his job waiting tables so that they could spend more time together while making plans for the future.

"Isn't he the handsomest thing?" she whispered to me one morning as we sat on the front porch. Joss was coming up the road, looking like the picture of health, except for a lingering limp that caused him to shuffle slightly as he walked. That limp was the reason for his therapeutic daily walk down to the mailbox and back—a good little hike. Now that the bandage on his head had been removed and only a faint scar remained, I had to admit that he was, indeed, darkly handsome. A pale olive skin, deep brown curly hair, soft dark eyes, and eyelashes that didn't seem quite right on a guy.

"Handsome, for sure," I agreed. "I guess he looks a lot like Arturo." *He about has to,* I thought; *he sure doesn't favor you.*

"Oh, yes, I think so—though you know, Lizzy, it sounds awful but it was so long ago that I hardly remember what Turo looked like—and when he never tried to get back in touch after the annulment, I burned all my pictures of him. But he had the same dark skin and curly hair, I do remember that much. And his eyes were gray—really striking-looking against his dark skin."

"Gloria, have you been in touch with Arturo recently? Phillip said—"

Gloria glanced down at Joss, who had paused on the road to throw a stick for James. James, as was his wont, had immediately attached himself to the latest arrival and now accompanied Joss faithfully on his daily mailbox excursions.

"Don't mention that to Joss, Lizzy, not yet." She was

almost whispering though we both knew that Joss was well out of earshot. "Yes, when I decided to try to contact my baby"—she laughed—"my baby girl Dana who turned out to be my grown-up son Joss, I got the strongest feeling that I should try to get in touch with Turo. I guess I was hoping to get closure on all outstanding business." Her eyes didn't leave Joss.

"*Any*hoo, it was ridiculously easy. I remembered that Turo's family had lived in Cartagena, Colombia, for generations. I mean, forever—since they first came over from Spain in the Dark Ages or whenever it was. Still in the same house, he told me. And I remembered that the house was called the house of the lion—Casa de Leon."

She giggled reminiscently. "I used to tease Turo and call him Lee-on."

"Glory, do you want to—"

"All *right*, Lizzy, it was when I was in Asheville, the day I got my hair done. I just borrowed Nigel's phone book, looked in the Yellow Pages, and found a private investigator. Her office was in a building nearby and when I called, she was able to see me right away."

She darted a look to where Joss was stretched out on the grass, with James on his chest. "She was a most attractive black woman—or African American, if that's what you're supposed to say now. Very well spoken—over the phone I had no idea—but I told her what I wanted and gave her my information and she just laughed. She asked if I didn't maybe have a teenager who could do this for me, it was so easy with a computer. And when I told her that it was a private matter, she just grinned and started tapping away on that computer and, I swear, Glory, it was less than five minutes and she handed me a phone number and an address: Arturo Rodriquez, Casa de Leon, Fernandez de Madrid Plaza. Do you know, she even showed me pictures on the computer of the front of his house? And when I asked what I owed her, she said I should make out a check to Big Sisters of Asheville for whatever I felt the information had been worth. So I wrote her a nice check and—"

"And you called the number . . ."

Gloria blushed. "Eventually. I had to wait till nighttime so he'd be home. And of course, I wasn't sure if I'd get Turo or his father, who *might* still be alive, or Turo's son, if he had one—"

"But eventually you got the right Arturo."

Joss was on his feet now and I wanted to finish this conversation without hearing a play by play that included maids and difficulties with Spanish and a possible wife—there, now she had me doing it.

"Yes, I did. And it was . . . well, it was amazing. We've talked several times since then, kind of reconnecting."

"And have you told him—"

I stopped myself just in time as James bounded up the steps, followed more slowly by Joss. He shuffled to the rocker by Gloria and plopped down.

"Whew! That's some walk, even with resting along the way. But, like they say, no pain, no gain."

He leaned back and shut his eyes. "Don't let me interrupt you two. Go on, Aunt E, has my mother told me what?"

"Phillip, there was something about the way Joss said that—well, it didn't exactly make my blood run cold but there was a definite edge to his voice that kind of creeped me out."

Phillip threw a handful of fish food into the pond and we watched the huge catfish appear, first rolling lazily to the surface then sweeping up the pellets with eager efficiency.

Since Joss had been staying with us, Phillip and I had

formed the habit, on the days he was home in time, of taking a stroll after dinner: into the woods, down to the pond and its little pavilion with two comfortable Adirondack chairs—anywhere for a little space.

He tossed out a second helping for the catfish and for the smaller bream that were beginning to appear at the edge of the feeding frenzy. Dropping into the chair by mine, he asked, "And did she tell him that she was in touch with his father?"

"No, and she actually sounded a little annoyed with Joss—told him rather pointedly that she wasn't talking about him. And she didn't go on. Later I was able to get her alone for a few minutes—sometimes I think Joss would follow her into the bathroom if she'd let him, just like a two-year-old not wanting his mother out of his sight. I remember when Laurel went through that stage—hollering *Ma! Whar you?* and pounding on the door while I tried to have a relaxing bath and—"

I caught myself as I saw Phillip trying to stifle a grin. "I'm running on, aren't I? Almost as bad as Glory or, Heaven forfend, Aunt Dodie. And yes, I wanted to call Aunt Dodie and ask about her baby—had Dodie been covering up the truth all these years? But Gloria insisted that *she* should be the one to do it, and she wasn't ready—yet. Okay, where was I?"

He reached over and took my hand then leaned back in his chair, his eyes on the bird's nest in the rafters above where a nervous little phoebe was doing her best to pretend we didn't exist.

"You were telling me whether Gloria had told Arturo about Joss."

"Oh, right. Well—and this was fairly unexpected— she said that she wasn't going to say anything to Joss or Arturo till she'd gotten proof. And she went on, in the most offhanded way, to say that she had that same private investigator—the one who'd gotten Arturo's phone number for her—on the case. I swear, Phillip, the girl has a lot more sense than I'd given her credit for. Do you know what she did?"

Really, my sister amazed me. Just as calmly as if she was a seasoned investigator herself, she told me how she'd managed to clip a bit of Joss's hair to send in for comparison with the hair in her locket—the hair a nurse who'd attended the birth had slipped to her, as a remembrance of the lost baby.

"Glory said that on the day after the birth, she hadn't been able to stop crying. And that was when the nurse gave her the little bit of hair, saying she'd clipped it before they took the baby away. The nurse told Glory she didn't agree with the way things had been handled—but that was all she'd say. So whether this nurse was talking about Gloria not being allowed to see a dead baby or not being allowed to see the baby she was giving up isn't clear—"

"But at least your sister's admitting a possibility here; that's good. The only trouble with the hair samples . . ."

He ran his free hand over his head in that characteristic worried gesture that I knew he'd tried to quit after I'd teased him about it. Catching my glance, he went on.

"Thing is, I don't know how useful those two samples will be. For DNA, you got to have the follicles and I'm assuming neither Gloria nor the nurse back then yanked the hair out by the roots. It's possible that the two samples could come up as a match but even a match isn't a hundred percent proof—and if they didn't match, it still wouldn't prove anything. I mean, the nurse might have felt like this would help Gloria stop crying and she could have gone to the nursery and gotten a little bit of hair from any baby. Or—"

"Glory said the P.I. warned her that it might not be definitive. Evidently the investigator's doing some more checking—birth and adoption records, that sort of thing. She's also going to have a chat with Joss's adoptive parents."

"How about a birth certificate? Or that driver's license Joss claims his doctor is holding on to?"

The sun had been behind the mountain for some time now and in the growing dusk, tiny bats had come out to dart above the pond, doing their part to keep the insect population under control. Occasionally one would swoop down and skim the water's still surface, whether feeding or drinking or both, I couldn't say.

"Supposedly Joss has sent for the birth certificate." I wondered if I should tell Phillip about the other thing Gloria had asked the P.I. to look into. *Later,* I decided and went on with the rest of my troubling news. "Joss got his driver's license back when he and Glory went into town yesterday. I've seen it."

"And . . . ?"

It was almost completely dark now, too dark to see the bats anymore. And in the darkness, all the night sounds seemed louder: the whirring and chittering of katydids, the distant calls of owls, the muted strains of *ranchero* music from Julio's house. I stood to start back up the road.

"And . . . ?" Phillip repeated as he pulled himself to his feet.

"And the dates match."

IX~The DeVine Sisters and Nellie Bly

May 17, 1887

"Doe! She'll be here any moment. You can't change your mind now!"

Theodora DeVine rapped again on the locked bedroom door, this time with urgent force, and hissed, "You'll spoil everything, you silly bitch. Surely you're not going to—"

The door opened and Dorothea emerged, her eyes red-rimmed but with her jaw set and her back straight. A step behind her, Lorenzo pulled the door shut and adjusted his cravat.

"Dear Doe has at last seen reason. These tedious vacillations of conscience are quite at an end, are they not, sister mine?"

Tight-lipped, Dorothea nodded and moved to take her place at the round table in the center of the room. In a whisper of purple silk, Theodora glided to her and brought her mouth close to her sister's ear.

"I thought we'd resolved this earlier. You know Miss Cochrane only wants assurance that her late mother is making her way to the upper planes—that there is no lingering business that detains her—"

"I've got it down cold," Dorothea replied, her face pallid above her green tea gown. She did not meet her sister's eye but spoke with every evidence of calm. "Your Miss Cochrane will receive the comfort she hopes for, never fear."

Her tone was uncharacteristically harsh and her pretty face grim as she spoke to Lorenzo. "Planchette and later, perhaps, the trumpets. Are you prepared?"

Assuring her that he was, Lorenzo turned to the window and drew the thick draperies, blotting out the early evening light. "This is a private session, I believe? No curious friends in attendance?"

Theodora nodded. "Quite private—Miss Cochrane is a recent arrival and, aside from myself, has hardly had time to take up intimate acquaintances. And, Doe— I believe that it might be well to leave some questions unanswered—Miss Cochrane's papa's purse seems capacious and I think we might stretch this to three or four sessions if you play this fish wisely." Her eyes moved over the room, taking careful note of the positions of certain key elements that would be vital to the forthcoming illusion. "The angel kiss? Shall we—"

"Yes, of course, at the conclusion. Renzo can handle that—you'll be busy manipulating the trumpets." Dorothea frowned. "You said there had been rappings in the chamber where Miss Cochrane's mother died. Perhaps we should begin with rapping—"

"Not possible." Renzo gave a last tug to the draperies. "The apparatus has disappeared. I haven't the least notion—"

Crack!

Renzo whirled and tore open the draperies he'd closed.

"That noise—it was the apparatus! But where . . ."

The sisters watched, both puzzled and amused as he fumbled at the cushions on the window seat. Dorothea leaned forward, narrowing her eyes at the slanting light.

"Theo!" she whispered. "Look there—just by Renzo's head. It looks as if—"

A determined knock on the door to the suite caused all three heads to snap round and Renzo hastily pulled the curtains back to cover the windows as Theodora hurried to the door. Only Dorothea remained still, her hands flat on the table before her, her eyes now closed. The medium was preparing for her trance.

"They are nothing but frauds, Amarantha! And I mean to expose them as such—but I'll need your help. That's why I booked another soak and massage—so that we could speak without being overheard."

The young woman's eyes flashed beneath her dark fringe as she stared at the impassive mountain woman seated on a low stool by the marble tub.

"Do you know what those women pretend to do? The cruel deceptions they practice on grieving mothers? It was the suicide of one such dupe that brought me here; she was the older sister of an associate at the newspaper where—"

She caught herself and hit the surface of the cloudy water that surrounded her. A spray of drops flew up and imprinted themselves on the long white skirt of the attendant, who allowed herself a little smile.

"You're powerful het up over these folks, ain't you? Are you sure about what you say? There's been quite a few going for these sessions, as they name them, and ain't none has made the first complaint."

Nellie Bly—for it was thus she thought of herself when she was at work as an investigative reporter; indeed, the name seemed more her own than the one she'd answered to since birth—looked up at the mountain woman.

"It's only because those people are suffering and want

so badly to believe that these DeVine sisters can get away with their hoax. Oh, they do the business well—but they are charlatans just the same!"

Amarantha nodded, almost imperceptibly, and Nellie continued, her indignation growing with each word.

"Dorothea—the green one—was the medium but Theodora and the brother were there as well. You know, when we first met, Theodora pumped me, oh so delicately and efficiently, for details of my life. And I obliged, filling her bucket to overflowing—but every particular was false. Oh, Amarantha, it was too comic for words! There was that pretty charlatan, moaning and swaying and rolling her eyes back, telling me that my dear mama was waiting just beyond this world and eager to contact me. Whereas I have it on good authority—a telegram received this very afternoon—that my dear mama is safe in Pittsburgh, packing for the coming move to New York and wishing to know whether she should dispose of my childhood books."

Amarantha made a snorting sound which was quickly transformed into a cough. Oblivious, Nellie Bly continued with her tale.

"Miss Dorothea and I each had our fingertips on the planchette. You should have seen it dashing about the little alphabet board with messages from Mama—no longer suffering, pain a distant memory, how she missed her darling Liza Jane—Liza Jane, indeed! Mama always calls me Pink. Oh yes, and 'Mama' expressed urgent hopes that our session might be repeated."

It was Nellie Bly's turn to snort. "I'll just bet they wish the session might be repeated—at the exorbitant fee they charge—oh, but I wanted to tell you about a strange thing, Amarantha. And I think I've soaked sufficiently now."

As soon as the young woman was wrapped in a robe

of fluffy Turkish toweling, she pulled up a second stool and sat knee to knee with the mountain woman.

"It was such a queer thing—and I'm sure that—unlike the faraway voice and the invisible kiss that came later—this was not something of the DeVines' manufacture. This was something real!"

She shivered and pulled the robe tighter.

Amarantha leaned forward. "What was it, honey?" The older woman's hand flew to her mouth. "I ask your pardon, miss. I didn't mean—"

"Fiddlesticks, Amarantha! I like it. But let me tell you of this queer thing—my supposed late mother had just begun a long message—probably quite wearisome for the medium who was dragging the planchette all around the alphabet board—she doesn't spell very well, by the by. The message had to do with the knocking sounds the Dear Departed was supposed to have been using in an attempt to communicate with me back home. And in the midst of all this nonsense, there came a whole series of knocks from the vicinity of the window seat. At first I assumed it was part of their ruse but Dorothea started like a frightened deer and the planchette slid off the table altogether. Then she jumped up and it seemed she wanted to go to the window where the sound was but her sister caught hold of her hand and pulled her back down. Of course, it was quite dark in the room—I'm interpreting the vaguest of perceptions."

Nellie Bly caught sight of the older woman's face. "Amarantha? Why are you smiling? Do you know something about this knocking?"

"It ain't the doing of them DeVine folks—that I'm sure of. They carried on with their foolery, you say?"

"Oh, yes. They were shaken, especially Dorothea, but the knocking lasted less than a minute and then there was a voice calling for Liza Jane—such a low whispering sound—I had goose bumps all up my arms in spite *of knowing it was a hoax and my dear mama was most probably sitting in the parlor reading a novel by her beloved Ouida."*

The young woman stood and stretched out a hand to Amarantha. "You will help me, won't you? All I need is for you to let me into their rooms at a time when the three are otherwise engaged. If you can manage it that the sisters are booked for the tubs and massage at the same time, I have an idea for dealing with Mr. DeVine."

From *The New York World*
October 21, 1888

Margaret Fox's Confession

"My sister Katie was the first one to discover that by swishing her fingers she could produce a certain noise with the knuckles and joints, and that the same effect could be made with the toes. Finding we could make raps with our feet—first with one foot and then with both—we practiced until we could do this easily when the room was dark. No one suspected us of any trick because we were such young children . . . all the neighbors thought there was something, and they wanted to find out what it was. They were convinced someone had been murdered in the house. They asked us about it, and we would rap one for the spirit answer 'yes,' not three, as we did afterwards. We did not know anything about Spiritualism then. The murder, they concluded, must have been committed in the house. They went over the whole surrounding country, trying to get the names of people who had formerly lived in the house. They found finally a man by the name of Bell, and they said that this poor innocent man had committed a murder in the house, and that these noises came from the spirit of the murdered person. Poor Bell was shunned and looked upon by the whole community as a murderer. As far as spirits were concerned, neither my sister nor I thought about it . . . I have seen so much miserable deception that I am willing to assist in any way and to positively state that Spiritualism is a fraud of the worst description. I do so before my God, and my idea is to expose it . . . I trust that this statement, coming solemnly from me, the first and most successful in this deception, will break the force of the rapid growth of Spiritualism and prove that it is all a fraud, a hypocrisy, and a delusion."

Chapter 27

Dreams and Dreamers

Sunday, June 3

Gloria looked at her the bedside clock. Ten-thirty
P.M. It was too late to call Aunt Dodie, who, like
others of her generation, made and expected phone calls
only between nine A.M. and nine P.M. Any call this late
would be construed as an emergency and would surely
send the old lady into palpitations. But it had been hard
to get a moment alone within the prescribed time frame.
Joss was so . . . was *attentive* the right word? It was
wonderful how eagerly he had claimed her as his
mother. And surely, his eager affection was just what
any mother would wish for on being reunited with a
long-lost child . . .

But still . . . she wanted to have it out with Dodie.
Sweet little Aunt Dodie, who'd always seemed so *good*.
Mama's best friend from school days and a constant
sender of birthday and Christmas gifts—this little porce-
lain doll of a woman had taken in the pregnant embarrassment that was Gloria without a word of reproof,
had cheerfully put up with her storms of emotion and
her moments of despair, had alternately bullied her into
walking for exercise and coddled her with delicious
food, all for the health of the baby. And then, that smiling, sweet little southern magnolia snake-in-the-grass
had lied through her teeth, saying that the child was

stillborn. The old bitch had *colluded* in keeping Gloria from her child all these years.

Maybe Dodie *deserved* to be awakened by a phone call. Gloria frowned, her mood growing blacker. It would be small payment for the years of her child's life she'd missed. So what if a phone call late at night startled the old woman? She deserved to be shaken out of her smug complacency.

Reaching over, Gloria turned down the exuberant strains of "I Dreamed a Dream." At home she would have turned it up full volume but Elizabeth and Phillip's room was just across the hall and they went to bed so unbelievably early—

What was that?

Gloria stabbed the pause button and sat up straight, listening hard. There were so many night sounds here, one reason she'd gotten the CD player in the first place. Elizabeth's darling dogs invariably had to go out at some point, or points, in the night, and James often broke into the weirdest peal of barking on stepping out the door. Then, of course, the creatures had to come back in. And there were always anonymous creakings and rustlings outside—the forest came down the mountain almost to the door of the guest room and god knew there were undoubtedly wild animals of every sort roaming around all night long. But this sound . . . was it in the hall . . . or outside?

And had she locked the door to the little porch? It was one of the few doors in the house that actually had a working lock and she'd made a habit of keeping it locked. But she'd stepped outside before supper to call Turo—had she locked it after that?

The sound that had caught her attention—she was sure now that it had been outside and close by—had not been repeated. Still . . .

What was she afraid of? Phillip had assured her that

the Eyebrow was in jail. It couldn't be him again. Nonetheless, it was a struggle to fight back the temptation to call for Phillip, so conveniently just across the hall but undoubtedly sound asleep. At last, winning the battle with herself, Gloria slipped out of bed, careful to make no noise, and approached the French door.

It took all the nerve she had, indeed, more than she'd known she possessed, to glide her hand under the curtain and feel for the little nubbin on the lever door handle. A quick twist established that it was already locked.

Fortified with this knowledge, Gloria flipped the light switch to the left of the door to turn on the outside light. She drew back the curtain, ready to take a look at whatever creature was poking around out there. In the morning she'd mention it—oh, so casually—to Lizzy. Let her see that her little sister wasn't the complete scaredy-cat she—

Gloria gasped. A huddled shape sat on the edge of the tiny porch, rocking back and forth.

"Joss?" She opened the door and stepped out. Her satin pajamas were perfectly modest—and anyway, this was her son, after all. Leaning down, she put a hand on his shoulder. "What are you doing out here? I thought you took some pills for your headache and went to bed."

His face was buried in the crook of his arm and she couldn't make out his muttered reply. As he continued to rock, she looked across the branch to the cabin where Ben and Amanda lived. No light showed; they'd taken themselves off for the weekend with some story about friends in another county. Provoking—but in time Ben would get used to this new family member. A shame that her two boys were so different.

"It was the dream." Joss lifted his pale face to her, his eyes huge and imploring. "I've had this dream over and over, as long as I can remember. My mother is getting on a bus and going away and I'm standing in the middle of an empty street and crying for her. When I was little I tried to tell Mom—the woman I thought was my mother—about it . . . I couldn't understand why the one in the dream didn't look like her . . . but Mom would just tell me to go back to sleep."

"Oh, Joss, I'm so sorry! I wish . . ." Gloria started to caress the young man's head then pulled back, remembering his recent injury. Instantly, his hand caught hers.

"Could you stay with me . . . just for a little while? Mom never would. When I was really little, I used to try to get in bed with her and Dad but they'd make me go back to my room. I just wanted her to hold me and help me forget the bad dream. I just wanted—"

Once again he buried his face in the crook of his arm. A brief sob escaped him.

Gloria tugged at the hand that was squeezing hers. "Joss, I wish I could have been there for you. You know I'd give anything to undo all that happened back then. Please talk to me."

He made no reply but held her hand uncomfortably tight. Gloria started as a giant moth tangled in her hair then escaped to continue its mindless fluttering around the porch light. With a shudder, she realized that the light was a beacon for night-flying bugs of all kinds and she made up her mind. She gave another tug on Joss's hand. "Please, Joss, I don't like standing out here. Get up and come in my room. We can talk there—but quietly, okay?"

She had turned the CD player back on to cover up the low murmur of their voices. Now, propped up on pillows beside her on the bed, Joss had whispered out more and more of his past—the feeling of not belonging to the family he lived with, confirmed by his overhearing a conversation between the woman he called Mom and a friend of hers.

"I heard her say they'd really wanted a little girl but they took me because they were afraid they might not get another chance since they were already considered borderline too old. And she told the friend that I'd never really bonded with them and that I scared her sometimes, with my strange dreams. She said I was just too *needy*."

He looked at Gloria again with those huge dark eyes and her heart overflowed. She put her arm around him, this big sad man, and pulled him closer till his head was on her shoulder.

"There, there, Jossie, Mama's here. It's all right; I've got you now."

He closed his eyes, let out a sigh, and lay still. "Mama," he whispered. "My mama. Let me just stay here for a while . . ."

Gloria shifted, trying to ease his weight off her arm and onto the pillow. This was uncomfortable, in more ways than one, but if it could make up to this newfound son of hers even a small bit of his lost childhood . . .

Closing her eyes she felt her breathing slip into alignment with Joss's. His head slipped a little lower to lie over her heart and his breathing grew slower and more regular. Gloria tightened her arm around her baby and began silently to weep for all the lost past, the might-have-beens that never were. She wept till there were no more tears, only a quiet acceptance and profound thankfulness. And then she too slept.

It was a familiar dream that she fell into—the dream of nursing her lost baby. As before, the infant pulled at her nipple with a ferocity that was at once deeply satisfying, surprisingly sensual, and at the same time, a bit frightening. In past dreams, the infant had always been a generic Everybaby—a pink blanket-wrapped bundle with dark wisps of hair, rosebud lips, and eyes that were long-lashed but closed.

In *this* dream—and somehow, she knew that it was a dream, even in the midst of it—the baby was a miniature adult Joss, baby-sized but fully clothed in the khakis and blue oxford cloth shirt she had bought for him on their last shopping expedition. And as he sucked, he regarded her with those great dark eyes.

It was disconcerting to have the old familiar dream change and she fought her way up from the depths of sleep to awaken.

To awaken to the realization that the real Joss was suckling at her breast, his great eyes on her face, just as in the dream.

Gloria shivered in spite of the heat of the morning sun. From her vantage point on the front porch she could see Joss setting off on his daily walk, down to the mailbox and back. She and Lizzy were alone in the house. This was her chance.

Last night's strange awakening had aroused in her a welter of conflicting emotions. Her immediate reaction had been to push Joss away and leap from the bed, hurriedly rebuttoning her pajama top and hoping that Elizabeth and Phillip hadn't heard her startled cry. But then Joss—so troubled and so deeply odd, yes, she could admit that to herself now—had curled into a fetal position, jamming his thumb in his mouth and refusing to budge. It had taken almost an hour of soothing him, of listening to more of what he called his "separation issues" and his ideas for their resolution, before he agreed to slip quietly out and return to his room.

And then she had spent the sleepless remainder of the night, worrying that her reaction would be seen as yet another rejection. Worrying—and wondering if she had made a very big mistake in bringing Joss here before verifying his identity. But that would have been another rejection, wouldn't it?

She watched Joss pass the chicken coop. He had seemed as usual this morning, as if last night hadn't happened. But she couldn't forget it and when he had said *I'm going for my walk now, Mama*—that same word that had sounded so sweet coming from him a few days ago now brought a feeling to the pit of her stomach that told her something was very, very wrong.

His walk—he'd be gone almost an hour. It was now or never. She saw Joss disappear around the corner of the barn and drew a shaky breath.

"Lizzy," she said, walking into the kitchen where her sister was kneading bread. "I have to talk to you."

Chapter 28

Aunt Dodie Speaks

Sunday, June 3

L izzy, I don't know what to do about Joss."
Gloria had finally spoken. It had been obvious
that something was on her mind and even more obvious
that she didn't want to talk about it. Especially with me.

Almost as if she'd read my thoughts, she went on.
"Well, I have to talk to *someone*."

I'd been expecting it. It was the reason I'd decided to
stay at the house and make bread rather than go down
and set out those new lavender cuttings. I'd babied them
along, hoping to expand my production and make more
of those pretty ribbon-woven lavender wands that folks
went crazy over. Now the unpromising sprigs had
turned into healthy bushy little gray-green balls on the
verge of being root-bound.

But they could wait one more day. At breakfast, Gloria had looked wretched, with dark smudges under her
eyes as if she'd slept badly, and I'd noticed that she had
tried to avoid Joss's good morning kiss. Something was
profoundly wrong in this idyll of refound motherhood.

She drew up her knees and wrapped her thin arms
around them, looking like a wistful little girl with a rad-
dled matron's face. "Joss has all these ideas, about re-
claiming his identity as my child. Weird ideas that he

probably got from all those strange people in Asheville. Of course, I want to help him but . . ."

I gave the dough a final thump and plopped it into a greased bowl, covered it with a dish towel, and set it in the pantry to rise.

"Exactly what sort of ideas, Glory?" I washed the flour from my hands and took a seat beside her.

She was struggling with telling me this stuff, I could see. I could also see that she was desperately unhappy. But I knew from past experience that she would have to find her way out of this situation on her own. Much as I'd like to, I couldn't just reach in with a big-sisterly hand and set things to rights—this had to play itself out.

"He wants us to do this thing . . . well, it's called a re-birthing ceremony," she explained with an unusual for Glory reluctance. "It's a kind of therapy for people with attachment issues caused by trauma at birth."

"Ahhh," I said, drawing the word out while I tried to think of something useful to say. "Is this a thing they do in Asheville? I know there's all kinds of New—" Just in time I managed not to say *New Age shit* and came out instead with ". . . new alternative healing techniques available there. Is this one?"

"I'm not sure." Gloria looked more haggard still and she was picking at her nail polish—something I hadn't seen her do since adolescence. "I guess there's a facilita-tor or something to guide the experience. I think this was something Joss heard about from Nigel . . ."

She looked even unhappier, which surprised me. Glory's usually big into these little quickie workshop fixes for broken chakras or misguided chi or whatever will promise instant enlightenment without all that bother of fasting and meditating for years. She adores a spiritual experience that will leave her with time to go out for lunch and shopping after.

Oh, shut up, Elizabeth. Stop being such a smug bitch and find out what's wrong here.

"So, how does this rebirthing thing work?" I was working hard at keeping my voice in the neutral zone: interested, not snarky. Gloria continued her assault on the dark red lacquer on her thumbnail as she explained.

"He's supposed to get all wrapped in blankets—to simulate being in the womb—and have to fight his way out, like a baby being born. And I'm supposed to be there to hold him when he breaks free—he says that probably all his insecurity and anxiety comes from the fact that he never had any contact with me at that crucial moment he came into the world. We didn't bond then and Joss believes that all of his bad dreams and relationship problems and commitment issues come from that . . . He thinks if we just did this . . ."

She stopped, as if there was more that she wasn't willing to go into. I could only imagine.

"Well, so what about it, Glory? Is it something you want to do?"

There was a long silence as she worked on those fingernails. The exposed unpainted areas looked deathly pale next to the gleaming red. As pale as her face, which had taken on the pasty look of someone about to throw up.

I was on the verge of asking if she was all right when she answered, "I just don't know, Lizzy. I suppose I should . . . if it could help him . . . but—"

She paused again and then the words came in a burst. "Lizzy—I'm just not sure anymore! What if he *isn't* my son? And what if he is? How do I find out for sure without seeming to reject him all over again?"

The anguish in her voice and on her face was so real— and so close to home. It reminded me of the unresolved question Aunt Dodie had asked about the mysterious Hawk . . . and my own dilemma.

"It's time to call Aunt Dodie." The words were out before I stopped to think but it seemed the only thing to do. "We can tell her about Joss. If she's been covering up a secret all these years, now that he's found you, surely she wouldn't stick to her story of a stillbirth."

"Gloria! My goodness, it's been—well. I suppose the last time I saw you was at your dear mother's memorial service. And you're at Elizabeth's farm? My goodness, I'll bet you girls are having a wonderful time catching up on things! Oh, I remember how your mother and I used to be—sitting up till all hours and chattering away. Such fun! Golden, golden days! And how is dear Elizabeth?"

"I'm on the line too, Aunt Dodie. We both wanted to talk to you." Gloria had placed the call from the phone in the office and I was on the bedroom extension.

"It'll be harder for her to lie to *both* of us," Gloria had told me. "I know how she is: She'll dither around and talk about everything in the world but what I want to know. You get on the other phone, Lizzy. You always seemed to enjoy her and get along with the old idiot."

We'd been in luck. Aunt Dodie had picked up almost at once and seemed delighted to talk to us—not that there'd ever been a time when Dodie *wasn't* happy to natter on and on.

"You dear girls! What a delight to hear from you! I suppose you're helping Elizabeth prepare for her wedding, Gloria. You have such good taste in wedding arrangements—I know I enjoyed all of yours that I could get to. When you married that dear Harold—oh, now that was a fairy tale scene if ever there was one! You were so lovely and every last detail was exquisite. Do you know, I wrote it all down: the blush roses, the bridesmaids in their Gainsborough dresses—just like that picture they call 'Pinkie'—the lovely string quartet on the balcony, and, of course, every *detail* of the food.

Those little asparagus sandwiches—you hardly ever see them these days."

Yes, Dodie was in her usual form. I opened my mouth to stem the flow so that Glory could ask her question but the busy little voice at the other end prattled on.

"And, Elizabeth, when's it to be? I'm so happy that my little false alarm is all resolved—you know, about the H-A-W-K—"

I broke in before we had to go any farther down *that* particular byway. "Aunt Dodie, Gloria has a very important question for you. Glory . . . ?"

There was a choked sound and then Gloria cleared her throat and tried again. "Aunt Dodie, I really need to know about that time—" She stopped, took a breath, and started over. "You told me that—"

Gloria broke off again with a fit of something that might have been coughing but Aunt Dodie remained silent—strangely silent. Normally this would have been her cue to dispense medical advice. This would have been the perfect moment for the story of the Old Gentleman and his favorite cough medicine of honey, lemon juice, and bourbon and what the Baptist minister had said and the Old Gentleman's wry comeback.

Instead, there was no response.

Then Gloria, her voice unsteady, spoke. "Elizabeth . . . you tell her."

So, after making sure that unnaturally mute Dodie was really there and listening, I launched into an abridged version of how I'd only just learned about the lost baby and then on to how Joss had found Gloria.

"The birth date is the same," I told Aunt Dodie, winding up this unlikely story. "We've seen his driver's license. So Gloria thought—*we* thought—that maybe you'd finally tell us what really happened when Gloria's baby was born. You *were* there, weren't you?"

More silence—undoubtedly a new record for Dodie—

broken only by gulps and sniffles from Gloria. Then, at last, Aunt Dodie spoke.

"Oh, my *dear*! My poor, dear, little Gloria! After all these years! I prayed that you'd put that time behind you. I have *so* wished so that I could talk to you about it but I'd promised your mother never to speak of it again. You know what a strong personality she had. And when she passed away—well, I thought I'd get you to myself after the service and we could have a nice talk but then I thought, what's the point of reopening that old wound? You seemed so happy with your life— Who could have known that you'd lose your dear Harold later that same year? Such a tragedy—"

Gloria interrupted her, speaking with cold fury, each word dripping with bitterness. "And when Harold died, did it ever occur to you that knowing that my child was alive might have helped me? Did you ever think that maybe—"

"But, Gloria," Dodie's horrified voice countered the venomous flow. "You don't *understand*. I never lied to you! Your child—a beautiful little girl—was stillborn. She never drew a breath but that nice nurse baptized her anyway and eventually, when they released the little body, she was buried in my family plot. It's just west of where the Old Gentleman is, with a little stone of pink marble. There's the sweetest lamb carved at the top and just the date and the word *Dana*—you had said when you were laboring that that was what you'd like the baby named, do you remember? I always take her a flower when I go to visit the Old Gentleman— But, oh dear, Gloria—who in the world is this young man Elizabeth was talking about? You haven't fallen into the snares of some sort of *confidence* man, have you, dear?"

Chapter 29

Breaking Up Is Hard to Do

Sunday, June 3

Gloria, we've got to decide what to do about Joss—right now, before he gets back to the house."

The call to Aunt Dodie finally ended, we were on the front porch, keeping watch against Joss's return. Gloria's pasty look had disappeared, to be replaced with something resembling a simmering rage.

"That's easy: I want him out of here. I never want to see him again. To think that he'd take advantage of me like—"

Her head jerked up and she stared down the road. "Oh, dear god, there he comes!"

She stood and looked around—for all the world like a trapped creature seeking its bolt-hole. "Lizzy, I *can't* talk to him. Please, *you* tell him that we know the truth and want him to leave— You can get Ben or one of the Mexicans to drive him back to Asheville. Please . . ."

Joss was past the barn now and plodding steadily up the road. The weird shuffling gait hadn't improved, I thought, in spite of his daily walk.

He looked up, almost as if he had felt my gaze on him, and raised a hand in a brief salute. I waved back.

"Glory," I said, "it's Sunday. Julio and Homero left hours ago to go to Mass and spend the day with friends. And remember, Ben and Amanda are over in Yancey

County this weekend with some of *their* friends. Of course, I could drive Joss into Asheville . . . but I don't know . . . I guess I'm a little concerned about how he's likely to react to being kicked out. He doesn't strike me as someone who'll shrug his shoulders and leave without a fuss. No, I'd feel better if we could wait till late this afternoon when Phillip will be back. I think things would probably go more smoothly—"

"Why the hell is Phillip working today? *Typical!*"

Glory was on her feet and pulling open the screen door. "You're probably right; we should wait. But I can't be around him! I *can't*! Tell him I'm not feeling good and I went back to bed. Tell him anything; just keep him away from me! Oh, *god,* keep him away from me!"

She disappeared into the house and in a few moments I heard her bedroom door slam shut, just as Joss came up the steps.

"Where's my little mother?" he asked. The same words that had seemed so touchingly innocent at first now set off alarm bells in my mind. Indeed, Joss's always intense gaze seemed to have taken on a mad glitter.

Don't overdramatize this, Elizabeth, I warned myself. *It's not Joss that has changed—just your knowledge of him. Don't let it make any difference till Phillip gets back.*

Somehow, we got through the rest of the day. Gloria stayed barricaded in her room and I hung about the house, doing chores that would allow me to keep an eye on Joss, who *would* insist on tapping at her bedroom door every hour to see if she needed anything.

"Do you think she should go to the doctor?" he asked me. "She said she just needed to sleep but—"

"Joss, that's exactly what she needs. Now just relax and leave her alone, for goodness' sake."

I was standing on a chair and leaning out of a screen-less dining room window, scrubbing the outside glass with vinegar and old newspaper. It was tempting to ask Joss to help me, just to give him something to do, but my conscience hinted that getting work out of someone I planned to evict later on in the day wasn't *quite* fair.

He hung about for a while, asking questions about Gloria and about our childhood and our parents. I answered briefly, trying to let him see that I didn't have time to chat. When he got onto the subject of my father, I began to wish that, like Gloria, I could just lock myself into my bedroom till Joss was gone.

At last, however, he grew bored. After tiptoeing down the hall to stand listening outside Glory's door, he returned to whisper that he *thought* she must be sleeping.

"She has her music on real low. I'm just the same way; I like music on while I fall asleep." He fidgeted another few minutes, watching me replace the screens, and then asked abruptly if he could use the office computer.

Delighted to have him out of my airspace for a bit, I told him to go ahead. Any sensitive info was password protected, so I sent him off to play Free Cell or surf the Net or whatever he was of a mind to do.

The day dragged on in fits and starts. Joss spent a goodish amount of time at the computer; he and I ate lunch together, during which I found it increasingly difficult to listen to his raptures about being a part of a family at last. Finally he returned to the computer and I was able to sneak a sandwich and an apple and a few bottles of Perrier in to Gloria. She opened her door and beckoned me inside, whispering to me that she was using this time to redo her nails as well as working on her Pilates exercises.

"Have you called Phillip to let him know about the situation?" she hissed. "Maybe he could get off early."

But I had to disappoint her by telling her that I ab-

solutely didn't bother Phillip when he was on duty unless it was the direst of emergencies—and this didn't
qualify.

"He usually calls me on his way home in case I need
something from the store," I told her. "I'll fill him in on
what Dodie told us then. And as soon as he's home,
we'll confront Joss."

"Not *we*, Lizzy." Her jaw was set in a familiar way.
"I'm staying in here till he's gone, do you understand
me? And listen." She picked up a fat teller's envelope
from the bedside table. "He doesn't deserve this, after
the way he tried to trick me, but I did encourage him to
quit his job. This is some cash to tide him over—not a
lot, Lizzy, so don't look at me like that."

I took the envelope from her—very fat, indeed. "How
much is 'not a lot,' Glory?"

She waved me off as if I were an annoying insect of
some sort.

"I don't know—it was just what was left of my mad
money for the trip. I really prefer cash to plastic, especially at restaurants where they disappear into the back
with your card. Harold and I were ripped off that way
once and he got me into the habit of always carrying
cash. I don't think there's more than two or three thousand there—I'll have to go by the bank tomorrow."

I opened my mouth to protest this lavish payoff but a
moment's reflection told me that the money would probably make the removal of Joss go much easier. He would
have a tidy sum to ease the pain of parting—Really, how
long had he thought he could get away with this little
scam anyway?—and we could close the door on this odd
interlude.

"And, Lizzy," Gloria leveled a turquoise gaze on me,
"what was Aunt Dodie talking about—a false alarm
about a hawk? Was it something about Phil?"

"Listen, you're supposed to be sleeping," I temporized. "I need to get out of here before Joss comes look-ing for me. With any luck, Phillip will be back in a cou-ple of hours and we'll deal with your problem." *And maybe, just maybe, I can deal with mine.*

I think she was starting to make some kind of apology as I slipped out of the door. I waited to hear the click of the lock and then hurried across the hall to my bedroom where the phone was ringing.

The welcome sound of Phillip's voice, asking if I needed anything from the store, flooded me with relief. As quickly and concisely as I could, I told him about the call to Aunt Dodie and Gloria's insistence that Joss be returned to Asheville today.

"No, we haven't said anything yet—Glory's hiding out in her room and has washed her hands of the whole mess. I was hoping you'd be home soon . . ."

I hated doing this—dumping Gloria's problem on Phillip, especially when I knew he was ready for a quiet evening after a day on duty. But he made me feel better about it at once by thanking me for waiting.

"I'm thinking your instincts are probably right on this, Lizabeth." His gravelly voice was at once amused and concerned as he went on. "Just hold tight—I'll be there in twenty minutes, sweetheart. Take care."

He hung up so quickly that I was left thanking a dead line. Or was it?

In the silence of my bedroom, just as I was taking the phone from my ear, I thought I heard the soft click of an-other receiver being set down.

Oh, dear god, I thought and waited, almost holding my breath, to see if there would be some reaction from Joss.

There's not a lot to do in my—our—room. I spent a little time looking in my closet, sorting out garments that were ready for the ragbag or the thrift store—far more of the former—and when that was done, I decided that I'd probably been mistaken about the click. Surely if Joss had overheard that conversation, he'd be back here pounding on Gloria's door with some more of his lies. No, it had been just my overactive imagination, I told myself, heading back to the kitchen.

Glancing into the office, I saw that the computer was dark and there was no sign of Joss. I continued on to the kitchen. No Joss.

I was wondering if I should go looking for him when I heard footsteps in the guest room above the kitchen and realized, with a surge of relief, that Joss had been upstairs napping—something he'd done almost every day after lunch to forestall the headaches he was prone to since his accident. The footsteps moved about and then started down the stairs just as James's characteristic combined bark-and-howl told me that Phillip was home. I hurried to the window by the sink to watch as he came up the walkway and wished that I could have saved him this end-of–the-day drama. He looked tired, poor thing; he'd looked tired ever since—

A hand settled on my shoulder and I jumped. Whirling around, I saw Joss standing there.

"If my mother wants to throw me away again," he said, his face white, his voice trembling, "so be it. But she'll wish she hadn't. And so will you, *Aunt* E."

Before I could answer, he turned to see Phillip coming in the door. "Hello, Phillip. My suitcase and other stuff is right here and I'm ready to go." In a split second, Joss's voice had changed from mad and menacing to matter-of-fact and almost lighthearted.

"Okay, then," Phillip stood aside to let Joss through the door. "Let's roll." He looked at me with lifted eyebrows and we exchanged puzzled shrugs.

"Well, that went better than I'd expected" were Phillip's first words on his return from Asheville. "You had me thinking I might have to cuff him or something but, whoever he is, Joss was a perfect gentleman. Thanked me for driving him in and apologized for what he called 'the misunderstanding.' "

Gloria and I were sitting on the porch with glasses of wine. In the two hours since Joss had left, she had gone through a bewildering variety of emotions—her initial anger giving way to concern—*You don't think this could make him suicidal, do you?*—and something quite like regret—*He was so sweet and I was so happy . . .*

She was still a little teary as she stood and hugged Phillip. "Thank you so much . . . I really owe you one." She hesitated and then whispered, "Where did you take him? I think he gave up the lease on his apartment. I had thought we—"

She couldn't go on but dropped back into her chair, pressing the back of her hand against her lips.

Phillip stared down at her with a somewhat paternal manner. "I was glad to help out, Gloria. As a matter of fact, Joss wanted to be taken to the bus station. Said he'd decided to go back home to his adoptive parents and try to sort things out. But I gotta say I'd have liked it a lot better if you'd pressed charges for fraud. And, if you don't mind my asking, what was in that envelope Lizabeth told me to give him?"

Gloria avoided his eyes. "It was just a note . . . saying how unkind he'd been to play such a trick and telling him that he should never attempt to contact me or my family again . . ."

Phillip continued to stare at her as if expecting something more.

My sister had the grace actually to look slightly embarrassed as she added, "Oh . . . and some money."

I stood to go inside and get supper ready. "Can I get you a beer, sweetheart? Or—"

Muttering something about a shower before supper, Phillip followed me into the house. Once inside, he jerked his head toward the back of the house, his lips framing one word: *Talk*.

Looking back through the screen door, I saw Gloria tapping a number into her cellphone.

Chapter 30

The Envelope, Please

Sunday, June 3

Okay, Elizabeth, where do we go from here?"

Phillip shut the door of our bedroom carefully and fixed me with an accusing look. "I got to tell you that your sister is making me crazy. I was thinking about it, driving back from Asheville. First she's on the run from her husband, then, about the time that looks like it's getting sorted out—what with the Eyebrow fella getting picked up—then there's this whole long-lost-child thing. Now that's over—what's next? "

I went to the window and leaned my forehead on the glass. "You've been so patient about this whole thing, sweetheart. I wish I could say it's over and she's leaving tomorrow. But she doesn't want to go back to Jerry. I think she's done with him—she says she still doesn't trust him . . . and anyway she's determined to stay and help with our wedding—"

"Oh, the alleged wedding." Phillip, who'd been shucking off clothes in preparation for a shower, pulled on his bathrobe and came to stand beside me. "I thought maybe you'd forgotten all about that."

Sarcasm isn't his usual mode: His words made me aware of just how angry he was. The man's a saint—he's put up with me for some time now—but even a saint, sooner or later, is going to be tempted to pull off his halo and beat someone over the head with it.

"Phillip—" I began, but he didn't look at me as he spoke.

"We're supposed to be getting married sometime this month and as far as I know, we don't even have a firm date for it. It would suit me fine to go down to the court-house but *you* said you wanted it at the farm with all the kids here."

I wanted to put in a conciliatory word but what that word might be completely escaped me and the ac-cusatory monologue rolled on.

"So, correct me if I'm wrong here but as far as I can tell, fuck-all has been done about any wedding. Shit, Lizabeth, Seth called today, wanting to know when he and Caitlin should plan to get here and I had to tell him I didn't have a clue."

The effort he was making to keep his voice down was obvious and when I laid my hand on his terry-cloth sleeve, I could feel the tension vibrating through his body.

It's time to put things out in the open, I told myself. Now or never, win or lose, do or die—faded old clichés but they suited the moment. All my life I'd prided myself on my rationality but at critical cusps or turning points, it had been my intuition—or call it my heart—that I'd followed. This was one of those times. Taking a deep breath, I plunged into the sea of doubt.

"Okay, Phillip, this is what's been on my mind— along with all of Glory's stuff. Bear with me for a few more minutes while I explain why I've been . . . hesi-tant."

The still afternoon beauty of the far eastern moun-tains, rosy with reflected light, seemed a ludicrous contrast to the turmoil of my thoughts. There should have been lowering storm clouds or driving rain. Tree branches should have been whipping in frenzied agony. Instead, the scene before me was one of pastoral calm. Red cows grazed on the green grass and just below the window, the bird feeder was a gentle flutter of doves, there for a last few sunflower seeds before darkness sent them to roost.

Peace . . . Would what I was about to tell Phillip change everything—call down the thunder, stampede the cattle, send the doves whirring off to safety?

No matter. I'd let this drag on too long. I held to his still-tense arm as if to keep him there and began.

"You remember when Glory first went to a private investigator in Asheville for help in getting in touch with Arturo? Well, that wasn't all she hired the P.I. to do. She was having so much fun with the detective stuff that she thought it would be a nice little hostess-gift-type thing for her to—oh god, I hate having to tell you this—for her to get the P.I. to find out more about what happened to Sam—"

Phillip looked at me now, his face a battleground of incredulity and frustration.

"Lizabeth, this is an old story. Sam's Navy friends have *always* suspected there was something weird about that crash. Shit, I know I told you that Del, my friend— Sam's friend too—has tried every avenue to investigate that crash, only to run into stone walls each time. And Del's high up at the Pentagon. What's some Asheville P.I. going to find out that Del—"

"And then there's this thing about the Hawk," I forged on, ignoring what he was trying to say. "A while back Aunt Dodie wrote me about a letter she'd found. The letter was from Sam to Dodie's husband—and Sam had written him about someone from the Navy called the Hawk that he—that Sam hadn't trusted."

Phillip was watching me closely now, his face expressionless. "Your aunt's husband was a retired admiral, right? I remember Sam mentioning him. Go on."

"Well, Dodie wanted to make sure that *you* weren't the Hawk—I guess it seemed kind of logical; after all, that's what Mackenzie calls you—but I just kept telling myself it was more of Dodie's foolishness. And then this morning when we talked to Dodie, she brought it up again, how she'd thought—"

I couldn't bring myself to finish the sentence. But Phillip could.

"That the Hawk was me, right?"

The muscle beneath the toweling sleeve hardened. Looking down, I saw that Phillip's fists were clenched and white-knuckled.

"What about you, Lizabeth?" His voice was flat—emotionless—as he made the challenge. "What have *you* decided?"

The first time Phillip and I had dinner together in Asheville—our first *date,* weird as the notion seems to me—I saw him lose his temper and smash his fist into a brick wall. My instant reaction had been to get away from a man capable of that kind of violence. But he'd apologized at once and, in the years since, there'd never been the least hint of the temper he'd shown that first day. If there was a demon within this man, it was on a short, strong leash.

As I said before, now and then I throw caution and reason to the winds and make a leap of faith. I made one when I asked Phillip to marry me. Now I was going to trust my instincts—or my heart—again.

"June the twenty-first," I told him. "Tell Seth and Janie that the wedding is Thursday, June the twenty-first—the summer solstice." I threaded my hand through his arm—noting that the quivering tension of the muscle had disappeared. "That is, if the day suits you. And if you still want to marry me, considering the sister-in-law you'll be getting."

"Are you going to take that shower?" I asked sometime later, wondering if Glory had noticed our absence.

Phillip gave me a final lingering kiss and stood up. "First, come down to the basement—I want to show you something I just remembered a few minutes ago."

Puzzled, I watched as, grinning like a madman, Phillip belted his robe tight again and unlocked the bedroom door. His bare feet pattered down the steep stairs and I followed, wondering what he could have in mind— what it was our recent . . . activities had reminded him of? There was nothing much in the basement but the washer and dryer and freezers—along with assorted boxes full of his possessions that had been ousted from the back bedroom to make room for Glory.

Shoving aside a laundry basket, Phillip pulled out one of the blue plastic storage tubs and began to root through it, muttering to himself, "It's in here somewhere—why the hell didn't I keep it out? I know I meant to . . ."

Stacks of assorted correspondence and various manila envelopes along with what looked like old income tax materials began to accumulate on the basement floor beside the blue bin as he continued his search.

"Where'd this come from?" He was staring at a newspaper he'd just unearthed—a newspaper that I recognized at once as *The Marshall County Guardian*. It was folded around a clump of assorted mail—and in that assortment was a shiny red mailing envelope.

Phillip raised his eyebrows, looked at the newspaper's front page, and shook his head in dismay. "January?"

He grimaced as he saw the little clutch of unopened letters hidden in the newspaper's fold. "Oh, shit, Lizabeth. It's your mail from early January." He held it out to me. "It must have gotten mixed up with my work stuff—been sitting in with all my old papers in that bedroom, waiting to get filed."

I took the little handful of letters. It was Dodie's missing red mailer—and inside would be the letter from Sam about the man called Hawk—the man he didn't trust.

As far as I could tell, the red mailer was unopened. Aunt Dodie never trusted simple adhesives and this flap was sealed tight with packing tape. My heart grew lighter.

Phillip had ceased his digging through the papers and was sitting back on his heels, looking deeply embarrassed. "Damn—what can I say? I hope there wasn't anything vital . . . missed bills or anything important . . ."

I tucked the red mailer under my arm and studied the other letters—junk mail and a reminder from the dentist. Fortunately Doc Adams left nothing to chance—his office always phoned reminders as well, so I hadn't missed that appointment.

"No," I said, "nothing important. But what is it you're looking for?"

"I know it's here," he said, returning to his rummaging. "Remember when I first called you? I'd just moved to Asheville and I wanted an excuse to see you so I offered to bring out some pictures I had of Sam back from our early days in training."

How long ago it seemed. I hadn't been particularly eager to see the pictures or to meet this old buddy of Sam's—a man I'd heard of for years but had never met till the memorial service and then only briefly.

I leaned against the dryer and watched him continue to excavate his past. "I kind of remember something about pictures. But what I mainly remember is how rude I managed to be to you that first time."

"Not rude, sweetheart—but definitely cautious."

Phillip winked at me. "You were . . . intriguingly aloof. And I love a challenge, so—" He pounced on something near the bottom of the bin. "Eureka! Here it is!"

Brandishing a manila envelope, he stood and handed it to me. "Take a look. There should be a picture of four guys in swim trunks."

It no longer hurt to look at pictures of Sam. A little twinge, perhaps, but Sam's loss was something I'd finally come to terms with. I would always love him but he was part of another time now. I couldn't say it to anyone, without sounding heartless, but I no longer missed him with that horrible, hollow longing that had permeated the early days of my widowhood. Now he was only a sweet and tender memory—like a faded dried rose that retains a whisper of its living fragrance.

So I shuffled through the little collection: Sam and Phillip shooting hoops, Sam and Phillip and three other sailors in front of some sort of brick building . . . Here it was: four men in bathing suits, standing on the edge of a large boat of some kind and squinting into the sun. Sam and Phillip, a tall black guy, and a wiry young man with gaudy tattoos on his chest.

"That one was taken in 'Nam. Check out the back."

X~Nellie Bly

Friday, May 20, 1887

*Nellie Bly, known to all at the Mountain Park Hotel
by her birth name Elizabeth Jane Cochrane, sighed and
laid her knife and fork across her almost empty plate to
signify that she had finished her meal. At once, George,
the ever-attentive waiter, whisked the plate away and returned with a pitcher.*

*"Mo' water, Miss Cochrane? Cain I temp' you folks
wif dessert? They got some mighty fine rhubarb pie. And
there's fresh strawberries, come on the train this morning—all the way from Georgia. Oh my, strawberry
shortcake! Lemme bring you folks a little taste."*

*Laughing, Nellie Bly waved him off. "Get thee behind
me, George! Not another bite!"*

*Addressing her companions at the table, she contin-
ued. "Don't you see that this place is nothing but a
fiendish snare? They put you to marching and dancing,
swinging Indian clubs, playing strenuous sports and
doing even more strenuous calisthenics—all in pursuit
of good health and an elegant figure—and then . . ."*

*She cast an expressive glance around the high-
ceilinged dining room where the chink of silver on china
played an accompaniment to the low hum of well-bred
conversation. Courtly black waiters in tuxedos and*

white gloves flitted back and forth, bearing trays heavy laden with delectable dishes in mounded plenty.

"And then! Three times a day they put the most delicious foods known to man before you and hire devils like George to sing the praises of the cuisine. I appeal to you, Doe and Theo, is this fair to frail womanhood— that we should be expected to exercise our willpower in addition to our muscles?"

A ripple of laughter ran round the table where Nellie Bly, the three DeVines, two portly middle-aged gentlemen, and a pair of women who appeared to be mother and daughter were seated.

Lorenzo DeVine leaned toward the vivacious, dark-haired young woman. "Surely a being as sylphlike as yourself need not deny herself the joys of strawberry shortcake? Allow me to suggest a solution . . ."

Raising a manicured finger, he caught the waiter's attention. "George! One shortcake, two forks—and be generous with the whipped cream."

"I declare, your sisters are monstrous poor friends— to desert me in favor of their afternoon naps." Nellie Bly smiled up at Lorenzo DeVine. "Ah, well, I suppose that I should go for a walk after such a dinner, but I believe I'll exercise myself in a rocking chair on the veranda for a while. There's a delicious breeze . . ."

"Allow me, Miss Eliza." Lorenzo proffered his arm and together the two strolled through the light-filled lobby. Persian carpets in glowing reds and blues muffled their tread as they wound their way through the spacious room. On every side, comfortable chairs and settees of cushioned wicker were placed in convenient groups for gossip, reading, or slumber and not a few of the guests took their afternoon rest in these congenial surroundings.

The veranda offered a view of the little golf course

where a few men in knickerbockers were ambling along the short fairways or bending over putters on the close-cut greens. Nellie Bly seated herself in a rocker well away from the other guests and patted the empty chair beside her.

"Now, as your punishment for leading me into temptation with that ambrosial shortcake, you are to sit here beside me and be amusing. What have you scheduled for the afternoon?"

Taking up a wooden paddle from the table at her elbow, she perused the printed schedule affixed to one side and began to read aloud.

" 'Three P.M.—Corrective and Medical Gymnastics followed by Games and Folk Dancing.' " She quirked a teasing eyebrow. "And will you be participating, Mr. DeVine?"

"Not I," he returned. "I must save my strength for the lecture on Spiritualism and the Life Beyond that the management has persuaded me to give this evening. At the moment, however, a stroll about the grounds with a fair companion is what I chiefly crave. And then I have a golf match at four with a Mr. Parsons who demands satisfaction for the trouncing I gave him yesterday."

"Do you, indeed?" said Nellie Bly, favoring her companion with a brilliant smile.

The Mountain Park Hotel & Sanitarium
Daily Program for Guests

(The following schedule is optional. There is no charge except for those treatments, entertainments, and sports marked by an asterisk.)

6:30 A.M.—Morning shower. Treatment room.

7:15 A.M.—Calisthenics and breathing exercises. Gymnasium or lawn.

7:40 A.M.—Morning worship.

8 A.M. to 9 A.M.—Breakfast.

9:15 A.M.—Corrective Gymnastics and Games. Walking and Mountain Climbing.

*9:00 A.M. to 1:00 P.M.—Men's Treatments.

1:00 P.M. to 2:00 P.M.—Dinner.

2:00 P.M. to 3:00 P.M.—Rest Period.

3:00 P.M.—Corrective and Medical Gymnastics, followed by Games and Folk Dancing.

*3:00 P.M.—Treatments for Women.

*4:00 P.M.—Tennis, Golf, Horseback Riding, Boating and other sports.

6:30 P.M.—Supper.

7:30 P.M.—Marching and Folk Dancing.

*8:00 P.M.—Moving Pictures, Lectures and Concerts, etc.

9:30 P.M.—Rest

Chapter 31

Seeking Closure

Sunday, June 3, and Tuesday, June 5

I flipped the picture over. Written on the back in faded ink that had been blurred by a moisture ring in one spot were the words: *Red Goodweather. Phil Hawkins. Boner Bonham. Jonesy (the Hawk) Jones.*

Phil. Of course. It came rushing back: Sam talked about traveling with *Phil* and some of the others to the Vietnam Memorial in DC—the Wall. It wasn't Phillip that Sam had been worried about. *It wasn't Phillip!*

"This Hawk fella you and your aunt Dodie are all worked up over—he was with our unit early on in 'Nam. Crazy guy—got the nickname when he fell asleep while he was sunbathing bare-ass naked. Literally. His butt was burned bright red and someone said something about a red-tailed hawk and before long, everyone started calling him the Hawk instead of Jonesy. An interesting guy—could talk your ear off and knew all the angles. Way too smart for his own good.

"He ended up with a dishonorable discharge and some brig time too—the creep was selling Navy property to the Vietnamese on a scale that finally couldn't be ignored. And it was Sam who figured it out. Not till he was out of the service, but he managed to get hold of someone with major pull who eventually reeled Jones in."

"That would have been the Old Gentleman—Aunt Dodie's husband. He'd been retired from the Navy a good while but I'm sure he still knew people . . ."

I studied the picture more closely. Sam and Phillip, both so young and untroubled, both so happy . . .

"Did your friend Del think that this Hawk had something to do with what happened to Sam?" I asked.

Phillip looked up from the messy piles of paper that he was shuffling into some kind of order before returning them to the container. "You know, that's something none of us ever considered. We've been pretty sure all along that we knew who the guy behind it was . . . and he was more or less untouchable because of his position in government . . . still is. But if Jones was involved and we can find him . . ."

Again, he rocked back on his heels and squatted there, thinking hard. "I'll give Del a call. See if going after Jones might get him anywhere . . ."

He stood and dumped the rest of the papers back into the container. "You understand, Lizabeth, it's a real long shot that Del will be able to prove anything—most likely nothing will change."

My heart, that most irrational of organs, was brimming with joy as I wrapped my arms around my soon-to-be husband. "Nothing . . . everything . . . what matters now is getting this wedding planned."

"*Lizzy?*"

Gloria's voice sounded from the top of the stairs. "Lizzy? What in the world are you two doing down there? Are you all right?"

"Better than all right, Glory. I've got a picture to show you . . ."

Later that night I had finally opened the mysterious red mailer from Aunt Dodie. There, just as she had said, was a letter from Sam with a reference to a person called the Hawk. There was also a duplicate of the picture of four men—though in this photo, there was an arrow drawn in ink pointing to the so-called Hawk. On the back, in Sam's precise printing were the words *This is him.*

Reading the letter had been bittersweet and I was happy to hand it over for Phillip to send on to his friend at the Pentagon. After all this time I could see little chance that justice would ever be done but there was always a hope.

Sunday had been a day of revelation . . . and liberation. Gloria and Phillip and I had talked . . . explained . . . apologized . . . and done it all over again till all that was left was love and laughter. By Tuesday all the doubts and what-ifs were laid to rest; at last I was able to turn my thoughts to the wedding—a wedding only two weeks away. Phillip had arranged time off for five days; his children had made their plans, as had mine. Nearby friends had been invited and I'd even asked Dodie, though I hadn't been surprised when she'd declined, saying that at her age the trip would be too difficult.

I'd managed to dissuade Gloria from flying her fancy florist friend in for the occasion, telling her that Laurel particularly wanted to take charge of decorating and that there would be plenty of flowers on the farm for her to use.

"What about food then?" Gloria had asked as we sat at the dining table, making lists of Things That Must Be Done. "I could have The Mountain Magnolia do the catering. Let's see . . ."

She pulled a notepad to her and began to scribble. "Poached salmon is always so elegant—perfect in this warm weather with the cucumbers and sour cream and little rye loaves. Quiche is good—do it in bite-size shells,

I think, with little roasted cherry tomatoes . . . and Ina has a divine strata recipe—"

"Ina?" I asked. "A friend of yours?"

"Ina *Garten,* Lizzy! The Barefoot Contessa—cookbooks, television—I would have thought even *you* would have heard of the Barefoot Contessa! Now, what do you think—champagne and mimosas—or have mimosas been done to death? And—"

Her pen was moving busily, filling the notepad. I hated to do it but I had to interrupt.

"Glory, Rosemary and Laurel and Amanda have already offered to do the food. They're actually looking forward to—"

Undaunted, she flipped the notepad pages and continued. "Your hair, then. I could get Nigel to style it—maybe next week take you in for him to figure out your look. And he could come out the morning of the wedding and do a comb-out. Did you know he used to be a stylist at the spa in Hot Springs? He could make you look *fabulous*! And I'll do your makeup."

I laughed and reached over to squeeze her hand. Somehow my sister's interfering little ways that had kept me on edge since her arrival seemed now nothing more than humorous, even lovable, idiosyncrasies.

"You know me, Glory: no hairstyling, no makeup. I'd hate for Phillip not to recognize his bride."

Her face fell—and for an instant I saw the child I'd locked out of my room because I wanted to read in peace, the little girl whose new pink dress I'd made fun of, the teenager I'd been too busy to worry about, the sister I'd let down again and again.

"Isn't there *anything* I can do?" she pleaded. "I'd like to feel that I had *some* part in the wedding."

Gloria's voice trembled—just slightly. She seemed on the edge of tears but looked down to busy herself with brushing invisible dog hair from her crisp linen cropped pants. An idea seemed to dawn and she brightened. "Tell me, Lizzy, what are you going to wear for the ceremony?"

I hadn't the heart to tell her that I'd planned on winging it with whatever I could find in the back of my closet. I knew there was a nice-looking long skirt and a pretty blouse that would work—but instead of disappointing Glory yet again, I summoned my better angel.

"Maybe you could help me find something in Asheville, Sissy," I heard myself saying.

"Do me a favor, would you, Lizabeth? Don't you and Gloria go in to Asheville for a few days. Not till say . . . Saturday. I want to make sure Joss really went home and stayed home. I've been in touch with the sheriff down there—it's a small rural town and he knows the parents. He said it would be no problem to verify that Joss had come back home."

I put down the book I'd just picked up and stared at Phillip. We were in bed—we'd been going to bed earlier and earlier these days, just to have a chance for a little private conversation. Between the overhead fan in our room and Glory's seemingly inexhaustible supply of show tunes, we could talk freely in slightly lowered tones. I'd been telling him how the wedding preparations stood as well as all about Glory's plans for a shopping trip.

He settled against the pillows and stared back. "I'm serious, Elizabeth. That Joss—oh, he went without making any fuss but, I don't know, he was so into the whole reunited mother-and-son thing—"

"He certainly *seemed* sincere," I agreed. "I would have sworn . . . Now, though, I'm wondering. Was it some kind of a scam? Looking back, there are a few things—like that license of his, showing he was born the same day as Gloria's child—I remember thinking it looked awfully *new.* But Joss didn't seem organized or . . . or street-smart enough to know how to get hold of a forged driver's license."

"What do *you* think, Sherlock?"

I landed a gentle punch on Phillip's bare shoulder. He was grinning at me now and I had the sensation—the comforting sensation—of playing a familiar part in this slightly corny version of almost-married life.

Settling against him, I began to think out loud.

"I think Joss is a sad case. I think he probably really is an orphan looking for his birth mother and I think he truly believes—or truly wants to believe—that Gloria *is* that mother."

Phillip put his arm around me and closed his eyes. "Go on . . ."

"I think . . . I think Nigel comes into this somehow. I mean, besides the fact that he told both Gloria and Joss about the séance weekend . . . and . . . Joss said that Nigel had some sort of vision of Gloria in a box . . . It was Nigel's call that told Joss where to look for her. But I don't see what . . ."

"If it was me, Sherlock," Phillip's deep voice rumbled softly in my ear, "and if I hadn't been told in no uncertain terms not to pursue the question, what I'd be wanting to know is who put little Glory in that box in the basement? And I'd start by asking *why.*"

Chapter 32

Old Friends

Thursday, June 7

I pondered that question as the busy week went on. At the time, the only reason I could imagine for Gloria's abduction was that it was meant to frighten her. She wasn't harmed and with a little determined effort, she could surely have freed herself. Or at least shouted. And that was another question that defied all my pondering: *Why hadn't Gloria called out?*

With Joss's departure, Ben and Amanda's hectic schedule mysteriously grew less full and they joined us for dinner most nights, lingering after the meal to sit on the porch with coffee, watching the fireflies winking in the dusk. Amanda's initial reserve with Gloria gave way to an amused affection and she delighted my sister with behind-the-scenes stories from her brief career as a highly paid fashion model.

"... A really scary-looking black leather *bustier* that laced up the back leaving the edges about six inches apart ... let's see ... and black and white checked tights with a short tiered skirt in a black and gray geometric pattern held out with black net crinolines. They'd skinned my hair back and pinned on a kind of crest of ruched black net—like a Mohawk—and the makeup girl did my face in dead white with slashes of red on each cheek. The white covered my lips and she painted a black butterfly in the middle, like a little rosebud mouth. I looked nothing like myself—but that's the point, when you're a model. You're the clothes hanger for the designer's creation—nothing more."

Gloria laughed with delight. At last, I imagined her thinking, a conversation that didn't involve planting things. "Oh, I *remember* that look. I saw pictures somewhere—"

Amanda raised her hand. "But here's the part I wanted to tell you: As I was waiting to step out on to the catwalk, the designer reached up to fluff my faux-hawk. She was really on edge—she'd just lit a cigarette even though there were signs posted everywhere. I started to warn her but just then the starter gave me my cue to go out.

"I was halfway down the catwalk when all this commotion broke out—*People are digging this outfit,* I thought. Cameras were flashing so that I could hardly see but I kept on with that weird slouchy walk we were all doing that year. It wasn't till I made my turn that I felt the heat on my head. And, at that same moment, I saw one of the stagehands running toward me with a fire extinguisher. Then the audience *really* went crazy."

"Oh, no! The thing on your head was on *fire?*" Gloria squealed. "And it was the designer herself, her cigarette—right? She must have been *devastated.*"

Amanda smiled and stood. "As a matter of fact, that incident made her reputation. Most of the audience thought the whole thing was planned. And the picture of me swaggering down the runway with my head on fire made all the trade papers."

She leaned against the railing where Ben was perched. "I never knew if the designer had done it on purpose or not. I wasn't burned. But that was when I realized I had to get out of the modeling game."

Ben reached out to put an arm around her. "Lucky for

me you did." Amanda turned to him with a smile of such breathtaking intensity that I felt like an eavesdropper on some private conversation.

Gloria, however, was hungry for more tidbits. "Didn't I hear that you'd worked for Versace once? Tell me, do you know if . . ."

I left them on the porch chattering away as Gloria pumped Amanda for more stories of the designers she'd worked for. I was lost amid the welter of names—*Pinar, Donatella, Tani, Samil*—but happy that Gloria and her son's girlfriend seemed to be enjoying each other's company at last.

A lot had changed with Joss's departure. Gloria, instead of darting off into Asheville every day on some pretext or other, began to relax, ever so slightly, into the routine of the farm—at least, the less strenuous, cleaner bits of that routine. She seemed to enjoy making wreaths and I was happy for her help and her company. We spent hours in the comparative cool of the fragrant workshop, filling in the blanks of our respective lives for each other and learning to enjoy and appreciate each other, warts and all—a quantum leap for both of us.

"Let me fix dinner tonight. I'll come with you to the grocery store and pick up some salmon," Gloria said Thursday morning, as we talked over our plans for the day while I made out my grocery list. "Salmon is one thing I know how to cook. And you've got asparagus in the fridge. That and some little new potatoes—what do you think?"

I thought it would be wonderful and told her so. Though I'm fond of cooking, it's a true luxury to eat a meal I had nothing to do with.

"Oh good!" she exclaimed. "And we can take my Mini. The poor thing's probably feeling neglected."

Cocking an eyebrow at me, she went on. "It should be

safe now, right? Now that all the baddies are accounted for."

I hoped they were.

Phillip had told me only the night before that Joss's arrival in the little town near the coast where his parents lived had been confirmed. Even better was the news about the Eyebrow who, as Phillip said, in best detective fiction style, had "sung like a canary."

"Those outstanding warrants I told you about—there were enough charges to keep him off the streets for a very long time. Finally his lawyer convinced him that a little cooperation might shorten his sentence and pretty soon they couldn't shut him up. Evidently he and Gloria's husband had a falling-out so the Eyebrow decided to get even by making Gloria think Jerry was trying to do her in."

Suddenly things began to fall into place. "So that's it! She was never in any real danger—because if something had happened to her, Jerry would have inherited her money. What the Eyebrow wanted was for her to leave Jerry—"

"And it was working. But now that the Eyebrow's looking at major time, he's spilling every last detail of Jerry's business dealings. I got a real feeling old Jerry's going to end up a guest of the state too. Probably one of those country club facilities for white-collar criminals. From what my buddy down in Tampa could tell me, Jerry stayed clear of the rough stuff—defrauding widows and orphans was more his style."

I had to admit Gloria's Mini was a hoot. Spinning along so low to the ground was quite different from my big Jeep. Though, as I quickly reminded myself, the Mini would be useless for my usual shopping trips which generally involved a week's worth of groceries and several fifty-pound bags of one kind of feed or another.

As we scooted past Miss Birdie's house, Gloria glanced at the tidy yard and the immaculate little garden patch where Birdie herself was wielding a hoe, scratching up invisible weeds. Always alert to every passing vehicle, the little woman turned her head in its protective sunbonnet toward the road and raised her long-handled hoe in a salute.

"She looks like something from another time," Gloria remarked as we returned the greeting and sped on toward the bridge. "I'd like to go visit her again. You know, seeing her just now, it reminded me of this workshop I did once about the Feminine Divine. Miss Birdie is like—and don't laugh at me, Lizzy—the Mother Goddess. "

"No arguments from me," I said, remembering the instant connection that had happened between my sister and Miss Birdie. "Tell you what: Birdie loves all sorts of exotic fruit but won't buy it for herself. Let's get her a fresh pineapple at the store—we can stop in on our way back."

And lay our offering at the feet of the Mother. The thought sprang unbidden but I resisted saying it out loud, lest Glory think I was laughing at her. Somehow, it sounded entirely appropriate.

As we turned onto the bridge across the French Broad, I caught sight of my old friend the great blue heron winging his stately way down the river.

"Pull over and stop for a moment, Glory. I want to see where he's going. They probably have a nest somewhere nearby." I was straining my eyes to follow the heart-stoppingly lovely bird—the immense wings, pale gray bordered in deeper steely blue-gray, the elegant curve of the neck, and the sweetly absurd trailing orange legs.

We leaned on the concrete railing, enjoying the fresh

breeze, the sunlight glinting on the fast-moving water. Far down the river a gaggle of rubber rafts were negotiating a series of rocks and rapids called the Maze. A few squeals drifted back to us.

"They sound like they're having fun." Gloria's eyes were hidden by her sunglasses but her voice was wistful. "Sometimes I wonder . . . if Mother hadn't—"

She stopped and we both turned at the approach of a work-worn black farm truck that slowed and then pulled over to park in front of the Mini. I took a deep breath as I saw Harice Tyler get out and come toward us, a lazy smile on his face.

"Lizzy!" Gloria's whisper was full of alarm. She had stiffened at the sight of Harice, who, in farm-dirty work clothes, was, I'll admit, enough to start the *Deliverance* banjos playing. I could only guess what Glory might be thinking. And she didn't even know about the snakes.

"You all right, Miz Goodweather?" Harice spoke to me but his eyes were on Gloria, no doubt taking in her sleeveless blouse, bare legs, gold jewelry—all forbidden to the women of the Holiness Church he pastored. "Thought maybe that little roller skate you uns is driving might have give out."

When I assured him that we didn't have car trouble, he gave Glory's legs one last odd look—disapproving approval?—and sauntered back to his truck. I watched him go, wondering why I had ever imagined myself attracted to him. The words of the old hymn *I once was blind but now I see* formed on my lips as I watched that conscious swagger of his that went over so well with the female part of his congregation.

As he pulled out and headed toward Bear Tree Creek, Gloria released the breath she'd been holding.

"Who was *that*? Those *eyes*! Clean him up and he could—"

"That," I said, looking down the river again, "was the pastor of a snake-handling church in Tennessee. Dang! I should have introduced you—he's between wives just now."

"You uns come up in the shade and get you a chair. Aye, law, what have you got in that big poke?"

Birdie's black and white dog Pup came wagging to greet us as we approached the porch where my neighbor was enjoying the virtuous rest of one with laundry drying on the line, a freshly mown yard, and a weedless garden patch.

"Gloria brought you a pineapple and some mangoes, Miss Birdie. If you don't care, I'll take them to the kitchen and cut them up for you while you and Glory visit."

"Well, what about that!" Birdie peered into the brown paper bag. "You know I do like them pineapples. My, I can smell it just as good . . . and these here—I like them things awful good. They put me in mind of a peach but they ain't peaches. What did you call 'em—something like banjo, ain't it? Why you girls is like to spoil me!"

In Birdie's cheerful kitchen I tracked down a cutting board and located a knife sharp enough to deal with the pineapple, as well as a couple of plastic containers to put the fruit into. As I stood by the sink, I could hear snatches of the conversation on the porch, just beyond the kitchen window.

". . . been thinking about what you told me . . . your babies that died . . . your angels . . ."

Gloria was telling Miss Birdie about her own lost baby—the stillborn girl she'd never seen. I could hear Birdie's comforting murmur and it seemed to me that Gloria was crying very softly.

". . . Honey, just you go ahead . . . do you good . . ."

By the time I'd dealt with the pineapple and turned to the mangoes, Gloria seemed to have recovered herself and was questioning Birdie about the "angels," as Birdie referred to her dead children.

I leaned a little closer to the window.

". . . talk to them—and seems at times they talk to me . . . Luther didn't believe in such . . . a comfort to me . . . like praying."

When I'd put the sliced-up fruit into the refrigerator and cleaned up the mess, I returned to the sink to wash my hands.

" . . . I will, Miss Birdie," I heard Gloria say, her voice filled with an eager joy. "I will . . ."

Chapter 33

Retail Therapy

Saturday, June 9

Saturday was upon us and I found myself on my way to a tour of Asheville's most expensive shops, in search of a wedding dress—or rather, a dress for an unsophisticated bride of mature years, embarking on her second marriage in an informal outdoor setting. I hate to shop, and do it so seldom that I always find myself suffering severe sticker shock at the prices.

For Gloria, on the other hand, shopping is like swimming in her chosen element. Despite the fact that she had been in Asheville only a few times, she was far more familiar with the shopping opportunities than I had ever been and a few days ago had laid out a plan of attack encompassing the various places that might have the sort of dress she deemed suitable.

"There's a wonderful place just a few doors down from Nigel's that I want to try. And, if you don't mind, I'd like to just pop into Nigel's for a quick shampoo and comb-out—my hair gets so out of control when I do it myself for too long. It wouldn't take over half an hour—forty-five minutes at the most. Surely you might have some shopping you could do while I was busy."

I had started to protest and then remembered my favorite downtown bookstore-slash-café near the library. I could while away a bit of time there—as well as pick up a few assorted books for birthday gifts.

"Sure, Glory!" the new, ever-accommodating Elizabeth had said. "Go on and make your appointment."

I insisted on an early start, having learned that weekends in Asheville tended toward the hectic at times. Recently, it seemed there was always a festival of some sort going on—Bele Chere, Goombay . . . I had no idea if something was up this weekend but with June came tourists and increased traffic.

We were passing by the Dewell Hill church, heading for the highway that would take us to the Interstate and on to Asheville, when Gloria slowed and nodded toward the graveyard that surrounded the old church.

"When I went with Amanda yesterday to see the herb garden she'd just installed at that B and B, on the way back I got her to stop here. Miss Birdie told me the other day how there used to be a grave up on a bank near the road that had a dollhouse built over it. She said if you looked through the little window, inside you could see the dolls sitting at a table like they were having a tea party. I wanted to see if I could find where it had been so Amanda and I walked around looking at all the gravestones there were for little children."

I opened my mouth to say that Birdie had told me that same story years ago and I too had gone looking for the dollhouse grave. But then I realized that this was Gloria's story. And how badly she needed to tell it.

Since our visit to Miss Birdie, my sister had been in high spirits, almost the same euphoria she'd exhibited during the days she believed Joss was her lost child. I'd hoped she would tell me just what it was that Birdie had said or done that had lifted her spirits so but she hadn't. And I hadn't wanted to pry.

But now the story was emerging.

". . . so many children's graves, some with little

lambs. Do you remember, Aunt Dodie said that the stone she put up for my Dana has a lamb on it?"

Her eyes were swimming with tears now, but Gloria brushed them away, careless of her mascara.

"Anyway, I've made up my mind. After the wedding, I'm going to go stay with Aunt Dodie for a while. I'd like her to tell me whatever she can about my baby—my Dana. Dodie actually saw her, you know ... She said she was beautiful ... And then I'll visit Dana's grave ... and talk to her ... the way Birdie talks to her lost babies. She says it gives her healing."

It took a moment for what my sister had said to register—and then I didn't know what to say other than, "Well, Glory . . ."

Gloria sniffed and fumbled in the side pocket for a tissue. "I know ... I could talk to her anywhere. If Giles were still here ... But he was just in North Carolina for the weekend and, according to his website, he's going to Australia for several months. Oh, when I think it might have been Dana trying to speak to me and then that crazy Joss interrupted . . ."

She dabbed at her eyes again. "But it doesn't matter. First I need to go back to New Bern, apologize to Aunt Dodie, and thank her for taking care of my baby's grave. Then I'll spend some time, just with Dana ... Turo might join me there ... We've been talking every night."

As she continued, it became apparent that once again, Gloria was moving on: putting her current relationship behind her and preparing to plunge again. She'd evidently been in touch with her friend Eleanor who'd confirmed what Phillip had been told—gone him one better, in fact. Jerry had been arrested. Rumor was that, even had Gloria been willing to throw resources into his defense, no lawyer, no matter how good, was going to get Jerry out of the tangle of fraud, extortion, and who knows what other felonious monkey business he'd been up to.

And Arturo, Gloria mentioned with elaborate casualness, was a widower now, and had been for some years . . .

"What about this Brice guy you were talking about— what is he, a cosmetic surgeon? I thought that was someone you were interested in?"

My question was innocent; when she'd first arrived Gloria had hardly let a day go by without speaking to Brice and she'd dropped some rather broad hints about their relationship—past and future.

I looked over to see that she had a white-knuckled grip on the steering wheel. She felt my gaze and lifted her chin.

"I was never really serious about Brice. He was fun to flirt with . . . but I knew he carried on that way with a lot of women. And anyway—"

She pulled down the sunglasses that had been perched on top of her head. "Well, Eleanor had all kinds of news for me. Along with the latest about Jerry, she also told me about Brice and his receptionist. It's almost funny: Brice used to brag that he never fooled around with anyone but married women because he wanted to stay single. Evidently he messed up and got his little receptionist pregnant— The wedding was last week."

There was a beat of silence.

"Oh, Glory . . ." I began, but she overrode whatever lame condolences I might have been about to offer.

"No biggie, Lizzy!" Her voice was suspiciously bright but she turned and grinned at me. "Let's *shop*!"

"We'll go out to Biltmore Village first," she explained, swinging the Mini off the Interstate onto the Tunnel Road exit. "Bravissimo might have just the sort of striking, arty-looking dress that would suit you. And there

are one or two other places . . . If we don't find anything, then we can hit downtown—and there are always
the malls . . ."

Bravissimo had that clarity of perfection—shining
glass, subtle lighting, gleaming metal and wood—that
warns the prospective shopper if they need to look at the
price tags, they're in the wrong place. But Gloria waved
aside my feeble objections.

"This is my treat, Lizzy. You look around and so will
I. The dressing rooms are over there."

Following her instructions, I avoided looking at the
price tags and let myself be seduced by gorgeous fabrics
and rich colors. Some of the styles seemed a little bizarre
but for the most part the garments depended on perfect
cut and simplicity. So, ignoring wistful thoughts of that
skirt and blouse languishing in my closet, I picked out a
garment that reminded me of the first leaves of spring
and took it to the dressing room.

I was indulging in a slight preen in the three-way mirror when Gloria appeared in the doorway, shaking her
head as she studied my reflection.

"No, Lizzy, that one doesn't do a thing for you—
unless you *want* to blend in with the shrubbery. You're
going to be outside in the garden—what you need is a
color that will really *pop* against the backdrop of plants.
Something like coral, maybe, or that blue your garden
benches are painted."

She pursed her lips and considered. "It's a pretty dress
but it makes you look like you have jaundice. Green just
isn't your color. Go on and take it off and I'll bring you
some others."

I fell in love with the third dress that she brought me.
A high-waisted, deep periwinkle blue linen bodice from
which fell graceful folds of a silky Liberty cotton. The
skirt gave the impression of an even deeper solid blue
but on closer examination revealed printed figures of

purple on a blue background. It was perfect. Comfortable, becoming, timeless—very much the way I hoped Phillip's and my marriage would be.

"Are you sure? We could have them hold it and look at some other places." Gloria was clearly disappointed to have our treasure hunt end so soon but I was adamant.

"This is it, Glory. I really love it." I was shamelessly admiring myself in the mirror and imagining what Phillip would say when he saw me in such splendor.

Gloria put her head on one side. "It *does* look like you, Lizzy. Just a little hint of a milkmaid . . . but quite becoming." Her face brightened. "Now that I know what you'll be wearing, I'll look for something for me. I haven't seen anything here that's what I have in mind, but we can buzz by a few more places here in the Village. And then that wonderful place right in Asheville not far from Nigel's salon . . ."

She glanced at her watch. "My appointment with Nigel is for three-fifteen. If we hurry, we'll even have time for lunch."

XI~*Nellie Bly*

The Mountain Park Hotel~Friday, May 20, 1887

Nellie Bly paced nervously up and down the shaded gravel path through the trees on the far side of the bathhouse. Renzo had stuck at her side till the last minute. Indeed, he had become so seemingly enamored of her company—Ha! enamored of the money he thinks I have—*that she had begun to despair of his leaving her for his game of golf. Only the fortunate appearance of Mr. Parsons as they strolled back to the veranda had freed her.*

She glanced at the little watch pinned to her shirtwaist. Four-ten—She was to have met Amarantha here at ten till but, though she had run almost all the way, had not arrived till five after. If all went according to plan, both DeVine sisters would be occupied with soaking and massage till five. And with that oily Lorenzo safely knocking gutta-percha balls about the nine-hole Wana Luna golf course, Nellie Bly, plucky investigative girl reporter, could go to work.

If only Amarantha had given her the key earlier! But the mountain woman had insisted she couldn't "lay her hands on them keys" till after dinner. And now, the whole endeavor—

The crunch of gravel interrupted her thoughts and Nellie Bly whirled round. A deep sigh of relief escaped

her at the sight of the tall, white-clad figure of Amaran-
tha.

"You wasn't here when you said and I had to see to
Miss Dorothea DeVine. They's both of them in the tubs
now—"

"Good, good! But—" Nellie glanced around to make
sure there was no one to remark upon this strange ren-
dezvous of a guest and a staff member. Then, lowering
her voice to an urgent whisper, she continued.

"Do you have the key? Oh, please, be quick! The
brother should be safely engaged with his golf for sev-
eral hours but I can't be sure the sisters won't wish to re-
turn to their rooms when their hour here is over."

It was 4:25. Amarantha had promised to keep the sis-
ters at the bathhouse at least till five—longer if she could
manage it. But to be completely safe, Nellie Bly needed
to be well away from the DeVine suite by 5:05.

She had hurried from the bathhouse as fast as she
could without exciting comment, made her way down
the long and mercifully deserted hallway to the DeVines'
suite, and slipped inside unseen by anyone. She stood in
the main room, looking from side to side for some sign
of what she sought.

There was the plush-draped table around which they
had all sat, right hands clasped to their neighbor's left
wrist to ensure that no one of those present could be re-
sponsible for the faraway voice, the angel kiss, or the
glowing hand that had floated above the table in a
ghostly blessing.

Nellie frowned. There had been a moment—Lorenzo,
who had been on her right, had asked to be released so
that he could adjust the draperies at the window. He had
returned to the table—or had he? The darkness had
been absolute. A hand had offered itself . . . surely she
had felt a man's coat sleeve as she resumed her grasp?

Quickly she turned up one side of the heavy cloth and secured it with several of the yellow-backed novels lying on the tabletop. Kneeling down, she subjected the underside of the table to close scrutiny, even running her hands over its surface.

Nothing. More time gone. She backed out from under the table, stood, and restored the tablecloth and books to their original state.

CRACK!

A sound from the direction of the window made her jump. She turned her gaze to the innocuous cushions of the window seat and the folds of the draperies. Could a person have concealed himself in that alcove? The DeVines had made much of the fact that they did not employ a so-called "spirit cabinet" in their séances. But could not this window seat have served? A concealed operator, manipulating luminescent items on black wires . . .

CRACK!

She moved to the window seat, curious to find the source of the sound. But though she shook the draperies and moved the cushions to look under them, there was nothing.

Now 4:37. More time wasted. She glanced out the window which overlooked a decorative lily pond and a part of the small golf course. Surely that figure at the tee box just beyond the pond was Lorenzo.

He swung and hooked the ball, then, with a shrug of his shoulders, moved aside for the other man to take his turn.

Oh, crikey, *she thought,* I've got to find something that's proof of how they work their séances. Maybe in the bedrooms—"

CRACK! CRACK, CRACK, *Crack, Crack, crack* . . .

The sounds began just at her ear and then seemed to

flow across the room to a small hallway. Puzzled, but somehow completely unafraid, Nellie followed.

Now the cracking sounds were frantic—almost like castanets. And they were coming from within the bedroom. Once again the key worked and Nellie Bly stepped into a room fragrant with the scent of lilacs. There was a confusion of female clothing slung across both beds and draped from the cheval glass while a clutter of toiletries crowded the single dressing table. To the side stood two steamer trunks—one of them emitting the same cracking sounds.

Locked! Amarantha's key was no good here. Would the sisters have left the key here in the room? Or did they carry it with them? Where did women always hide things?

CRACK! The sound came from an elegant chiffonier standing at the side of a huge wardrobe.

In a moment, Nellie Bly had opened the top drawer and was feeling beneath the folds of the fine linen handkerchiefs—

CRACK! CRACK!

No? The next drawer perhaps . . .

Kid gloves—white, dove gray, black. Nellie Bly ran her hands beneath them, exploring the drawer.

Nothing. Perhaps among the chemises—but wait!

As she withdrew her hand from the stacked gloves, there was a tiny tap. *Not the whisper of thin kid falling but of something solid, muffled by the soft leather.*

CRACK! The sound was almost exuberant as she drew forth a long brass key from a white evening glove. She looked again at her watch—4:54! Eleven minutes.

She flung herself at the steamer trunk, her hand shaking so that the key rattled in the lock. Rattled . . . and turned.

As she raised the lid, Nellie Bly laughed aloud. Yes! It was all here, from the heavy paper speaking trumpets to the stuffed glove painted with some phosphorescent paint. There was a thing like a collapsible fishing pole with black fishing line, and yes, oh, the clever dogs! Here was a length of a man's coat sleeve with shirt cuff and links attached. Easy for one of Lorenzo's sisters to slide onto her arm in the dark and—

"My dear Miss Cochrane."

She started up. Lounging against the door, Lorenzo DeVine was regarding her with an appraising look.

"I thought I glimpsed your elegant form at the window and, conceiving you were eager to see me again, I cut short my match and hurried back, hoping we might enjoy a pleasant interlude before my sisters returned."

He strode into the room, his walking stick under his arm. "But I find that you are not as simple as you seemed."

The walking stick clattered to the floor and at once he was on her, one hand over her mouth, the other twisting her arm behind her. The pain was excruciating. And through the roar of blood in her ears, she heard him say in a voice that was at once amused and chilling, "Now, what shall *we do with you, my dear Miss Cochrane?"*

Chapter 34

The Kindest Cut

Saturday, June 9

We wound our way through the low-ceilinged floors to almost the very top of a parking garage in downtown Asheville. As I'd suspected, there was, indeed, a street festival of some sort going on and the garage was almost full. The air was full too, with the sounds and smells of music and cooking from a dizzying variety of ethnicities.

Somehow I hadn't been surprised when, after visiting three shops and trying on eight dresses, Gloria was still searching for the garment that met all her requirements.

"Coral, I think, though yellow *could* work. But coral has always been such a favorite of mine. And sleeveless, because it might be warm, but maybe with a light jacket for later in the evening."

A thought struck her. "Lizzy, what are your girls wearing? Are they going to be bridesmaids—oh, and what about Phillip's daughter? And then there's Amanda— Are they . . ."

At the thought of a kind of chorus line decked out in matching bridesmaid dresses, I suppressed an unladylike snort. "No, Glory—this ceremony is going to be pretty much bare-bones. We do have friends coming to play some music before and after. But, basically, Phillip and I will stand up together and say some words. And then the judge will say we're married. No bridesmaids or flower girls or ring bearers and, for bloody sure, no one to, quote, *give me away*—just friends and family to share our happiness and stay around for a bit of a celebration."

After several more fruitless stops, at last Gloria found the object of her desire in a little boutique that was tucked away down a crooked one-way street lined with enticing shops of every ilk. Enticing to Gloria, that is. I'd never realized what an endurance sport shopping can be, and I was dragging behind, dreaming of the iced coffee concoction I'd soon be enjoying at the bookstore. Gloria, however, was clicking along the sidewalk in her high heels like a long-distance runner with her second wind.

"Lizzy, don't you think this dress is absolute *perfection*!" She patted the huge shopping bag that dangled from her elbow. "It's so worth all the looking when you end up with just the right thing. That delicate balance between pink and orange has always been my favorite. So festive too! It'll set off *your* dress *and* look good against the greenery. But, you know—I'm not happy with the way those copper highlights Nigel put in my hair look with the coral. I think they need to go; a *silvery*, moonlight sort of blond would be better, don't you think?"

The narrow sidewalks were already awash with tourists and shoppers as well as some spillover from the street festival crowds a block away. The muted roar of many people filled the air, while the percolator sound of reggae fought with the twang and thump of a bluegrass band, while over all, the amplified voice of an announcer repeatedly asked spectators to move be*hind* the yellow barricades as the parade would be coming that way soon.

Before I could weigh in on Gloria's highlights, however, I was halted by a gaggle of ladies-who-lunch types emerging from a doorway just between me and Glory. Blocking the sidewalk, they stood in a chattering knot, trying to determine whether to go on to the QuerY gallery or to do the Art Museum first. I was puzzled by the fact that all of them were wearing purple and every last one had on a bright red hat of some sort, mostly fancy models with wide brims but there were a few baseball caps too—one completely covered with sparkling red sequins.

By the time the club or sorority or whatever it was had dispersed (the QuerY won out) like a flock of chattering red-crested birds moving on to another feeder, Gloria was half a block away, peering through the glass door of another storefront. A quaint hanging sign over her head showed a pair of golden scissors and the words: THE KINDEST CUT.

When I caught up to her, she was frowning at the CLOSED sign on the door. A note posted just beneath it said that Nigel was relocating to the DC area. He thanked all his customers for their friendship and their patronage and invited them to check out his website for news of his new salon.

"I don't understand— When I made my appointment the other day, he never *mentioned* that he planned on moving . . ." Gloria leaned in close to the glass of the door, peering through a slit left at the edge of the closed blind. "Oh, good—he's in there. I'll let him know I'm here. Why don't you come back in about forty minutes? I'd love for Nigel to take a look at your hair, Lizzy—he might have a suggestion or two."

As Gloria moved aside and began to rap on the doorframe, I could see for myself a tall man with a ponytail waving a blow-dryer over his client's blond mop of curls. He didn't seem to hear my sister's knocking nor her "Nigel—it's *Gloria*. I have a three-fifteen."

But then the blonde in the chair nodded her head in the direction of the door and the ponytailed man put down the blow-dryer and brush he'd been wielding and headed our way, his mouth a thin line of annoyance—or was it some other emotion?

I heard the click of a lock and the door swung open. At the same moment, the cellphone in my purse sounded its jingling tone. As no one but Phillip and my family have my number—and none of them ever call just to chat—I tend always to answer the rare calls right away—and always with a bit of trepidation.

Scrabbling through the odds and ends in my shoulder bag, I located the little leather holster that held my phone and stepped away to answer.

"Forty minutes!" Gloria called cheerfully before disappearing through the doorway. The door shut behind her just as I finally managed to hit the right button to answer the call.

"Sweetheart, where are you?"

Phillip's voice held an unmistakable urgency and I braced for the worst.

"Glory and I are in downtown Asheville; she's just gone into Nigel's salon and I'm headed to the bookstore. Is something wrong?"

I had moved away from the door and was standing by one of those little glass-fronted boxes of the type restaurants use to display menus—a vitrine, I think they're called. Inside were several clippings pertaining to Nigel's past triumphs: his course of study with Vidal Sassoon, a picture of Nigel holding a trophy of some sort and standing next to a young woman with a strange asymmetrical hairstyle . . . a kind of outdoor brag wall.

On the other end, Phillip was hesitating—and, no doubt, running his hand over his bald scalp as he always did when he had something he didn't know how to say.

"The thing is . . . now I don't want you to get rattled;

I know you two are having a nice day together but the thing is . . ."

Another picture in the vitrine caught my eye. It was a picture of half a dozen people standing in front of the Hot Springs Spa. The photo was on a page cut from one of those glossy lifestyle magazines and it was part of an article about the spa, dated two years ago. The people pictured were the staff—and in the article a great deal was made of the qualifications of the spa's hairstylist: Nigel.

Phillip's voice was drowned out by a roar of applause and the *oompah* of a marching band passing by at the end of the street. I looked again at the picture and started toward the door of Nigel's salon. The person who had abducted Gloria had to be someone familiar with the spa. And it was Nigel who'd been responsible for sending both Gloria and Joss to the spa . . .

And Gloria was in there with him. As soon as the blonde's hair was done, she'd be on her way and Gloria would be alone with Nigel.

No, I couldn't let that happen.

The tinny chatter in my ear was unintelligible and the noise on the street was getting louder.

"Phillip, stay on the line. I've got to go get Gloria."

Dropping the open phone into the little pocket at the top of my shoulder bag, I put my hand on the shining brass latch of the door. As long as that customer was in there, I doubted that Nigel would . . . would what? I had no proof that he was responsible for the incident at the spa in Hot Springs but now it seemed likely that he was more deeply involved than I'd thought. Still, no one had been *harmed*. The more I thought about it, the more likely it seemed to have been a charade to allow Joss to rescue Gloria.

We could sort that out later. The important thing was to get Gloria back outside. As soon as she was out the door, I could tell Phillip about Nigel's connection to the spa and see what he thought.

I tried the latch and to my surprise, the door wasn't locked. Assuming a casual demeanor I was far from feeling, I pushed the door open and stepped in.

Gloria was perched on one of the chairs in the waiting area, leafing through a glossy magazine and speaking to Nigel who was standing behind the blonde and putting some finishing touches on her coiffure. His tanned face was strained and he seemed nervous—like a trapped animal.

I bet he thinks she's onto him and his little scam. Probably that's why he had the closed sign up—trying to avoid her. Well, serves him right.

"No, I made an appointment and here I am. I would *not* prefer to come back later. I don't mind waiting till you finish up there."

Now the stylist was simply standing—staring at the back of the blonde in the revolving chair. "You shouldn't have come in, Gloria." His voice was flat and emotionless. "I did *try.*" And he put out a hand to swing the chair around.

As the blonde's face came into view, I was suddenly struck by a feeling of—not déjà vu but recognition. Surely I knew this woman from somewhere, some previous encounter. A past customer, perhaps? Had I done the flowers for her wedding?

Her clothing was mostly covered by one of those pink capes hairstylists always drape their clients in, but I could see the hem of a flowered skirt, a pair of white, rather thick-ankled legs and red low-heeled sandals.

Nigel stepped forward with a hand mirror and the blonde studied the back of her head in the wall mirror at her back.

"Yes," I heard a familiar voice say. "Yes, *that's* who I really am."

The blond head turned toward me. At the same time, her . . . his other hand came from beneath the concealing cape, aiming a revolver in my direction.

"Well, if it isn't my sweet aunt Elizabeth," said Joss. "And my own loving little mother."

Chapter 35

The Bolitar Ploy

Saturday, June 9

Was she even listening? Phillip shook his head in frustration. Adjusting the cellphone at his ear, he spoke louder.

"Elizabeth, did you hear what I said? The sheriff just called—the one from Joss's hometown. The parents got in touch with him to say that Joss has completely flipped out— The shrink they'd taken him to says it's a delayed reaction from the blow to his head. The way he shuffled when he walked—that was a tip-off that there was damage. But anyway, Joss is convinced that he really is Gloria's child and everyone—his parents, the shrink, you, me—are all plotting to keep him and Gloria apart. He got violent with his parents and then stormed out and they haven't seen him since—and here's what has me worried, sweetheart: They're pretty sure he took some of the father's handguns and a rifle."

At the other end, he could hear a confusing babble of sound and finally Elizabeth's voice telling him to stay on the line.

What the fuck is she up to? She said Gloria was going into Nigel's salon— Is that the hairdresser guy who's a friend of Joss?

"I got a bad feeling about this," he muttered, pulling his car out of the parking lot of the fast-food place where he'd just gotten a late and unsatisfactory lunch. Keeping the phone to one ear, he keyed the mic of the car radio to call the Sheriff's Department.

"Brenda—I need an address ASAP. A beauty parlor in downtown Asheville—guy who runs it is named Nigel . . . No, sorry, that's all I've got . . . Probably a pretty high-dollar place . . . Well, do what you can and get back to me—this is top priority."

He pressed the cellphone hard against his ear and tried to make sense of what he was hearing: Gloria speaking pretty sharply to someone about an appointment . . . an unfamiliar male voice with a British accent—Nigel?—telling her she shouldn't have come.

Where the hell is Lizabeth? The voices seemed remote, even slightly muffled, as if the cell at the other end were concealed or—

Holy shit—the concealed cellphone! It's the Bolitar Ploy! Did she do this on purpose?

Only a few days ago they'd been joking about the book he was reading. The Coben novel had reached a crucial moment and the hero—the improbably named Myron Bolitar—was in Big Trouble. But—and this was the part Lizabeth had nicknamed the *Bolitar Ploy*— Myron had left his concealed cellphone on with his psychotic sidekick listening in. There had been some discussion as to whether this so-called ploy would actually work . . .

Hold on—there was another voice; male . . . female . . . hard to say—but it sounded familiar.

". . . *my aunt Elizabeth,*" the high-pitched voice was saying, "*and my own loving little mother . . .*"

Sweet Jesus, it's Joss. Phillip reached for the switch to activate his siren and emergency lights. "Get out of there, Lizabeth!" he shouted into the unhearing phone as the voices continued.

Once again he keyed the car radio. "Have you got anything yet, Brenda?"

He was on the Interstate now, emergency lights and siren going, speeding toward Asheville. The car radio crackled and Brenda spoke. "... *Thirty-three Wall Street* ... *near the intersection with Haywood and* ..."

Time. How long would it take him to get there? And Joss was presumably armed. *Oh, Jesus, what are you doing, Lizabeth?*

"Brenda, alert the Buncombe County Sheriff's Department that we have a possible hostage situation at that address. I'm on my way."

Cutting the dispatcher short, he punched in the info on his GPS, silently thanking the department for this recent addition to his official vehicle.

On the cellphone, the British male was speaking again, almost babbling—agitated words falling over one another.

"... It was only a harmless scam—Joss was to pay me if it worked—if Gloria believed him. No harm done. I'd be making two people happy ... and there'd be a little something for me ... I'd got a lease on a salon in Arlington, Virginia—a really upscale place but I couldn't quite swing it without a bit of a cash infusion. I knew Gloria would never miss twenty-five K. Once she'd accepted Joss, he was going to ask for help with some outstanding debts—maybe make it sound as though some thugs were after him. When she came through, he'd pay me—that was the deal we had."

There was a shocked exclamation from Gloria and then Elizabeth's voice, much clearer than the others. *The phone must be in her pocket or shoulder bag.* Again he wanted to warn her but stayed silent so he could catch her words.

"So, Nigel—what did you *do* that was worth that

much money—aside from sending both of them to the séance weekend? Were you responsible for putting my sister in that box in the basement? She could have—"

"She was never in any danger—never! It was all so that Joss could be a hero and 'save' his mother. And it wasn't me. Jeremy, a friend of mine who works at the spa, did the abduction and he let me know the minute she was in place and I called Joss. Really, it was little more than a prank—"

The agitated voice was interrupted by Joss. His tone was low and controlled but menacing.

"Nigel, shut up. My mother and I don't want to hear any more of your lies. Elizabeth, move away from the door and come over here with us."

Was he holding a gun on her? Something in the assurance of his words suggested that he was—on her or on Gloria.

The New Stock exit flashed by. How long would it take the Buncombe County Sheriff's Department to respond? He had said it could be a hostage situation—would they handle it right?

Lizabeth. Stay cool. I know you will. I'm coming.

The Brit was talking again—and his voice was easier to hear now.

Damn! That meant that Elizabeth was closer to the others, that she had done as Joss had directed. Which also meant that Joss almost surely had a gun.

"Joss, you know they're not lies. We planned it all, sitting right here. I arranged the driver's license—and that didn't come cheap, since it was at such short notice. I was the one who knew the right date—you mentioned it yourself, Gloria, when you told me about your lost baby—"

"Nigel, don't make me say it again. There is no Joss. I'm *Dana*. I've always been Dana inside and now I'm transitioning so that I can be the daughter my mother wants."

What the fuck is this guy talking about? What transitioning?

Phillip swerved around a lumbering school bus and shot onto the Patton Avenue exit ramp.

"I've given it some thought," the calm, ladylike voice went on. "I always knew I was meant to be a woman. The man I used to call Dad hated that. He tried so hard to make me just like him—hunting, sports—he even tried to get me to walk like him. *Be a man, son,* he used to say. But it was all a lie, all of it. Joss is gone now—and if there are none who remember Joss, then my little mother and I can go off together and begin again."

Mother of God, this lunatic is capable of anything. Phillip beat at his horn in frustration, forcing a minivan and two bikers up onto the sidewalk. Somewhere, not too far away, he heard more sirens added to the sound of his own.

As he neared Haywood, yellow barriers directed him to an alternate route. Beyond the barriers, a costumed, banner-carrying crowd was swirling haphazardly after a marching band and several overcrowded floats.

Phillip groaned and pulled his car into a loading zone. The noise was making it almost impossible to hear the voices on the other end of the cellphone but he kept it pressed to his ear as he checked the GPS system once more to pinpoint his location and the route to the salon.

The situation was headed for a complete meltdown. On the phone it sounded as if all four were shouting at once—shouting, wailing, pleading—a confusion of words in his ear as Phillip hurled himself from the cruiser and ran in what he prayed was the right direction.

The noise on the streets was almost tangible. He

seemed to be pushing his way through dense masses of sound. And in his ear . . .

And in his ear two shots sounded.

As the reverberations died away, Joss spoke.

"Soon it will be the way it should have been from the beginning—just my little mother and me . . . Don't you understand? It had to be done to stop the lies. Say you understand, my little mother."

And the sound of weeping—inconsolable weeping. Then a woman's voice: Gloria.

"*Lizabeth!*" Phillip shouted into the telephone as he ran, elbowing his way through heedless groups of merrymakers. "*Lizabeth!*"

XII~Amarantha

Friday, May 20, 1887

It was nigh on six o'clock and no Miss Cochrane. All my ladies was done and had gone back to make ready for the evening meal but still no sign of that feisty little somebody what had convinced me to lend her my keys. My treatment rooms and the tubs was all scrubbed clean and everthing was in readiness for the next day. Yet still she didn't come.

I begun to have a sickly feeling about it. Miss Cochrane knowed I must have them keys back to return to the head housekeeper afore I went home. She should have been back long since . . .

So I decided to take a look. Once more I filled the little basin with rubbing oil and set before it, waiting to see what it might show me. In the quiet of the bathhouse I could hear my own breathing, seeming loud.

The oil shivered under my breath and at first it was dark. I waited, trying to breathe slower and to see what came—trying not to lead it.

The first picture that came weren't Miss Cochrane—it was a little yellow-haired woman with her hair short cut, like they do when a body's had a fever. She was wrapped in rags and closed up in one of those steam boxes they use for treatments. But it weren't in a treatment room; it looked like to be in some dark cellar. The yellow-haired woman was scared most to death, poor thing, but somehow I knowed that this was a seeing from another time. Was I to go looking, I'd not find the yellow-haired woman—not now. And then I seen a tall woman with a long dark braid moving in the depths of the oil and I knowed she was coming after the other one.

"Be still, honey," I whispered to the one in the box. "Hit'll be all right. Jest you sleep."

The picture begun to change and I saw the DeVine sisters and that feller they call their brother. They was all standing about and looking at something and the green one was carrying on like one thing. The purple one slapped her and the picture got hard to read—the sisters was in the dining room, and the brother was hauling poor Miss Cochrane down the back stairs and to the doctor's special treatment room.

I didn't wait to see no more but lit out running for the back door of the hotel. Now I understood why I'd seen the picture from another time and I knew, sure as anything, that Lorenzo was aiming to put Miss Cochrane into one of them steam boxes. And there weren't no one coming to get her out unless it was me.

At this time of day there weren't a soul to be seen there on the back porch of the hotel. Any other time and they'd be one or two of the housemaids or kitchen girls, taking themselves a little break—rolling a smoke or eating a cold biscuit. But at suppertime, all the outside staff had gone home and all the others was busy in the dining room or the kitchen. It takes a right smart of people to feed that many folks and get the food to them hot and all at once.

I slipped through the screen door, not worrying about the squeak for the sound of nigh on three hundred people, all eating and talking at once, drowned out any little noise I might make. No one saw or heard as I hightailed it up the back stairs and ran down the long hall—past the offices and the parlors, the music room and the billiards room and the smoking room, and around the corner to where the gymnasium and the doctor's special treatment rooms was.

The door was shut but it opened when I turned the knob. I could hear the hiss and rattle of the steam pipes—the same ones that heated the hotel in winter—coming from the boiler. Now that the hotel had hot water in most of the rooms, the boiler run night and day, keeping a crew of men busy with bringing in wood to burn.

The front room had all kindly of strange-looking machines but the hissing of the steam pipes was coming from the room beyond—the room with the steam boxes.

At first I thought that I'd been mistaken, that she wasn't there after all, but then I heard a groaning and a knocking and a weak voice calling for help.

"I'm coming, honey," I called out and ran like a crazy woman from box to box, wasting time by pulling the doors open till it come to me that they was all cold—but I was still hearing the hiss of the steam.

They must have been several dozen of the plagued boxes and I ran along the row, just touching each long enough to know if it was heated. The knocking and the calling out had stopped by the time I reached the last row. And here too ever last box was cold.

I stood there panting and swinging my head around, trying to think where she could be. I didn't doubt the seeing I'd had—

And then I saw in the corner of the room there was a pile of exercise mats. At first I thought they was laying across a table but then I saw the steam trickling out here and there.

I ran to the corner and began throwing the mats off. The last of them was hot to the touch and damp from the steam. The hole where the person is supposed to stick their head out had been stopped up by the heavy pile of mats and through it I could just make out the striped bodice of Miss Cochrane's dress.

The devil who'd put her in there had jammed the latch so she couldn't open it but I tore at it with all my strength and soon pulled her out of the steam-filled box. She was a mess—wet all over, red-faced, and her hair all a-straggle. But she was alive, coughing and gasping for air and saying words I'd not think to hear from a young lady's mouth.

I got her up and took her to the shower room for I was feared of what could happen if she didn't get cooled down right quick. She sputtered and cussed some more as the cold water hit her but in time she begun to catch her breath and come back to herself.

"Well, Amarantha," says she when I'd got her out of the nasty wet clothes and into a bathrobe. "I found plenty of proof but as I don't have it in my possession, it would be my word against theirs."

Miss Cochrane set there a minute, just a-fuming. She put me in mind of a little black hen I once had. That biddy purely hated the rain and would shake her feathers and fuss like one thing everwhen she got wet.

Finally she said, "I don't know—I'm very much of a mind to attend their lecture on Spiritualism and stand up and denounce them as the frauds they are. But I'm afraid that any accusation I might make could too easily be dismissed as the fabrications of a muckraking reporter."

She looked up at the Regulator clock on the wall. "Twenty after seven. Supper is almost over and people will be pouring out of the dining room soon. I'd better get to my room—I look such a fright. Oh, how I wish I could have—"

"Miss Cochrane," I said, for a thought was forming itself in my mind. "If you don't care, I believe I might have an idea for a stunt that will be the undoing of those three."

I went to the cabinet in the corner of the room where I knew the supplies was kept. There I found a great tin canister of the talc the doctor sold in little envelopes for the easing of rashes. Then I picked up the bundle of Miss Cochrane's wet clothes.

She was looking at me all amazed but I just smiled and put a finger to my lips. "I'll explain when we get to your room. And then I'll fix you up so's you can go to that lecture. And won't they be surprised when they see you!"

Chapter 36

My Sister, My Hero

Saturday, June 9

Gloria and I stood frozen in place, watching as Joss looked from Nigel's body sprawled beside the revolving chair to the gun in his—her—hand as if wondering how it came to be there. Under the blond hairdo—a perfect copy of Gloria's, copper highlights and all—Joss's face was drained of color, except for the bright lipstick and the two slashes of rouge—also a perfect duplication of my sister's makeup.

As Joss stepped down from the chair, he reached behind him with his free hand and tugged at the ties securing the pink cape. Pulling it off, he dropped it over Nigel with a flirtatious swirl. Then he looked at Glory and me.

"He shouldn't have tried to take the gun away from me. I really didn't have a choice, did I?" He sighed and shook his head in peevish annoyance. "Well, *anyhoo* . . . we'll just have to make the best of a bad situation, won't we, girls?"

To my dismay, I realized that Joss had exactly caught Gloria's accent and mannerisms. What had been at first annoying, then almost endearing, in my sister was nausea-inducing seen through the deeply disturbing carnival mirror likeness that was Joss.

I put one arm around Glory and hugged her to me. Her entire body was trembling but she managed to put an arm around my waist and give me a weak, terrified smile. Joss seemed not to notice. He was the center of his own tiny spotlight, strutting in his finery and caught up in some fierce, sick game of make-believe.

Putting a coy finger to his glossy red lips, Joss raised his newly shaped eyebrows in mock perplexity. "I wonder what dear old Dad would say if he knew I'd actually *killed* someone? Maybe he'd think I was a man at last. *There's* irony for you."

He giggled. Stepping carefully around Nigel's body, Joss studied his face and hair in the wall mirror once more. "Such a waste—he was a genius colorist, don't you agree, my little mother? Look at those highlights— exactly like yours."

Gloria gulped. "Yes, they're beautiful. But, Jo— I mean, Dana, hadn't we better leave right away? There's just a chance you and I could get out of here and to an airport. And then we could go anywhere you like—South America . . . or Thailand or . . . anywhere. But we need to go *now*. Don't you hear the sirens?"

Joss lifted his head, his dark eyes glittering with manic excitement. Mixed in with the carnival sounds there were, indeed, sirens. But whether they were wailing for us, I couldn't say.

I knew what my sister was doing: She hoped to get Joss out the door and away from me. Little Glory, whom I'd always dismissed as the most frivolous of lightweights, was showing unimaginable courage. In spite of that, I couldn't let her slip out into those crowds with this delusional bastard who'd already killed once.

"No, Glory." I tightened my grip around her shoulders. "No way. You can't walk out of here with him. You see what he's capable of. He's insane and god knows what he might do—"

The ludicrously tall imitation of my petite sister snarled at me, the perfectly made-up face contorting into a hideous caricature. "You can shut your mouth, Aunt E. You've been against me from the beginning, haven't you? We both know that."

With appalling clarity, I saw the revolver rise till I was looking down the black hole of the barrel. From a long way off I heard Joss say, "You're another I need to be rid of."

There was a shriek. "Not my sister!" Gloria cried and I felt a jolt as she twisted free and pushed me to the side. At the same time, another shot rang out and I saw her collapse on the floor in front of me. Outside, the sirens were screaming and an amplified voice was shouting for Joss to put down his weapon and come to the door with his hands up.

Glory lay on the floor at my feet, blood pumping from the great wound . . . so much blood . . . soaking her blouse and spreading . . . my sister's blood . . .

I snatched the pink cape from Nigel's body, then fell to my knees and tried to stanch the hopeless wound . . . to stop the seemingly unstoppable tide . . . so much blood.

Outside, the shouting intensified and the continuing sound of the festival music played a strange counterpoint to the voice on the bullhorn.

Slowly Joss knelt beside Gloria, his rage spent, his painted face a cartoon mask of anguish. "Oh, my little mother. Why? Why did you jump in front of her? I didn't want to hurt you. It was Elizabeth who should have died . . ."

He leaned over her, keening as he stroked her head, oblivious to the blood that was everywhere. My eyes were full of tears as I too leaned close, desperately pressing the darkening fabric to the horrible wound.

The voice on the bullhorn was calling my name now, but it didn't seem to matter. I was trapped in this bubble of time at the side of the sister I'd just discovered—only, it seemed, to lose her. Joss also seemed oblivious to the clamor outside. It was just the two of us, caught in the terrible moment at the side of the woman we had both loved.

"I won't let you win, Aunt Elizabeth. I won't let you keep me from my little mother. It was you and your family who separated us—but now we'll be together for eternity."

As he spoke the words, once more I saw him bring the revolver up. Once more I stared into the black O of the barrel, helpless to act.

And the barrel continued to rise. Joss's red lips closed around it in an obscene parody of a lover's embrace.

Once again, a deafening roar filled the little salon. Then Joss fell across Gloria's limp body, his shattered head beside hers.

My ears were still ringing when the door burst open and uniformed men swarmed into the room. And Phillip came to me and held me as the EMTs carried Gloria away.

My sister. My hero.

XIII~*Amarantha*

Sunday, May 29, 1887

Amarantha sat on her porch, the letter and newspaper in her lap, her lips moving as she read the letter yet again. A smile spread itself across her usually severe countenance.

My dearest Amarantha,

Here is the piece I wrote and, as you wished, I did not mention your name nor reveal all of your part in our glorious exploit. My lips are sealed forever. But, oh my, you were wonderful and I only wish I could have the benefit of your Sight to guide me in the future months and years! Ah, well, I understand your objections. But should you ever "take a notion" to travel, the offer remains open.

Your own,
Nellie Bly

Laying the letter aside, the mountain woman took up the newspaper and looked once more at the drawing of her young friend—the dark eyes and hair, the straight back, the waving hand.

Was it hello or good-bye?

Hard to say—and in her experience Amarantha had found them to be much the same.

She began to read the newspaper, sounding out the unfamiliar words.

SENSATION AT SPA!!!
By Nellie Bly

On Friday night last, the packed audience at a lecture on Spiritualism was witness to the unmasking of a trio of heartless rogues, the callous exploiters of many a mother's grief and many a bereaved spouse's sorrow.

The pair of mediums known as the DeVine sisters and the man (alleged to be their brother) who acted as their manager had been resident at The Mountain Park Hotel for some weeks, "resting," it was said, after a triumphant tour of the Eastern seaboard. (See related story, special from *The Charleston Courier,* on page 2.)

Your reporter, having been moved by the plight of a mourning young mother, driven to self-destruction by the ruses of these cold-blooded frauds, came to the Mountain Park under her own name and took care that none should suspect her true purpose nor connect her with the exploits (see related story "Nellie Bly in Mexico" on page 2) that so recently stirred the imagination of the reading public.

Putting her very life at risk, your reporter was on the brink of collecting the needed evidence—the very apparatus used to produce the supposed wraiths of the departed—when she was overcome by the man known as Lorenzo DeVine, stuffed into a steam cabinet, and left to perish. (Note: this reporter in no way wishes to imply that The Mountain Park Hotel bears any responsibility for the actions of the "DeVines." On the contrary, one of the hotel employees was instrumental in saving this reporter's life as well as in the public exposure of the charlatans. See paid notice at the bottom of the page.)

All three were on stage before an audience of almost three

hundred. Mr. DeVine had spoken briefly on the principles of Spiritualism and one of his sisters was demonstrating the trance state by relaying messages from the departed spirit of a Cherokee maiden who had drowned in the previous century, it is said, not a quarter of a mile from the hotel itself.

When the gas lights flickered and dimmed to a Stygian gloom, doubtless many in the audience assumed it to be a part of the demonstration. And when a ghostly form in trailing white, with streaming tresses, appeared at the back of the hall, gliding silently toward the speaker's dais, surely there were those who believed themselves to be viewing the veritable manifestation of the sad Cherokee princess. (Continued on page 2.)

Amarantha laid aside the newspaper and closed her eyes. For a little somebody, that Miss Cochrane—or Nellie Bly, to give her the name she'd chosen—could surely use some big words.

But, oh, how fine it had been to see that Lorenzo jump at the sight of the woman he'd thought dead and out of the sight of prying eyes till the following Monday. He must have thought that he and his sisters would be well away by then. How he'd grabbed for his throat as Nellie Bly, white with talc from head to toe, came toward him.

"Murderer!" she had called out in a trembly voice loud enough to wake the dead. "Murderer!"

Amarantha felt the hair rise on her arms as she remembered the sound. She would never forget the fuss that followed—Lorenzo's crazy talk, the sister in green swooning, the manager and several of the younger and stronger waiters hurrying to the scene.

And then Nellie Bly, taking the stage while she, Amarantha turned the lights back up. Nelly had stood there before that crowd, bold as a preacher, and told just what these scoundrels had been up to and by the time she was done, had the sheriff and his men not have arrived, it would have gone hard for Lorenzo.

Lorenzo was still in the jail and happy to be there with all the talk there was in town of tar and feathers or worse. The green sister, Little Dorry, as all the ladies had taken to calling her, had cried for mercy. She swore the other two had put her up to the tricks and had made her go on, even when she had begged them to stop.

Little Dorry had become a great pet with the church ladies and had even stood up several times in meeting to beg forgiveness and to witness. There was talk that one of the guests at the hotel was courting her right heavy but others said that Dorry had been called to do the Lord's work and would soon be traveling to all the big camp meetings and revivals, as soon as she got done grieving for her sister.

It must have been just before the manager had brought his black fellows in to quiet things down that the purple sister had slipped away. Folks figured that she'd planned to follow the tracks to the next railroad stop and board there. It was said she'd made off with a fine diamond jewel bracelet but likely that was at the bottom of the French Broad now. An evil woman and a fool to think she could cross the trestle bridge in the dark.

People mostly gets what they deserves, mused Amarantha.

Chapter 37

Summer Solstice

Thursday, June 21

Yes, we did consider postponing the wedding because of Gloria. It just didn't seem right . . . but
Janie and Seth and Caitlin already had their tickets and
Rosemary had taken time off . . . Who knows when we
could have gotten all of them here at the same time
again . . . Well, after a lot of thought and discussion, it
made sense to go ahead as scheduled."

I had repeated this little speech till it was beginning to
sound like a recording. The very next day after the
nightmare events in Asheville, friends had begun calling
or emailing. It hadn't taken long for the news about
Gloria to get around. My little community of friends
had all responded as I'd known they would, offering as-
sistance and comfort in every form.

It had been a rocky, emotional time but we'd come
through it. I'd even been in contact with Joss's adoptive
parents, who seemed to feel the need to apologize for
their dead son's actions. Poor people—he had been their
only child. Coming to terms with his loss, as well as the
delusion-fueled destruction he had wrought, had been
heartbreaking for them. The presumption that this delusion and subsequent psychotic behavior had been
caused by the head injury, rather than something in his

upbringing, was the sole crumb of consolation they had to comfort them.

And somehow, in the busyness of preparation for the ceremony, I had found myself feeling closer to Gloria than ever. I saw all the lovely little refinements of food and decoration that had been her ideas and felt the bitterness of her absence. Gloria. How she would have enjoyed making sure that Laurel put the flowers *here* rather than *there,* and what wonders she would have worked supervising the arrangement of beautiful foods on the buffet tables.

Ah, well, I told myself, life goes on. And we were moving minute by minute toward the ceremony in which Phillip and I would publically affirm the union, the partnership of heart, mind, and body that already existed between us. *Had* existed, for some years now . . .

"Miz Goodweather—time you were getting changed." Phillip pointed to the clock on the kitchen wall. "Though if you want to stick with the casual look, the T-shirt and jeans look fine to me . . ."

I finished filling the big coffee urn with water and gave a last look around. The house was awash with hydrangeas in every shade of blue and lavender, as well as creamy greenish-white. There was champagne on ice out back; the dining table was set, buffet-style, with Gramma's silver and linen, awaiting the trays of food safely stowed in the refrigerator and in the array of coolers in the basement. Little sandwiches—chicken salad, cream cheese and nuts, asparagus—lovingly made by Rosemary and Amanda; an array of beautiful salads, courtesy of Laurel; a baked ham with little biscuits— "Honey, you can't do a wedding lunch without one of these," Sallie Kate had insisted; little lemon tarts, and a stack cake Miss Birdie had sent over by Calven . . .

"Let me just check the dessert table—I'm not sure there're enough forks." I headed for the table in the living room, where a three-tiered, white-frosted carrot cake was the centerpiece. It had been a gift from Phillip's children and Janie had spent the morning pressing fresh-picked wild violets one by one into its thick-swirled cream cheese icing.

"Come on, woman; we don't want to be late for our wedding." Phillip caught my hand and pulled me to him for a quick kiss, then propelled me toward the bedroom. "Go! Five minutes!"

The dress—the one Glory had insisted on buying for me on that last day—was exactly what I might have dreamed of. Almost a period piece: Somewhere between a Jane Austen heroine's Empire-waisted frock and the romantic flowing robe of a Pre-Raphaelite heroine, it still managed to look appropriate for a fifty-something bride at a small outdoor wedding on a farm.

I surveyed myself in the big mirror over the dresser. The periwinkle blue of the simple square-necked linen bodice brought out the blue of my eyes, just as Gloria had insisted it would. And the ground-sweeping skirt of Liberty cotton—a riot of tiny fruits and trees and fantastic birds in deep blues and purples—was a celebration unto itself.

"Thank you, Glory," I whispered, pulling on the beautiful garment. "Thank you from the bottom of my heart."

As I came out to the porch where Phillip was checking his watch, he looked up. "Is that the one your sister . . ." He stared, his eyes taking in every inch of my magnificent dress. Then he smiled. "Lizabeth, you look beautiful. The dress is—"

The smile disappeared and he slapped his pocket. "Holy shit! The ring—I left it in the office. Right back." And he vanished through the front door at a run.

I walked to the end of the porch to survey the garden below. Simple wooden benches were placed between the beds of flowers and herbs—all of which, for a mercy, were lush and beautiful, thanks to a little last-minute filling in with blooming plants. Jake and Sarah were off to the side, their banjo and fiddle filling the air with old-time mountain music. The cheerful lilt of "Under the Double Eagle" rang out accompanied by the chatter of the wedding guests as they took their places. The three dogs wound their way among them, greeting friends.

My friends—now our friends. And our family—Rosie and Laurel flanking the indomitable Aunt Dodie. She had giggled like a little girl at surprising me and had made Phillip actually blush by planting a robust kiss on his cheek. Seth, Phillip's handsome son, was there with his fiancée Caitlin, and his sister Janie. Janie—soon to be my stepdaughter—a relationship that I hoped would blossom into friendship rather than the wary neutrality we seemed to have achieved so far.

As Miss Birdie, Dorothy, and Calven were taking their places just behind Dodie and my girls, I saw Laurel introducing the two octogenarians who seemed to take to one another right away. I found myself straining to hear that conversation but it was no use; the music and the many happy voices were all one joyful symphony of sound.

The glorious noise was suddenly stilled by a peal of barking from James. Heads turned at the crunch of gravel as the Jeep crept slowly and carefully up the road. And there, being helped out of the Jeep and ushered like royalty to a cushioned armchair by Ben and Amanda, was Glory.

Dear, dear, infinitely dear Glory. Still a little pale, still a little shaky, she was wearing the coral silk dress, its accompanying jacket draped elegantly around her shoulders. Her right arm was in a sling covered by a brilliant Hermès silk scarf and her left arm was gesturing imperiously as she directed the placement of her chair. Glory was obviously on the mend.

Dearly beloved. All of them.

"Are they here?" Phillip came through the front door and I turned to admire my groom. *Most dearly beloved . . .*

"They just got here and she looks great! Talk about a grand entrance. The doctor wasn't thrilled about releasing her so soon but you know Glory . . ."

"It took a while but yeah, I think I do now." Phillip put his arm around my waist and we stood, watching the wedding guests below. "It's strange; when I first met her, I didn't see how she could be related to you at all, but it turns out that you two were . . . what's that saying . . . 'sisters under the skin' all along."

He glanced at his watch. "Aren't we supposed to get on down there? Seems like they're ready for us."

"Almost. We start down to the garden as soon as they play 'Haste to the Wedding.' "

Right on cue one tune ended and another began. "And there it is now."

Phillip's lips brushed my cheek then he stepped back and offered his arm. I bit my lip to hold back the tears. Happiness . . . such happiness as I'd never thought to know again.

My heart was so full I couldn't speak. Even if there had been time to say all the words that were tumbling over one another, trying to be heard. *Thank you for your patience . . . Thank you for believing in me . . . Thank you for loving me even when I was unlovable.*

But all that I could manage was a husky, heartfelt "Thank you, Phillip, for everything," as I hooked my arm through his. His dear familiar face was turned toward me and through the shimmer of my tears I could see his reassuring smile.

He drew my arm in close to his body and we began our stately walk down to the garden. Down the rock steps to the grassy road that led to the garden steps, pacing in slow and careful unison toward the rest of our lives together.

The lively dance tune ended and the fiddle began the slow, achingly sweet "Ashokan Farewell." I could see the little cluster of family and friends hushing one another and turning to watch as we climbed the rock steps and made our way to the flower-bedecked arbor where the judge waited.

The music stopped; the judge cleared her throat and began.

"Dearly beloved, we are gathered today . . ."

The sweet old words ran on, like a river flowing in its course to the sea, so inexorable, so fitting. And when it was my turn to speak my vows, it was with all my heart and my mind, my soul and my body—reason and faith reconciled at long last.

"Do you, Elizabeth . . ." said the judge.

And I did.

"Vicki Lane shows us an exotic and colorful picture of Appalachia from an outsider's perspective—through a glass darkly. *Old Wounds* is a well-crafted, suspenseful tale of the bygone era before 'Florida' came to the mountains."
—SHARYN MCCRUMB,
New York Times bestselling author

If you enjoyed *Under the Skin,*
please read on for a look
at Vicki Lane's acclaimed novel *Old Wounds.*

Available online and at your local bookstore

Prologue

Saturday, October 1

The glowing computer screen, the only light in the dim gloom of the tiny, windowless office, cast a sickly green hue across the young woman's exhausted face. She slumped back in her chair and let out a profound sigh that spoke of surrender . . . and relief. At last it was done: the story that had, against all her careful defenses, clawed its way into existence. The story that had haunted her for too many long years, tapping with urgent, insistent fingers on the clouded panes of her memory, the story that she had pushed away like an unwanted and unloved child. Now, at last, she had allowed it into the light, had unbound it, had let it speak.

The words crawled down the screen and she scanned them critically. Enough details had been changed; it would pass as fiction. But the heart of the unresolved matter was there. She had put down all she knew . . . all she remembered, after so long.

She watched as the account of that terrible time passed before her blurring eyes. As the last page came into view she paused, pulled off her reading glasses, and wiped them on her sleeve. She drew in a long, shuddering breath, fighting back unwelcome tears. It had been worth it—painful but cathartic. It had been necessary, she told herself. And the story was powerful—her best work ever.

Rereading the last words, that desolate closing paragraph, she frowned. This was it, wasn't it? What more was there to say? For a moment she sat frozen, paralyzed by the flood of memory and emotion that threatened to overwhelm her. Then, with sudden decision, she clicked on the PRINT icon. The machine stirred into action and as the white pages pattered into the tray, the young woman's lean body began to tremble.

"Maythorn?" It was a tentative whisper. Shoving her chair back, she felt held in place, mesmerized by the growing stack of paper before her. The soft murmur of pages falling one upon another mocked her. *You think this is all but you're not done.*

So many questions remained unanswered. *You have to keep going. This won't be enough for her.*

The final sheet of paper inched its way out of the whirring printer.

"Mary Thorn."

Her voice was stronger now. The name was a declaration of the buried grief and doubt of the past nineteen years.

She pulled the sheaf of paper from the tray and stood, clutching the pages to her heart. Closing her eyes, she tilted her face to the ceiling and cried out, in a voice to wake the dead:

"Mary Thorn Blackfox, I *see* you!"

Still gripping the pages, Rosemary Goodweather reached for the telephone and punched in her mother's number.

Chapter 1

Dark of the Moon

Monday, October 3

Bloody hell!"

The three dogs raised their heads, startled by the vehemence of Elizabeth's unexpected outburst. Their morning reverie disturbed, they looked at one another as if considering abandoning the sun-warmed porch for more peaceful surroundings. But when no further words, angry or otherwise, were forthcoming, heads sank back to outstretched paws and the three resumed their private contemplations.

Elizabeth Goodweather sat on her front porch, staring unseeing at the distant Blue Ridge Mountains that disappeared into ever-hazier rows along the eastern horizon. She was blind to the nearby wooded slopes with their first gildings of copper and gold, oblivious to the clear blue sky marked only by a pair of red-tailed hawks riding the cool autumn currents, and deaf to the birds' shrill, descending calls. The breakfast dishes in the kitchen behind her were still unwashed; the mug of coffee she held had grown cold without being tasted. She sat motionless but her mind whirled in tumult—a congregation of seething thoughts, feelings, and desires, all unresolved.

Two days ago she had been on the verge of . . . *on the verge of what, Elizabeth? Phillip asked if I was still grieving for Sam, if I would ever let someone else into my life. And I said something really profound about being willing to take a chance. And I was . . . I am . . . but then, just then . . . Oh, bloody hell!*

But at just that exquisitely crucial moment, Rosemary had called. Her brilliant, reliable, *sensible* older daughter. Assistant professor of English at UNC–Chapel Hill and not yet thirty, Rosemary had been writing a story based on the disappearance of a childhood friend almost twenty years ago. *And in the writing, something let loose. All those years that she wouldn't talk about Maythorn . . . and then Saturday . . . oh, god, it was awful to hear Rosie so . . . so unhinged.*

"Mum!" Her daughter had whispered, sounding more like the ten-year-old she had been than the self-assured academic she had become. "Mum! I have to find out what really happened to Maythorn."

Rosemary had been all but incoherent, babbling about her lost friend, about memories that had resurfaced . . . *and Maythorn's granny and something called the Looker Stone . . . and what was the really weird-sounding thing? . . . the Booger Dance? Whatever the hell that is.*

Maythorn Mullins, the child of a neighboring family, had been Rosemary's friend—*she's my best friend, Mum,* and *she's my blood twin! We were both born on January 11, 1976, and we both have brown eyes and we are exactly the same tall! We cut our fingers and swapped blood and now we're blood twins!* The pair had been almost inseparable for two idyllic years. Then had come the Halloween of 1986 and with it the disappearance of Maythorn from her family's home.

A massive search through the hollows and coves of Ridley Branch and adjoining areas had revealed nothing. Some believed that the child had run away—there were whispers of an unhappy family situation. Others were sure that a kidnapping had been attempted and had somehow gone wrong. Still others shook their heads. They swore that the child was somewhere on the mountain—dead or alive.

But as a weary Sam had said to Elizabeth, on returning from the steep slopes and thickets of Pinnacle Mountain, "Liz, she could be hiding . . . or hidden . . . anywhere out there. There's just no way of searching every inch of these woods."

Wide-eyed, but remote, Rosemary had watched mutely as the futile search continued. Her responses to questions about Maythorn, from Sam and Elizabeth, as well as from the authorities, were little more than monosyllables. Tearless, she had shaken off attempts at comfort. Elizabeth could still remember the sudden stiffening resistance of her daughter's thin body when she'd tried to gather the child up in her arms for consolation.

"Don't, Mum," Rosemary had said briefly, gently removing herself from the embrace and retreating to her own room. And though she had eventually returned to her usual talkative self, any mention of Maythorn was met by a blank stare or an abrupt change of subject. Soon it seemed that she had simply chosen to forget the existence of the little girl she had called her blood twin. Elizabeth and Sam, caught up in the thousand details of their new life, had gratefully accepted Rosemary's return to normalcy. By unspoken mutual agreement, they no longer mentioned Maythorn around their older daughter.

A local man was questioned by the police and released for lack of evidence. The Mullins family drew in on itself and, after a year had gone by with no ransom demand and no sign of the child, they moved away, eager to leave behind the unhappy memories that haunted their home. Marshall County put the mysterious disappearance away in a seldom-visited drawer and life resumed its pleasant and accustomed shape.

Rosemary's unexpected and unsettling call on Saturday had alarmed Elizabeth deeply. All thoughts of romance and Phillip Hawkins vanished like dry leaves before an icy wind. She had listened in baffled incomprehension to her daughter's frantic chatter till Rosemary had run down, had calmed and begun to sound more like her usual self.

"I'm sorry, Mum. I didn't mean to spring it on you quite like this. Really, I'm fine. It's just that I've been so immersed in the story and when I printed it out now— well, I felt like I had to talk to you about Maythorn. Stupid, I should have waited. Listen, Mum, I've got to go. I'm meeting a friend in a few minutes. I'll call you tomorrow or the next day when I've made some arrangements and figured out exactly what I want to do."

Rosie finished talking and hung up and I . . . I just stood there holding the phone and staring. She had stared at Phillip Hawkins who, at the insistent ring of the telephone, had released her and tactfully moved to the cushioned nook at the end of the kitchen to busy himself with her three dogs while she answered the call. She had looked at him in bewilderment, as if she had never seen him before, as if he were a stranger who had unexpectedly materialized in her home. Granted, a stranger whose right hand was scratching behind the ears of James, the tubby little dachshund-Chihuahua mix, while his left was busy fondling Molly's sleek head. The elegant red hound's amber eyes gazed soulfully at Phillip as if *she* knew him very well indeed. And at his feet, shaggy Ursa lay on her broad back, offering her black furry belly to be scratched.

"What?" He'd looked up with a quizzical smile, which was rapidly replaced by a puzzled frown and a look of concern. As she continued to stare silently at him, he had disentangled himself from her dogs and come toward her. She'd stared at the burly man with the soft dark eyes and nut-brown balding pate, trying to re-assemble his pleasant features into a familiar face.

"Elizabeth, sweetheart, what's wrong?" Suddenly the stranger was replaced by the familiar friend, the good man she'd come to rely on. She put down the phone and burst into tears.

He had put his arms around her again and she had relaxed against his comforting bulk. When her voice was under control, she asked, "Did you ever see that movie years ago—*Alice's Restaurant?* Well, like Alice said, I feel like a poor old mother hound dog with too many puppies snapping at her tits. I mean, I'm already worried about Ben and Laurel, after what they've just been through, and now *Rosie* . . .

"Sam and I thought it was all over—that she'd for-gotten that awful Halloween and the days and weeks that followed. We were so grateful that she seemed . . . seemed *untouched* by it all that we just pretended it never happened, let *her* pretend there'd never been a lit-tle girl called Maythorn. But now it's all come back. I should have known. . . .

"Don't you see, Phillip? . . . I owe it to her . . . to both of them . . . to see it through to the end this time."

Somehow it had gotten sorted out. Phillip had listened as she explained and, before she could finish, had pulled her to him again. She hid her face on his broad shoulder and wrapped her arms around him, trying unsuccessfully to capture the joyous abandon she had felt before Rosemary's call.

His fingers traced a path along her cheek. "Hey, Eliz-abeth, it's okay. This is something you have to do. And if I can help, you know I will."

Gently, he cupped her chin in his hand and raised her head. "Elizabeth, what we were . . . where we were

heading just before that call . . . where I hope we're still
heading—that can wait a little longer."

The deep brown eyes were steady on her and he
smiled tenderly as he said, "Miz Goodweather, I want
your full attention for what I have in mind."

Elizabeth could still see his crooked smile as he had said
good-bye. This man, an unwelcome stranger in her life
not so long ago, had over the past year, in almost imper-
ceptible increments, somehow become very dear to her.
Almost even . . . necessary.

The thought was disturbing and she brushed it aside.
*But he's added something to my life . . . and he's always
been patient and kind, even in the beginning when I
kept trying to ignore him.*

Phillip Hawkins and her late husband, Sam Goodweather, had been buddies during their years in the
navy, and when Hawkins, a former police detective,
had moved to the Asheville area, he had tried very hard
to befriend Elizabeth. Her emotions still raw with the
pain of her widowhood, she had rebuffed him until the
suspicious death of a neighbor had forced her to seek
his help.

*The more time we spent together, the better I liked
him. And then this nightmare we've just gone through
in Asheville . . .* She shuddered at the vivid memory of a
chase through dark corridors—a memory of blood and
mirrors and madness.

*Thank god for Phillip! A very solid bit of comfort
and sanity to hang on to in a world gone askew. And if
Rosie hadn't called just when she did, I'm pretty sure
he'd have still been here the next morning. I was so
ready. . . .*

Impulsively, she jumped to her feet and hurried inside
to the phone. She put in his number, her thumb flying

over the tiny keys. *He might not have left for school yet— Didn't he say his first class isn't till ten?*

The line was busy. She hit REDIAL. Still busy. Again. Busy. *Maybe he's trying to call me. Okay, Elizabeth, put the phone down. Go do the dishes and—*

The shrill ring of the phone in her hand startled her and she fumbled eagerly for the ON button.

"Phillip! I've been trying to—"

"Mum? It's me, Rosemary. I've come up with a plan."

Shit! said Elizabeth to herself. She sat down heavily on the cushioned bench. "Hey, sweetie. Okay, tell me about it."

"All right, Mum, here's the thing. I've got a few Fridays free this semester and my only Monday class is in the afternoon. So that will give me some long weekends to be there at the farm and I'm going to work through this—I have to do it if it kills me. I've been making a list of places to visit and people to talk to—things that will help me remember. I do have a seminar this Friday, but I still want to come on and get started. If I leave right after class, I could be there in time for dinner. Then if I leave the farm Monday morning around eight, I'll make it back with time to spare. One thing I know I want to do eventually is go over to Cherokee. I need to find out more about the Booger Dance."

Elizabeth Goodweather frowned. The frantic whisper of Saturday's call was gone—Rosemary's tone was calm and perfectly controlled—maybe a little too controlled.

"Sweetie, you know I love for you to come home whenever. We've hardly seen you at all since you bought your house. Laurel was complaining just the other day that it's been months . . . and I'd love to go with you to Cherokee—someone was telling me recently how good the museum is—but, Rosie, did you say *Booger* Dance? Are you serious? What's a Booger Dance and what does it have to do with Maythorn?"

"I'm not sure, Mum . . . but I think it's important. It's something that came to me as I was writing the story. You know I went with Maythorn a few times to visit her grandmother over in Cherokee. Remember, she was called Granny Thorn and she was a full-blood Cherokee—living on the Qualla Boundary. Anyway, one of my last memories of Maythorn is her telling me how she was making a mask for the Booger Dance so she could stop being afraid of someone. I went online and found out what I could about the dance. It all seemed really familiar . . . like I'd seen it. I'm not sure; maybe Maythorn's granny took us to one that last weekend we stayed with her. Or, I don't know—it's vague; maybe she just told us about it.

"And then . . . it seemed like more and more memories of those two years started coming back to me, from the first time I saw Maythorn to right before . . . right before she disappeared . . . and I remembered a bunch of things she told me. Mum, I don't know what's important and what isn't but I do know I have to follow this to the end."

Phillip Hawkins looked at the clock. This was his first semester of teaching criminal justice at AB Tech, Asheville's two-year community college, and he had a class at ten. There was still time. He reached for the telephone.

No. He clicked off. *What was it she said? Like a hound dog with too many pups? I need to back off— Elizabeth's got enough on her mind right now.*

He stared at the phone, still undecided. Saturday night had been the first time he'd seen her cry—*Sam mentioned that about her, how she almost never cried, tried to hide it, like it was a weakness.*

Back in their navy days, during those last long months before they were discharged, back when the one thing that loomed in their minds couldn't be spoken of, he and Sam Goodweather had fought against the boredom, the danger, and the loneliness by talking about their girl-friends. Phillip had not met Elizabeth—would not meet her till years later at Sam's memorial service—but he had known from the picture Sam carried that though she was not really beautiful, her long dark brown hair and startling blue eyes compelled you to look again.

Sam had told the story over and over—how he'd gone into a used bookstore in Tampa, while home on compassionate leave, in search of something to take his mind off the past, something that might give him a new direction. He'd been browsing the cluttered back room when he spotted a battered copy of *Walden,* a book he'd been meaning to read for years.

"I reached for it just as this tall girl with dark hair down to there reached for it too. My hand touched hers, and I swear to god, it was like a goddam jolt of electricity. Then she looked at me with those blue eyes and that was it. It was like I couldn't get my breath."

The tall girl had insisted that they flip a coin for the book. She had won the toss but when Sam invited her for coffee that turned into lunch and she learned that he was on his way back for his final tour of duty, she gave the book to him, first writing her name and address in it. A correspondence had ensued, and a little over a year later, soon after Sam's discharge, they had married.

And me, I married Sandy. No electricity there. Just a pregnancy that wasn't. A pretty, empty-headed little cheerleader with a cute giggle . . . at least, it was cute for the first month or so. Hawkins glanced toward the bookshelf where he kept framed photos of his son and daughter. *Still, there were some good times—and the kids, they were worth it. I don't know, maybe if I'd had a different job, we'd still be together. Maybe.*

He shrugged his shoulders and ran his hand over his shiny scalp. *Nah, Sandy's happier with her life now than she would ever have been with me. She's got a nice tame husband who goes antiquing with her and plays bridge and crap like that.*

Phillip looked again at the pictures of his children. *Good kids, both of them. But they've got their own things going now—Seth keeps talking about bringing Caitlin to Asheville so I can meet her. And Janie—*

Abruptly he picked up the telephone again and hit the familiar number. The harsh burr of the busy signal taunted him. He waited briefly and touched REDIAL. Once again the mocking busy signal rasped in his ear. Glancing at the clock, Phillip Hawkins muttered a brief imprecation, threw down the phone, and hurried out the door.

Rosemary and Maythorn

June 1984

Why are you living in a barn? The solemn little girl stared down at Rosemary from the top of the granite outcropping. My mama says you're hippies.

Eight-year-old Rosemary, climbing laboriously up the slopes of the mountain pasture, a stout hickory stick clutched in one hand, was deep in her pretend of an explorer in unknown lands. At the unexpected sound of a voice, she glanced up in surprise. Two dark eyes in a brown face, half-hidden by a thick shock of black bangs, regarded her steadily from the top of the big rock that she had marked as the goal of her exploration.

We are not either hippies. My grandmother says that, too, but we're not! We're the Goodweathers. And this is Full Circle Farm. My mum named it. And we're just living in the barn till Pa and Uncle Wade can get our house built.

Rosemary pointed down the mountainside to a flat, bulldozed area where two shirtless, tanned men in work boots, straw hats, and cutoff jeans were busy installing a window in the unfinished shell of a modest house. A tall, slender woman in a blue work shirt and faded jeans toiled up the steep road that led to the building site from the barn below. A thick braid of dark hair hung nearly to her waist. In one hand she carried a thermos jug while with the other she held tightly to the unwilling fist of an energetic redheaded toddler. The child broke loose and tried to outpace her mother but soon took a tumble and sat down hard on her overalled bottom. Resisting any attempts to help her up, the child staggered to her feet, and ran. Once again her tiny boots slipped on the gravel and the scene was repeated.

That's my mum and my little sister. Rosemary jerked her head negligently in their direction. Her name's Laurel. She's only three and a half and she can be a pest.

I have a little sister named Krystalle and she's a pest too. The dark child patted the rock beneath her in a proprietary manner. You want to come up on Frog-head?

Is that its name? Rosemary scrambled up the steep slope and climbed onto the tilted surface of the big rock protruding like a granite thumb from the mountain pasture. She moved cautiously up the incline and lowered herself to lie on her belly beside the other child. Who named it?

Me. The dark girl patted the rock again as if it were a living creature beneath her. It's one of my special places. I know all about this mountain. My mama stays so busy with Krystalle that she doesn't care what I do. Long as I get home for supper. A lean brown arm indicated a knapsack that lay beside a pair of binoculars. I pack my lunch and sometimes I stay out all day.

I'm Rosemary. What's your name? Rosemary cast an admiring glance at the other child's long straight black hair and bronze skin. You look like an Indian.

I am an Indian. Granny Thorn's a full-blood Chero-kee and my real daddy was mostly Cherokee. My true name is Mary Thorn Blackfox but mostly everyone calls me Maythorn. My mama told them at the school that my last name is Mullins now, 'cause my real daddy's dead and she's married to Moon.

Moon? Is he an Indian too? Rosemary propped herself up to look at this interesting stranger more closely.

No, he's just ordinary. Maythorn pulled the binoculars to her and trained them on the big pear tree near the house site. The two men, the woman, and the red-headed child were sitting on a stack of lumber in the shade of the tree while the men drank from tall glasses.

Is one of those men your daddy? Slim brown fingers adjusted the binoculars for a closer view.

He's the one wiping his face with the red bandana. Now he's tickling Laurie. His name's Sam but I call him Pa. The other one's Uncle Wade. He's Pa's brother and he's staying here this summer to help build our house.

Hmmph. The binoculars stayed in place. I figured they were brothers—both with red hair and all. The lenses turned toward Rosemary. Do you like your uncle?

Rosemary wrinkled her brow at the glittering lenses. What do you mean? He's my uncle! He's really funny and nice and he tells dumb jokes all the time. The impassive lenses continued to hold her gaze. And he's teaching me how to play the harmonica. Why wouldn't I like him?

Dunno. The binoculars turned back to survey the scene below. The tall woman was rising and the toddler shook her head violently, stamped her foot, and attached herself, limpetlike, to her uncle's leg. The mother squatted down to look her daughter in the eye, spoke a few words, and slowly Laurel released her hold. The storm passed and the little girl grabbed the empty jug, waved a cheerful good-bye to the two men, and set off pell-mell down the road, the jug bumping the gravel with every step. Her mother hurried after her, pausing to look up the mountainside in Rosemary's direction.

Instantly Maythorn lowered the binoculars and flattened herself against the rock. Rosemary lifted up and waved in her mother's direction. I'm up here! It's really cool! There's a—

Below, Elizabeth, with one eye on Laurel, who was nearing the old tobacco barn—their home for the duration—waved abstractedly at her older daughter and called out, Okay, Rosie, just don't go any farther off. I'll ring the bell when it's lunchtime. Be careful up there.

She turned and hurried after the fast-moving little redhead, who was disappearing through the open doors of the barn loft.

Mum's got to watch Laurel all the time. There's holes in the barn floor she could fall right through. Pa and Uncle Wade fixed a safe corner for her—kind of like a corral. There's an old rug that covers the floor and we put her bed and all her play things on it. There's a kind of fence around the rug and she's not supposed to try to get out.

Where do you sleep? Maythorn's binoculars moved to the barn and studied the picnic table and rocking chairs under the raw new shed at the side of the barn.

We all have mattresses on the floor and sleeping bags on top of them. Except for Uncle Wade—he has his own tent in the other barn, that little one behind those trees. My special place is in the corner across from Laurel. I have a rug, too, and a bookshelf with my favorite books—the rest of them are in boxes down below till the house gets done. And I have a trunk for my clothes and a box for my very most important stuff. It's like camping out, except we don't have to worry about rain. And when it does rain, it sounds cool hitting the

*metal roof, like a million fairies tap dancing. Sometimes
I wish we could live in the barn forever. We have
kerosene lamps at night and we sit outside and watch
the lightning bugs. And we bathe in the branch or in a
big round tub if we want hot water. It's really fun.*

Maythorn abandoned the binoculars and rolled onto
her side, leaning on one elbow to study Rosemary. *Do
your mama and daddy yell at each other much? Mine
do. I'm glad I have my own room to get away from
them. I wouldn't want to live all together like you do.
That's why my mama said you all are hippies.*

No, they don't yell at each other! Rosemary was
aghast at the idea but, after brief consideration, added,
*Sometimes Pa yells when things mess up—like when
the truck wouldn't start yesterday. He yelled and said
bunches of bad words but he wasn't mad at any of* us.

What were the bad words he said? Maythorn gazed
with interest toward the house site, where Sam Goodweather was hoisting another window into place.

*I'm not allowed to say them. But I guess I could spell
them for you. He said D-A-M and S-H-*

A cowbell clanked and Rosemary jumped to her feet.
I have to go now. She paused, reluctant to leave her
newfound friend. *You could come down and eat lunch
with us. There's plenty. I could show you my books and
stuff.*

*No, thanks, I've got my lunch right here. And I've
got some other jobs before I go home, some other
things I have to see about.*

*What do you mean? You're just a kid—and it's sum-
mer vacation! What do you* have *to see about?*

*Things. It's my job. Maybe I'll come down another
day.*

The bell sounded again, louder and longer. Laurel
was standing at the edge of the shed, waving the cowbell wildly from side to side.

Okay, maybe another day. See ya. Rosemary slid off the rock and started down the slope. A thought struck her and she whirled to address the binoculars that were following her retreat.

Maythorn, what kind of job? What do you do?

The sun glinted on the lenses, throwing bright lances into Rosemary's blinking eyes.

I'm a spy, said Maythorn. *I find out stuff.*

Lunch was on the table in the welcome shade of the new shed. Bread and cheese, cold cuts, crisp green lettuce, and thick slices of tomato were heaped on two old iron-stone platters. Elizabeth was fixing a plate for Laurel—five carrot sticks, half a cheese sandwich with tomato, no lettuce. No mustard, mayo on the slice of bread next to the cheese, not *the one next to the tomato. Perched on a cushion atop the picnic table's bench, Laurel swung her legs and drummed her plastic cup on the table while singing the ABC song, loud and tuneless.*

Hey, Rosie, did you have a good adventure? I saw you up on that big rock. Her father smiled his crinkly smile at her. *Better wash your hands, Punkin.*

Uh-oh, Sam, don't you remember? Uncle Wade's mouth turned down in a sad expression. *We used up all the water in the branch. Rosie'll have to wash her hands with something else. Maybe leaves . . . or rocks . . . or—*

Uncle Waa-ade, that's silly. You couldn't possibly use it all up! Rosemary made a face at her uncle and hurried off to the little stream, where a wooden trough set over a big rock provided a steady flow of icy, clear water. A bar of soap sat on a nearby rock and a faded green towel hung from a convenient spicebush.

When she returned, her mother had already made her

a sandwich—just right—with lettuce, tomato, sliced turkey, and mayonnaise. She slid onto her place on the bench and the family held hands as Sam said, Let's be thankful.

The brief blessing done, they ate. Everyone was starving—it had been hours since breakfast—but Rosemary was full of her news. She swallowed her first huge bite of sandwich and announced, I have a new friend. She's a real Indian and her name is Maythorn.

VICKI LANE is the author of *The Day of Small Things, Signs in the Blood, Art's Blood, Old Wounds,* and the Anthony Award finalist *In a Dark Season.* She lives with her family on a mountain farm in North Carolina, where she is at work on her next novel.